A Duty

to the Dead

ALSO BY CHARLES TODD

Inspector Ian Rutledge Mysteries

A Test of Wills
Wings of Fire
Search the Dark
Watchers of Time
Legacy of the Dead
A Fearsome Doubt
A Cold Treachery
A Long Shadow
A False Mirror
A Pale Horse
A Matter of Justice

The Murder Stone

A Duty

to the Dead

CHARLES TODD

wm WILLIAM MORROW *An Imprint of* HarperCollins*Publishers*

A DUTY TO THE DEAD. Copyright © 2009 by Charles Todd. All rights reserved. Printed in the United States of America. No part of this book may be used or reproduced in any manner whatsoever without written permission except in the case of brief quotations embodied in critical articles and reviews. For information address Harper-Collins Publishers, 10 East 53rd Street, New York, NY 10022.

HarperCollins books may be purchased for educational, business, or sales promotional use. For information please write: Special Markets Department, HarperCollins Publishers, 10 East 53rd Street, New York, NY 10022.

FIRST EDITION

Designed by Joy O'Meara

Library of Congress Cataloging-in-Publication Data

Todd, Charles.
  A duty to the dead / Charles Todd. — 1st ed.
    p. cm.
  ISBN 978-0-06-179176-5 (hardcover)
  1. Nurses—England—Fiction. 2. World War, 1914–1918—England—Fiction. I. Title.
PS3570.O37D87 2009
813'.54—dc22   2008055909

ISBN 978-0-06-193384-4 (international edition)

09 10 11 12 13 OV/RRD 10 9 8 7 6 5 4 3 2 1

This book is for—

Pauline and Brian Gadd, two terrific people, who shared their England with the authors, including a wonderful day at the Imperial War Museum and hot chocolate, pork pies, the fox in the back garden, and making us feel we were family . . .

Moses and Monty, the most enormous, warmhearted kitties, who purred when we needed a cat fix and ours three thousand miles away . . .

Fran Bush, bookseller extraordinaire, who isn't afraid of anything, including driving on the left and having adventures in Romney Marsh, Battle, and the wilds of Sevenoaks . . .

Don Bush, who did without Fran so that she could go with Caroline, an act of love if ever there was one . . .

The wonderful landscape of Kent, which has been the inspiration for more than one Todd novel . . .

And not least, Robin Hathaway, author of the Dr. Fenimore and Dr. Jo Banks mysteries, who offered us Gum Tree and other adventures, when we needed a sanctuary to finish *Duty* . . .

With much, much love always.

CHAPTER ONE

Tuesday, 21 November, 1916. 8:00 A.M.

At sea . . .
This morning the sun is lovely and warm. All the portholes
below are open, to allow what breeze there is to blow through the
lower decks and air them. With no wounded onboard to keep
us occupied, we are weary of one another's company. Beds are
made up, kits readied, duties done. Since Gibraltar I've written
to everyone I know, read all the books I could borrow, and even
sketched the seabirds. Uneventful is the password of the day.

I lifted my pen from the paper and stared out across the blue water. I'd posted letters during our coaling stopover in Naples, and there wasn't much I could add about the journey since then. I'd already mentioned the fact that Greece was somewhere over the horizon and likely to stay there. Someone had sighted dolphins off the bow just after first light, and I'd mentioned that too. What else? Oh, yes.

We discovered a bird's nest in one of the lifeboats, no idea how
long it had been there or if the hatching was successful. Or what

variety of bird it might have been. Margaret, one of the nursing
sisters, claimed it must surely be the Ancient Mariner's albatross,
and we spent the next half hour trying to think what we should
name our unknown guest. Choices ranged from Coleridge to the
Kaiser, but my personal favorite was Alice in Wonderland.

I always tried to keep my letters cheerful, even when the wards
were filled with wounded, and we were working late into the night,
fighting to save the worst cases. My worries weren't to be shared.
At home and in the trenches, letters were a brief and welcome respite from war. It was better that way. And now we were in the Kea
Channel, just off the Greek coast at Cape Sounion, and steaming
toward our final destination at Lemnos. It was the collection point
for wounded from Greek Macedonia, Palestine, and Mesopotamia.
There, post could be sent on through the Army.

I'd grown rather superstitious about writing to friends as often
as I could. I'd learned too well just how precious *time* was, and how
easily someone slipped away, dying days or weeks before I heard
the news. My only consolation was that a letter might have reached
them and made them smile a little while they were still living, or
comforted them in their last hours. God knew, the Battle of the
Somme over the summer had been such a bloodbath no one could
say with any certainty how many men we'd lost. I could put a face to
far too many names on those casualty lists.

A gull flew up to land on the railing close by me, an eye fixed on
me. Most were nearly tame, begging for handouts. In the distance,
over the bird's shoulder, was a smudge that must be Kea. The sea
here was a sparkling blue and calm, *Britannic's* frothy wake the only
disturbance as far as the eye could see in any direction. Sailing between the island and the mainland was a shortcut that saved miles
and miles of travel.

Or as Captain Bartlett had told me on my first voyage out, "Keep
Cape Sounion on your left and Kea on your right, and you can't go

wrong." And so I looked for it every voyage thereafter, like a marker in the sea.

One of *Britannic*'s officers paused by my deck chair, and the gull took flight with an annoyed squawk. "I see you're already enjoying the morning air, Miss Crawford. The last time we passed through here, it was pouring rain. You could hardly see your hand before your face. Remember?"

Browning was sun browned, broad shouldered, and handsome in his uniform. We'd formed a friendship of sorts during the voyages out, flirting a little to pass the time. Neither of us took it seriously.

"Much pleasanter than France this time of year," I replied, smiling up at him. "No mud."

He laughed. "And no one firing at you. We should be safe as houses soon."

"That's good to hear." But I knew he was lying. It was a game all of us played, pretending that German U-boats weren't a constant threat. Even hospital ships like *Britannic* were not safe from them, despite our white paint and great red crosses. They were said to believe that we hid fresh troops among the wounded or stowed munitions in the hold amongst the medical supplies. There was no truth to their suspicions, of course. And this channel was well traveled, always a temptation. For that matter, mines paid no heed to the nationality or purpose of the hull above them, when a vessel sailed too near. You couldn't dwell on it, or you'd live in fear.

He moved on, overseeing the change of the watch, and I capped my pen.

There was something about his laugh that reminded me of Arthur Graham. When it caught me unawares, as it had done just now, the gates of memory opened and Arthur's face would come back to me.

During training, we'd been warned about letting ourselves care too much for our patients. "They are yours to comfort, yours to heal, but not yours to dream about," Matron had told us firmly. "Only foolish girls let themselves be drawn into romantic imaginings. See that you are not one of them."

Good advice. But Matron hadn't foreseen Arthur Graham. He'd been popular with the other wounded, the medical orderlies, and the nursing staff. It was impossible not to like him, and liking him, it was impossible not to feel something for him as he fought a gallant but losing battle with death. I wasn't foolish enough to believe it was love, but I was honest enough to admit I cared more than I should. I'd watched so many wounded die. Perhaps that was why I desperately wanted to see this one man snatch a victory out of defeat and restore my faith in the goodness of God. But it wasn't to be.

And truth be told, I had more than one reason for remembering Arthur Graham and his laugh. There was a promise I'd made. Freely.

If you gave your word so freely, my conscience argued, *then why have you never kept your promise?*

"There's been no opportunity!" I said the words aloud, then in embarrassment turned to see if anyone had overheard me.

Liar. You never made the time.

It isn't true—

You traveled through Kent on your last leave. You could have kept it then.

I resolutely uncapped my pen and tried to distract myself with my letter. The seagull returned to keep me company.

There's a cheeky seagull on the railing every morning. I've christened him Baba, for the man who sat outside our gate in Agra and examined the goods the merchants brought to the house. Afterward he'd come round to the back garden and talk Cook into giving him

The gull flew up just as there was a deafening explosion, and the ship seemed to rock on her spine. The deck lurched where I was sitting, pen and paper flying from my lap. It was all so unexpected that I was thrown out of my chair as it too went over. I struck the bulkhead with such force that I rebounded hard against the stairs just behind me. My right arm took the brunt of that, and pain shot up to my shoulder.

I cried out in alarm, trying to scramble to my feet. The explosion had left me stunned. I could hear the shouts and screams all around me, but they seemed to come from a great distance. And then I was standing upright, holding on to the stairs with my left hand. My hearing gradually returned, and I forced myself to think clearly, to remember all those drills we'd attended again and again, and sometimes laughed about over tea.

My life belt. It was in my cabin. I had forgot to bring it on deck with me.

A rating ran by, stopping every few feet to look over the railing.

"What is it?" I called to the young seaman. "What's happened?"

He didn't answer, his attention on the ship's waterline. But I really didn't need to hear it from him. A submarine had found us and torpedoed us somewhere near the bow. It was the only explanation. Was there a second torpedo already on its way?

There was no time to stand and speculate.

Still dazed, I stumbled through the nearest sea door and went toward my cabin for my life belt. The dark-haired Irish nurse, Eileen, came running toward me in the passage, crashing into me as if she hadn't seen me at all. It jarred my arm, and I smothered a cry. I tried to steady her, but she shook her head and ran on, disoriented and badly frightened.

I came to the next set of stairs, and it struck me suddenly that all this elegance surrounding us—elegance intended for happier voyages, for travelers dancing the night away without a care in the world—might wind up at the bottom of the sea.

Like *Titanic*. Or for that matter, *Lusitania*.

No, that mustn't happen here—this great ocean liner would survive.

As the General Alarm was being sounded, the orderlies were collecting under the Major's sharp eye while the rest of us were hurrying to take our stations. Since I was coming from the open deck, everyone asked me for news as they passed, but I could only shake my head and tell them I knew as little as they did. Dr. Menzies stopped me and reached for my arm.

I hadn't noticed that my arm was cut, much less that it was bleeding rather badly. His fingers ran quickly, surely, over the skin closest to the gash. I winced at his touch.

"I rather think it's broken. Have you got something to stop the bleeding? I'll set it for you as soon as we know what's happening." And he was gone.

I reached my cabin, found my life belt on its nail, and cursed Dr. Menzies as I struggled to put the vest on properly. I hadn't had time to notice how my arm was beginning to ache until he drew my attention to it. Now, it hurt like six devils, and I felt a first inkling of nausea from the intensity of the pain. He was right, it *must* be broken. I wasn't about to touch it myself and find out.

And this wasn't the time to be a problem for others. Using my left hand and my teeth, I managed to wind a scarf around the gash to contain the bleeding.

My kit bag lay at the foot of my bunk. Holding my right arm close to my chest, I reached into it and pulled out the small oilskin packet in which I'd learned to keep my papers and money. Shoving that down the front of my shirt, I turned and hurried back into the passage.

It was eerily quiet, as if no one was left onboard but me.

"Anyone need help?" I shouted to be sure no one was lying hurt somewhere. If I'd been thrown to the deck, it was possible that others had been tossed about as well. I listened and heard only the sounds of the ship herself. I opened the nearest doors, only to find the cabins empty. Their occupants were all on deck, then, trying to see what sort of damage we'd sustained, getting to their stations in some sort of order, waiting for instructions. Time that I joined them.

As I turned to the companionway, Captain Bartlett began speaking to the ship's company, and I tried to make out what he was saying. My ears were still full of cotton wool and I couldn't distinguish all the words. Something about assessing damage and no need to worry. The Abandon Ship alarm hadn't sounded, and that was reassuring. *Britannic* had watertight doors. Wounded she might be but certainly not doomed. Of course they'd said the same about *Titanic.* . . . At least there hadn't been a second torpedo. Yet. I didn't want to think about what that might have done to us.

I reached the lifeboat station as someone just ahead of me remarked, "I expect we hit a small craft. A fishing boat, most likely." There was a nervous edge to her voice. "This is probably nothing more than a precaution."

Marilyn Johnson answered, "I wish the captain would tell us more. But then he probably doesn't know himself, yet."

Most of the nurses were wearing their life belts, but several still clutched them in their hands.

The crew was busy with the boats, not lowering them yet, just preparing them. And then ahead of our station, a working detail of ratings panicked, racing to get a boat launched early, and I realized with a shock that they were intending to commandeer it.

My next thought was, *Had they been down below, and did they know how bad it really was?*

An officer was trying to deal with them, his voice hard and calming. "There's no need to panic. Do your duty, damn you, and your turn will come!"

I thought it was my friend Browning, but there was tension and anger in the voice as well, changing its timbre. Not encouraging, surely.

Behind me Dr. Brighton joined the queue. He was an older man, a very good doctor, and unflappable. I'd watched him in the operating theater. He noted the scarf around my arm. "What's this?"

I saw that blood was seeping through the pretty pattern of lilacs. "A cut," I told him, unwilling to admit to more.

He began to unwind the scarf, then saw for himself what lay beneath. Rewinding it more efficiently, he confided to me in a low voice, "I don't think it's a good idea to go below for something to stabilize that bone. The portholes on E and F decks are still open, worst luck, and there's no chance of closing them now. We'll sink fast if the watertight doors are damaged."

"Where was the explosion?" I asked as quietly, striving to keep my arm steady as he worked. "Starboard side, I think, near the bow—not far from where I was sitting."

"Yes. Bartlett has just sent a distress signal. Meanwhile, damage reports are still coming in. They aren't good."

The ship was turning now, toward Kea in the distance, but I wasn't sure we could make it. Something didn't feel right about *Britannic*— she seemed heavier. I'd sailed in her often enough to recognize a difference. I prayed it was only my imagination running away with me.

Dr. Paterson, nearer the rail, called to Dr. Brighton. "They're using the screws to turn, not the rudder. I don't think that's a good sign." Dr. Brighton finished tying up my arm and then hurried over to join him, staring down into the water.

How many of these people can swim? For that matter, could I, with this arm?

That thought flashed through my mind as I watched the crew at their work as they readied the great arms of the lifeboat launching system.

Everyone knew the drill, but no one had believed it would ever be necessary. Five voyages into the Mediterranean, with no trouble. That had given us a false sense of security.

I watched one of the younger seamen fumble the ropes, and an older rating swore at him to mind what he was about.

Browning was by my side, saying, "I don't like the look of that arm, Miss Crawford. Ask someone to help you into a boat, if the time comes."

I turned. "Does anyone know what happened? I'd swear *Britannic* seems sluggish, as if she's taking on water."

He didn't answer me directly. "U-boat. Mine. Does it matter?"

"Are we sinking? Is this a precaution or real?"

"Damned real," he said tightly, and was gone.

There was a nurse just up ahead with bruises on her face. Someone had tied an impromptu bandage around her head, and already the blood was seeping through. Serviettes from the dining room? They gave the woman a rakish air, and I wanted to laugh.

No, that's hysteria. Stop it, I warned myself.

The Irish nurse had come up beside me, trying to edge her way up the queue. Her face was so pale the freckles across her nose stood out. "I don't like the water," she was saying, "I'd rather take my chances *here*—"

I put a hand on her shoulder. "Don't be silly, Eileen. If anything happens, the lifeboats are the safest place for us to be."

Eileen froze, fear stark in her eyes. "Then it's true, we're sinking—"

I could hear shouting now, and saw that Harry Dyke, one of the officers, was looking up at the poop deck, where firemen from below were trying to launch a lifeboat for themselves.

"You fools!" he yelled. "Stay onboard—we're trying to beach her—"

But they were frantic to be gone, and without waiting for orders or other passengers to join them, they launched anyway.

"Stay away from the ship," Dyke was shouting to them now. "And for God's sake, try to pick up any of the crew who've already jumped!"

Surprised, I turned to look at the sea and could see bobbing heads treading water, those who hadn't waited for a boat to be lowered. From the look of them, they were already tiring. The water was November cold, after all, in spite of the sun's warmth.

Eileen fled before I could stop her.

The firemen were paying no heed, but I thought they'd heard Dyke. I saw one reach out an arm to drag a swimmer inboard.

Then the third officer, Lawes, was trying to prevent two of his boats from automatically launching. So far the Abandon Ship signal still hadn't been given. We were all at our stations, worried and waiting for instructions. None came. I eyed the distance to Kea. Could we make it that far, wounded as we were? Or was the submarine lurking nearby, watching, ready to try another shot if it looked as if we'd be successful? I shivered at the thought.

I saw that Lawes was too late—the boats dropped to the water with such violence that spray swept the side of the ship. By a mercy, both stayed upright. To my surprise, Eileen was in one of them.

Britannic was listing now, it wasn't just my imagination, and it was harder to understand why the Captain hadn't ordered the boats away. I could appreciate how the passengers on *Britannic's* sister ship, *Titanic,* must have felt in the cold darkness of the North Atlantic. At least here there was daylight—

Someone behind me was pushing hard, eager to be nearer the lifeboat, as if afraid she'd be left behind. She jostled my right arm, and I felt faint from the stab of pain.

I stepped back, letting her have my place, then sat down on the deck, lowering my head, swallowing hard. Nausea was there, all too close to the surface, dizzying in its intensity. I hadn't realized that a break in a bone could be so exquisitely painful. I'd feel a greater tolerance for the wounded after this.

One of the other nurses came to bend over me, and then we heard people shouting and screaming a warning. I managed to get to my feet and turn to look over the railing.

The two boats from Lawes's station were in trouble, and Bartlett was bellowing to them through the loud-hailer. "Mind the screws, damn it!"

I stood there, unable to turn away, as one of the lifeboats caught in *Britannic's* wake was being dragged inexorably back toward our three propellers, already partly out of the water, their great brass wings shining wet in the sun as they went round.

Like everyone else along that rail, I cried out in horror, staring down at the frightened, helpless faces turned first up to us and then back toward the stern. There was nothing that anyone could do. No way to stop what was about to happen. In what seemed to be slow motion, but must have been only a matter of seconds, the first boat was swept into the screws. The sound of wood rending reached us. Screams echoed across the water, and then there was silence.

I don't think anyone on the ship moved.

Wood debris and torn bodies churned into the bloody wake.

I felt sick. In five sailings with severely wounded onboard, I had never seen anything quite so terrible. The image stayed with me, repeating itself over and over again.

Dr. Paterson, swearing like a trooper, raced toward the stern, looking over into the water for survivors.

The Abandon Ship alarm was sounding now, and I realized that while we'd been absorbed by the drama on the water, *Britannic's* list had increased alarmingly. Someone came up to me, cursing me, telling me to get into one of the lifeboats before it was too late to lower them.

It was Lieutenant Browning, harried and angry, his expression a mask of duty but his mind already leaping ahead to what we were about to face.

It was the last thing I wanted to do now—leave this ship. I could see other boats in danger of the same fate as the first one. It would be better to drown than to face those churning blades. But when I turned, drawn to stare at them, I was surprised to see that the screws were barely moving, that someone had ordered all engines stopped. It was then I knew with cold certainty that we were sinking.

Collecting my wits, I said, "Look—the boat I'm assigned to is full—"

Browning shook me, and I cried out from the pain in my arm.

He stopped, saw how bloody my scarf was, and ripped my apron off below my vest, using it to fashion a makeshift sling.

"This way, Sister!" He took my good hand and led me through the ship to another boat station, lifting me bodily into the first one we came to just as it was ready to lower. "This one has a better chance of making it."

What he didn't add was that with the ship listing it would be touch and go on the other side.

The occupants reached up to pull me safely aboard.

"Be safe—Godspeed!" he told me, and then he was gone.

We hit the sea heavily, bobbed dangerously, then steadied. Someone was calling frantically to us from the water, and I turned to see that it was the Irish nurse, clinging to a shard of wood from one of the broken boats.

I leaned forward to touch the shoulder of the officer in charge of our boat and pointed. Looking around, he saw Eileen.

Nodding, he tried to steer the boat nearer to her. She was having a dreadful time staying afloat as the plank perversely danced away on the next swell. Afraid of losing her, several of us leaned over at once to try to reach out for the bit of wood she gripped so frantically, and nearly capsized ourselves in the process. The officer shouted a warning, and then I saw the boat hook lying in the bottom. I picked it up, swung it over everyone's head, and out toward Eileen. She hesitated, reluctant to let go of the only security she knew, and then in a final desperate lunge that took all her strength, she grasped the curved end of the hook. I could see the despair in her eyes as she held on for dear life. With Barbara Mercer's help, I dragged her to the side of our boat.

Because I was nearest her, I passed the boat hook to someone else and put out my left hand to catch Eileen's. Barbara did the same, and with an effort I hadn't dreamed I was capable of, we began to haul the girl up over the side. Eileen was crying, begging us not to let her go. Nurses on either side of us caught at her wet clothing as it tried to pull her down, and we soon had her safely aboard.

Other hands lowered her gently into the well. It was then I saw the lacerations on her legs, and the tatters of skirt and petticoat that only half covered them.

The wounds were deep and bleeding profusely. It must have been a torment for her almost beyond bearing. But the coldness of the water had helped stanch the rate of bleeding long enough for her to be rescued.

Barbara and Margaret began to bind up the wounds, but the pain was intolerable now. Eileen fainted.

"Just as well," Barbara muttered as she worked.

Our boat crew began to row now with vigorous strokes, pulling us as far from *Britannic* as possible, their backs arched over the oars and the muscles in their shoulders straining with the effort.

There was nothing more I could do. I sat back, nursing my arm. I'd damaged it picking up the boat hook with both hands, trying to reach Eileen and pull her to us. The ends of the bone felt as if they were grinding together now. But what else could I have done? In the closely packed lifeboat, there had been no time or space to shift places. I tried to touch the area around the break, but it hurt so much I stopped. It was too late to worry now.

Besides, the little lifeboat was rolling in a fashion that *Britannic* never had done, even in storms. I was feeling increasingly uneasy. Or was it the agony in my arm? It was overwhelming, and seemed to have reached a crescendo. I closed my eyes, trying my best to cope.

Think of anything but your arm, I commanded myself. *Anything—*

England? No, don't think of home. Something else . . .

My great-grandmother had danced at a ball in Belgium on the eve of Waterloo, while Napoleon was racing north across the French border. She had watched my great-grandfather slip from the ballroom to ride to meet his regiment, then smiled to hide her fear from the others present, and turned to dance with a new partner. Later she'd had her portrait painted in the ball gown she wore that night. I tried to picture her floating across the polished floor in the arms of another man while the one she loved was facing the greatest battle of his career. Would I be painted in my torn, bloodstained uniform, after surviving *Britannic*? My mother would have a fit—

There was a single blast of the ship's whistle, and I opened my eyes in time to see that her bridge was almost on a level with the water. *Britannic* was going. That beautiful ship—

Tears began to run down my face, salty on my lips. I shook my head to clear it, and unable to turn away, watched the great liner die. On all sides of me other people were crying as well, their eyes fixed on the ship, not ready to absorb what this meant—or what lay ahead of us.

We could hear the boilers exploding as the cold water reached them and the splash of gear and equipment sliding down the decks to crash into the sea. The ship itself was creaking, as if she were alive, protesting.

The engineers, last to leave, were madly scrambling out of funnel four, after holding their positions until the end.

Lucy, across the boat, exclaimed, "Oh, my God. Just like *Titanic*."

Barbara, beside me, said dryly, "No, dear, *Lusitania*. There aren't any icebergs in the Mediterranean."

"Was it a mine?" someone else asked.

I was shading my eyes against the sun's glare as one of the officers assigned to our boat cleared his throat and answered the question.

"Must have been. None of the lookouts saw any sign of a U-boat or reported a torpedo's wake. But if it was a submarine, thank God it didn't attack again."

"Bloody U-boat wouldn't have picked us up, even so." It was the rating at the helm.

We had moved smartly in a dash to put ourselves beyond reach of the great ship's death throes, afraid of being pulled under with her, but she filled our world still.

Then someone said, "There's the end of her!" in a hollow voice, as if they couldn't believe their eyes.

Britannic seemed to roll uncertainly, then bow first she raced down through the water, as if she had a rendezvous below and was late. The roar of her passing was like something human, a cry like nothing I'd ever heard. The sight and sound were heart wrenching, and as I looked out at the turbulence where the great ocean liner had once been, I knew I'd remember those last appalling moments until the day I died.

The sea seemed lonely now. Wide and endless and unfriendly. We were in the middle of nowhere. Kea was off on the horizon, and this was a busy sea lane, but the water was so desperately *empty.* Even crippled, *Britannic* had been comforting, a place we knew, large and able to hold its own against the vastness of the sea. Or so we'd wanted to believe.

"Did everyone get off?" Lucy asked anxiously. "Oh, my God, what if we'd had more than three thousand *wounded* onboard?" She began to tremble.

We were all shaken, uncertain, trying not to think about that. We'd had enough lifeboats, and we knew the procedures by heart, but it was a daunting prospect in the face of our present situation.

Attempting to shift the subject, I said, "Did anyone respond to the Captain's distress call?"

"There was no mention of other boats in the area, as far as I know," Margaret replied. "They must have learned about the mine laying. . . ."

In the bottom of the boat, Eileen moaned a little, and Barbara asked, "Is there a medical kit onboard? She needs something now for the pain."

There was a swift scramble to find the kit, and I let myself go for a few minutes, drifting on a tide of sickness and pain. Even so I could hear Barbara talking as she worked on Eileen's limbs, worried that the girl would bleed to death.

I tried to recapture the image of that ballroom in Belgium, and my great-grandmother whirling past long candlelit windows in a daring waltz, smiling up at a young lieutenant while out of the corner of her eye, she watched another officer slipping out the door and hurrying away. But behind my lids now was only the red glare of the sun.

As I opened my eyes again, other lifeboats had drawn within hailing distance of ours. One of them called to us and asked if everyone was all right. I thought it was Lieutenant Browning—prayed it was.

The officer in our boat bellowed, "We'll do."

Someone else called across the water, "How many boats did we lose?"

"Four." The number seemed to hang in the air like signal flags on a lanyard.

"Try to stay together, then. We've a better chance."

I was nearly sure it was Captain Bartlett speaking now, but water tended to distort voices. Would he be blamed for what happened, like the captain of *Titanic*? You couldn't see a mine in time, could you? They were purposely low in the water, bobbing, hiding in the froth, a cruel and unseen killer.

We roused ourselves and began taking stock. Three others in our boat were wounded, in addition to Eileen. The only doctor among us had sustained a blow to the head, the knob rising like a small hill, and he was slow to respond to questions about how he felt. Two of the nurses had rather serious cuts. Barbara was already ripping apart her skirts for makeshift bandaging, and others followed suit.

"Salt air is a healer," Lucy was saying, trying for cheer. "But I doubt it was meant this way, medically."

Barbara said succinctly, "Bloody Germans!"

I said, noticing that somewhere I had lost my cap and the heat was beating down, "We need to shield our heads and faces from the sun. Try to rig something if you can. We'll burn in no time."

My apron was around my arm, but I borrowed a pocketknife from the man at the helm, and with a little help managed to hack a strip from my skirt that I could wind, turbanlike, around my head.

"You look like an Arab," one of the other women told me, and there was a general nervous laugh. But I noted that others were following my example. I managed to cut another strip and handed it to Barbara to shield Eileen's face from the sun, rigging it over the bucket used for bailing. The glare from the water was very different, this close to it, and I found I was squinting horribly until I'd created my own shade.

We fell silent for a time, overwhelmed by events. There seemed to be no one else in the world but ourselves, a cluster of small boats at the mercy of the sea.

Thank God it was not raining or stormy.

I felt myself drifting away again on the thought, the wash of the sea against the sides of the boat and the warmth of the sun surprisingly soothing for a little while. My great-grandmother seemed to have abandoned me, leaving me to my own devices, and for a time I tried to pretend we were on the ship that had brought us back from India, lying on deck with our backs to the mast, watching moonlight streaming across the dark sea. It had been too hot to sleep below, and the passengers had come up to find a breath of air, counting stars until that palled.

POSH . . . I hadn't thought of that in ages. It stood for Port side Out, Starboard side Home. The best cabins, the cooler ones, were on the port side of a vessel traveling out to India, and on the starboard side coming home. And still there were nights when not a breath of air stirred, and if the ship hadn't been moving, we'd all have surely died of heat exhaustion.

The image of a dark ship on a dark sea faded, abandoning me too. I came back to the present, unable to escape for very long.

My arm had settled into a dull, constant ache as long as I kept it close to my body and braced. I think all of us were feeling the exhaustion of the last hours. God knew, after what we'd been through, it wasn't surprising.

Then suddenly I was awake again, overheated in the full strength of the sun, and thirsty. I wanted to dip my hands in the cool water surrounding us and bathe my face. But I knew better. Not only would it dry my skin more, but it would also make it burn and blister.

People were sleeping for a few minutes at a time as I'd done, or staring out to sea without actually seeing it. No one seemed inclined to talk now. I wondered what memories they were chasing, and if theirs had succeeded better than mine. I turned my head to look forward, at the officer. He was anxiously scanning the horizon. The ratings were trying to keep us on course with the other boats, but I didn't think we were making much progress toward Kea. I looked around and found that several of the boats had even drifted away. The rhythmic slap of the waves against the sides of ours was the only sound.

Surely Kea was farther away than before? It had looked closer from the decks of *Britannic*. Hadn't it? I couldn't be sure.

Where I was sitting, my back had very little support, and soon it began to ache in concert with my arm, in spite of my sling. I straightened, trying to ease both. Why had the mast on the ship from India seemed comfortable, and here there was no comfort to be had?

Barbara, stretching, turned to me and said, "The arm hurts, I daresay. But from the looks of it, this isn't the best place to try and set it."

"A little, yes," I answered, managing a smile. "But nothing like what Eileen must be feeling."

"More than a little. I broke my arm when I was twelve, falling out of the apple tree while trying to emulate my brothers. As for Eileen—" She shrugged expressively.

"Yes." If we weren't found soon, if she didn't have proper care . . .

"We were lucky," Barbara went on, as if to convince herself. "We got off, and no one in this boat was terribly hurt." She glanced down at Eileen. "Except of course for her. We'll have to bathe her legs in seawater again soon, to keep the wounds from suppurating. It'll have to do."

I knew what was in Barbara's mind. The Irish girl might survive, but she could lose one or both legs to infection.

Barbara was older than most of us, an experienced nursing sister before the war had begun in 1914. She had told me once that her family had been horrified when she decided to train as a nurse. Now, with the war on, it was socially acceptable to tend the wounded. But not then, not a woman of her class, not in 1905.

With a sigh I leaned back as best I could, still trying to find comfort for my spine. The life belt was cumbersome and very little help.

One of the nursing sisters moved a little, as uncomfortable as I was. "We will be rescued, won't we?"

"Of course we will," I answered to cut off the rising fear in the girl's voice. "There must be shipping, fishing boats—"

Barbara added, "There are so many of us. If a ship finds one lifeboat, it will begin to search for others. If you must worry, ask yourself how we are to get home, with no *Britannic* to carry us to England."

A very good question. Her words turned all of our thoughts from rescue to passage back.

Lucy said, "They're chronically short of nurses. That's in our favor."

"I'd rather not be sent to Egypt," Margaret put in. "I hear hospitals there are appalling."

Most of us understood appalling conditions. We'd worked in

them, more often than not. "Egypt is no worse than the others," I said.

Fishing boats out of Kea began to appear over the empty horizon. A cheer went up. After what seemed to be an eternity, the first one arrived on the scene, and then others, spread out behind it. Watching them move past us, I realized that there were people bobbing in the water, even though from our position we couldn't see them, and the boats went first to pull them out. But there wasn't much space on the little craft, and so they couldn't manage taking any of us from the lifeboats.

While we were watching them turn back for Kea, wondering how long it would be before we saw them again, HMS *Scourge* steamed into view and began to pick up survivors.

Our boat wasn't one of them. But *Scourge* was followed soon enough by HMS *Heroic*, which seemed to tower over us as she came up.

The worst of the wounded, including Eileen, were sent by motor launch to Korissia, the port on Kea. We were taken aboard, climbing the ladder if we could or waiting our turn on the sling if not.

From *Heroic*'s deck, I watched our progress in, the mountainous interior growing higher, the numerous small coves and bays giving the shore a ragged outline. What sort of medical care would we find here? I wished I had two good arms. It rankled that I was a burden. There were enough injured without me.

"We're forty nautical miles from Piraeus," one of the officers said reassuringly, as if he'd read my thoughts. "You'll be all right."

The doctors and nurses already landed there had begun working frantically to save the most critical cases, making use of whatever they could collect among themselves to bind up the severest wounds, some including loss of limbs. Supplies were being off-loaded from the naval vessels now, and that was a blessing. I was a little unsteady when I got to shore but went directly to do what I could to help. Then someone noticed my swollen hand, discovered it came from a broken arm, and ordered me to step aside.

"We've enough nurses," Dr. Paterson told me. "I'll see to you directly. Meanwhile, there's a little shade over there. And Eileen could use the company. She's awake now. We've given her something for her pain, thanks to *Heroic*."

Silently cursing my uselessness, I did as I was told, pausing to speak to a pair of ratings lying on blankets and to the nurse with the bandaged head before sitting down by the Irish girl.

Eileen recognized me and said, shakily, "Well, we're alive. It counts, doesn't it?"

I smiled. "I should say it does."

"I made such a fool of myself, didn't I?" she added after a moment.

"I don't think there's any way we can predict how we'll behave in an emergency until we're there," I answered judiciously.

"You didn't panic."

"My ancestors were battle-hardened soldiers. I wouldn't dare panic," I said lightly. "They'd rise up from their graves in horror."

That brought a flicker of amusement, quickly gone. "I've never been hurt before. Not like this. It's odd, you know. To be one of the wounded."

"I was just thinking the same thing myself, not half an hour ago."

"I'm not enjoying the experience." There was a pause. "Will I lose my legs, do you think? Dr. Menzies wouldn't answer me when I asked."

"I doubt it. He's always been the cautious one, you know."

"Yes." But I didn't think she believed me.

One of the island women brought us cold water to drink, which was pure bliss, and then a little later gave us bread baked only that morning, with a small dish of almonds and olives. I was surprised to find I was hungry, and I dipped little chunks of bread into the water, sharing it with Eileen, insisting that she must keep up her strength, even if she didn't feel like eating. Another woman brought us fruit, and gesturing with a smile, mimicked biting into it.

"Will I lose my legs?" Eileen asked again, as if she'd forgotten she'd spoken to me before about it. Looking at her, I could see she was groggy, and perhaps a little feverish.

"There will be scars," I said, avoiding the question. "But who will see them? Here, have a little more of this orange. It will help ward off scurvy." But she barely noticed my little joke.

Just then I realized that Lieutenant Browning had arrived, bringing in one of the last boats, and he began to take charge almost at once. I thought he was actually speaking Greek, but it was French, and he'd found someone among the local people who could translate for him. I smiled, thinking that it was just the sort of thing he would do, find a way to cope.

At some point in the afternoon he came over to speak to me, asking how I was.

No one had had time to set my arm, and I said nothing about it, although he could see my purpling hand, and the swelling. By that time Eileen had been taken to someone's home where it was cooler, and I was sitting with one of the engineers, who'd broken his leg jumping into the water, listening to his tale of another sinking before the war.

Lieutenant Browning came back shortly with Dr. Brighton, and although I protested that it could wait, my arm was cleaned and braced and wrapped, and I was given a stronger sling. It looked suspiciously like a part of someone's tablecloth. But there was no morphine to help, because we didn't have enough.

I slept for a time after that, in spite of the pain. It was beginning to put my teeth on edge. And so my sleep was restless at best and my dreams were filled with mines and explosions and fear.

In late afternoon, two more warships came in, and I was among those taken to Piraeus. Crowds of people had come down to the grimy little port to watch us disembark, as if word had run before us like wildfire. A number of us were put up in one of the small hotels near the harbor. It was called the Athena, and the staff was very kind. Margaret shared my room and helped me undress and bathe and dress again. She also cut my meat (it tasted suspiciously like goat) and broke my bread. Four times I was taken to hospital for my arm to be seen and treated and rebound. I could tell no one liked the look of it, but there was no infection, and I thought perhaps the bone was beginning to knit. Pulling Eileen into the boat, I'd managed to turn a simple fracture into a compound one, and it appeared for a time that I'd need surgery. Thank God the doctors were wrong.

Several days after our arrival, someone came to tell us the final death toll: thirty men. It was astonishing, and I put the good news into a letter home, written with my left hand and barely legible.

The question now was how to get us back to England. And how soon.

CHAPTER TWO

As it happened, I arrived in England before my latest letter, traveling aboard a smaller hospital ship where I was given light duties, from reading to patients to sitting with the surgical cases. It was an odd experience to stand aside while other nursing sisters did what I could do with my eyes shut, but I also had the opportunity to observe techniques or oversee the skills of new probationers, who were still struggling to remember all they'd been taught.

My father met my train at Victoria Station and tut-tutted over the bandaged arm strapped to my side under my cloak. He reached into the carriage for my valise, saying gruffly, "Well, it could have been worse, Bess. *Britannic* was in all the newspapers, you know, and speculation has been rife that she was torpedoed. They'll be giving you a campaign ribbon next. Captain Bartlett is already in London, facing an inquiry." As we made our way through the throngs of people—most of them families greeting soldiers or saying good-bye to them—he added over the uproar of the next train pulling out, "I told you to stay out of harm's way!"

"Yes, well," I said dryly, "I was trying. The mine had different ideas."

"Damned efficient Germans." He studied my face. "Still in pain?"

"A little," I lied. The train from Dover to London had been

crowded, and my arm had been jostled in spite of the sling and every care.

He tried to shield me from the bustle of people coming and going. "Let's get you out of here, then."

We threaded our way through the valises and trunks and people cluttering the platform, and he handed in my ticket for me. Then we were outside, in the street, and London was cold, wet, and rainy. A far cry from the warmth of Greece. All the same, I was so thankful to be home. The journey from Athens to Malta to Dover had been long and arduous, and somehow a ship no longer seemed to be a haven. We had spotted submarines on three different occasions, but they had been after more important prey.

My father was saying, "My dear, there's not a hotel to be had anywhere. We'll have to make do."

"There's the flat for me. What about you?"

"I'll stay at my club. Tomorrow the train leaves at some ungodly hour, seven, I think. We'll have to be down again by six-thirty."

"Wake me up at five-thirty, if you will. It takes me longer to dress."

He was trying to conceal how worried he was about me, but he said only, "Growing conceited about your looks, are you?"

"Quite vain," I retorted. It was an old argument. Richard Crawford, career officer in the Army that he was, had wanted a son to follow in his boots. Instead he'd got a strong-willed and determined daughter. We had battled ever since I was three.

He waved to a cab that was waiting down the line, and it pulled up for us. "In you go. At least you haven't a great deal of luggage to worry about. That's a blessing. But your mother has already bethought herself of that. The house is full of female things, and she'll expect you to make a fuss over all of them."

"I shall." The war wasn't over for me, whatever Mama might hope. I'd have to find myself new uniforms, or have them made up.

We stopped at the flat I shared with four other nursing sisters, and I made a clumsy dash through the rain for the door. My father, at my heels, got there first and opened it for me.

Mrs. Hennessey, in the ground-floor flat, answered my knock and was on the point of sweeping me into a copious embrace when she glimpsed the strapped arm.

"Oh, my dear!" She hardly came to my chin, an elderly widow who had lived in this same house since her husband died in 1907. It had been converted into flats in 1914. She reached out and took my left hand. "You'll be wanting the key, and with that arm, who's to see to you? None of the others are here just now, you know. But I'll be glad to come up and clean, cook a little, whatever it is you need." She hesitated. "We heard that *Britannic* had gone down. Was it very bad?"

"We were so fortunate there were no wounded onboard," I answered. "But for the rest of us it was a little wearing. Still, we were very lucky." A response I'd given so often it was like a parrot repeating a lesson and not a part of *me*. Of my experience.

"Indeed." Mrs. Hennessey peered into the hall. "Is that your father with you, dear?" She had strict rules about men coming up to the flat. If we wanted to say good-bye to any male over twelve and under sixty, it had to be done at the foot of the stairs, in plain view of anyone coming and going. Diana called it the cruelest blow to romance she'd ever encountered, but none of us had so far complained to Mrs. Hennessey's face.

"Who else?" I asked with a smile. "There are no handsome young men left in London to meet my train. He's dragging me home tomorrow, but I'll have to stop over tonight."

"Then here's the key, my love, and if you need anything, just ask. I'll be bringing up a bit of hot soup later. Tell your father I'll keep an eye on you."

I thanked her and let my father see me up the stairs to the flat under the eaves.

"A mercy it was a broken arm and not a broken limb," he said as we reached the last landing. "I couldn't have carried you another step." He unlocked the door for me and stuck his head inside. "I'll have dinner sent round to you. I expect the larder is empty."

"Mrs. Hennessey is bringing me soup. That will do. There's tea," I said, glancing toward what we euphemistically called our kitchen. "I'd do anything for a cup."

He laughed and came in, shedding his coat. He was not presently a serving officer, he'd retired in 1910, but they had found work for him at the War Office nonetheless. A tall, handsome man with iron gray hair, broad shoulders, and the obligatory crisp mustache, he wore his uniform with an air. We called him Colonel Sahib, my mother and I, behind his back.

He made tea quickly and efficiently while I pored over the mail collected in the basket on the table.

Three of the letters were for me, friends writing from the Front. I wasn't in the mood to open them and set them aside. The war seemed too close as it was, the streets filled with soldiers, some of them wounded on leave, the drabness of late November feeling as if it reflected the drabness of another year of fighting. For a little while I just wanted to forget that somewhere bodies were being torn apart and people were dying. We could hear the guns as we disembarked in Dover, and I had no way of knowing whether it was our artillery or the Germans'.

Something of what I was feeling must have shown in my face.

My father misinterpreted it and said, "Yes, you've had a rough time of it, my dear. Best to think about something else for a bit. Your leave will be up soon enough."

"Soon enough," I echoed, and took the cup he brought me.

It was a souvenir from Brighton, with the Pavilion painted on it. I had never understood where Marianne, one of the nurses with whom I shared the flat, had found all of them, but the shelf in the tiny kitchen held plates from Victoria's Jubilee, Edward VII's coronation, and half the seaside towns in England. My father held a cup with Penzance on it.

He raised his eyebrows as he noticed that himself. "Good God, your mother would have an apoplexy. No decent dishes?"

"We do very well," I answered him. "Didn't you notice the teapot? It's Georgian silver, I swear to you. And there are spoons in the drawer that are French, I'm told, and the sugar bowl is certainly Royal Worcester."

He joined me at the table, stretching his long legs out before him. "Bess."

I knew what he was about to ask.

"It wasn't bad," I said, trying to put a good face on all that had happened to me. "Frightening, yes, when we first hit the mine, and then when we had to abandon ship." I didn't mention the boats pulled into the screws. "And worrying, because there were so many who were hurt. The papers said we were lucky in the circumstances that only thirty died while over a thousand lived. But what about those thirty souls who never came home? Some are buried near Piraeus, in the British military cemetery there. Others were buried at sea or never made it out of the water at all. I think about them. On the whole, everyone behaved quite well. And it was daylight, and sunny, though the water was cold. That made an enormous difference to those who jumped."

"Do you want to go back to duty?"

He was offering to pull strings and keep me at home to work with convalescents.

"Yes, I do. I make a difference, and that matters. There are men alive now because of my skills." And one who died in spite of them . . .

I changed the subject quickly. "Do you know the Graham family? Ambrose Graham? In Kent." Too abrupt—I'd intended to broach the subject casually. But his concern had rattled me.

He frowned. "Graham . . . Rings a bell somewhere."

"He had something to do with racing, I think—a horse called Merlin the Wise."

"Ah. One of the finest steeplechasers there ever was. That Graham. He died some years ago. His first wife was a cousin of Peter Neville's. He lost her in childbirth, and Merlin had to be put down that same year. Neville wrote me that it turned his mind." He finished his tea and sat back. "Any particular reason why I should remember the Grahams tonight?"

My father was nothing if not all-seeing. His subalterns and his Indian staff had walked in fear of him, believing him to have eyes everywhere. I knew better—it was a mind that never let even the tiniest detail escape his notice.

"Not especially." I was fishing for words now, the right ones. "His son Arthur was one of my patients, you see."

"Arthur? Was that the child's name?"

"Arthur was a son of the second family. Ambrose Graham married again."

"Ah. Go on."

"At any rate, Arthur was healing quite nicely. Then his wound went septic almost overnight, and he—died," I ended baldly.

"And you felt that somehow it was your fault. You must have been very tired and upset, my dear, to believe such a thing. Men do die from wounds. I've seen perfectly hardy souls taken off by the merest scratch while others survive against all odds. Even Florence Nightingale couldn't have done more. You must accept that as part of the price of nursing." His voice was unusually gentle.

"No. Not that. I mean, yes, I felt—it was appalling that he died, that we'd failed, although we'd done all that was humanly possible. . . . There is something else. As he was dying, Arthur made me promise to give one of his brothers a message. He was insistent. I don't think he would have died in peace if I hadn't agreed."

I could see Arthur's face again, taut with suffering as he reached for my hand, intent on what he was saying, urgent to make me understand why I must carry out his wishes. He'd died two hours later, without speaking again. And I'd sat there by the bed, watching the fires of infection take him. It was I who'd closed his eyes. They had been blue, and not even the Mediterranean Sea could have matched them.

"What sort of message?" He knew soldiers, my father did, and his gaze was intent. "Something to do with his will? A last wish? Or more personal, something he'd left undone? A girl, perhaps?" When I hesitated, he added, "It's been some time, I think, since you made your promise. Is that what's worrying you, my dear? There were no wounded on *Britannic*'s last voyage."

"It was the voyage before that—if you remember, I had only a few days in London before we sailed again." I should never have brought up the subject tonight. I don't even know why I had, except that as our train rumbled through Kent, and I was finally safely back in England, I faced for the first time the unpalatable truth that I could very well have died out there in the sea, one of those thirty lost souls. And if I had, and there was any truth to an afterlife, it would have been on my soul that I'd failed Arthur. I was sorely tempted to change trains there and then in Rochester, and make my way unannounced to Owlhurst. It would have been a foolish thing to do—my father was waiting for me in London, and for all I knew, Arthur's brother was in France, out of my reach. But the urgent need to assuage my sense of guilt had been so strong I could hardly sit still in my seat. I knew what it was, of course I did. It was the taste of near failure, and to my father's daughter, failure was unthinkable.

I tried now to find a way of disentangling myself from what I'd begun, but I was in too deep and heard myself saying instead, "The message—how am I to judge it? How can I know if I waited too long, if I'm already too late? Arthur wasn't delirious, he knew what he was telling me and why. What we'd been giving him hadn't affected his brain. I know the dying dwell on small things, something left undone, something unfinished. This was different. He was still in command of his senses when he held my hand and made me swear. I think until the last minute, he still believed he'd live to see to it himself. He desperately wanted to live. He turned to me as a last resort."

"If the moment made such an impression on you, why have you put off carrying out his wishes?"

I rubbed the shoulder of my bad arm. "I don't know," I said again. And then was forced to be honest. "Fear, I think."

"Fear of what?"

"I was still grieving, not for the man his family knew, but for the one I'd nursed. They'd remember him differently, as their son, their brother, their friend. I wasn't ready for that Arthur. I wanted to hold on to my memories for a little while longer. It—I know that was selfish, but it was all I had." I looked at my father, feeling the shame of that admission. "I—it was a bad time for me."

"You cared about this young man, I can see that. Do you still?"

I hesitated, then made an attempt to answer his question. "I'm not nursing a broken heart. Truly. It's just—my professional detachment slipped a little. I—it took a while to regain that detachment." I stirred my tea before looking my father in the face. "You've commanded hundreds of men. There must have been a handful of them who stood out above the rest. And you couldn't have said why, even when you knew you oughtn't have a favorite. They're just—a little different somehow, and you want the best for them. And it hurts when you lose them instead."

"Yes, I understand what you're saying. God knows, I do. I've sent men into danger perfectly aware that they might not come back, and equally aware that I could not send someone else in their place. If you remember, when you first decided to train as a nurse, I warned you that the burden of watching men suffer and die would be a heavy one. Young Graham just brought that home in a very personal way. It happens, my dear. He won't be the last. War is a bloody waste of good men, and that will break your heart when nothing else does. I'd have liked to meet this man. He sounds very fine." He cleared his throat, in that way he had of putting things behind him. "As to the message. Would you like to tell me what it is, and let me judge?"

I considered his suggestion, realizing that it was exactly what I wanted to do. I took a deep breath, trying to keep my voice steady. "I had to repeat the words two or three times, to be certain I knew them by heart. 'Tell Jonathan that I lied. I did it for Mother's sake. But it has to be set right.'"

My father frowned. "And that's it?"

"Yes. In a nutshell." I was tense, waiting. Afraid he might read something in the words that I hadn't.

"I don't see there's been any harm done, waiting until now to pass it on to his brother," he replied slowly. "But you have a responsibility not to put it off again. A duty to the dead is sacred, I needn't tell you that."

I lied. I did it for Mother's sake. I repeated the words in my head. I couldn't tell my father that with time those words had become sinister. It was only my imagination running rampant, of course. Still, I was relieved that he'd found them unremarkable.

"It's not your place to sit in judgment, you know." And there it was again, that sixth sense that told him what I was thinking. "There must be a dozen explanations. Perhaps he tried to make himself seem braver than he was. Or safer than he was. Or perhaps there's a girl involved. Someone his mother had hoped he might marry one day. And he'd lied about how he felt toward her. Men do strange things in the excitement of going off to war. Make promises they can't keep, get themselves involved more deeply than they might have done otherwise. If Arthur Graham had wanted you to know more, he'd have explained why his message mattered so much. For whatever reason, he didn't."

And that was the crux of it. Arthur had never told me anything. And I'd been afraid that it meant there had been someone else. . . .

It wasn't merely vanity.

I had listened to too many men in pain, in delirium, on the point of being sent home, dying. The dying often regretted a hasty marriage that would leave the girl a widow. Sometimes they regretted not marrying. And how many letters had I written to girls who had just told the wounded man that she was expecting his child, and he would turn his head to the wall. "It can't be mine," they sometimes murmured in despair. Or they were in a fever to find a way to marry her before the baby came. War and women. They seemed to go together.

There were other worries facing the wounded, of course. Debt, a family's need, a mother's illness, how to live with one arm or without sight. But Arthur had said, *It has to be set right . . .*

I heaved a sigh, not of relief but of self-knowledge. Arthur Graham had confided a responsibility to me. I'd made a promise to carry that through. And there was an end to it. His past was never mine to judge, and caring hadn't altered that.

I *must* go to Kent. I'd done both Arthur and his family a disservice by putting off doing what I'd sworn to do. If nothing else, they should have a chance to carry out Arthur's last wish. Their duty. And not mine.

Honor above all things. I'd heard my father drum that into his subalterns and his younger lieutenants.

What I needed now was to hear my father say that it wasn't selfishness that had held me back after all, it had been a matter of another duty, and I'd had to answer that call first. That Arthur hadn't misplaced his trust.

To put it bluntly, I wanted comforting.

But he didn't answer that need. And I couldn't ask.

My own guilty conscience nattered at me instead. And the Colonel was right, there was no excuse for failing in one's duty. No comfort to be given. I thought bitterly, whatever I discovered in Kent would teach me that dying heroes sometimes had feet of clay.

Then my father said gently, "Bess. If you'd gone down with *Britannic,* there would have been no one to deliver his message."

Which brought me back to the nightmare that had haunted me on my long journey home. Full circle.

"I can't go now—" I gestured to my arm.

"You aren't fit enough to travel again just now, and you must write to this brother first and ask if the family will receive you. Your mother would tell you that war or no war, the rules of courtesy haven't changed." He smiled. "You do know how to reach the Grahams?"

"He made me memorize the address as well."

My father studied my face. I wanted to squirm, as I'd done as a child when I'd got caught in a mischief. He said, "It's not wise to get close to a soldier, Bess. Ask your mother."

I wanted to cry, but I forced myself to smile, for his sake. "Yes, so you've told me. A solicitor, a banker, a merchant prince. But never a soldier."

But in my mind I could still see Arthur's face. The worst of it was, I knew very well he'd have done everything in his power to carry out *my* last wishes. How could I have let him down?

Besides, I would probably have never known about that other girl, if he'd lived.

Chapter Three

Somerset, Late December 1916

My arm was stubborn and refused to heal properly. By Christmas, I still couldn't brush my hair with that hand, it was so weak.

Dr. Price fretted over it, threatening to send me to a specialist in London.

My mother urged me to go anyway, to see what could be done. "You're lucky there's been no infection, what with the cut. There will be a scar, I'm afraid. We'll ask Nora for some lotion or ointment to make it look a little less angry." The gash had gone deep, very deep. The scar was raised and ugly still.

"I'm not worried, Mother. Bones take their time, you know. Let's wait another week."

But it was the duty of mothers to fuss, and truth was, I was glad to be home for a bit, leaving decisions to others. My father, on the other hand, was after me to exercise my arm.

"They'll not take you back again until it's strong enough," he warned me. "You can't swim in this weather, worst luck, but we can have you sit by the bath and move your arm back and forth in warm water. That should help. It's what they did for my leg in India."

He'd broken it playing polo.

"I'll try," I promised, and did. I also had my own ways of keeping the arm working. Exercises I'd learned aboard *Britannic,* listening to doctors instruct wounded men.

"Muscles atrophy without use," they'd explained. "Leave a limb in a cast too long, and it will be worthless. A baby could knock you over. But *this*—"

And men had done their best, crying sometimes from the pain or the frustration as they worked. I'd learned an entirely new vocabulary from my patients. Most of it unacceptable, even to tease my father.

I found myself thinking at one point that in coming home wounded, I'd somehow stepped back into the old pattern of parent and child. It was strange, after being responsible for life-and-death decisions in a hospital ward. I'd grown used to responsibility and consequences, to holding back my own emotions in order to give comfort to someone else, to handling recalcitrant patients or men so far gone in delirium they thought they were still fighting the Germans. Now I was tucked up in bed with a glass of warm milk, just as I'd been at seven when I had measles.

The truth dawned on me slowly: my mother and father missed the old Bess, and they were still recovering from the shock of *Britannic* going down. It must have been days before they had had news of me, whether I was alive or drowned. And so I drank the milk without complaint and let them heal too.

One day my father stopped by my chair in the small parlor where I was trying to read.

"Have you done anything more about your promise?"

"I wrote to Jonathan Graham. I asked to meet him, adding that it concerned his late brother."

"You want to see this girl for yourself, I think. The one Arthur abandoned." He was half teasing, half serious.

"Not at all," I answered with more heat than I wanted to hear in my voice. "I must deliver my message in person. It's what I was asked to do. Arthur told me over and over again—a letter was use-less, I had to speak to Jonathan face-to-face."

"Jonathan may be at the Front."

"No, I've asked friends. Apparently he's at home as well, conva-lescing."

"Then go before your leave is up."

"Yes. I shall."

He said nothing more. But a week later he brought me a letter from the post and dropped it in my lap.

I took it up, dreading it, thinking it must be my orders.

My father said, "They've answered."

And I turned over the envelope. The sloping handwriting was unfamiliar, but the return address I knew all too well.

Opening the letter, I scanned the contents quickly.

"It appears that Jonathan Graham is willing to see me." To con-ceal my relief, I added dryly, "He's probably bored to tears, or else he's already got his orders to return to the Front. I'm to come at my convenience, and Thursday next will do very well."

My father laughed, then added, "You aren't ready to drive."

My own motorcar, the one I'd fought my father for, was now in the stables, collecting dust, tucked safely out of range of the zeppelin raids on London.

Since the Colonel refused to sanction the purchase, I'd had to ask one of my male friends to advise me. I wanted the independence a motorcar could give me.

I hadn't counted on it breaking down during my first visit home.

My father, *I told you so* written all over his face, had brought Simon Brandon with him to ferry me home while he consigned the offending motorcar to a nearby smithy. Simon Brandon was younger than my father by more than twenty years. He'd risen in the ranks to become the Colonel's regimental sergeant major, and was nearly as domineering, but much easier to cajole. He treated my mother like the Princess Royal, and rumor had it that he was in love with her, because he'd never married. As usual, rumor had got it wrong.

"I can manage quite well," I told my father now. "There were times when I drove ambulances in France, and anything at Gallipoli that needed being driven. Including an officer's motorcar, when he lost his leg."

"My dear, it's the train or else I drive you."

I didn't want him going to Kent with me.

"Very well, the train, then."

"I'll see to it. Meanwhile, Simon's invited you to luncheon."

My father drove me to the station and saw me off with misgivings he kept to himself. My mother had scolded me, warning me against taking a chill, worried that the Grahams wouldn't look after me properly, wanting to keep me home and safe for as long as possible. She didn't see me off, claiming the press of getting my uniforms ready before my orders came. But I knew she was afraid of crying. If it had been left to her, I'd never be out of her sight again. It was a measure of how frightened she'd been.

She had said to my father once when she thought I was not within hearing, "With that arm broken, she would have drowned." It had been a cry for comfort, but my father had answered her, "And she didn't. Don't make her timid, my dear. Courage will keep her safer than fear."

My mother had said to me afterward, "Your father is a fool."

When I asked her why, she'd shrugged. "Men generally are," she'd retorted, and changed the subject.

I had found myself wanting to hug her, but I didn't dare, knowing she would have wondered why, and probably guessed. She is good at reading hearts, my mother.

The train's carriages were filled with eager young men on their way to war, leaning out their windows and talking excitedly to others boarding at each station. I looked at their faces and felt sad. The captain of artillery sitting next to me said under his breath, "Little do they know," when a rousing cheer went up as we pulled out of the next small town.

We weren't winning, and the killing would go on and on. That was the fate of trench warfare, of a stalemate neither we nor Germany could break.

I'd seen that the captain wore one arm in a sling as well, and I asked him where he'd served. "France," he answered. "I'm on my way back again."

"Is your arm healed?"

"Near enough. I don't have to carry a rifle or a pack. It'll do. How is yours healing?"

I had to admit it was not doing as well as I'd hoped.

He knew Jack Franklin, as it turned out, and we spent the journey to London in conversation. Jack had been our neighbor before he'd married and gone to live in Warwick. My father had had high hopes for him in the Army, and Captain Banks promised to give Jack our best wishes when next they met.

In London I changed trains for Tonbridge, and we rolled through a dreary rain that lasted almost all the way, lashing the windows and dampening my spirits.

After Sevenoaks, I was alone in the compartment, and I removed my sling, tucking it in the small case beside me. Flexing my fingers, I gingerly tested my arm. If I was careful, it would do.

The early dark caught up with me long before I'd reached my destination, but through the rain-wet windows I could see rolling downs, the lights of farms, and the houses of villages through which we passed with only the briefest of stops.

The fruit trees were bare, but I had seen clouds of blossoms, coming up from Dover the spring we arrived in England from the Colonel's last posting in India, and their beauty had taken my breath away after the dry featureless expanse of the Northwest Frontier.

Now the hop fields were flat and hardly recognizable save for the oast houses, like broken windmills. In one pasture, sheep huddled, backs to the wind and almost invisible in the shelter of a stone wall. A man in a cart crouched wretchedly under his umbrella as he waited for the train to thunder past a crossing. I think my resolution dropped with the weather and I wished myself home again, sitting by the fire in comfort.

In his letter, Jonathan Graham had told me that I would be met. But when the train pulled into Tonbridge the winter dusk had turned to darkness, and there was no one waiting as I stepped out onto the windswept platform. For a mercy the rain had stopped. I could see the station master talking with the engineer, and so I walked into the booking office where it was warmer. It too was as empty. Then through the front window I saw the flicker of a lamp in the street beyond and heard the sound of a horse being turned. I went through to find a small dogcart there, and a driver muffled to the teeth against the cold.

"Miss Crawford?"

"Yes, I'm Miss Crawford."

He grudgingly got down to fetch my valise and my small case from the platform, then returned to hand me up into the cart. But I shook my head. "I'll ride with you, instead." Reaching for the blanket folded on a seat, I realized that it was colder than I was.

Without a word he settled me into the seat next to him. As he climbed up to join me, his bulk blocked the worst of the wind. I huddled beside him and set my teeth to stop them from chattering. In the cold air, my arm ached. Broken bones tend to do that.

The horse snorted and began to walk on, and I said to the man holding the reins, "What is your name, please?"

"Robert."

It was all the information I got for several miles as we left the lights of Tonbridge behind and the darkness settled around us like a cloak. The blanket across my knees began to unthaw and I kept my gloved fingers cradled in an edge of it. I watched houses and then the occasional farm pass by, windows lit, people no doubt just sitting down to their tea. I felt remarkably alone, and even unwanted. I could sense Robert's hostility and in a way understood it—it was my fault he'd had to drive out on a night like this.

We must have traveled five miles or more beyond the last village when we came to a large, rambling house set back in the trees behind a high wall. It was brick, and every window seemed to be blazing with light. At first I thought it must be my destination, ready to welcome me, but as we passed by, Robert must have sensed my surprise.

"The asylum," he said, and fell silent again.

The horse trotted on, the sound of his hooves and the cart wheels filling the night.

Robert reached behind him into the cart and brought out a rug I hadn't seen in the darkness at the station. He thrust it toward me, and I took it, gratefully wrapping it over my shoulders. The wind seemed to cut straight through my traveling coat, touching my skin with sharp fingers.

Some time later, the cart's nearside wheels dropped off the road into a deep rut. The jolt caught me off guard, and I was nearly thrown from my seat onto the verge.

Robert's hand came out in the nick of time and caught me, holding me back as the horse regained the road and the cart stopped rocking wildly. I hadn't even had time to cry out, it had all happened so fast. But for the quickness of the man beside me, I'd have been pitched out on my head. Or worse, perhaps, on my still-healing arm.

I shuddered at the close call, and Robert said, "Beg pardon. I must have dozed off."

My heart was racing, and I could still feel his fingers in that bruising grip.

I'd have been happy to see a stoat or a fox along the road, any living thing, by the time I could glimpse the lights of another village ahead of us.

Cottages, houses, then a pub, The Bells, its sign swinging in the wind, a cricket pitch on the other side of the road, and then the tall silhouette of a church set on a slight rise behind a low stone wall. To one side was what must have been the rectory, a lovely tall black and white Tudor house, and through the mullioned windows I could see a comfortable parlor done up in blue and cream, with a pair of china dogs set on the windowsill, their backs to the stormy night.

We turned the other way, under the sheltering limbs of two great trees overhanging the wall, and then another turning brought us into a lane with four or five houses in a row. The largest of them was Georgian and backed up to the far side of the churchyard. Gardens that must have been colorful in summer lay in the shadow of an iron fence, and a gate set into it led up the walk to an elegant door.

A single lamp burned above it, and the horse drew to a halt, as if he knew he had come home.

Robert got down and came around to help me, taking the rugs from me. Then he opened the iron gate for me and carried my valise and case up the walk before lifting the knocker.

A maid answered the summons almost at once, opening the door wide and welcoming me inside. Robert set down my bags, then disappeared into the night as the door shut on him.

"Mrs. Graham asked me to show you directly to your room, Miss Crawford. There's dinner in half an hour. I'll come for you to show you the way."

"And you are?"

"Susan, Miss." She bobbed a curtsey, smiling in welcome.

"Thank you, Susan." I was glad not to have to present myself to Arthur's mother travel worn and with muddy hems.

The hall floor was patterned parquet, and on a gateleg table between two doorways stood a vase with dried flowers arranged in it. Above it was a fine oil painting of a black horse, and I wondered if this was Merlin the Wise. As I followed Susan up the lovely curving stairs and down a wide passage, I thought of my mother's last words of advice.

If you wish to make an impression, my dear, wear the blue gown.

As always, she was right. The blue gown suited this house very well.

There was a fire on the hearth of the room I was taken to, and warm water in the pitcher on the stand. I washed my face and hands, then changed my clothes. I was just tidying my hair when Susan came to collect me.

We went down to a dining room where only one end of the long table had been set. A woman was standing near it, waiting for me. Arthur's mother.

She was not at all as I'd pictured her in my mind. Somehow the words "I did it for Mother's sake" had prepared me for someone small and fragile and perhaps more than a little domineering.

Instead she was younger than I'd expected, and tall, with graying dark hair, blue eyes, and a confident carriage that spoke of years of managing her family on her own after her husband's death. I looked for any resemblance to her son and decided it was in the height, the dark hair, the strong chin.

She greeted me with a warm smile of welcome, but I knew very well she'd been examining me even as I examined her.

"Hello, my dear! Robert tells me you came close to a nasty fall. Are you all right? Should I send for Dr. Philips?"

"No harm done," I said lightly. "Thank you for asking."

Her eyes were searching my face. "You knew Arthur well, did you?"

I'd met that look before, from mothers and sisters and wives wanting to know how their dear boy had gone to his death, wanting some crumb of comfort and love to fill the emptiness that lay ahead of them.

"He was very brave," I said. "When he was wounded, he took it well. I often read to him and a few of the others, when I had time.

Or wrote letters for them. I wrote his last one to you. He couldn't hold a pen, you see, and he wanted desperately to tell you how much he cared."

"Yes, I've cherished that letter. A fine young man. I think in many ways he was my favorite. Though a mother shouldn't say that, should she?"

"He was a man any mother could be proud of," I answered with sincerity, though I had said it many times in many letters to women I would never meet.

"Yes. Yes, he was." Remembering her manners, she said, "Please, sit here by me. Jonathan will be down before long. He's here on convalescent leave."

"Arthur told me he had three brothers. Are they all in the Army?"

Her face clouded. "Timothy isn't serving—he wasn't allowed to join the army, you know. He was born with a clubfoot, and although he walks very well, he was considered unsuitable. He feels rather cut up about that, with everyone else enlisting or already at the Front."

"I'm sorry—"

"Don't be! To tell you the truth, it's one less worry for me. I've suffered enough with Arthur and Johnnie."

Before she could tell me about the last son, Jonathan walked in. I knew him at once because of his wound. He was a paler version of Arthur, his hair a lighter brown, his eyes a less vibrant shade of blue.

He had a terrible scar across his face. Shrapnel, at a guess. It was still half covered by bandages, but I could see where the wound began high on his forehead near the hairline, and then the last thin line of it passing down his jaw and back to his chin. His mother made the introductions, and he shook my hand.

"Where were you wounded?" I asked before I thought. But I was used to talking to bandaged men, and more often than not they wanted it known where they had served.

"Mons," he said shortly, and went to kiss his mother's cheek. She turned to him with a softness that spoke of her love for him, and I glanced away. It was such a private moment, and touching.

Another man, leaning on his cane, came in at that moment. He was fairer than either of his brothers, with gray-blue eyes.

Again I was introduced, this time to Timothy, and he said at once, "Mother tells me you knew Arthur?"

"I was his nurse for some time, yes."

He nodded. "We were grateful for your letter afterward. It's hard to think of him dying so far away. We expect him to walk through the door any day, smiling, calling to one of us."

They spoke of Arthur with such warmth, almost as if he were still alive.

It occurred to me that under different circumstances, I might have been brought here after the war, Arthur's arm linked with mine as he presented me to his family. What would they have thought of me, then? Not as Florence Nightingale, who had nursed their brother, but as someone who mattered to him? Arthur had asked me to marry him, before he lost his leg. He'd been in high spirits after the doctor moved him from guarded to satisfactory condition, believing he'd heal now. I'd smiled and lightly given my usual response to impetuous proposals. "You must speak to my father first. He outranks you, you see."

It hadn't put him off, as I'd expected. On the contrary, he'd wanted to write to the Colonel directly, but nothing more had been said about that after the amputation.

Susan appeared with the first course as we were sitting down. As she served us, we talked about people we might know in common, about London, about the sinking of *Britannic*. I found myself thinking that this was a family like so many others in Britain tonight, trying to pretend that life was going on as it had before, despite the empty chair at the table and the shadow hanging over Jonathan's future.

The door opened again, and I thought that the third son must be making his appearance at last, but it was an older man who stepped into the room and nodded to Mrs. Graham. He was tall, with broad shoulders and a barrel chest, a handsome man with thick fair hair that was graying. I realized all at once that this was Robert. I hadn't seen him clearly in the dark, muffled as he was in scarves, his hat pulled down against the wind.

There was an air of impatience about him, and his manner was very different from that of the man in the cart.

Hardly a servant, was my first thought. Yet he'd been sent to fetch me.

"If you need me, I'll be in my room," he said, and was gone.

Mrs. Graham turned to me. "I don't know if Arthur told you about Robert. He's a Douglas, a cousin on my father's side. He was such a blessing to us when my husband died. There was no one to take my sons in hand, and Robert saw to it that they were given the opportunities my husband would have wished. Robert taught them to ride and to shoot and to be men."

Arthur had said nothing at all about him. But I made polite noises, and she turned to another subject, the journey from Somerset.

I could see that I wouldn't have an opportunity tonight to speak to Jonathan privately. *Tomorrow,* I thought, *would be best.* I had the feeling as the evening wore on that Arthur's mother was anxious, as if she'd wanted me to come here and, now that I was under her roof, wasn't certain how to entertain me. She was often silent as Jonathan and Timothy talked to me about the war, and I tried several times to change the subject for her sake.

We finished our meal and went into the parlor where the tea tray had been taken. After another hour or more of polite conversation, I excused myself, saying that the journey had been tiring, and went up to bed.

I carried with me the picture of a close family still grieving for their loss.

In the morning, Susan tapped lightly on my door and took me down to the dining room where breakfast was waiting.

Jonathan and Timothy must have come and gone, judging from two empty cups and saucers on the table. Mrs. Graham was just helping herself to a dish of eggs from the sideboard.

I filled my own plate and sat down, taking up my cup. Mornings aren't my best time, and I let the tea flow through me, waking me up. Mrs. Graham was cheerful and the conversation general until we'd finished eating.

And then she said, setting her knife and fork across her plate, "You have a message, you said. From Arthur."

I set down my knife and fork as well, though I hadn't finished eating. "The message is for Jonathan, Mrs. Graham. Though Arthur sent you his dearest love."

"Yes, I understand. But surely you could share it with me?"

"I'm—I'm not sure that was what Arthur wished me to do. But I think Jonathan should be the one to answer that."

She was frowning at me, her back straight, her shoulders squared, as if bracing herself for an argument. And then she relaxed.

"Of course. You're right, my dear. It's just that I'm hungry for any crumb of comfort. You can't imagine what it is like to know your child is buried at sea in a foreign place, and will never come home again. I haven't been able to believe he's gone forever. I tell myself, and then I slip into the habit of putting it out of my mind."

I thought she was cajoling me. But I was saved from an answer when Jonathan came into the room and said, "Miss Crawford? If you've finished your breakfast, perhaps you'd like to see the memorial to Arthur in the church."

"Yes," I said—not too quickly, I fervently hoped. But my relief must have been plain on my face. "I would like that."

"I'll ask Susan to fetch your cloak, while you finish your toast."

"Thank you."

While Mrs. Graham watched with a mixture of frustration and worry, I drained my cup and rose to leave the room.

As I reached the door, she said, "Forgive me for pressing, won't you?"

"Yes, of course, I'm sorry to have made you uncomfortable."

And I was gone, hurrying to the hall, where Susan was just bringing down my cloak. Jonathan was standing there, his face unreadable, but one hand was clenching and unclenching, as if he dreaded what was to come.

I wondered fleetingly if he already knew about the girl . . . or was she merely a figment of my own runaway imagination? I was beginning to think she was. Certainly Susan, who must have been closer to forty than thirty, wasn't a likely candidate for Arthur's affections.

We went down the front steps and turned toward the churchyard. The wind had dropped, and the air was crisp. I said, as we walked, "I'm afraid I've upset your mother. But Arthur was still very much in command of his faculties when he asked me to speak directly to you. I don't think he intended—" I broke off.

"We were close," Jonathan said, but somehow I hadn't got that impression from Arthur. He'd not spoken of his brothers except in passing. I knew very little about any of them.

We opened the iron gate and walked through it into the churchyard, my boots crunching in the cold, dead grass. Above us the golden stone of the church apse led the eye upward to the pinnacles gracing the top. Against the blue-gray sky, they stood out like sentinels.

The church door was not locked, and we went inside, where the cold stone seemed to hold on to the stormy chill of last night. I pulled my cloak around me as Jonathan led me to the brass plaque that had been set in the wall between two windows. The stained glass spilled color onto the floor at my feet, and I looked up to the figures of saints high above my head before I could bring myself to look directly at Arthur's memorial.

He was gone.

There was a finality to that as I read the name and dates engraved into the brass. Beneath them were the words *Beloved son and brother* in graceful script.

I very much wanted to reach out and touch it. But not with Jonathan there.

I had not been at the service when his body was committed to the sea. I had been standing in the operating theater fighting to save another life. I had felt the ship slow, then resume her speed, and not allowed myself to think why.

I swallowed my tears and said as steadily as I could, "He would have been pleased."

"Yes."

We turned away without another word and walked back into the sunlight. Standing in the shadows of the west door, Jonathan said, "I expect I'll be as ready now as I ever will be. What was it Arthur entrusted to you to say to me?"

CHAPTER FOUR

I TURNED AWAY, looking at the gleaming white walls of the rectory in their black framework, the tiny panes of glass set into the windows like small diamonds glittering in the morning sun.

"Go on." There was impatience beneath the urging.

I took several seconds to think. To wonder if I'd done the right thing in coming here. The message seemed different suddenly. Futile, and somehow infringing on something I didn't understand.

I tried to set the stage, so that Jonathan Graham could see what I had seen. "He had finished his medicines, and he took my hand, pulling me closer. I thought at first that he was having difficulty seeing me, but it was only to drop his voice so that no one else could hear him. He asked me if I'd carry a message to his brother for him. It was very brief, I had no difficulty remembering it. 'Tell Jonathan I lied. I did it for Mother's sake. But it has to be set right.' And afterward, he made me promise to deliver the message to you in person."

He was watching me, his gaze intent.

"*Tell Jonathan I lied. I did it for Mother's sake. But it has to be set right.*"

"Yes, exactly as he told me."

"And what did you make of his request?"

I could feel my face flushing. I could hardly say what had gone through my mind over the weeks that had passed. It would have sounded presumptuous even to hint at it. I answered only, "I don't know, Lieutenant Graham. I'd hoped you would."

"And he didn't explain to you what it was he was trying to convey?"

"No. To be frank, I don't think he would have said anything at all, if he hadn't realized he was dying. But something was preying on his mind, I could see that. And it was disturbing enough for him to try to do something about it while he could still speak."

"Then why not write it in your letter?"

"I don't know," I said again. "It was almost as if—" I stopped.

"As if what?"

"It was almost as if *he* hadn't wanted to put it in writing. He was insistent that I come to you personally."

"But Arthur has been dead some months. If it were a pressing matter, surely it would have been better to come here at once?"

I prevaricated. "You were in France, Lieutenant Graham. And there were my duties as well. And this—" I indicated my arm.

"I'm sorry, I wasn't thinking." He continued to stare at me, but his mind was elsewhere. Then he said again, "And that's all of the message? You're quite sure?"

"Yes. I've given it word for word."

"Thank you, Miss Crawford. It was kind of you to carry out my brother's wishes. But I think you liked him, a little. Is that true?"

"He was a very likable man," I answered honestly. "Very popular with the men and with the nursing staff."

"And he said nothing about this matter until he was—dying?"

"To my knowledge, no. None of the other nurses told me anything about promises."

"But then you didn't tell them, either, did you."

"No."

"Why do you think he chose you?"

I knew I was pink again. "Because I took the time to be with him during his last hours. I assure you, he wasn't the only one I watched over or read to—or wrote letters for. It's hard to explain, Lieutenant Graham, but when you are sitting by a wounded man and he's telling you what to say to his mother or his wife or his sweetheart, there's an intimacy that can't be avoided. I have had men say things to me that were terribly personal, messages to their wives that they would never have shared in any other circumstance." I paused. "It's almost as if I'm not there, they're simply talking aloud. But I hear these things and try not to listen at the same time. If you understand what I'm saying."

Jonathan Graham nodded. "Yes, I've asked the nursing sisters to write letters for me, when the bandaging covered my eyes." After a moment he roused himself from whatever thoughts were distracting him, and said again, "Thank you. It was a great kindness. I hope you'll consider staying the weekend. I think my mother would be grateful if you could."

"I don't wish to impose—"

"It's no imposition. She would take it as a great favor."

We walked on, the wintry sun trying to peer through the bare trees.

"Have you been to Owlhurst before, Miss Crawford?"

"No, it's my first visit to this part of Kent."

"We were once famous for our owls. On the far side of the churchyard there's what's left of the great expanse of wood that covered much of Kent in the distant past, an almost impenetrable forest. When my parents were first married, I'm told they could walk through it of an evening and count two or three species of owl calling in the dusk. I daresay they're still there, those owls. I like to think of the continuity of life here. It helps, a little, in the trenches."

"I remember Arthur saying something about them. He could never find where they nested."

Jonathan smiled. "That was Arthur for you. Always trying to get to the bottom of things. My mother will tell you he was a very clever child, interested in science but with a leaning toward the law. I expect he'd have become a solicitor but for the war."

I said nothing. Arthur had told me that he had turned away from the law as a profession. I tried to remember his words.

"There's evil in goodness and goodness in evil," he'd said. *"I've seen too much of the evil in the law to be comfortable with it."*

"What would you like to do, then, when the war is over?"

"I think I'd like to grow coffee in East Africa. Somewhere new where I could start over."

"Why should you wish to start over?"

"Because there would be no memories of the past infringing on the present."

I'd thought he meant memories of the war. Now I wondered.

"Lieutenant Graham, I'd like very much to ask you a question. Though you needn't answer if you don't wish to."

"Of course. What is it?"

"Can you right this wrong for your brother? Is it in your power?"

"Why should you doubt me?" His voice was cold.

"It isn't doubting you so much as wanting to believe that his faith in both of us wasn't misplaced. I saw his distress. This was on his conscience, if you will. He was helpless to rectify what lay in the past. But he thought you might be able to do that for him. I'd like to leave here with the feeling that Arthur will rest easier now."

"Your sense of duty does you credit, Miss Crawford. You can rely on me to see to it that Arthur's last wishes are treated with the greatest respect."

"Indeed. Thank you, Lieutenant."

We made our way back to the house in silence, and I tried to tell myself that I had faithfully kept my promise. There was, after all, nothing more I could do or say. And if Arthur had trusted his brother, I must believe he knew he could.

Then why did I have this feeling that treating Arthur's last wishes with the greatest respect wasn't the same as promising to carry them out?

I could almost hear the Colonel Sahib's voice: *Walk away, Bess. If Arthur had wanted more from you, he'd have told you more.*

The question really was, would *Arthur* have felt satisfied?

Well, to be fair, it was possible that Jonathan Graham knew what it was Arthur wanted but not how to go about it. After all, he'd had only a matter of minutes to digest my message.

Who are you *to talk?* my conscience demanded. *After leaving your duty to the eleventh hour. What would you have done, my lass, if Lieutenant Graham had died of his own wounds?*

I sighed as we walked through the door and would have liked to go directly to my room for a bit.

But Mrs. Graham was standing there waiting for us, as if she'd watched our progress from a window, and she rushed me into the sitting room the instant I'd handed my cloak over to Susan.

"You must be freezing, my child. Come and sit by the fire. Would you like something warm to drink?"

"No, I'm fine, Mrs. Graham, thank you."

"You saw the memorial?"

"It was—touching," I said, trying to think how to answer.

"Yes. I think he'd have been glad of it."

Jonathan had gone to some other part of the house, and I wondered if he would tell his mother any or all of that message. Or what he would tell her. I was just grateful now that she hadn't brought up the subject again.

After lunch, she asked if I'd care to walk around the village. "For the sun is stronger now, and it will be more comfortable."

It was the last thing I wanted. The cold, after the Mediterranean Sea, was penetrating. My arm preferred to sit by the fire. But I smiled and said that I would, and she sent me up for my coat.

Muffled once more in scarf and gloves, I followed her down the lane and into the churchyard. I thought at first she was going to take me back to see the memorial.

Instead we walked a little way among the gravestones, and I could admire the lovely mellowed stone of the church above us. Its air of age was comforting, like an anchor—or a rock—that spoke of centuries past and centuries to come.

Neither of us mentioned the raw graves marking where men had come home to die. Arthur might have been among them, if his leg had waited another few weeks to turn septic.

In the sea there were no markers for the dead. No place in the deep to mourn, no place to leave flowers. Just degrees of latitude and longitude on a chart.

Mrs. Graham nodded toward the rectory. "We have a new rector now. And a new doctor. Times are changing. But then nothing stays the same forever, does it? Even one's children grow up and go off to die."

"You're worried for Jonathan," I said.

"Dr. Philips tells me the bandages will be off in another fortnight. After that, it will be a matter of days before his orders come." I could hear the pain in her voice and for once was thankful that my own mother had not had a son.

"They're in desperate need of men," I said.

It was not what she wanted to hear.

She gave me a sharp glance and didn't answer. We walked on down the street, where brick houses lined the road. One of them, set back a little, was covered in what would be honeysuckle and roses in summer. Their bare branches arched across the front of the house, trembling in the wind.

Mrs. Graham caught the direction of my interest and said, "That's the doctor's surgery. And just down there is the house that Arthur would have had, if he'd lived. It's part of our property, going to the eldest son on his marriage. There's a caretaker now, one of my school friends who fled London at the start of the war. She was that certain the Kaiser would sail up the Thames before she could pack her boxes."

It was a handsome house, with a front garden set off by a low wall and a cat curled on the doorstep, waiting to be let in. I smiled without realizing it, and she said, "Yes, the cat goes with the house. It or its ancestors have always lived there. Arthur was fond of cats, did you know?"

But he hadn't said anything to me about cats or dogs. I would have replied, if anyone had asked me, that we'd spoken of everything under the sun. I realized now that "everything" hadn't included his childhood or his family. How much had I told him about the Colonel? I couldn't remember. . . . We'd lived in the present. It turned out to be all there was, though he'd wanted a future.

At the next corner, where a row of shops began, we paused. "Did you know this was once a famous smuggling area? Goods were brought up from the coast and hidden wherever the Hawkhurst Gang believed they were safe. There's a hotel now where the inn stood—it provided the horses and wagons for the smuggled goods, and the story has come down that an underground passage ran between The Rose and Thorn and the church. We couldn't find Arthur and his brothers one afternoon—he must have been twelve or thirteen at the time. We finally discovered them in the church, searching for the secret door to the tunnel. I had to explain to them that nearly every village with a smuggling past has such stories of underground passages. They were sorely disappointed."

I smiled as we turned back the way we'd come. "It was probably a story the smugglers themselves invented to keep Customs officials busy searching in the wrong places."

A little silence fell. I could sense that Mrs. Graham was on the point of asking me about what I'd told Jonathan, and I was bracing myself to meet her pleas. I was grateful when a young man came out of one of the other houses we'd just passed and called a greeting to her, heavy with relief.

"Just the person I was after. Could I borrow your Susan, Mrs. Graham? I've got an emergency on my hands, and Betsy is with Mrs. Booth, awaiting the baby." He caught up with us, nearly out of breath and flushed with worry.

"Certainly not," Mrs. Graham answered him. "We have a guest at present, and Susan is indispensable." She turned to me, her face stiff with disapproval. "Miss Crawford, this rude young man is Dr. Philips."

"My pleasure, Miss Crawford. And my apologies. But I'm short-handed, and there's little time for polite exchanges—"

I interrupted him. "I'm a trained nurse," I said. "Can I help in any way?"

The doctor stopped short. "Are you indeed? Oh, thank God. Will you come with me?" He hesitated. "You aren't put off by swearing, are you?"

"Not at all."

"Then I must take her, Mrs. Graham, and return her to you later in the day. Forgive me, but it's urgent."

Mrs. Graham wanted no part of this arrangement. She said, "Dr. Philips. Miss Crawford will not accompany you. You may have Susan—under protest—but you must make certain she's back in time to serve our luncheon."

He glanced at me and then said, "Miss Crawford volunteered, I believe. I'll have her back to you, no harm done, as soon as possible. Come along, there's no time to waste."

"Dr. Philips—" Mrs. Graham was indignant.

"It's quite all right, Mrs. Graham. I have a duty to help. Forgive me, but I must go." I could see the anger in her eyes. I'd disappointed her in some way, but there was nothing I could do about it now. "Dr. Philips?"

He touched his nonexistent hat to her, then took my arm and led me away, his strides twice the length of mine.

"I expect I've caused you no little trouble, Miss Crawford. But I'm rather desperate, and my patient comes first. I'll do my best to smooth matters over for you."

He was a tall man, prematurely graying, with dark eyes. A strong odor of pipe tobacco swirled in his wake as I tried to keep pace with him. We'd reached the house he'd just come from and were hurrying up the walk. "What's the matter with your patient?"

As I spoke I looked back. Mrs. Graham was standing where we'd left her, staring after us. I turned away and followed Dr. Philips through the door of the house.

Dr. Philips was saying, "This is a man who suffers from shell shock. You don't have any preconceived notions about that, do you? Cowardice, and all that? No? That's good. He terrifies his poor wife, but there's nothing she can do when he has one of his spells. I'll give him an injection and he'll calm down. But you'll be there to see to it that he does himself no harm meanwhile."

I had had some experience with shell shock. None of it the sort of thing I wanted to walk into the middle of, not knowing the circumstances.

"Who is in the house with this man—besides his wife?" I asked.

"No one at the moment, worst luck. It's the housemaid's day off, and she's gone to Cranbrook to visit her sister." We stepped into the cold entry, went through the inner doors, and turned down a passage on the left side of the stairs.

A harried young woman stepped out of the nearest room. She had been crying. She said, "I'm sorry, I'm sorry, I didn't know what else to do—I left him there, I couldn't watch him any longer."

"You did just the right thing, Mrs. Booker. Now run along to your mother's house and let her take care of you. Miss Crawford and I will see to Ted."

He was walking on as he spoke, opening the last door along the passage, pushing it wide for me to enter. It was a small back parlor where a man sat in a chair in front of the windows, a shotgun across his knees.

I stopped, surprised. I hadn't expected to find him armed. Small wonder the man's wife had been terrified.

"Come along, Ted," Philips said in a strong voice. "You aren't going to kill yourself here, in the house. Certainly not in front of this young woman. You don't want to upset her, do you? Let me take the gun and give you something for the pain."

From across the room Ted Booker stared at him, unaware who the doctor was. I could see the blankness in his eyes. Ignoring us, he went on talking to invisible companions, men *he* could see clearly and appeared to know well.

He was arguing, vehement and insistent and profane. It appeared that a sniper had already killed three of his men, and he was on the field telephone, asking someone to do something about it.

"I can give you his range, damn it." His voice was ragged, close to the breaking point. "We can't hold out much longer. I tell you, the Hun's got us in his sights—"

He ducked then, swearing, and shouted, "Someone stop that bastard! *No, not you, Harry*—" There was a garbled exchange, as if he were struggling with another man, the shotgun jerking wildly in his grip. And then he cried out, screaming Harry's name over and over again, springing to his feet and finally bending to someone lying there in front of him, pleading with the man not to die.

I said quietly to Dr. Philips, "Who is Harry?"

"His brother."

Dear God, no wonder this poor soul was distraught!

The doctor tried again, but I could see he wasn't getting anywhere asking the man to buck up and put the past behind him. Ted Booker was in a dark place no one else could reach. But there might be a way. . . .

Ignoring the shotgun, I crossed the room to take Booker's arm. "We must get him to the dressing station," I told him urgently. "Hurry, he's bleeding badly."

He shook me off. "Harry, speak to me, for God's sake, speak to me."

"If you wait any longer, he'll die." I reached out and took the shotgun away as his hands flexed open, trying to help the wounded man. I put the weapon behind me, and Dr. Philips was there, I could feel his grip above mine, then he stepped back. I held on to Booker's arm. "What rank was he? Do you know?" I asked Dr. Philips in a low voice.

"Er—lieutenant, I think."

"Don't stand there staring, Lieutenant Booker! Here, take his shoulders, I'll get his feet."

He seemed to rouse himself, looking up at me, then telling Harry it would be all right, there was help now.

And then between us, we lifted the wounded man I couldn't see, and Booker started out the door and down the passage with him between us, urging me in his turn to hurry, *hurry.*

Confused as we entered the passage by the stairway, Booker hesitated.

I said, "That cot. Over there. *Doctor! This case is critical.*" We put Harry down at the foot of the stairs, with Dr. Philips hovering in the background.

"Well done, Lieutenant. Look, here's someone to see to Harry now. Sit down over there—yes, out of the way." I led him to a chair against the opposite wall, put out a hand, and Dr. Philips set the needle into my palm. "Here, you're exhausted. You must be calm when you see him again. Let me give you this—" The needle went home, and Ted Booker started up. I thought for an instant he was going to strike me. "Steady, young man, or I'll make you wait outside the tent," I said harshly, the voice of Matron and not to be trifled with. "Now sit down and be quiet while we do our work."

But he shook me off, still calling to Harry.

Dr. Philips came up, took his arm as I had done, and said, "Soldier, you're in the way. I can't work—sit down. See, you're distressing the wounded man—"

I turned my head to stare at him—it didn't sound like Dr. Philips's normal voice at all. It sounded like a medical orderly giving orders. We had found ourselves swept up in Ted Booker's nightmare, playing our roles to an invisible audience.

Booker, distraught, clung to him. "Harry—" he began.

"Harry's in good hands. You mustn't let your men down, you know. Good example and all that."

We finally got through to Booker, and then he sat down on the floor and began to cry, holding his dead brother in his arms and rocking him like a child. It wouldn't be long now before the injection took effect.

I said softly to Dr. Philips, "The shotgun. Get rid of it."

He turned to do as I'd asked, and I bent over to touch Booker's shoulder.

"Lieutenant. Come in here, out of the rain."

Ted Booker got up, stumbling a little, and let me lead him toward the dining room.

Halfway there, he twisted free and went back, calling for Harry. But his words had already begun to slur, and it was just a matter of minutes before he was half conscious and easily led up the stairs to the nearest bedroom. We got him onto the bed, his shoes off, his collar loosened, and a blanket over him against the chill. By that time he was out, and snoring from the drug.

Dr. Philips said, "Thank you for your help. You must have done this before—you got through to him."

I couldn't tell him I'd never dealt with such a severe case before. Not alone. But I'd learned from Dr. Paterson not to interrupt whatever world the patient inhabited. It was easier to enter it, and use it to help.

"They're accustomed to the sisters. They usually mind well enough." I was suddenly very tired, a reaction to the tension we'd been under.

"One of these days, he's going to do himself a harm. He thinks he got his brother killed. Most of the time he's all right, but today something set him off. His wife sent the man next door to call me. He was as bad as I've ever seen him."

"He's in torment," I said. "And it won't go away. You can't keep him drugged."

"No. I'll take the shotgun home with me and bury it in a closet. I should have thought of looking for a weapon before this, but truth is, I didn't know it was even in the house until today."

We sat down on the two chairs in the room, one by the window, and the other near the bed. Dr. Philips looked as tired as I felt.

"A long night?" I asked him.

He roused himself to answer. "A difficult delivery, and another biding its time. There's no doctor in the next village. I work there as well, when I'm sent for. Where did you serve? France?"

"I was on *Britannic*."

"Good God. That explains why you're visiting the Grahams. Arthur Graham died on that ship."

"Yes, I was there."

"A putrid wound, from what I hear."

"The doctors tried amputation, but the infection had advanced too far."

"Yes, sadly, once it has got a grip, there's not much hope. Arthur was a strong young man, but that seems to make little difference."

"Did you know Arthur well?" I asked him.

"I came here just before his first leave. Dr. Hadley had died. From overwork, if you want my opinion. Another doctor I know suggested I take over his practice. Because of the need."

"I'm surprised you aren't at the Front."

"Yes, well, I'm not fit enough to go. So they tell me. I have a heart condition."

"And yet you're working yourself into exhaustion. Because you feel guilty about not serving?"

He smiled. "You are to the point, aren't you?"

"I was hoping to find someone who could tell me more about Arthur Graham. I took care of him when he was wounded, and I got to know him. So I believed then. I realize now how little that was."

"Wrong person. Dr. Hadley, now, had been the family physician for most of Arthur's life. He could have told you about measles and falls from a horse and whatever else you desired to know."

I smiled. "I've met Jonathan and Timothy. But there's another brother, isn't there? I'm sure Arthur told me he had three brothers. I was reluctant to ask—he might be dead."

"They don't mention him. Apparently he did something rather dreadful and was sent away."

"To prison?" I asked, taken aback.

"No. He's in an asylum. If you came down on the train, you must have passed it on the road here."

The house ablaze with light. "How awful for the family."

"Peregrine is the eldest, a half brother to the younger three. A tragedy that we can't cure minds."

My father had told me that Ambrose Graham's first wife had died in childbirth. Peregrine would have been her son, then.

"But what did he do?"

"He's said to have killed someone. One of the old spinsters here in Owlhurst, Mrs. Clayton, told me all about the family skeleton. She said he strangled a girl in a moment of passion." Disconcertingly, he grinned.

"Small wonder no one mentions Peregrine."

"I have to take most of that with a grain of salt," he added in apology. "By my calculations, Peregrine was hardly more than fourteen when it happened. Mrs. Clayton is a wonderful old gossip, I love her dearly, but she has a lively imagination, fed in part by senile dementia. Still, he *was* banished from Owlhurst at a young age, and in the dark of night, according to what I've gathered. Would you care for some tea? It's the one thing I can manage, along with toast. If my cook left me, I'd starve to death."

Ted Booker was deeply asleep. After making certain, we went down to the kitchen and Dr. Philips found the tea things, blew up the fire in the stove, and soon had the kettle on the boil. It was fairly decent tea, and I told him so.

Afterward, we went to sit with Ted Booker for another half hour, then Dr. Philips stood up, stretched his shoulders. "I'll leave you here, shall I? Until I can find someone to replace you. He won't be any trouble for several hours. He'll be dry as a desert and have a thundering headache when he wakes up." He took my hand. "Thank you for volunteering. I hope I haven't upset any plans Mrs. Graham may have made for your entertainment. How long are you staying?"

"Just the weekend."

He nodded. "Wretched beginning to your visit. But there you are."

And he was gone, his footsteps echoing on the stairs. I looked out the window and saw he had the shotgun under his arm, broken open.

I went back to my chair and made myself as comfortable as I could, listening to Booker's heavy breathing, thinking about his anguished obsession with his brother's death.

And in the silence, I also considered what Dr. Philips had told me about Peregrine.

"A tragedy that we can't cure minds . . ."

Arthur's words came back to me then.

Tell Jonathan I lied. I did it for Mother's sake. But it has to be set right.

What had to be set right? Had Arthur objected to his brother going to the asylum instead of prison but said nothing? Was that it? But if he'd gone to prison, surely he'd have been hanged. No, not that young—

I knew little about prisons, but enough to understand that an asylum might well be a better choice for a deranged man. Perhaps the authorities had tried to spare the family the nightmare of a trial and conviction by sending Peregrine to where he might—or might not—get the treatment he needed. At least there he was no longer a threat to anyone. He wouldn't be the first nor the last to be put away in that fashion.

I shivered, remembering the lights in every room. *Was* a madhouse better than hanging?

Only Peregrine could answer that. If he understood at all what he'd done and what choices had been made for him.

And then it occurred to me that I'd worried about trouble with a girl—and in a way, perhaps my instincts had been right. But in a far different sense than I could ever have guessed.

Had the dead girl's family been considered? Or had their wishes, their feelings, been swept away in the rush to protect Mrs. Graham and her children from scandal?

Belatedly, faced with his own death, had Arthur suddenly come to realize that they hadn't been consulted, that they had been wronged? He would have wanted Jonathan to recognize that revelation as well. At the same time, he wouldn't have wished for this to distress his mother—and he must have felt that he couldn't confide the family skeletons to me. Or to paper.

If the girl had come from a poor family, what recourse had they had against the Grahams and their money or influence?

I found myself feeling a new respect for Arthur.

I'd been sitting in that same uncomfortable chair for another half hour, wrestling with my own thoughts, when the outer door opened and a voice called tentatively up the stairs, "Where are you?"

I stepped to the door and answered quietly, "Who is it?"

"I'm Sally Booker's mother."

"We're in here. The bedroom nearest the stairs."

She came up, heels clicking on the treads, a small, gray-haired woman with lines of worry on her face. "Is he all right?"

She peered in the room, then sighed. "I don't know what's to become of him. He was the most wonderful young man. I was so happy when Sally married him. And now look at him."

"He can't help it," I said, in defense of Booker.

"Yes, I know that. It doesn't matter, does it? He'll never be the same, and Sally is at her wit's end. I feel so deeply for both of them."

"Are there any children?"

"Yes, a boy. He's away at his cousin's, thank God."

She took a deep breath, then said, "I'm Marion Denton."

"I'm Elizabeth Crawford. I'm here to visit the Grahams. And Dr. Philips commandeered me to help."

"Yes, that's what Dr. Philips told us when he looked in to let us know how Ted was faring. Thank you for your help. I don't know how we would have managed. The doctor said it was easier with a woman here. That surprised me. Sally isn't able to cope with Ted in these moods."

"She's his wife," I said simply. "That's harder."

"True."

Ted coughed, and then moaned a little in his sleep.

"He doesn't rest at night, you know. That's the roughest time for him."

"He lost his brother, I understand."

"They were twins. I'm told it's harder with twins."

She came in to take the chair that Dr. Philips had occupied, and we sat in companionable silence for a time. Then she said, "How did you come to know the Grahams? Are you a relation?"

"No, I was a nursing sister on *Britannic,* when Arthur was brought onboard. I was with him when he died."

"I was fond of Arthur. A very nice boy, who grew into a very nice young man. Timothy and Jonathan seemed to collect trouble the way a dog collects burrs. They're closer in age, of course, and what one couldn't think of, the other could. Their father died when they were very young. It isn't surprising they ran a little wild. Mrs. Graham's cousin did what he could to manage them, but they were headstrong. Of course they turned out well enough, I must say. I thought for a time that Sally might choose Johnnie or Tim. I didn't know Peregrine well. The family always claimed he was a little slow. A little different. But I never saw it myself. Still, his tutor despaired of him, and he must know better than I."

She turned to stare at the man on the bed. "So was Ted a nice boy. I was that fond of him, and he was a good husband to Sally. Look at this house—he saw to it that she wanted for nothing. And now she can't bear to come here, to him. She's begged me to send him back to hospital, where they know what to do with his kind. Maybe it would be best after all if he used that shotgun. I don't know what peace he'll ever have."

I was shocked. "He can't help but relive his brother's death. He feels the burden of responsibility. It's not something one gets over easily."

"But that's the point, isn't it? His brother is dead. It's time to move on and live for his wife and son."

"It's not that easy—" I repeated, trying to make her see that his memories were beyond Ted Booker's control. But she had no experience of war or any other horrendous event that shocks the mind, and her callousness was in defense of her daughter. I might as well have been talking to the wall.

She turned to me. "What's not easy about remembering your family? The boy is afraid of him, and Sally's told me that when she promised to love him in sickness and in health, there was nothing said about madness."

"It isn't madness. Shell shock is an affliction of the brain."

"I call it madness, to sit in a dark room and talk to the dead and threaten to use that shotgun. I tried taking it away once, but he came raging over to my house and demanded it back. And I was afraid to say no."

"It takes time."

"No, it doesn't. He needs to brace up, like a man, and say good-bye to his brother and remember he's still alive, with a family looking to him for love."

I lost my patience. "You weren't in the trenches with him, Mrs. Denton. You don't know what it's like when one mistake kills dozens of men right in front of your eyes, where a simple lapse in concentration means you're hanging on the wire, dying, and no one can bring you back without dying beside you. You don't smell the dead with every breath and know that some of what's nasty under your boots were your friends before they were blown to bits."

She replied righteously, "Yes, that's all very well, isn't it? That's in France, where such things happen. This is Kent, and he must learn the difference."

It was useless. Instead of trying to persuade her, I suggested that she have a long talk with Dr. Philips to see what could be done to help Ted Booker cope.

"*He* doesn't have any answers, except for the powders he gives Ted that make him like this—asleep and useless for hours at a time. How is he ever to earn a living and support a wife and child, I ask you!"

"Perhaps you and Sally ought to visit such a hospital yourselves, before deciding where your son-in-law belongs," I suggested. I trained in one, and it was heart wrenching. But this woman could only see her daughter's misery, and the anguish that drove Ted Booker into the past was as foreign to her as the monkey gods of India or the typhoons that killed thousands in the flat deltas below Calcutta.

The outer door opened, and Dr. Philips's footsteps rang on the stairs. He came in, looked at the two of us sitting there in a huffy silence, and then crossed to the bed to examine Ted.

"Be careful he doesn't choke," he said. "He can't fend for himself just now."

"Yes, I'll be careful."

"Mrs. Graham is very upset with me. She wants you to come back to the house straightaway. 'She's a guest,' she tells me. 'And not here for your convenience.'"

"Surely you've found someone to sit for a while. He's harmless, poor man, as he is."

"Yes, I've found someone. But she's nearly as frightened of Ted as his wife is. She needs the money, and so she'll come."

"What's to become of him?"

"Back to hospital, I fear. Mrs. Denton here and her daughter have had enough. I can't say that I blame them, but Booker is my patient, and I had hoped that in surroundings he knew from before the war, there was comfort."

"What set him off this morning?"

It was Mrs. Denton who answered me. "It's their birthday—his and his brother's."

I felt a wave of sadness. Poor man.

I went on, out of compassion, "I'll sit with him a little longer, if you like."

But the doctor answered with a shake of his head. "Mrs. Graham will nail my medical degree to the church door, if I leave you here a moment longer. Can you find your way back? Or do you need a guide?"

"No, I'll be all right. Stay with your patient. Good-bye, Mrs. Denton. I hope that all will be well with your daughter's marriage before very long."

She thanked me, and I went down the stairs and into the street. The wind was at my back as I walked, and I looked at the houses on either side of the Bookers'. Arthur had told me that this was once iron-making country, and so it had prospered. But the trees that fed the furnaces had gone long ago, and now it was pasturage for sheep and fields of corn and hops that kept the villages flourishing.

I found myself thinking that the Grahams had secrets as painful as Ted Booker's. It wasn't surprising now that Arthur hadn't told me about his brother. He'd have had to explain too much, and so it was easier to say nothing. Had Arthur and Peregrine been close as children? They were nearest in age. How had Mrs. Graham managed to tell her remaining sons why Peregrine was being sent away? Surely not the truth, not until they were older. I understood now my feeling when I met her, the feeling that she carried a heavy burden.

The church door was open as I came by, and for a moment I stepped inside out of the wind, not quite ready to return to the

Graham house. I stood in the nave and looked up at the stained-glass windows, shining in the bright sun, before walking a little way down the aisle. I didn't want to go as far as Arthur's memorial. I just needed the silence here, to wipe away the stress of dealing with Ted Booker and then listening to his mother-in-law wish him dead. She didn't know how near she'd come this time to getting her wish.

Someone was moving over my head, the sound of a bench being dragged across the wooden floor, the rustle of papers, and I realized that whoever it was must be in the organ loft. Then, without warning, the stone walls filled up with the raw scrape of a saw biting into wood. It was so unexpected that I walked down the aisle and looked up at the loft. All I could see was a man bent over something, and then as the sawing stopped, hammering began. As he stood up, I could see his clerical collar and shirtsleeves rolled to the elbow. He was looking down at his handiwork as if satisfied, and then he gathered up his tools, and moved toward the stairs. I strode quietly up the aisle and was out the door before he could encounter me in the nave.

CHAPTER FIVE

I HAD MISSED luncheon and was beginning to wish Dr. Philips's culinary skills had extended to more than making a cup of tea. But Susan met me at the door with the news that Mrs. Graham had asked her to set my meal aside.

"Mrs. Nichols—she's our cook—has gone to have a little nap. Come along into the kitchen. It's warmer there," she urged, and I followed her.

As she took my plate out of the warming oven, she went on shyly, "I've been wanting a chance to ask you about Mr. Arthur. How it was at the end. I've not got over his dying. It doesn't seem real to me, somehow. I think of him away fighting, as I always did, and then must remind myself that he's not."

I told her what I'd told the Grahams, and she listened with tears in her eyes. "He never gave up hope," I ended, "and everyone who knew him was saddened by his death. He was as popular a patient as he was an officer, and it was some time before the staff got over what had happened." I could feel my own throat tightening. "I don't believe he suffered," I lied, for Susan's sake. "And he was unconscious for the last hours. That was a kindness."

She nodded, turning her back to me. I saw her lift the corner of her apron and wipe her eyes. She busied herself about my meal until she was sure her voice was steady, then said huskily, "Thank you for telling me. I didn't feel right asking Mrs. Graham. She took his death hard."

She set a bowl of soup before me, thick with barley, and then slices of chicken with potatoes and swede. After the tension of dealing with Ted Booker, I was hungrier than I'd imagined, and Susan watched me eat with pleasure.

"Nice to see someone enjoying their food," she said with a smile. "They never say much, above-stairs. I try to please, but it's hard to find the meat and vegetables they're used to. The war and all. I'm at my wit's end, sometimes."

"How long have you worked here?"

"Since I was sixteen. I came with my mother, and after she left to live with my brother, I took over as housekeeper, more or less. They don't call me that, but they might as well give me the title. I do the work."

"Were there others in service here, before the war?"

Her face clouded a bit, but she said, "Half a dozen. Except for Mrs. Nichols—and she was too old to consider war work—the women left one by one as the men went off to fight. The footman died on the Somme, and we lost the coachman soon after. You've only to walk in the churchyard to see how bad it's been for us."

"Yes, I noticed the graves."

"And that's only them that died at home."

As I was finishing my pudding, there were footsteps on the stairs, and Mrs. Graham came into the kitchen, frowning. "My dear! I didn't intend for you to be served here. Susan, what were you thinking?"

Susan went red in the face, and I said quickly, "The kitchen was warm, and I didn't wish to put her out. It's my fault, truly."

As I'd finished my meal, she carried me off to the sitting room, apologizing again for Dr. Philips's demands on my time and skills. "He has no sense of what is right. You didn't come here to deal with Ted Booker. A tragedy, I'm sure, but not ours. I don't know what your parents will think of me, letting such a thing happen."

"They will understand. I'm trained to help. It would have been difficult for me to say no." To change the subject, I asked about the rector and the work he was doing in the church.

"It's the war," she said with a sigh, as if that explained everything. "Our sexton lost an arm at Ypres, but he can still carry out most of his duties, and so he was given his old position back. But the church needs constant upkeep, and when no one is looking, the rector, Mr. Montgomery, sees to it. There were protests at first, but he reminded us that Christ was a carpenter. And I must say, he's got quite good at what he does, and it has saved church funds time and again. But it isn't right, somehow. Call me old-fashioned if you will, but this making do at every turn is trying."

I said, "Of course his own duties come first, but it must give him a sense of satisfaction to know that the fabric of the church isn't suffering from the war."

She tilted her head as she considered that. "I hadn't looked at it quite that way. But I'm sure you're right. He was on a ladder, inspecting the stained-glass windows last week, when I went to see to the flowers, and he said the saints were taking the war in stride. I see now that he was pleased. I'd taken his remarks to be rather— irreverent."

She got up to poke at the fire, though it didn't need it.

"Perhaps I ought to ask Robert to speak to him. To offer help, if he'll accept it. Robert has been my right hand for so many years I don't know how I could have survived without him." There was a warmth in her voice that conveyed the closeness of that relationship. "He was always my favorite cousin, you know, and the only one who stepped forward in my time of need. I was so young when my husband died, and the responsibility was overwhelming. The estate to run, my sons to care for. I hardly knew where to begin. And all these years later, Arthur's loss to endure."

I wondered where she was going with this unexpected confession of vulnerability. She was a strong woman, I'd felt that from the beginning. I should have guessed what her purpose was.

Turning from the fire, she came to sit by me. "Jonathan has spoken to me. Are you sure Arthur didn't tell you the circumstances surrounding his message?"

"Absolutely. He entrusted me with that, and nothing more." I didn't add that my imagination had been busy filling in the blanks.

"Yes, well, it's rather a mystery. Was he perhaps being given morphine? Or was he out of his head with fever?"

"He'd been given something for pain, but he knew what he was saying. I think he died more comfortably, knowing his duty was done."

"Duty. That's an odd way of putting it." She sighed. "I really don't know what to make of it."

I found myself wondering if that was true and she was intentionally blinding herself to what Arthur wanted. On the other hand, I couldn't help the growing suspicion that she was probing to discover how much I knew about the matter. It was hard to judge what lay behind her sad smile as she stared into the fire, and I was feeling rather uncomfortable.

What surprised me was that Jonathan had confided in his mother. Had she importuned him until he had given in?

I couldn't stop myself from commenting, "Perhaps he expected Jonathan to understand. The message was meant for him, after all."

"*I did it for Mother's sake. . . .*" She repeated the middle of it, as if trying to work it out. "But what was that?"

"Sometimes it's a girl. . . ."

Her eyes flicked to my face.

"What makes you think such a thing?"

"I've sat with many wounded men, Mrs. Graham. And some of them were in love when they went off to war. But their family or the girl's family refused to let them marry. That sometimes weighed heavily on their minds, at the end. They often wanted the girl to know that they regretted not marrying her."

"My sons haven't been involved with any young women." Her voice was harsh. I'd met that resistance before. Mothers who believed that their sons had formed no attachments because they were too young . . . I knew better, I'd written passionate letters to sweethearts from men barely old enough to enlist.

"I didn't mean to suggest—we were speaking of what men at war talk about at the end. When they know they're dying."

She smiled. "That was pompous of me, my dear. Certainly there was no one in Owlhurst for whom Arthur and Jonathan had feelings, and it was natural to assume. . . ." There was a brief hesitation. "Of course there's Sally Denton. Timothy was quite taken with her for a time. But I can't believe it was a serious attachment."

"Then perhaps it was something left undone, something that he'd expected to set right when he came home again."

"Undone? No, surely not. Typical of Arthur, he'd put everything in order before he sailed. Well. I expect we'll never know what was in his mind. You must be tired, my dear, after your experiences with Dr. Philips's patient, and I've selfishly kept you sitting here talking. Would you like to go up and lie down for a while?"

I wouldn't, but it was a dismissal, as if she preferred to be alone with her thoughts, and I was very happy to escape this conversation. I said, "Yes, that's very kind of you. If you don't mind . . ."

"Not at all." She put out her hand to take mine. "I can't tell you how happy it has made me to have you here."

I closed the sitting room door behind me and walked toward the stairs. Timothy was standing in the shadows of the hall, and he turned as he heard me approach.

"How is Booker?" he asked.

"Resting quietly when I left."

"What a nightmare it must be. Is there nothing to be done for him?"

"I'm afraid not. Somehow he must find the will and determination to let go of the past. And often even that isn't enough. His wife is afraid of him, which doesn't help matters. They say time . . ." I let my voice trail off. We didn't know enough about shell shock to offer hope. But I didn't want to admit that.

"We were friends before the war. I've seen little of him since he came back."

"Perhaps he needs his old friends," I suggested tentatively. "To take his mind off his brother."

"What do I know about war?" Timothy asked bitterly. "It's not something I could share with him, is it? The experience of the trenches, the fear of dying when you go over the top."

"It isn't war he needs to talk about, you see. It's ordinary things, the life that was."

"I'd have married Sally, if she hadn't chosen Ted. There's that as well."

Men and their wretched self-importance.

"If Ted Booker shoots himself, there may be another chance for the two of you."

That shocked him, and he looked at me with surprise and distaste. "I don't want her that way."

"Well, think about Ted Booker in his dark world, will you? An effort on your part to save her husband's sanity will be a gift to her. If you loved her, you'd want to do that."

He swore under his breath.

"I wasn't trying to distress you. But I just spent several hours watching a man who wants to die. There are too many dead, Mr. Graham, and I'm heartily sick of bodies to be buried."

I turned to walk away, and he called to me, "Did you see through Arthur as easily as you see through me?"

"I don't know that there was anything to see through. He was dying, and that tends to sweep away the trivia of living. He wanted something done, and that's why I came, because it was so important to him."

"Were you in love with him? Most of the girls were. He was the pick of the Grahams, you know. Better than all of us."

I answered carefully. "I liked your brother very much. Perhaps more than I should, but I watched him believe in his future, and then I watched him give up all hope. That made me feel something for him, compassion, pity, affection. Sometimes you see briefly into someone's heart, and it becomes a bond between you that goes beyond friendship. But not as far as passion."

"You're blunt."

I smiled. "Am I? It's my training, I suppose."

And this time I walked on. He didn't stop me from going.

My intent was to go up to my room, but the house seemed airless, suffocating. I went to the kitchen instead and begged Susan for a cloak from the entry pegs, and walked out again.

This time I didn't turn in the direction of the rectory but went down the lane on which the Graham house stood. It ran for a short distance, then split, and I took the left fork. The houses here were comfortable, but not as fine as the Grahams'. At the end of this lane, where another crossed it, I found myself in a row of small cottages, some of them very old but well kept up.

I had walked almost to the end of these when a door opened and someone called, "Susan, is that you?"

I turned to see an elderly woman peering out at me, squinting to make out who I was. It was then that I realized that Susan must have lent me her cloak.

"No, I'm afraid not," I answered. "I'm staying at the house and borrowed her coat to walk a bit."

"Then you must be half frozen. Come in to the fire, do, and I'll make you a cup of tea."

I debated accepting, but she was holding the door open for me, and I turned up the path with a word of thanks as I gave her my name.

"Mine's West, Matty West." She shut the door behind me and shivered. "I think it's colder this winter than last. Though it's probably my bones a year older."

Leading the way into the kitchen, she pointed to the kettle on the boil. "It's nearly ready. Sit down and warm yourself. I'll see to the pot."

As she bustled about, she said, "You're at the house, you say? I didn't think they were taking on more servants at present."

"Actually I came because I knew Arthur Graham and was with him when he died."

She stopped, her hands holding the saucers. "You knew Mr. Arthur? Oh, my dear, tell me he died peacefully!"

"Yes, it was very peaceful," I replied. "Did you know him well?"

"I was housekeeper there while the boys were young. Then my son lost his wife and I came to keep house for him and his children."

"Oh. You're Susan's mother." When I'd been told she'd gone to live with her son, I'd assumed distance, as in Dorset or Hampshire. Not in Owlhurst.

"Indeed I am." She went on setting cup into saucer, finding a spoon and the jug of milk. "He was my favorite of the lads, though Mr. Peregrine was the eldest, you know. Mr. Peregrine was— different. I was never sure why. His father blustered and tried to make out that the boy was bright, nothing wrong, but his tutor said it was a shame about him. It must have been true. I put it down to his mother dying so young. But then he never knew her, did he? When his father married again, he was still hardly more than a baby."

"They never speak of Peregrine," I ventured. "Is he dead?" I felt guilty for lying, but my curiosity got the better of my conscience.

"As good as. I remember him well—happy and busy and strong, he was."

"Where is he now?"

She looked away. "It's not my place to tell you, Miss. He got himself into some trouble, and was taken away. Mrs. Graham sobbed and cried, and the doctor feared for her. But I thought it was no more than an act. She never loved Mr. Peregrine the way she loved the others. If she had to lose one of the boys, it would have been Mr. Peregrine she'd have sacrificed."

"She admitted to me that Arthur was her favorite."

"He was mine as well. A finer young man you'll never see. When the word came he was dead, she took to her bed for two days."

I left the subject, and said, "Susan has worked for the family a long time. She would make a good wife and mother."

"She's devoted to the Grahams. They're all the family she needs. I'd hoped there might be something between her and Mr. Robert, but there never was."

"It was Robert who brought me from the station."

"He's a strange one, keeps himself to himself. But he's never failed the family, I will say that for him."

"Mrs. Graham told me he was a blessing, dealing with the boys after her husband died."

"They were a rowdy lot, right enough. Just the wrong age to lose a man's firm hand over them. Mr. Jonathan was the worst, always coming up with this bit of mischief or that. I was that surprised he went into the army. Not one to care for discipline, was he? His mother tried to get him off, but he was determined to go. And he got a medal for bravery, as well. Hotheaded, I'd have called him, but I expect in a war that's useful."

I smiled. "Sometimes, yes."

The tea was ready, and she poured my cup, then her own.

"I'm supposed to be having a nap," I confided to her.

"Yes, well, you're young. Old bones feel the wind more. How did it happen you were with Mr. Arthur when he died?"

"I volunteered as a nurse. I was assigned to *Britannic* until she was sunk by a mine. I didn't want to drive omnibuses or till the land. My father had been in the army, you see, and I felt I had to do something for his sake. Nursing was much harder than I'd dreamed it was. Helping people, yes, I liked that, but watching them suffer and die was dreadful. I'm still not used to it."

Susan's mother nodded. "I was midwife for a time. I just fell into it, because I was the eldest of seven, and my auntie had six, and there was never time to call the doctor to them. When a baby died, I felt guilty, as if I'd done something wrong. I still dream of it, from time to time. Not as much as before, but sometimes. Those wee little faces, so still and pale. No future for them, no love nor laughter nor happiness."

"I understand."

"I expect you do."

We talked for another quarter of an hour, and then I took my leave. She asked me to remember her to her daughter. "For she has no time for visiting just now, with the maids all gone. That's why I was glad to see what I took for Susan coming down the road."

I promised and walked back to the house, coming in again through the kitchen and passing on to Susan her mother's greetings.

"My brother's children are grown now, and she keeps house for him. But this is still her family as well. I expect she was as glad of news of Mr. Arthur as I was."

"Hardly happy news."

"No. Would you like some hot chocolate, Miss, I was just about to put the kettle on."

"Thank you, no." I was awash with tea. "I'm going up to my room."

Susan grinned at me. "Mrs. Graham said you was sleeping. I didn't tell her otherwise."

I got to my room without encountering anyone, and Susan brought me a pitcher of hot water shortly afterward. I sat down in a chair by the window, and the next thing I knew there was a tapping at my door.

It was Mrs. Graham, inviting me down to the sitting room. I went with her, and we sat by the fire, talking about the war and any expectation that it would be over by the spring.

"Will you be going back to sea?" she asked me at one point.

"I expect to be assigned to another hospital ship, yes. But the decision isn't mine. I might be sent to France."

"You're a brave young woman," she said thoughtfully. "I shouldn't have cared to be sunk, as you were. It was in all the papers, you know. But what do you expect of the Hun?"

"I'm sure the mine was intended for bigger game, not an empty hospital ship."

"Where did you live as a child? In Somerset?"

"No, I traveled with my parents. We lived in India for a time, and then wherever my father was sent by the army. I had a few friends my own age, but most often I got to know the country through the servants."

She raised her eyebrows at that.

I explained. "We had any number of servants in India. My ayah, what you would call a nanny, was particular about where I went and what I did. But sometimes the gardeners or the grooms would take me to market with them. Our cook was a man, and quite good. He would bargain ferociously, and he had a reputation for being a hard man to cheat."

"You enjoyed this way of life, did you? Among the heathen and their idols?"

"I knew nothing else, you see. Since I was an only child, my parents preferred to keep me with them rather than to send me to England to be educated. I realize now how fortunate I was."

Jonathan came in at that point, and the subject was changed. He was fretting over his wound. It seemed to be irritated by the wind, and he'd stopped in at Dr. Philips's, in the hope of being given an ointment for it. "But he has his hands full—two births, and of course Booker. The man's a coward, he should be shut away with others of his kind."

I opened my mouth to argue—and shut it firmly.

His mother said, "That's unkind. You've known Ted almost all your life. He's not a coward."

"It's different, Mother, when you're fighting. You see a man in his true colors then. Whether or not he lets his side down."

"Your own brother has been called a coward, because he isn't wearing a uniform. It has hurt him very deeply. Surely you don't believe it's true."

"Tim was born with a club foot. It's not his fault. That's very different."

His brother came in at that moment, and we all sat there with feathers on our faces, as if we'd eaten the canary.

Timothy looked from his mother to his brother and said, "What is it?"

"We were talking about Ted Booker. It's a painful subject for your brother," Mrs. Graham answered him.

"Yes, sometimes I think that medal has gone to his head."

They glared at each other, but there was a tap on the door, and Robert stepped in.

"There's been a message. Peregrine has pneumonia."

There was a stunned silence.

"And what are we expected to do about it?" Mrs. Graham asked after a moment.

"He needs nursing. They would like to bring him here."

Jonathan said explosively, "No!"

Mrs. Graham spoke over him, saying, "We don't have the staff to look after a sick man. Tell them that."

"They think he's dying. They would prefer that he do it elsewhere."

I could hear Timothy swearing under his breath. "Then we have no choice," he said to his mother.

Her face was set, grim. "I want no part of this business. For one thing, it's not safe."

"He's no danger to himself or others, in his present condition."

"Tell the messenger it isn't possible."

Timothy said, "Mother." It was a warning, and a glance passed between them. "If he's delirious—"

"If you like, I could stay a day or two, and care for him," I said before I'd thought. "I've some experience with pneumonia."

They turned to stare at me as if I'd offered to climb to the roof and sweep the chimney.

"It's what I do," I said. "Nursing."

Robert considered me. He said to Mrs. Graham, "It's true. She helped Dr. Philips to manage Booker this morning. I saw Mrs. Denton in the stationer's shop. She was regaling the Marshalls with a full account."

"You know that's not possible. Bringing Peregrine back. God knows what thoughts or memories it might trigger," Mrs. Graham added forcefully.

"He's going to be sent here, whether we like it or not," Robert retorted. "I've told you. They don't have the staff to care for a dying man."

"It will most certainly kill him to bring him out in this cold," Jonathan put in.

His mother turned to him, her mind working.

It was an odd feeling, sitting in the midst of a family that was deciding the fate of one of its own as if he were a stranger. But it occurred to me that after all these years, he might seem to be.

"If he's wrapped up well, and there's a way to keep the air he breathes warmer, he could travel," I said, doubt in my voice. "I wouldn't recommend it, but if he's not likely to be given proper care . . ."

"He's in the asylum," Timothy answered. "You must have seen it last night when you came from the station."

Robert had pointed it out. As if I should know its significance. As if he was certain that Arthur must have told me about Peregrine.

"The messenger is waiting," Robert reminded them quietly.

I was beginning to see that he had more influence in this family than a cousin ordinarily possessed.

Mrs. Graham bit her lip. "No," she said finally. "It can't be done."

"Perhaps Dr. Philips could care for him," I suggested.

"Absolutely not," Mrs. Graham responded, not looking at me.

"Perhaps I should leave you alone while you decide what to do." I started for the door, but Robert was blocking it.

"It might be the best course," he said, ignoring me. "If you think about it."

Mrs. Graham stared at him as if she could read his mind. And then she nodded once, as if she understood what he was suggesting.

"All right, then. Let them bring him here. If Miss Crawford will be kind enough to see to him until it's over, I would be very grateful."

"Mother—" Jonathan began.

"No, Robert's right. As usual. This is perhaps the answer we were looking for."

"That's settled, then." Robert shut the door.

Mrs. Graham said, "Timothy, if you don't mind—I'd like a whiskey and water." She sat down, as if her knees were about to give way. He went to the drinks table and poured a little whiskey into a glass and added the water. She drank it almost thirstily, as if she needed the support it offered.

Then she turned to me. "I have imposed on you, my dear. It is not something I would have wished. If I'd known—" She broke off, and looked at her empty glass. "When Peregrine arrives, we must do our best to make him comfortable. Timothy, would you ask Susan what is needed to open his room?"

He left us, and Jonathan said, "Mother, I hope to God you know what you are about."

I asked, tentatively, why their son and brother was in an asylum. It was expected of me, and I didn't want them to know what Dr. Philips had already told me.

"Because, my dear, he murdered someone. In cold blood, but not in his right mind." The suffering on her face was real.

She hadn't beaten about the bush. I hardly knew what to say. "That's—it must have been a terrible time for you."

"Peregrine's never been—he had difficulties as a child, you see, but we never suspected—the truth is, you don't suspect your own flesh and blood of—of having that sort of nature." There was distress in her voice, a tightness that must have been a mixture of shame and of inexpressible shock as she looked back at the past.

Her emotional confession made me wonder if perhaps I'd been a little hasty in offering my services. She knew better than I just how safe her stepson was. But I couldn't take back my offer now. The Colonel Sahib would tell me that retreat was the better part of valor, but I knew for a fact he'd never retreated in his life. I wasn't about to spoil the family record now.

She must have read something in my expression because she said at once, "You needn't fear him. They say he's become quite docile—he's accepted his fate." She squared her shoulders, as if preparing herself to face what was to come. "Robert is right. They don't have the means to care for my son as ill as he is. So many of the orderlies and the nurses went off to war that they're fortunate at the asylum to be able to function at all."

After that we waited in an uncomfortable silence, expecting the knock on the door at any time that would announce the arrival of the sick man. I thought—belatedly—that I must send a telegram to my parents. I wouldn't be coming home as planned.

Finally, almost when we'd given it up for the evening, the door knocker sounded like the crack of doom.

I went out into the hall with Mrs. Graham, and she opened the door herself.

A man in a heavy coat stood there, and behind him were two stout men with a stretcher between them. Their breath steamed in the cold air.

On the stretcher lay a tall man, swathed in blankets.

Just then I heard him cough, and I knew the worst. His lungs were terribly congested. And the cold air during the journey had done them no good. Nor had standing there in the winter night.

The stretcher bearers were coming through the door, now, and somehow between them they managed the stairs, grunting and struggling every step of the way. I thought how difficult it must be for the man they jostled and tilted like an egg carried in a spoon, but he never complained.

I went up after them, but Mrs. Graham stayed below, talking to the third man.

Somehow Susan had managed to make a room ready, and I watched the stretcher bearers settle their burden in the bed, drawing up the sheets to his chin.

He lay there, exhausted, his face gray.

I went to the side of the bed as the two men left, and looked down at Peregrine Graham. As murderers went—and I was most certainly no authority—he didn't appear to be any different from the dozen of pneumonia cases I'd dealt with on *Britannic's* next-to-last voyage.

He opened his eyes then, and they were dark, pain and exhaustion mixed in their depths. As he struggled to speak, I wondered if he was dumb. His mouth moved, but he appeared not to know how to shape words.

Finally he managed, "Where am I?" His voice was a husky whisper, I could barely hear the words. "Where have they taken me?"

I realized that no one had told him what was happening. "You're in your own home, at Owlhurst. I'm here to take care of you."

"Home?" His eyes looked around, as if trying to place his surroundings. "I must be dying."

"Early days," I said, and then watched him start to shiver as the fever came on again.

I ran to the stairs to see if the men had left any medicines for me, but they were gone, and Mrs. Graham was still standing in the hall, her face turned toward the door.

I said, "Could you send Robert to Dr. Philips? I need something for a heavy fever, and something as well for a cough and congestion in the lungs."

She turned to me, looking up the stairs with shadows on her face that seemed sinister in the low lamplight. "I was told he was dying. That medicines were of no use."

"We need to make him comfortable to the end," I pointed out.

After a moment's hesitation, she said, "Robert will see to it."

And an hour later, Timothy was at the door with a small box containing the medicines I'd requested. But he wouldn't come into the room. It was as if he had no wish to see his brother.

It was a measure of the family's feelings.

Chapter Six

I lost count of time. I had almost no rest, sitting up through the nights and again through the days, eating the meals that Susan brought up to me and working hard to make the poor wretch on the bed as comfortable as possible. I'd expected Dr. Philips to appear at some stage, or even the rector, but no one came, not even Peregrine's mother.

But then she was his stepmother, wasn't she? And this son had disgraced the family.

The only respite I had was a letter sent on to me by my father. It was from Elayne, one of the women with whom I shared the small flat in London. I recognized her sprawling hand at once. Tearing open the envelope, I was immediately lost in her words, so like her voice.

> *I hope the arm is healing as it should. I'm eager for news. Here's mine. You'll never guess, darling, what has happened to me. I'm in love, and he's wonderful. I met him on the ship bringing the wounded back from France. He broke his shoulder wrestling a mule. Judging from the size of him, I wonder how the mule fared. Did I tell you he's Staff? Quite safe behind the lines, so I shan't fear losing him. He's coming to visit when he's out of hospital, and meanwhile, I'm off again to France. He's asked me to smuggle a*

bottle of good wine back for him. I've left a small package at the flat for you—something I found for you in Dover. If you haven't received orders by the time I'm home again, come to London and meet Anthony. But mind you don't fall in love with him yourself—he's claimed.

Smiling, I folded the sheets of blue paper and returned them to the envelope. Elayne, dear friend that she was, was tall and plain and had told me she thought she would never marry, like one of her favorite Jane Austen characters.

Just then, Peregrine twisted in the bed, choking on his own phlegm. Tossing my letter on the bedside table, I bent over the sick man, lifting him, turning him to slap his back, forcing him to eject the heavy plug.

That exhausted him, and I settled him again, adding an extra pillow under his head, to help him breathe.

Where was Dr. Philips?

I asked Susan the next time she brought my meal, but she shook her head and replied that she hadn't been told he was expected.

Peregrine's breathing filled the room, raucous and painful, my only companion, and there were times in those early days when I thought it had stopped altogether. And then he would cough and struggle to find air, and finally slip back into the steady, rough pattern as before.

Fighting to help him, I used all the skills I'd learned since entering my training. Hot water with the fumes of pungent oils that made my own eyes water, poultices on his chest, cool cloths for his head, aspirin to ease his fever. He soaked the bed time and again with a sour sweat, and I changed the sheets, setting them outside the door to be washed and brought back to me. With an invalid cup, less likely to spill, I fed him sweet tea and broths that Susan brought to me in Thermoses, although much of both wound up on the towel I put across his chest. Still, each time he swallowed a little, it gave him the strength to keep fighting.

It was easy to see why the asylum had despaired of him, without the staff to sit with him hour after hour, and fearful that the Grahams would accuse them of neglect in his death. How were they to know his family wanted no part of him?

Despite his thinness, Peregrine Graham was a strong man, and in the small hours of the morning of the fifth day, his fever broke.

He lay there in utter exhaustion, trying to breathe, still coughing when the breath was too deep, unable to care for himself or even speak. I considered what to feed him, but I didn't think he could keep anything down, and that the effort of trying would be too much. The broths and the tea would have to do.

His eyes followed me about the room, and I wondered what was going through his mind. Was he aware that if he lived, he must return to the asylum? Would he have preferred to die? Still, people often clung stubbornly to life, willing themselves to live despite severe injuries or illnesses. Even though he'd appeared coherent in that brief moment on his arrival, Peregrine hadn't spoken since, and it was possible that he didn't completely understand his situation. Perhaps it would be a blessing if he didn't.

It was not until late into the afternoon of the sixth day that he had the strength to whisper, "Are you Arthur's wife?"

I turned quickly from the window where I'd been watching the light fade into the early winter dusk.

"No. But I knew your brother. I was with him when he died."

His dark brows rose. "Arthur is dead? How?"

Had no one told him? Surely they had! Or was it that his mind couldn't absorb family news? "In the war."

"It isn't over? The war?"

"No, sadly, it hasn't finished."

"What day is this? What year?"

I told him. He frowned, as if he'd lost track of time.

"How did he die? Arthur?"

"Bravely. At peace."

"You're lying."

Surprised, I said, "Why should I lie to you?"

"Kindness."

I wasn't sure how to respond. It was a remarkably rational exchange. But I was saved from answering as Peregrine began to cough. I offered him a drink of water and said, "You must rest now. You're a little better, but not out of the woods yet. Sleep, if you can."

Obediently he closed his eyes and was quiet for some time. Then he said, still in that painful whisper, "Why was I brought here?"

"I don't think there was anyone to take care of you where you were."

"I want to die."

"Well, I don't think it's up to you," I said briskly. "Modern medicine can work wonders without your help."

"I'd rather be dead."

"No, you mustn't say that," I replied, coming to the bed to look down at him. "If God sees fit to spare you, then there's a reason. Something you need to finish—" I stopped. For him all there was to finish was his life sentence in an asylum.

His mouth twisted. "Indeed." There it was again, that logical comment, with its touch of irony.

But he slept after that, and when Susan came to the door with my dinner, asking how he was, I said only, "There's no change. Still, if Mrs. Nichols could prepare a soup for me—nothing too heavy, chicken stock and rice to thicken it, and a little meat, minced fine, and perhaps a little wine too, I'll see if he can keep it down. He's frighteningly weak, we must do something."

"There's fresh bread as well, for sops," she told me, and then left without asking to see the sick man.

Two hours later, she brought the soup in a covered bowl and half a loaf of bread wrapped in a linen cloth, handing them in at the door.

I was able to cajole Peregrine into trying a little, and it must have been to his liking because he took nearly a third of a cup. And he kept it down, which I told myself was a good sign. Close to two o'clock, I brought him more, and again at six, finishing the container a little after eight the next morning.

I spent the night in my chair where I could watch him and hear the slightest sound, though by dawn, my cot beckoned, and I felt the stiffness across my shoulders and in my back. The chances of a relapse were very good, and I couldn't risk that. But as the new day dawned, he was cool to the touch and resting well.

I rested myself that morning, realizing how hard a vigil it had been, and was grateful for the hot water that Susan brought with my breakfast so that I could wash my face and hands. It did very little to wake me fully.

My patient studied me in silence as I moved about the room, and I grew accustomed to finding those watchful eyes on me whenever Peregrine was awake.

"Why are you here?" he asked me late in the afternoon.

"To look after you."

"No. Why are you *here*?"

"I was with your brother when he died. There were messages he wanted me to carry for him."

"Messages?"

"Personal ones. To his brother."

"Do you carry such messages to the family of every soldier you nurse?"

I could feel myself flushing. "No. But in Arthur's case, you see, he thought he was recovering. And then everything changed."

He didn't reply, and I thought perhaps he'd fallen asleep. If I'd had any doubts about his ability to understand his surroundings, they were erased now. He could think, he could reflect on what was said and draw coherent conclusions, and he spoke like a rational man. But madness had its rational moments, I reminded myself. What's more, I had no knowledge of what he was like before entering the asylum. Or what help, if any, he was given there.

If his tutor had despaired of him, why was he able to use his brain so well now? And if he had been given treatment that produced this mental agility, why did he not know his brother had been killed, how the war was progressing, or what year it was? It was a contradiction I couldn't quite fathom.

What he said next shocked me. "A pity it wasn't Jonathan who died, rather than Arthur." His eyes were still closed.

"You can't mean that!" I said, thinking how cruel it was.

"I do. I've hated him for years. Ever since I can remember."

I didn't know quite what to say. And then I recalled that others had called Peregrine "different." Perhaps that was why he disliked his brother so intensely—if Jonathan had been held up as an example of what Peregrine ought to have been, and failed to achieve, it would breed jealousy. Frankly, I wouldn't have put it past Jonathan to tease Peregrine unmercifully. Not after what he'd said about Ted Booker.

Finally, I replied, "He's your brother."

"I doubt it."

I smiled. I had heard children quarrel in much the same vein. But then those dark eyes flicked open, and he seemed to pin me there in my chair. "I was separated from my brothers at an early age. There was little love lost between us."

"Do you know why you were kept away from them?"

He turned his head to look out the window, agitated. "I always believed it was because my father died."

I had the feeling that this wasn't a safe subject for conversation. Until now, Peregrine had made good sense. Sometimes madness turned on small grievances, and I didn't wish to provoke him into violence.

"That must have been a difficult time for you. You must have been little more than a child—" I'd meant it as conciliatory, but he didn't take it that way.

"Later I wondered if she killed him or if she persuaded Robert to do it for her."

That was surely a madman speaking—

There was a tap at the door, startling both of us. We turned toward it, as if expecting—what? After the briefest hesitation, I went to open it. It was Susan with another covered jar of soup.

I took the jar from her and set it on the hearth. By the time I'd spooned half a cup of it into his bowl, Peregrine seemed to have forgotten what we were talking about. I wasn't about to bring it up again. He drank the soup without comment, and lay back against his pillows, tired enough to sleep.

I went back to my chair. I hadn't been trained in the field of various forms of madness. We'd been more concerned with the destruction of the body, by illness or weaponry. I wished I could ask Dr. Philips for his opinion.

And now I was uneasy in this sickroom, where I hadn't been before.

But I needn't have worried. That was the only time my patient broached the subject of his brothers or his father's death.

Later that evening as I sat by the fire, Peregrine cried out. It was so sudden I nearly leapt out of my skin. But when I turned toward the bed, he was lying there asleep, one arm flung out and his body half twisted to one side. I realized that he was dreaming. I heard him say, his voice muffled, "Please—," and again, as if pleading, "*Please*—." After that, he was quiet and didn't rouse again until it was time for his soup at ten o'clock.

It was while Peregrine was finishing the cup that Timothy came to the door, knocking tentatively, to ask about his brother. But when I opened it, he stepped back, as if afraid he might find himself looking into the room beyond.

It occurred to me that the family had expected that my nursing skills were not up to saving Peregrine Graham, and they were now wondering why I hadn't appeared with the sad news of his death. They had made no effort to send Dr. Philips to the patient. I wondered if they would have, if I'd sent down to ask for his help.

"I'm cautiously optimistic," I responded to his question. "It's too early to say what the outcome may be."

It was a habit I'd fallen into, working with the wounded. Orders were to find them fit again as quickly as possible and send them back to the fighting—men were in short supply, malingerers not tolerated. I often sought to keep a man who was exhausted, still weak, or pretending he was healed when I knew very well he was not. It made no sense to me to send someone back to die his first day. And I wasn't convinced that *this* patient was well enough for the long, cold ride back to that tall, forbidding house behind its high walls. As well, the building clouds at dusk had spoken of snow, and I had seen the winter birds huddled in the bare trees, out of the wind, a sign of foul weather.

Timothy nodded, thanked me, and quickly walked away.

Peregrine, who had overheard the brief conversation, said with some bitterness, "I expect they're eager to see the back of me. Or else he's afraid I must be well enough now to overpower you and run amok in the house."

"We shan't worry about that until you can overpower your soupspoon," I retorted. For his hands shook with the palsy of weakness as he tried to drink or feed himself.

When he didn't reply, I said, "Mr. Graham. Would you wish to see the doctor or the rector? I'll ask for them on your behalf, if you like."

The answer was emphatically no.

"I don't think they are the same men you remember," I told him. "Your mother made some mention of newcomers."

He remained adamant.

"Would you like for me to read to you? I'm sure I can find a book that might interest you."

He shook his head, drifting into sleep almost as soon as I took away his bowl and cup.

I debated leaving him for a while and going to my own room. I hadn't had a change of clothes for days, and a bath would have been heaven. But I was afraid to leave him alone. I didn't want to address the reasons why.

And so I settled back in my chair, falling asleep myself to the rise and fall of his even breathing.

I woke sometime later with night creeping through the window and the lamps unlit. As I stirred, I could sense movement from the bed, and an instant of panic swept over me.

Then I realized that Peregrine had pushed himself back on his pillows and was asking if there was any of that soup left.

I got up and drew the drapes across the window, then found and lit the lamp. Susan had brought me a spirit lamp to keep the soup from thickening, and I heated it a little before giving him the cup to drink.

His hand was steadier now, and I left him to hold it for himself.

Over its rim his eyes were speculative, and I was suddenly nervous.

"If they told you what I'd done," he asked, "why did you allow yourself to be shut in here with me? I don't remember much about the events leading up to my removal to the asylum. Dr. Hadley kept me heavily sedated. But I have nightmares all the same. If they are true, then I'm a monster."

"It's Dr. Philips now," I reminded him. "Dr. Hadley is dead. As for my agreeing to care for you, I hardly expected a man with terminal pneumonia to present a problem. I've had to deal with men raving from pain and from night terrors. I'm stronger than I look. And my father would tell you I didn't have the good sense to be afraid." I hesitated, and then asked, "Have you tried to harm anyone since the—the events that put you in the asylum?"

He moved restlessly among the bedclothes. "I'm not a lunatic."

"I never suggested you were—"

There was a determined knock at the door, and I went to open it. Mrs. Graham stood there in the passage. I thought her eyes were nearly as darkly circled as my own.

"Timothy tells me that my son is going to live. Is that true?"

I thought she was glad, and was on the point of telling her that he would.

But she went on with a coldness in her voice that I was sure Peregrine could hear from his bed, "I shall inform the director of the asylum to send someone to fetch him at once."

"I don't think he's ready to travel—"

"Nonsense. He survived his journey here and he will survive his journey back where he belongs."

She turned on her heel and walked away.

I shut the door slowly, not wanting to see the look on Peregrine's face.

He said, "There's an end to it," in a clipped voice. I did turn then and caught the expression of despair before it was smoothed away.

His keepers came for him the next morning.

It was the first time I'd ever seen a patient of mine manacled before he was taken away. Yet Peregrine Graham was too weak to walk down the stairs unaided. It took two stalwart warders on either side, and still he was in danger of falling to his knees. Yet somehow he managed it, and I wondered if it was sheer pride.

There was no one in the passage, by the stairs, or in the hall to bid him farewell. I threw a blanket around my shoulders and went out to the ambulance they had sent for him. In the end, I put the blanket around him on the bed to which he was chained, for there was nothing to cover him against the cold.

The driver waited impatiently, and I could see clearly what it was he was thinking—that I was wasting pity on a man who should have been hanged, if his family hadn't had the money or position to send him to an asylum for the insane instead.

I went back into the house and slammed the door, unwilling to watch the ambulance pull away and turn back the way it had come.

Timothy appeared at the head of the stairs.

"He's gone, then."

"An animal would have been treated better," I snapped without thinking about the fact that I was a guest here and should hold no opinions about circumstances of which I was ignorant.

"He *is* an animal," Timothy said. "You saw him ill and weak. Not in his full strength."

"I'm a nurse," I said, trying to rein in my anger. "Not a keeper. I look at a patient, not a prisoner."

"As you did with Booker."

"Yes."

"Which says much about your capacity for compassion."

Timothy turned away and was gone.

I went back to the room to clear away the bedding and the spirit lamp and what was left of the broth, but Susan was there before me.

She said, "I'll boil these sheets, Miss, and see that everything's put away."

I thanked her and went about collecting my own things.

"We was all amazed that he didn't die. Mrs. Graham said it must be your fine nursing that did it. To tell truth, I don't know how you could bear it!"

"He was ill. A nurse doesn't ask who her patient is, or if he's acceptable in Society."

"No, Miss. I think his mother would have preferred to see him dead. It was a terrible blow to the family, to have a son of the house taken up for murder."

"I don't understand why he wasn't sent to prison—or hanged."

"Because he was so young and never right in his mind, Miss. And the doctor and the rector and his tutor all spoke to the magistrate. It was decided that the asylum was for the best."

"But who did he murder?"

"I don't know, Miss. It didn't happen here. Mrs. Graham had taken him to London, to see a specialist. He hadn't been well, there was nausea and vomiting, and he walked like a drunken man, hardly able to keep his feet. Dr. Hadley didn't know what else to do.

When she came home from there, she was as distraught as I've ever seen her, and Mr. Peregrine was locked in a room at the rectory. She sent for the rector and then for the magistrate, and I never saw Mr. Peregrine again, not even when they brought him here the other night. Mrs. Nichols and I were told to stay belowstairs."

"And then what happened? After Mrs. Graham spoke to these people?"

"He was taken away. And Mrs. Graham cried for days. It was the saddest thing."

"Arthur was here?"

"Oh, yes, Miss, as grim as I ever saw him. He didn't speak to anyone for days. Master Timothy tried to comfort his mother, he kept putting his little arm around her shoulders. Master Jonathan paced the floor until Mr. Robert came and spoke to him, and after that he was quiet. Still, he sat in his room, pale as his shirt, worrying about his mother because she was crying. I tried to tell him that she was a strong woman, she'd be all right. But he wouldn't hear me. He was angry with everyone, because he didn't understand what was happening. Mr. Robert explained that Master Peregrine had been taken away because he was ill in his mind, but they were too young, they blamed him for everything, especially for having to cut their holiday in London short. But Mrs. Graham was strong, she stood up to all of it like the lady she is. All the gossip, the stares. I heard her tell Mr. Robert that those were the worst days she'd ever lived through. No soldier could have been braver. I couldn't help but admire her."

"But what about the victim, the person he murdered? Surely the victim's family came to the inquest and gave evidence against him?"

Susan was confused. "I don't know—I never heard they were there. And she wasn't killed here. That's why the inquest was in London."

"What was the finding?" I asked.

"I don't know, Miss, I wasn't there. But Mrs. Graham came

home, her face red from crying. Mr. Peregrine was already in the asylum, had been for days, and she told us all that he'd never leave it, he'd stay where he couldn't harm anyone else."

I was more than a little confused. "The inquest was held in London, but Mr. Peregrine had already been taken away?"

"Yes, Miss, it was decided in London that he was in no state to be shut into a prison. There was a doctor at the asylum who treated such cases, and it was his opinion that Mr. Peregrine should be brought to him straightaway. That doctor, and Dr. Hadley, here, the rector, the tutor, the local magistrate, they all sent depositions to London, asking that Mr. Peregrine remain in that asylum where he could be cared for properly. I heard Mrs. Graham tell Dr. Hadley it was a great kindness. She said she couldn't have faced her husband in heaven, if she'd let his son go to the hangman. But I don't think it would have come to that. I don't think they've hanged anyone his age in a hundred years. Not at Maidstone, they hadn't."

I shivered at the thought. "How old did you say he was?"

"He wasn't even fifteen when it happened and not well, in the bargain. If he'd been taken away and put into prison, it would have been a terrible burden for the family to carry, wouldn't it?" She collected the bundle of sheets. "I've said enough, more than I should."

I handed her the pillow slips that I'd been removing, and asked, "You aren't going to have to do all these by yourself, are you?"

"No, Miss, thank you for asking. There's a laundress comes to see to the washing and ironing."

After Susan had gone, I stood in the empty room and thought about the man who had lain so ill in that bed.

Perhaps it wasn't the first time Peregrine Graham had attacked someone. But that was neither here nor there. His brothers had had to grow up in the shadow of his crime of murder, and it must have been exceedingly difficult. While Peregrine had for the most part been civil and seemed perfectly sane, as far as I could judge, who knew what lay beneath the surface? I had glimpsed the force of his anger once, and that had been enough.

It was to his credit that Peregrine acknowledged what he'd done. He hadn't tried to pretend to me that he was an innocent man, or that he didn't deserve his fate. He knew very well that he must return to the asylum, and he went back peaceably. But his family, knowing his history better than I did, must have spent a good many uncomfortable nights while he was under their roof.

Chapter Seven

When we gathered in the dining room for our noon meal, Mrs. Graham was profuse in her apologies for using a guest so poorly, and added her gratitude for saving her son's life. I wasn't sure I believed the latter. The Grahams could decently mourn the dead, and admit that they'd loved him. Even if they choked on the words.

How would my own parents feel if I were taken up for murder?

A sobering thought that made the Grahams' dilemma strike home. And yet I couldn't forget that they had protected themselves—at whose expense?

"My training wasn't solely for the battlefield, Mrs. Graham. I was taught to work with the sick as well," I reminded her.

"We heard almost nothing from the sickroom except the endless sound of his coughing. Did—was Peregrine able to speak? I worry that they were treating him well, that he'd had proper care."

I knew what she was fishing for. She could have come and asked him about his care herself.

"He was hardly able to speak more than a few words," I told her. "He asked where he was, and if the war was still going on. He asked what year it was. . . ." I let my voice trail off, as if I were having trouble remembering anything else. I most certainly couldn't tell her that he believed she or Robert had killed his father.

She seemed to be surprised that he didn't know what year this was. "But surely they tell him—" She stopped, then went on in a different direction. "Well. He's always been troubled in his mind. Even as a child. At least he doesn't appear to be any worse—violent, difficult to manage."

"I don't think he had the strength to be difficult."

We had just finished our pudding when Dr. Philips came to the door and asked to speak to me.

While I was playing angel of mercy, Ted Booker had tried again to kill himself, and it had been necessary to strap him down to a bed and keep him at the surgery.

"I don't know what will happen to him. I feel I've failed him in some fashion. He wants to see you. Meanwhile I must contact the clinic and tell them to hurry. Booker can't wait six weeks for space. Not now."

"He's asking for me? I'm surprised he remembers me at all."

"I expect his wife may have told him. Will you come?"

Mrs. Graham protested, but this time it was more form than substance.

I went to fetch my coat and stepped out into the still, cold air.

"When I heard that Peregrine was ill," Dr. Philips said as I preceded him down the walk, "I offered to come. They told me you were managing very well. I wasn't surprised. I'd already witnessed a little of your skills."

I turned my head to look at him. "But—I kept wondering why you hadn't at least overseen what I was doing."

"I'm sure Mrs. Graham would have sent for me if she'd believed he was truly in danger. It was a compliment that she trusted to your training."

I opened my mouth to tell him just how ill Peregrine Graham had been, how I'd lain awake hour after hour, worried as he struggled to breathe. And then I stopped myself in time. What good would it do to make him wonder why Mrs. Graham had turned him away?

It hadn't yet begun to snow, and I made some remark about how heavy the clouds were. Dr. Philips told me snow was unlikely. The awkward moment passed.

We walked in silence to his surgery, cutting through the church-yard. I told him about the rector's carpentry.

"He's quite good with his hands. I could wish him a stronger force—he's sometimes of two minds about what should be done when he ought to be taking a stand."

"Perhaps he's chosen the wrong profession."

"You haven't heard his sermons. They're quite good as well," the doctor assured me. "It's solving problems of a practical nature where he's something of a paradox."

I wondered if he was thinking about the rector's views on Ted Booker.

The doctor's housekeeper met us at the door and let us into the surgery, saying as I entered, "You're the young woman who knew Arthur."

"I did, yes."

"We all mourned him. Such a shame."

What do you say in response to that? I smiled, and she took my coat before leading me back to the small room where they had put Ted Booker.

He lay on the bed, his eyes closed, but he opened them when Dr. Philips said quietly, "She's here."

I saw such misery in their depths. My heart went out to him. But I said in my brisk voice, "What's this I hear about you doing yourself a harm?"

He looked at the doctor, and both Dr. Philips and the house-keeper withdrew, shutting the door softly after them.

Lieutenant Booker said, "I'm a coward. Just as they say. A brave man would have got it done properly."

"Perhaps it isn't your time to die," I replied. It was an echo of what I had said to Peregrine Graham. "Had you thought about that?"

"No." It was blunt.

"Well, it's something to consider. Hasn't your poor wife suffered enough? Even for Harry's sake? He would be the first to tell you to put the living before the dead. You won't bring him back by sacrificing yourself as well, you know. And he doesn't have a son to carry on his memory. But you do, and it's your duty to see that your own son remembers his uncle with pride and honors him for his courage."

He held up his wrists, bandaged now. "I couldn't do it. Not even for Harry."

"Then I'm proud of you. Something deep inside prevented you, and that means in time you'll heal. The living must go on living, or we fail the dead."

"It wasn't that. I heard my brother crying out to me. As clearly as I hear you now. He stopped me, I didn't stop myself."

I digested that, then said, "Which proves I was right. There *was* some reason for you to live."

"It shook me to the core."

I could see that it had. "Of course it did." I pulled up the only chair in the small room and sat down by the bed. "I expect he watches over you. And always will."

He stared at me. "I told myself it was proof of my madness."

"I'd say, rather, proof of your sanity. Why did you send for me?"

"Because none of them has been to war. You've come close." He frowned. "I thought I'd seen you in France. When Harry was taken to the dressing station."

"It was dark, you were very upset. We look alike in our uniforms."

"That's true. . . ." He hesitated. "Will you tell the doctor that I won't try again? He won't believe me. My mother-in-law is set on sending me back to the clinic. I want to stay here."

"Dr. Philips has already given you one chance. And Mrs. Denton is sick with worry for her daughter. Wouldn't you be in her shoes?"

"I tried to make her understand about Harry," he said defensively.

"Oh, don't be silly, Lieutenant. If you had a daughter and she'd married a soldier who seems bent on breaking her heart if he doesn't frighten her to death first, what would you do?"

He gave me a twisted smile. "I'd try to knock some sense into the bas—" He broke off. "Beg pardon, Sister."

"That's precisely what Sally's mother feels."

"Tell them I'm sorry. Tell them to give me one more chance. I won't let them down." His eyes pleaded, and I tried to judge whether he meant it at this moment but would succumb to his nightmares again.

There was no way of telling. "I'll speak to Dr. Philips."

"I can't help that the trenches come back—"

"That's not your fault," I agreed. "*This*"—I gestured to his surroundings, the bandages and the straps holding him down—"*this* is your doing."

He shut his eyes, and I could see tears beneath the lids. Men don't like to be seen crying. I turned and quietly left him alone.

I wasn't sure Dr. Philips believed me when I told him that Ted Booker had promised not to do anything rash again. I could read the skepticism in his face. After all, I was a nurse, and he was the medical man.

Walking back to the Graham house, I was overtaken by the rector—he called to me, introducing himself in the same breath.

"Miss Crawford? I say, I'm Christopher Montgomery, the rector."

I turned to meet him as he caught me up.

He was a man of middle height, with light blue eyes and fair skin. I put his age at forty, perhaps forty-five.

"I understand you were with Arthur Graham when he died."

"Yes, I was. I came to Owlhurst with messages for his family. We nearly met before, Rector. I was in the church the other day, when you were repairing something in the organ loft."

He smiled ruefully. "I must have been making a terrible racket.

But the bench was wobbly, according to my organist, Mr. Lessing, and I took it upon myself to find a solution. Thankfully, all four legs of the bench were even when I finished."

I laughed. "I'm sure they were."

"I saw you leaving the surgery just now."

"I was looking in on Lieutenant Booker."

"Yes, I sat with him earlier. A sad case. I don't understand what shell shock does to the mind, but I can see very clearly how much he's suffering. I was a chaplain in the first months of 1915. They sent me home because I had a very bad case of trench foot. Embarrassing, to say the least. But I've thought for some time that it might have also been my reluctance to convince men that God intended for them to die for King and Country."

"There are worse cases than Mr. Booker's."

He shook his head. "That's beyond my ability to imagine."

We had turned to walk together toward the church gate, where I would take the shortcut to the Graham house.

The rector said after a moment, "I wanted to ask you about Peregrine Graham."

I was immediately on my guard. It wouldn't do to gossip about the Grahams behind their backs.

"It came to my ears that he'd been brought home and is not expected to live. Is it true?"

"He's much improved, I'm happy to say. Someone came for him only this morning."

"Yes, the neighbors were quick to inform me that the ambulance had returned, but they couldn't tell me whether it took him away alive or dead. I tried to call one morning, but was turned away. They told me Peregrine had no wish to see me."

I hadn't known that he'd called. I said, trying to be judicious, "I don't think he was really well enough for a visitor."

"It was kind of you to help the family in their hour of need."

It hadn't been kindness, it had been necessity. "I was glad I was here to step in," I answered instead.

"Where have you served?"

I told him, trying to keep my voice neutral—an experience, but stiff upper lip and all that.

We were halfway across the churchyard now.

He stopped. "It must have been a very nerve-racking experience. I can't imagine coming so close to drowning. And how is your arm? I see you aren't keeping it in a sling."

"Much improved." I smiled. "Friends at the Front are exhausted from deciphering the letters I wrote with my left hand. It will do much for fighting morale when I am legible again."

The rector chuckled. Then he said, going back again to Peregrine, "I've always been of two minds about Mrs. Graham's son, and what he did."

"I didn't know that you were here, er—at the time."

"I was not. But my predecessor kept journals for his own guidance, and left them to me for mine. I have read the pertinent passages. He writes that Peregrine had been taken away quietly. He seemed to be comfortable with the decision, he felt that the family had suffered enough. I wonder if that was fair to Peregrine."

"Would prison have been better? Surely not, if there were doctors at the asylum who could work with him."

"As to that, I can't say. My predecessor—Craig was his name—spoke of a damaged mind, and the fact that the poor soul had never successfully been educated. That would have been taken into account, certainly."

I knew my surprise showed in my face. "Is that what he wrote?"

"He felt Peregrine Graham had the mind of a child."

Hardly the man I'd just dealt with!

"Was that the generally accepted view? Or just Mr. Craig's?"

"I can only tell you his given opinion. Apparently the boy had been having some difficulties while his father was alive. The tutor complained he was slow to learn, unable to concentrate on his lessons. But when his father died, the boy's mind broke with his grief. And so they kept him close to home after that. At any rate, I thought, while Peregrine was ill, I could offer him Christian solace before he returned to that place. I went to Barton's—the asylum—soon after I took up the living here, but they told me he wasn't allowed visitors. I was astonished. I thought the family would have—but I was told he was allowed to see no one."

"Were these the terms of his confinement?"

"That's possible, of course. Ted Booker told Mr. Craig that one day he was passing the asylum, and there was Peregrine, sitting on a bench under a tree, manacled to it. This was some years ago, well before the war. Booker could see him through the gate, and called to him. Peregrine turned his head away. Booker was shocked by his appearance, and said something to Arthur about it. The rector reported in his journal that Booker was the only person to have seen him since he was taken there."

And I'd just missed my chance to ask Ted Booker about Peregrine Graham.

I next expected the rector to ask me what I thought of my patient, but he didn't. It was the journals that were on his mind. I could see that he was fascinated by his predecessor.

"Well, water under the dam," he went on. "I've never spoken to anyone else about the journals, you know. It seemed best. There are comments in there that are more honest than most people could stomach. Mr. Craig believed in the truth at any price."

"I understand." I wasn't to chatter about them.

"I think you do. Thank you."

We had reached the far gate of the churchyard. He opened it for me, and said rather shyly, "Perhaps you'll call at the rectory, before you leave. I'd be glad to show you the journals."

"I should be leaving shortly. I'm awaiting my orders now. With *Britannic* at the bottom of the sea, I'm sure London is at sixes and sevens trying to decide where to put all of us. One of the nurses on the ship with me has just been posted to Poona, in India."

"That's a long way from home," he said.

I didn't tell him I'd spent part of my childhood in the East. I simply agreed, and he said good-bye, but then called me back to ask, "Do you think Peregrine Graham lacks spiritual comfort where he is? Is he capable of recognizing his needs in that direction?"

"I think," I responded slowly, "that he despairs of comfort. But it's a matter you must take up with the family. Or the doctors at the asylum."

"Mr. Craig was also chaplain there, but I've not been asked to fill his position. Perhaps I ought to speak to someone in charge and see what the need is."

"Yes, that might be wise," I said. "Good-bye, Rector."

We shook hands, and I turned away to walk the rest of the way alone.

There was much curiosity at the house regarding my summons to speak with Ted Booker. Susan was the first to ask, and then over our meal, Mrs. Graham brought up the subject.

Not wanting to add to any gossip about his attempt to kill himself, I merely said, "He felt that I'd been closer to the war than his family. I think he wanted reassurance that his problems are not his alone."

"I should think a rational man would do his best to heal quickly and return to the fighting. God knows, we need soldiers." Would she have wished her own son back before his time was up?

I could have answered that it wasn't surprising—the casualty lists continued to be unbearably long. But I said instead, "It takes time to heal the mind, just as it does the body."

"Did he ask you about Peregrine?"

"About Peregrine? I don't believe he even knew your son was at home, ill."

"No, I meant Dr. Philips."

I think my guilty conscience for having spoken of Peregrine with the rector must have shone in my face, but I said resolutely, "He complimented me on my skills."

"You needn't avoid the question, you know."

"But I'm not. He did tell me he'd called, to see if I needed his help. I wish I'd known it at the time."

She nodded. "Thank you for your honesty. And I'll be equally honest in return. I didn't wish people in Owlhurst to gossip about my son. I'm well aware that a medical man must keep matters concerning his patients in strictest confidence, but I don't know Dr. Philips that well yet."

Timothy came in just then and said, "Did you hear? Booker tried to slash his wrists. Fool that he is. His wife must be in despair." He sat down to take his tea, and then too restless to be still, stood up and carried his cup to the window.

"She made her choice, Timothy. It's not for you to judge her decision. I've always felt one of the Loftlan girls would be more suitable. We could invite the family to dine with us . . ."

It must have been an old argument, because I saw Timothy twitch one shoulder, as if trying to shrug off her words.

"I'd just like to think she's happy," he said brusquely. "More to the point, safe."

"How can she be, under the circumstances?" Mrs. Graham turned to me. "Sally was quite popular. Everyone liked her, and she had a sweet nature that I thought spoke well of her upbringing. She and Ted Booker were an excellent match. Everyone was pleased for them."

"She saw him in uniform, and that was that," Timothy added sourly.

Jonathan came in, late as usual, and said, "Sorry," to his mother, before nodding to me.

Taking his cup, he said, "There was a message from the asylum. Brother Peregrine made the journey back safely. I don't know who is more disappointed in that, the asylum or us."

"Jonathan!" his mother said sharply.

"What sort of life does he lead, Mother? I'd hate to be caged up. And if he complains, it's Maidstone instead. The poor devil could live to be eighty in that place. Is that what you want for him?"

"Do you think prison would have been better? Do you want that on the family escutcheon?" Timothy asked from the window.

Jonathan wheeled on his brother. "Peregrine is an albatross about our necks, alive or dead."

"Jonathan." His mother spoke his name in such a cold tone that both of her sons stared at her. "We'll hear no more about Peregrine, if you please. The matter is closed."

"Yes, well, he's still Father's heir when you die, Mother. We haven't got round that problem yet, have we?"

"Peregrine could well outlive us all," she told him. "As you said. Which reminds me. Someone needs to bethink themselves of a guardian for him, if anything happens to me."

Jonathan said only, "Let Timothy see to that. I'm not setting foot in that place."

"Don't ask me to go. That's why we have a family solicitor," Timothy retorted.

I sat there in embarrassed silence, trying to pretend I wasn't hearing such a private family issue being discussed.

Robert came in to speak to Mrs. Graham. He stood there, leaning against the doorframe, as if he belonged in this room and was not happy at being excluded. Remembering his gruffness when he met my train, it occurred to me that he hadn't wanted me to come to Owlhurst. He was close to this family—it was possible that he'd guessed what Arthur would say on his deathbed, and knew it would open old wounds. Even I could see that Robert felt free to express his views. His had been the deciding voice in allowing Peregrine to come home to die.

Watching him there as he and Mrs. Graham discussed a problem with a tenant's cow, I was reminded of what Peregrine had said about who might have killed his father—his stepmother or her cousin. It was hard to give credence to his words—they hadn't married, after all, and I couldn't think of another reason for killing a husband. Yet they were close, as cousins sometimes are. Clearly the two of them were of the same mind in this problem with the cow, and Robert had come out of duty rather than from a need for guidance.

When they had settled on a course of action regarding how to treat the animal, he nodded to me and left.

Mrs. Graham's gaze followed him to the door, a frown between her eyes.

Then she turned back to me and said, "You've heard us speak of things that are private, my dear—in regard to Peregrine. I must apologize. But his circumstances make it necessary for us to think and act for him, painful as it may be."

Was she testing me again, to see if I'd noticed—or failed to notice—something in regard to her stepson?

It dawned on me that perhaps the talk about Peregrine's mental deficiency during his childhood might have been the family's way of covering up something worse. Better to tell friends and neighbors that the boy was slow than that the boy was dangerous. It explained too why I'd not found him deficient—if anything, articulate and sensible.

I smiled with understanding. "It must be very difficult. I don't envy you."

Jonathan said, "I don't wish to appear to cut short your visit, Miss Crawford, but I'll be traveling to Tonbridge tomorrow. I'll be happy to take you to the train, if that's your wish."

Mrs. Graham said in protest, "Jonathan, that's not necessary. Robert will drive her when she's ready."

But I knew what was expected of the guest who had stayed overlong.

"It would be lovely if I could go with you, Lieutenant Graham. Much as I've enjoyed my visit, I must have everything ready to return to duty when my orders come."

There was protest, but halfhearted. I smiled, told Jonathan I'd have my luggage closed before I came down to breakfast, and the subject was dropped.

I wasn't ready to leave. But I didn't know how to prevent it.

Beware what you wish for.

Dr. Philips was at the door just before dawn, pounding insistently until Susan answered the summons, then awakened me.

Ted Booker had stripped away his bandages in the night and succeeded, finally, in killing himself.

I was shocked.

"There's to be an inquest," Dr. Philips was saying urgently. "You must tell them that he was not in his right mind. That he didn't know what he was doing."

"He promised," I said. "He told me he understood what his wife was suffering. I believed him." I could feel hot tears stinging my eyes. "Poor man. Poor, poor man."

"You'll be the only one to weep over him," Dr. Philips said. "His mother-in-law is telling the world that he's gone to a better place. . . ." He stopped. "I'm sorry, Miss Crawford, I am so sorry to bring you this news. But I have nowhere to turn. I don't quite know how to take it in."

He was upset. I understood losing a patient. "I'll fetch my coat and come with you."

Dr. Philips shook his head. "There's nothing you can do, not now. I've seen to the—er—necessary steps that follow on the heels of sudden death. I am refusing to sign the death certificate until another doctor has seen the body. Dr. Blessing is coming from Tonbridge."

"Dr. Philips. Come with me."

He seemed almost grateful to follow me to the kitchen, where Susan was just stoking the fires. I gave him a cup of tea and with Susan's permission, eggs and bacon and toast as well.

He kept murmuring, "This is most kind—most kind."

When Susan had taken the tea tray up to Mrs. Graham, I said quietly, "Something more than Ted Booker's death has upset you. What's wrong?"

"Someone came into the surgery in the middle of the night. I was asleep, I'd had a long day. Then I woke to the sound of something heavy falling, and when I went down, I found a muddy print in the passage, and it wasn't mine, and it wasn't Booker's. His shoes were still where I'd put them, in the small closet where I keep my coat and Wellingtons. I don't want to believe that someone came into my house and talked to Booker, and left him in a state of mind where he killed himself. But the evidence is *there*."

"What size print? A woman's? A man's?"

"I can't judge. A muddy smudge is more descriptive." He rubbed his face with his hands. "I don't want to believe it was Mrs. Denton. But who else? And what am I to do?"

"You said you'd spoken to her. What was she like? Anxious? Unsettled? Afraid that you knew what she'd done?"

"As usual she was full of concern for her daughter. Glad that her suffering was over. Claiming this was a blessed release for Booker. Sometimes I think she could have killed Booker for her daughter's sake and never blinked an eye. And then I look at her and tell myself she's not vicious, just a mother fearing for a child's situation."

I tried to bring Mrs. Denton back to mind. I thought it very likely that she might have tormented Ted Booker to the point he chose to die and release his wife. Not intending, perhaps, to kill him, but driving home what she considered to be the truth, that he was a poor husband for putting his brother before his wife.

"Sometimes the Mrs. Dentons of this world get their way through sheer cruelty," I said with resignation. "And then they deny what they've set in motion because they blotted out the possible effects of their words. They convince themselves."

"Do I tell the police? It would create a sensation if I did, and if I am wrong, I've done to his mother-in-law what she may have done to Booker." He looked up at me, pain clear in his eyes. "I've never had to deal with the murder of a patient before. And I don't know why I should turn to you—"

"Because I'm an objective observer? And I did have a long talk with Lieutenant Booker. Whether it helped or not, we'll never know now. I thought at the time I had his full attention, that he was listening." I considered for a moment. "The police must know whatever you can tell them about Ted Booker's state of mind. As for the inquest—I was leaving today. I've trespassed long enough on the kindness of the Grahams."

"I've more than enough space in my house. But I'm afraid as a single woman—"

"No, it would cause talk. I understand. Is there anyone else I could stay with? Preferably someplace where I'm needed. It will look less like the Grahams had pitched me out."

"Mrs. Turner has just had appendicitis. But what she needs isn't a nurse, so much as someone to cook and clean until she's on her feet again."

"That will do. I've done as much onboard ship, when we were shorthanded. I must draw the line at doing the wash." I indicated my arm.

"You can use the laundress who comes to the Grahams and sees to my needs as well. Mrs. Abbot."

"Then I'll break the news to the Grahams." Somehow I was sure they wouldn't be best pleased. "You can come and collect me at ten. That's when I was leaving for Tonbridge with Jonathan Graham."

"Very well." He got up, smiling. "Women always know what's best, don't they? Food and a willing ear. Are you single, Miss Crawford? You would make an admirable doctor's wife."

He was smiling as he said it, and I gave him my answer with a matching smile.

"Why, Dr. Philips, whatever would you do if I said yes?"

We laughed, and he went out the kitchen door rather than

through the house again. I thought he didn't want to encounter the Grahams.

Susan came down the back stairs and said, "What brought the doctor here at such an early hour? I've never seen him so agitated."

"Ted Booker killed himself last night. Despite all our precautions."

"Oh, my dear Lord." She set down her tray and shook her head. "I'm that sorry. He was such a nice young lad. I was quite fond of him. Well, there's the war, of course. It's taken so many young men. . . ."

I went to see Mrs. Graham just before breakfast, and told her that Ted Booker appeared to have killed himself, and I would most likely have to give evidence at the inquest. "I'm so sorry," I added. "It's an inconvenience to everyone. But Dr. Philips is making arrangements—"

Mrs. Graham frowned. "I don't like the way Dr. Philips is using you, Miss Crawford. That's what it is. You're a young woman of good family. What would your father have to say to the doctor's inconsiderate behavior? If you stay in Owlhurst, you remain with us. That's all there is to say."

She pressed her fingers to her face for an instant and then added, "I must call on Mrs. Denton. It's my duty. Perhaps you'd like to go with me?"

"I don't think she will care to see me at such a time. I've defended her son-in-law to her."

"Yes, well, perhaps you're right. I'll dress and go directly after breakfast. There will be arrangements to make. Robert will know what to do about that. I'll ask him to come with me. How tragic, Miss Crawford—it could have been Jonathan, you know, scarred in his mind. The wound on his face could easily have affected his brain. It was deep, very deep."

I didn't try to explain that shell shock didn't begin with a physical wound.

She excused herself, and I went to my room, to write to my parents, then realized that I'd be giving my father an excuse to come and rescue me. Shell shock, murder, inquests—the Colonel Sahib couldn't have stayed away. If need be, he'd bring the Household Cavalry with him.

I had packed my belongings the night before but didn't have the spirit to take them out again. Instead I sat at the desk by the windows of my room and began a letter to Elayne. When it was finished I left it on the silver salver on the little French table in the hall, where someone would see that it was posted.

After that, what to do with myself? I opened the door of the house and stepped out, looking at the sky. To my surprise the clouds had broken, the winds had died down, and after the long spell of frosts and cold, the day was warming quickly. I went up to my room, collected my coat and hat and gloves, and set out for a walk.

As I did, I saw Mrs. Denton and her daughter leaving the rectory. *Arranging poor Ted Booker's services,* I thought. I would have liked to offer them my sympathy.

This was my first opportunity to observe Sally. She appeared to be a little younger than I was, but she had a small son and was now a widow. I thought about Ted's promises to me, and felt sad. He had wanted to heal. I wished I could tell his wife that. For her sake . . .

Her future bleak, her life a shambles now, it was still possible that Sally Booker might find happiness again. In time . . .

With Timothy? a little voice in my head asked.

Chapter Eight

THE RECTOR, WALKING briskly across to the church, waved to me, and when I waved back, he waited for me to catch him up.

"Lovely weather. I see you're enjoying it," Mr. Montgomery said as I came within earshot. "Come in, if you will. I need to work for a bit. This business of Ted Booker's death has disturbed me."

I joined him, and we turned toward the church. "I thought it was your duty to comfort the ill and the grieving."

"Yes, so it is. But to tell you the truth, I feel very uneasy in my mind."

"He killed himself while devastated by the death of his brother," I said, bristling on Ted Booker's behalf. "I can't see how he could be held accountable for his actions, given his state of mind."

"That's not what I was driving at. No, I wonder if we couldn't have made a greater effort, taken the burden from his wife and her mother. I understand twins are very close, closer than brothers even. Harry's death was a terrible shock to Ted. It was wrong of us to expect him to recover from it quickly."

"I don't know that he would have done. I've had some experience with what he was suffering. It's not as simple as grief at the loss of a loved one. It's a measure of guilt, and the mind dwells on what was done or not done, trying to find a way to change the outcome. But of course that's not possible, and so there's no way to escape what happened." I found myself thinking of Peregrine Graham. "He might have had problems for years. And I think that frightened him as much as Harry's death."

"You are very understanding for one so young," he said, smiling.

"I've dealt with broken bodies and broken minds. You learn how to cope. And how to care."

"Are you staying on with us for a time?" We went into the church and felt the cold in the stones that today's sun hadn't begun to warm. I reached in my pocket and pulled on my gloves.

"I was to leave today. But with Mr. Booker's death—it's possible I'll be called to give information at the inquest."

"Indeed. That's very kind of you."

Before thinking, I blurted, "It isn't kindness. I thought he had turned a corner, so to speak, and was better. But in the night, the darkness must have come down again. I should have stayed with him. I thought Dr. Philips would have arranged for someone. . . ."

"He tried, but it wasn't possible."

"I would have come, if he'd asked."

"But he did. Mrs. Graham told him you were leaving this morning, and that she wouldn't interrupt your rest."

I would have sworn, if I hadn't been in a church, with its rector.

Before I could answer that, Mr. Montgomery went on. "Did you know that Jonathan went to speak to him around ten o'clock last evening? I was just coming home from Mrs. Turner's sickbed when I saw him. He waved in my direction but didn't wait to speak to me. I thought perhaps their conversation had brought the war back to him as well. Still, I was glad he'd gone to see Ted. The two families had grown apart, with the war."

"It was kind of him," I said doubtfully.

"Jonathan can be very blunt and to the point, without sympathy, sometimes. But there is good in everyone." We walked down the aisle, and he paused to examine the cushion on one of the kneeling benches. "I'm afraid I was partial to Arthur. He was such a good man."

"Yes, he was," I responded sadly.

He removed the cushion and took out a needle and thread. We sat down in one of the pews, and he mended a corner that was worn. I watched his hands deftly ply the needle, and the work was as good as I might have done. But the next cushion was beyond his skill and he set it aside. "I could ask the women to do this task, but most of them are busy trying to help the war effort. Bandages, knitting scarves and stockings for the men, even vests. But I must admit to the sin of pride when it comes to my church, and I quietly do what's possible before asking for help."

We moved on, and I found it soothing to watch him at work. And I think he enjoyed the companionship as well.

My mind wandered in the stillness, my eyes on the memorial brass that caught the early-morning sun.

Arthur. Ted Booker. Peregrine Graham.

Three men to whom Fate had not been kind. Arthur should have lived, Ted Booker should have been given time to heal, and as for Peregrine—as for Peregrine, he had been lost at fourteen, and there was no way to bring him back.

I sighed, and Mr. Montgomery said, over his shoulder, "That's the point of working with one's hands, you see. It gives the mind something else to do besides worry."

"That's a very comforting philosophy when you enjoy mending and carpentry."

He laughed and gave me the end of a cushion to hold while he repaired a seam. The needlepoint pattern was floral, nasturtiums and petunias entwined in a vine of leaves. A subaltern in my father's last command had been fond of gardening, and his mother had sent seeds for him to plant. Only the nasturtiums survived the heat. I wondered where Linford might be now. Dead?

The rector had set aside two cushions that were beyond his skill.

He put away his needle and said, "There, enough for today." Collecting the cushions he said, "You're concerned for Peregrine. That does you credit."

I hadn't realized that I'd spoken the three names aloud.

Then something occurred to me. There was a new rector, a new doctor. Was there as well a new policeman here in Owlhurst?

I asked the rector, and he said, "Yes, how did you know? Inspector Gadd, a wonderful man, died of a brain injury some two years after Peregrine was taken away. Inspector Howard is our man now. Not as sharp as Gadd, you know, but early days. Early days."

All of which meant that those who might have had some part in sending Peregrine to the asylum had died—policeman, doctor, rector. "And what about the magistrate? Is he still here?"

"She. Yes, of course. If you're concerned about the coming inquest, it shouldn't be terribly difficult for you. Would you like to go with me while I deliver these cushions? It's partly pastoral call and partly a way of dispensing charity in a way that doesn't offend. Mrs. Clayton needs the money, and she's a wonderful seamstress. And I think she might be glad to hear about Arthur from you."

Dr. Philips had mentioned her name.

"I've nothing else to do," I agreed. "If you don't think she'll mind my coming along."

"She'll be delighted. You'll see."

We walked from the churchyard down past The Bells, and along the cricket pitch, to a cottage tucked away down a narrow lane. It sat with five of its neighbors in a tiny cul-de-sac that time had passed by. The cottages were, like the rectory, Tudor in style, their roofs running together and almost swaybacked with age. Mrs. Clayton had just stepped out to sweep the large stone that was her stoop, and Mr. Montgomery hailed her.

She looked up and said, "What brings you calling, Rector? Discovered my secret sins, have you?" And she cackled like one of the hens scratching in the grassy patch of land at the end of the lane.

Her eyes were watering in the cold air, her teeth had gone, and she was as wrinkled as a prune, but her spirit was still young.

"I've brought more work for you, Mrs. Clayton. And a visitor."

She passed from her inspection of him to me, standing a little behind the rector, and said, "Is this the lass who came about poor dear Arthur?"

News travels fast in small villages.

"Yes, it's Elizabeth Crawford, Mrs. Clayton. How are you this morning?" From the start he'd raised his voice a little, to accommodate her loss of hearing. "Is there anything you need?"

"I'm poorly, but still breathing, thankee." She turned to me. "Was it you nursed Mr. Peregrine when he was sent home with that pneumonia?"

"It was fortunate I was there. He had a close call."

If she knew and repeated this much gossip, how was I to ask her about Peregrine?

But I needn't have worried. She invited us in for tea, took the worn cushions from Mr. Montgomery, and then as she set cups in front of us, followed by the teapot, she said, "I was once maid in that house. I knew Mr. Graham, and his first wife, Margaret. Now there was a lovely one, was Miss Margaret. She died in childbirth, you know. They feared for his sanity. But men are fey creatures, six months later he was in love again, this time with the present Mrs. Graham. A Montmorency she was, before her marriage. And they had three sons of their own, in quick succession. Hardly one lying in past, and it was near time for the next. It was a house full of joy. But it didn't last. First Mr. Graham was taken, and then Peregrine, you might say, and now Arthur. He was so like his father, Mr. Peregrine was, and may still be for all I know. I'd say that Arthur favored his father as well. I can't say as much for the other two. Very like their mother, both of them. Then Mr. Graham died after his carriage horse bolted and threw him out on his head. A Gypsy woman had foretold his death, you know. 'A horse will kill you, and you will not see the hand that sends you to your death.' Well, it was a child with a hoop run out in the road that startled the horse into bolting, and I doubt Mr. Graham saw her until she was under the hooves of his horse. It was all too quick. Both dead in the blink of an eye."

Mrs. Clayton loudly sipped her tea through pursed lips, and sighed. "I always did like a nice Darjeeling. Susan sends me a packet now and again."

"Tell me about Robert," I said, curiosity getting the better of me.

"Robert? He came to Owlhurst with Mrs. Graham. It was said, to look after her. Her father didn't want her moving to Kent. If you ask me, if that was his fear, he shouldn't have given her a London season. But the Montmorency family comes from Northumberland, and whatever nonsense they get up to there, it makes them a suspicious lot. It's been whispered that Robert was a poor cousin and Mr. Montmorency was looking for a way to keep him employed. Mr. Graham took him on to run the farm."

The rector smiled into his cup, and I thought perhaps I ought to drop the subject of Robert.

I needn't have worried. Mrs. Clayton was off again. When she learned I had lived in India for much of my childhood, she said, "And I've never been as far as Chatham, though I came that near to seeing London, once."

She pinched her fingers together to indicate how close it was. I didn't need to prod her, she launched into the story of her own accord.

"Mrs. Graham was to take a house in London, to show her sons the sights and so forth. We'd heard she was having Mr. Peregrine seen by a specialist as well, but nothing came of that. I was to accompany her, and I was that excited I told all my acquaintance they could write to me at Number 17, Carroll Square."

She spoke the address as if it were a talisman, grinning toothlessly at me, then went on. "I should have saved my breath. Mrs. Graham changed her mind and decided to keep the servants who came with the property, and leave us behind. I don't think I've ever felt such disappointment, because that chance wasn't likely to come my way again."

I wanted to ask if this was the visit to London that had turned out so disastrously but I'd reckoned without Mrs. Clayton's sense of drama.

She added, "Now that was when Mr. Peregrine was said to have killed one of the London maids, and I was grateful it was none of *us* dead at his hands. Still, I've always been of the opinion he wouldn't have harmed someone brought from Owlhurst. He was used to us and our ways."

Comment was expected from me, I could see it in her face.

"How terrible for everyone," I said. "Did the poor girl have any family?"

"I never heard of any."

"How sad. Was Mr. Peregrine considered dangerous, before this murder?"

"Not dangerous, that I was ever told, no. But given to anger sometimes, and not clever at his studies. Mr. Jonathan, he was younger, but he'd torment Mr. Peregrine when no one was looking. And Mr. Peregrine, he'd fight back, then Mr. Appleby, the tutor, would send him to his room as punishment. It was Mrs. Graham who decided they should be taught separately, so that Mr. Peregrine wouldn't hold the other lads back in their studies."

We had finished our tea and had no excuse to linger. We thanked Mrs. Clayton and rose to leave.

She said, "A shame about poor Mr. Ted, isn't it? I was that fond of him and of Harry. Have they set the day for the services, Rector?"

"Not yet. I'll be sure to let you know, Mrs. Clayton."

I hadn't considered the fact that she would have known the Bookers as well as the Grahams. I said, "Would you tell me a little about Harry? What he was like? How the two boys got on together?"

We were standing at the door, the rector with his hand on the latch.

Mrs. Clayton said, "They was so alike you couldn't tell one from the other. What one did, the other was his shadow. And close? They could read each other's thoughts, I'll be bound. I remember once, Ted was in the greengrocer's talking to me, and almost in the middle of a sentence he said, 'I must go, Mrs. Clayton. Harry wants me.' And I said, 'Where is he, then?' And Ted told me, 'He's over by the cricket pitch.' I followed the boy out of the shop, and he was walking straight toward the cricket pitch. I could see Harry in the distance, standing there watching for him. So I said to him, when he came back from France, you must miss your brother something fierce, and Ted answered, 'He's still there, inside my head, and he calls and calls, but he can't find me.' I wanted to weep for the two of them. Nasty war!"

I shivered. "I'm surprised they were allowed to serve together."

"I don't see how anyone, even the Army, could have kept them apart." She thanked us for coming to visit and, as we stepped out the door, wished me a safe journey home, adding, "Perhaps it's a kindness that now they are together again, those two."

It was as good an epitaph as any.

"It's so sad, isn't it?" I said to Mr. Montgomery. "What war does to families."

Mr. Montgomery replied, "You mustn't take our burdens on your shoulders, Miss Crawford. I was warned when I went to France as chaplain not to dwell on all I saw or heard. It was a hard lesson. But it has stayed with me here in my parish. I am the better for it."

But I thought he mended his church because he couldn't mend the broken lives and minds brought to him for comfort.

We walked in silence for a time, and then he asked, "Did you want to save Ted Booker because you couldn't save Arthur Graham?" His eyes were on my face. "Dr. Philips has told me how hard you tried. And you worked a miracle, saving Peregrine Graham. You must count your debt paid in full."

"I—don't know if that's true or not. I won't know until I've left here, when there's distance between me and Owlhurst," I said, unwilling to discuss my feelings with him. Then I heard myself admitting, "I kept putting off coming here, oddly enough."

As if acknowledging my confession, Mr. Montgomery made one of his own. "I wasn't cut out to be a chaplain, although I did all I could for the men who came to me. I just didn't let them see the cost of helping them."

We walked on in silence, and I said good-bye to him near the rectory, before turning in the direction of the Graham house.

Something he'd said earlier came back to me. That he'd seen Jonathan leaving the surgery later in the evening. I thought grimly, *Had he undone all that Dr. Philips and I had tried to accomplish? Jonathan hadn't shown any sympathy toward Ted Booker. Why the need to visit him? Timothy I might have understood. But Jonathan . . .*

And speak of the devil—

Here he was coming toward me.

I stopped a few paces from him, and asked the question that was on my mind. "I didn't know you'd visited Ted Booker last evening. I wonder—was he in better spirits? Or had the depression settled over him again? How did he strike you?"

Jonathan looked at me with a frown between his eyes. "I didn't go to the surgery last night. Why should I? I had nothing to say to the man."

He nodded and walked on. I stood there, staring after him. The rector had just told me— But perhaps he was wrong, and it was someone else. He might have assumed . . . That made no sense either. I somehow hadn't had the impression that the rector was guessing at the visitor's identity.

A little unsettled, I had just reached the Graham house to find a man turning away from the door and coming toward me. He was lifting his hat to me, as if he knew me.

"Miss Crawford, if I'm not mistaken?"

"Yes?" I didn't know *him*. Tall, middle-aged, dark hair already thick with gray, and blue eyes that were pale with a darker rim. Disconcerting.

"Sorry to have to introduce myself here in the street. I'm Inspector Howard. I was just asking for you. Susan told me you were having a walk. I must speak to you. Would you be more comfortable in the house with Mrs. Graham present?"

Of course I wouldn't, but I couldn't say so. "Perhaps we might continue to walk a little," I said.

"Certainly. Thank you." He seemed relieved at my suggestion. We turned back the way I'd come, along the church wall, toward The Bells. "I'm here, as you might have gathered, to ask you about Lieutenant Booker. Dr. Philips tells me you had a good grasp of his medical situation, and that you had spoken to him several times, in fact just after his initial attempt at suicide."

A formality? What was I to say, that Ted Booker had been driven to his death by well-meaning people who believed that a stiff upper lip, and all that it entailed, would set him right again? That a good husband and father ought to know what was expected of him and do his duty, however painful?

Inspector Howard waited.

Finally I said, "I don't think he wanted to die. He just didn't know how to go about living. It was too overwhelming. I was just speaking to Mrs. Clayton, and she told me how close the two—Ted and his brother, Harry—had been all their lives. Do you have a brother, Inspector?"

He grimaced. "Three sisters."

I had to smile. "Then you can't very well put yourself in Lieutenant Booker's place."

"Do you feel that Dr. Philips did everything possible to prevent Booker's death?"

So that was the way the wind was blowing. Mrs. Denton must have said something to leave the impression that Dr. Philips was to blame. On the heels of her own spoken wish that her son-in-law would die! How like her now to try to make a case for neglect, so that her daughter wouldn't be burdened with the stigma of a suicide.

We had come to The Bells and walked on past their garden gate toward the cricket pitch.

"Not only was he convinced that Lieutenant Booker was on the mend, that his word could be trusted, I was as well. Neither of us would have left him if there had been any doubt in our minds. He was contrite about frightening everyone—he said as much."

"Then why the turnaround?" He kept his pace matched to mine, and watched my face without appearing to do it. "It must have taken some determination to tear off the bandages and reopen his wounds. I take it the restraining straps had been removed."

"When he was calmer, yes."

I could have told Inspector Howard that according to the rector and Dr. Philips, there had been a late visitor to the surgery. But there was no proof that whoever it was had even spoken to Ted Booker. The police would believe Jonathan Graham if he claimed he was nowhere near the doctor's house. And it would add tinder to the fires of doubt regarding Dr. Philips, that his surgery was not properly secured.

I knew I had felt my own share of guilt for what had happened. But it was emotional, not rational. Dr. Philips must have experienced the same thing. People died, however much you tried to save them. . . .

"Sometimes," I said, "Lieutenant Booker was unable to tell the present—today, his wife, his son, his responsibilities—from the past—his duty to the men serving under him. He could easily have awakened, confused, not understanding where he was, or why he was bandaged, and tried to return to his unit. Not realizing that in the attempt, he was going to die."

We stopped, and the inspector stood there, his eyes on the cricket pitch. "You think it was confusion about where he was and what he was doing, that led to his death?"

Remembering how hard Ted Booker had fought to save Harry, I nodded. "He would have done anything, sacrificing himself if need be, to keep his brother alive. It's the only explanation I can offer. As for Dr. Philips, I've known him only a very short time, but he's well trained and compassionate. I'd trust him with my own life."

"And yet I understand that when Mrs. Graham's son Peregrine was very ill, she didn't call in Dr. Philips to oversee his care."

The gossips had been busy.

"You are well informed," I said.

"Well, yes, the asylum notified us that Mr. Graham was ill and in the care of his family. There were constables within call as long as he was in Owlhurst. It was reported that Dr. Philips came to the house once but was turned away."

"Hardly turned away. Not really needed is closer to the mark," I answered, my voice nearly betraying my surprise at news of the constables. "I was in charge of the sickroom." I didn't add that Peregrine Graham's case had been such a near run thing that I'd had my hands full. Dr. Philips's presence would have been reassuring. Besides, the Grahams weren't turning him away as much as they were keeping Peregrine behind closed doors. Out of sight and out of mind.

"And Jonathan Graham isn't attended by Dr. Philips, in spite of a rather nasty war wound."

"Dr. Philips isn't a surgeon, Inspector Howard. Lieutenant Graham's bandages haven't been removed, and he may require more surgery before he's fully healed. I daresay he'll remain with the medical staff in charge of his case until they are satisfied that there is no infection."

"I see." He nodded, as if he did.

I ventured one last remark. Let the crows come home to roost. "I'm sure Mrs. Denton is distraught over her son-in-law's death, but it's unkind to blame Dr. Philips. In my opinion, for what it's worth, she was not as sympathetic as she might have been during Lieutenant Booker's illness, and perhaps that's weighing on her mind now."

He smiled. "You are very forthright, Miss Crawford."

I knew then the crows had found their rightful nest. Yes, Mrs. Denton had been busy protecting her daughter. That was as it should be. But she had also been partly responsible for Ted Booker's plight. I wasn't about to let her ruin Dr. Philips's reputation as well.

"I spent several hours in Mrs. Denton's company one afternoon while we watched over Mr. Booker. I had the opportunity to witness her feelings about him."

A little silence fell. Finally Inspector Howard turned back toward the church. "Let me walk you home, Miss Crawford. You've been very helpful."

He asked what had brought me to Owlhurst, and I told him. He said, "It's a great sadness, this war. So many young men lost to us. My sister's son, for one. He was a bright boy. He could have made something of his life. Now we'll never know what it might have been."

"Are you married, Inspector?"

"Indeed I am. And I've been blessed with three young daughters."

We laughed together.

"Will you speak at the inquest?" He appeared to be offering me a choice.

"If my opinion carries any weight, of course I shall."

Ahead of us was the church. He said, "Would you mind if I left you here? You know your way, I think?"

"I'll be fine. Thank you."

He turned to go and then had one last question for me. "In your opinion, was Ted Booker mad?"

"Not mad, no." I looked toward the church steeple, thinking about Peregrine Graham. "Not as we think of madness. He was as wounded in spirit as Jonathan Graham is wounded in the flesh."

Inspector Howard touched his hat to me as he thanked me, and then walked on toward the High Street of Owlhurst.

Looking after him, I wondered how much good I had really done—and how much harm. On the whole, I thought the Colonel Sahib would have been pleased with his daughter's handling of that interview. Inspector Howard was no fool.

When I reached the house, I could almost sense the curiosity welling behind that front door, and the questions I'd be asked about what the inspector had had to say to me. The very thought was enough to make me keep on walking. I wasn't ready to answer them, and I refused to add to any speculation about police interest in Dr. Philips. And so, with nowhere else to go, and my feet feeling like numb blocks of ice, I called on Susan's mother. It was the only other sanctuary I could think of where there was a fire and a warm welcome.

No one had told her the sad news about Ted Booker, and tears came to her eyes as she sat down in the nearest chair.

"Oh, my good Lord. No."

I tried to comfort her, but she took his death hard. "I was that fond of the Booker twins. The truth is, I liked them better than the Graham boys, barring Arthur of course. Steady lads, honest and caring, that's what they were. Sons a mother could be proud of."

I was surprised. But then Peregrine was a murderer, Jonathan seemed to be callous and uncaring, and Timothy—Timothy I hadn't really understood yet. He seemed to be open and honest, but sometimes that appeared to be what was expected of him. As if to show he bore no ill will to Fate for having given him a club-foot. Again, that English insistence on stiff upper lip, pretending nothing is wrong.

Susan's mother sat there for a time reminiscing about the Booker twins, and then said, "I don't know how many more shocks I can bear. First Arthur and then Harry, and now Mr. Ted." She shook her head. "I ought to count poor Mr. Peregrine as well. He's as good as dead, isn't he?"

"I was talking to Mrs. Clayton earlier. She told me she had

expected to go to London with the family, until plans were changed at the last minute. Were you to go as well?"

"I was to stay here. I can tell you, I was more than a little envious of Hester Clayton, at the time. As it turned out, I was glad I wasn't there. It was a terrible shock. I heard Mrs. Graham speaking to Inspector Gadd, describing how he'd ripped that poor girl to pieces in an orgy of lust and blood. Very like Jack the Ripper, it was, that's how she put it. I didn't sleep for two nights, picturing it. And Mrs. Graham walking in to find the body and Peregrine there with blood all over him. It's a wonder she didn't lose *her* mind."

Shocked, I said, "I thought—" But I don't know what I thought. A nice quiet killing with no blood and the victim someone I didn't know and never would? Appalling and all that, but somehow until now, not *real*.

"Mrs. Graham cried all night, saying she wished he'd died there and then, so she could bury him beside his father and have done with it, and never have to think about it again. Ever."

There were tears in her eyes again, and she bit her lip to hold them back. "I was that fond of him, as a boy. Very like his father, he was, when he was young. I tell you, it was such a blow. But then he went away, and we all tried to go on as if nothing had happened. It wasn't as if we'd seen him every day, even when he was young, running about and coming in from some lark, muddy and looking for a bite to eat. I used to save a little treat for him, setting it aside, before he was found to be different. After that he never came down to the kitchen, and his tutor told us that he must be quiet, or it would damage his brain."

"Damage—" Medically, unless he was subject to seizures, that didn't make much sense. But of course the tutor was not trained to deal with such a child, and he probably meant well.

"I never liked that tutor," Susan's mother was saying. "Sly, he was, and not much one for conversation in the servants' hall. He took his meals separately, a step above the rest of us. But he would come down sometimes and speak to one of us about Mr. Peregrine's needs. As if the Prince of Wales was wanting something, mind you, and the tutor was the Lord Chamberlain. I never resented it, knowing what the poor boy must be suffering. His brothers running and shouting about the house, or in the back garden, while he must sit by his window and watch. There was talk that little Prince John had such seizures and was sent away. I remember that. And I thought, Poor Mr. Peregrine, and wondered if he was to die young too."

She seemed to tire, her face drooping a little. "I should never have told you such things. You won't let on to Susan, or to Mrs. Graham, will you?"

"No, I wouldn't dream of speaking of it—truly. I wouldn't wish to remind any of them—"

"You're kind, Miss. It's been bottled up in me all these years, and I thought I'd carry it to my grave, but I've been that upset over Mr. Ted."

"Will you be all right, if I leave you?"

"Yes, go, if you don't mind. I need to rest. Thank you for coming, Miss."

I made my farewells and slipped out. The cat jumped into her lap as I latched the door, and she bent her head, as if nodding.

I walked back to the house and went up to my room without meeting anyone. I was grateful for the respite.

Small wonder no one in the family wanted to see or speak to Peregrine Graham while he was there, ill. Even after all these years, the memory of what he'd done must still be raw.

It explained too why there were constables on watch. And why at the first sign of recovery, Peregrine had been sent directly back to the asylum. While he was still too weak to do anything frightful again.

Chapter Nine

The magistrate, the aging relict of the man who had held that position before her, was nearing seventy, hunched and sharp-tongued. Dr. Philips pointed her out seated nearest the roaring fire, one of her grandsons beside her.

She had commanded that we hold the inquest at once, so that she could visit her granddaughter in Canterbury in time for the birth of her first great-grandchild. And everyone, from the Grahams to the police, agreed without argument.

It was the day after poor Ted Booker had been buried. *Indecent haste,* I thought, but perhaps no more than a duty to Lady Parsons.

I didn't know the Coroner, a dour man of fifty, who, according to Dr. Philips, had come down from Tonbridge to conduct the proceedings.

I listened to the evidence given about Theodore Russell Booker's state of mind, as if he were a stranger the witnesses barely knew. An embarrassment, something to put behind us quickly, so that we get on with living.

Dr. Philips gave a very clinical report on his mental state, and then added, "I think perhaps we haven't considered the whole man. He and his brother were close, and Harold's death must have been appalling. Theodore Booker was not in another part of the Front, word coming secondhand, he was there, a witness, he held

141

his brother in his arms as Harold died. We must accept as well our failure as a member of the medical profession to find a cure for horror and heartbreak. If Theodore Booker took his own life while in the grip of such painful memories, it was not his fault. It was the fault of war and of our inability to understand how to save him."

There was silence as he stepped down and walked to his place next to me. We were in The Bells, in a parlor that was more often the scene of parties and filled with laughter, not talk of death. The dark beams over our heads and the dark paneling of the walls, added to a dreary day with rain coming down in sheets, fit our somber mood.

I reached out to touch the doctor's arm as he sat down, then heard my own name called to give evidence.

I did so, to the best of my ability, remembering that I was under oath. But I also told the truth as I'd observed it: on the night of his death, I had felt so strongly that Lieutenant Booker had turned a corner. Then, like Dr. Philips, I added more than I was required to tell. "He loved his wife very much. He told me that. He tried to heal for her sake. I felt a great pity for him, because he wanted to be a good husband."

There were two questions for me—one to do with my training and whether or not I knew enough about such cases to judge the circumstances surrounding Ted's death, and the other to do with whether or not Theodore Booker was, in my view, of sound mind.

I answered, "Grief is difficult to bear at the best of times. Ted Booker was perfectly sane but so overwhelmed by what he saw as his responsibility for his brother's death that he couldn't find his way back to the man he was." I wanted to add that a little more understanding from his mother-in-law might have gone far in saving him. But I held my tongue.

She was seated in the front row with her daughter, her face smug with satisfaction that the troublesome man was dead. Sally was so shrouded in widow's weeds that her feelings were hard to read. There was no way of knowing whether she felt relief or despair.

Indeed, most of the people attending the hearing seemed to be unsympathetic to the dead man. I had a fleeting thought that the poor man was well out of it. These were neighbors and friends, they had known him since he was a boy, and yet they had turned away from him when he most needed them.

Was that what had happened to Peregrine Graham in his own hour of need?

In the end, the finding was that Theodore Booker, while not in his right mind due to grief over his brother's death, had taken his own life. The stigma of suicide had been lifted from the survivors. That was all Mrs. Denton had wished for.

No mention was made of Dr. Philips or his skill as a physician. I hoped that my conversation with Inspector Howard had well and truly spiked those guns.

As I was walking out of The Bells, glad to be away from the crowded room inside, I looked out at the rain and thought about going back to the Graham house, then decided to sit in the church for a few minutes until I felt a little more tolerant. Jonathan Graham had said nothing about going to see Ted Booker, and the Coroner hadn't called on him to give evidence. I had seen Mr. Montgomery look at him several times, as if expecting him to add what he knew, but he didn't speak up. And neither did the rector.

I had closed the churchyard gate behind me and was walking toward the stained-glass windows of saints, when I heard someone shouting. I turned to see who it was.

It was a rider, coming fast, and calling to Jonathan Graham as he was escorting his mother home. They had reached the large trees that overhung the churchyard wall—not twenty yards from where Ted had been buried—when they heard the shout.

They turned as one, and the rider came up to them, reaching down to hand them a letter. As Jonathan opened the envelope, his mother was questioning the man on horseback. I realized then that it was Robert Douglas, holding the horse steady as he answered.

Jonathan's face was flushed with something very like fury, but he nodded curtly, passed the letter to his mother, and she bent over it, trying to see it in the shadows cast by the bare limbs and her black umbrella. I thought for an instant she was going to faint, but she steadied herself, said something more to Robert, who wheeled his horse and went back toward the stragglers just coming out of The Bells. I realized that he was looking for Timothy, who was speaking to Mrs. Denton while Sally was being handed into a carriage by the young man I'd seen with Lady Parsons during the proceedings.

Timothy broke off, excused himself, and spoke sharply to Robert, who answered and pointed. Timothy Graham turned toward where his brother and his mother were standing and without a word of farewell to Mrs. Denton, strode away to join them, rigid with emotion.

Robert lifted his hat to Mrs. Denton, with a brief word, then put his horse to a trot to follow Timothy.

No one had seen me there by the church nave. And I stood watching the little scene play itself out as Timothy also read the letter and then passed it back to his mother. The Grahams walked briskly toward home, Robert riding ahead to stable his horse.

From their posture, heads together, backs rigid, I knew that the news was bad.

All I could think of was that the journey back to the asylum had been too much for Peregrine Graham, and that he had got his wish—he'd succumbed to his pneumonia after all.

CHAPTER TEN

I HURRIED INTO the church and sat down in a corner near the pulpit, where no one could see me, huddled into my cloak for warmth and comfort.

This wasn't the right moment to go to the house. Let them have their time to grieve. But it was cold in the church, as cold as the tomb, I couldn't stop myself from thinking, and so after a time, though the rain was coming down hard, I left the church and crossed to the rectory, my shoes wet to my ankles, and the hem of my skirt dragging.

A middle-aged woman opened the door when I knocked and ushered me into the hall, clucking over how wet I was.

The rector wasn't to home, she informed me. He'd gone to speak with the widow, to offer what comfort he could after the inquest.

At first I thought she meant Mrs. Graham, and then I realized she was speaking of Sally Booker. I turned away, wondering where I could go now, and she said, "No, you mustn't leave here so wet as you are, Miss! The kitchen is warm, I'll dry your shoes and your cloak while you have a bite of something. I've a nice bit of soup that's just the right thing on such a day. Rector wouldn't like me to send you away just because he's not to home." She glanced at the sky. "I don't think this will last for more than a quarter of an hour. See, it's brighter to the west."

I smiled, trying to hold back tears of gratitude. "Thank you—"

"There's nothing to thank me for. It's Rector says turn away no one in need."

Was I in need? Yes, in a way. I wanted to go home, to see Colonel Sahib, to listen to my mother being sensible and comforting at the same time. Right now, being tucked into bed with a glass of warm milk would have been the epitome of happiness. Ted Booker was dead, there was nothing I could do to change that, and now Peregrine Graham had died, because he had been sent back to the asylum over my objections. Coming to Kent had been a bad decision—I was sure no one would carry out Arthur's last wishes. Nothing would be done about whatever it was he wanted set right.

I tried to come to grips with my despondent mood, and couldn't.

The housekeeper took me down the passage to the kitchen, and as I glanced over my shoulder, I could see the two china dogs in the parlor window, staring back at me. I'd glimpsed them on my first night in Owlhurst, and this was most likely my last night.

She introduced herself as Mrs. Oldsey, housekeeper here for many years, because the last two rectors hadn't been married. "Not that I've lost hope for Rector," she added as she helped me out of my heavy wet cloak and draped it in front of the kitchen fire. "He's young yet. We've six bedchambers in this house, did you know that? And only one of them being used. I long to see children about the house. I wasn't blessed with any myself, but I sincerely do love the little ones."

She bustled about, setting the kettle on to boil as I removed my wet shoes and looked around.

It was an old-fashioned kitchen, with no wife to complain and have it redone. But Mrs. Oldsey seemed not to mind.

"What brought you out on such a morning as this?" she asked as she set down cups and saucers from the cupboard.

"I was at the inquest—"

"Yes, the poor Booker lad. Sad. I didn't have the heart to go. I remember him and his brother. Imps, they were, but good-hearted. What was the verdict brought in?"

"Death by his own hand in the throes of grief for his brother."

"Ah, well, best that way. He can be buried in holy ground, and his widow doesn't have his memory hanging about her neck like something to ward off the plague."

Amused by her way of seeing life, I said, "That's what her mother hopes as well."

"Mrs. Denton? A piece of work, that one, though it isn't Christian of me to say so. But a spade's a spade, for all that."

I kept my opinion to myself, but the twinkle in Mrs. Oldsey's eyes told me she suspected I shared her views.

She fed me tea and toast and a cup of soup warmed up from the night before. I ate because I was hungry, and because I dreaded going back out in the rain to the Graham house.

Mrs. Oldsey rambled on, sitting across from me as if we were old friends having a gossip.

I found the courage to ask her about Peregrine.

She frowned. "That was another tragedy. He used to come to services with his father. A handsome child with good manners. And then he stopped coming, and later the whispers began that he wasn't quite right in the head. I thought, often enough, that Mrs. Graham was ashamed of him. Else she'd have seen to it that he lived as normal a life as possible, gossip or no gossip. But she didn't, and as I never set eyes on him again until he was almost fourteen, who's to say what was right and what was wrong?"

"You saw him when he returned from London?"

"Oh, yes, they brought him here. He was in such a state of shock—white as his shirt, shaking with fright, and unable to utter a word—that I thought he ought to be in his own home and his own bed. But Mrs. Graham wouldn't hear of it. 'I've three boys to think of,' she told me, 'and I can't go to them until I've settled Peregrine.

147

I've sent Robert for Inspector Gadd, and Dr. Hadley. Can you find the rector for me, please?' And she asked me to send for Lady Parsons, Sir Frederick's widow. I kept the boy down here in the kitchen, trying to warm him up a little, and wash his hands, but he wouldn't let me touch him, whatever I said. Then they insisted on locking him in one of the bedchambers, without so much as a word of comfort to him. After a bit, they went up for him and took him away, him still all bloody and without a coat, and Rector told me later he was in the asylum. I wouldn't wish my worst enemy in a place like that, not to speak of my own child. I didn't learn until later that he'd killed someone. I thought somehow he'd done himself an injury, all that blood. They never said who he'd killed, and when I asked Rector, he told me it was best I didn't know. That it was horrible beyond human imagination. I never forgot that. Horrible beyond human imagination."

She repeated it, as if the words had been imprinted in her memory.

"Most folks have forgotten Mr. Peregrine, you know. Perhaps that's for the best."

But they'd remember all the whispers soon enough, when he was brought back to Owlhurst to lie next to his father. I had a feeling it would be a brief graveside service, with few mourners, though the curious would be there to gawk.

She went on with other stories about her years as housekeeper, and after a while, since the rector hadn't returned, I put on my still-damp shoes and my cloak and set out for the Graham house. The rain had let up, just as Mrs. Oldsey had prophesized, and I was grateful.

I let myself in the front door. There were no sounds to greet me—no conversation somewhere in the downstairs rooms, and no voices on the first floor as I quietly went up the staircase. I wanted to find Susan and ask her what was happening. But she too seemed to have vanished. I expect she had gone to visit her mother and give her the outcome of the inquest. She had one afternoon off a week.

I sat by the fire in my room and waited. There was nothing else I could do.

But it wasn't Mrs. Graham who came to speak to me—it was Robert. He knocked at my door, and when I opened it, he said gruffly, "Mrs. Graham's apologies, Miss Crawford, but there's been terrible news. Mrs. Graham would take it as a favor if you could be in Tonbridge in time for the six o'clock train tonight. I'll be taking you myself, as soon as you're ready."

I had expected this—and I hadn't.

All I could manage to say was, "I can be ready in an hour. I'd like to say my farewells—"

"Mrs. Graham begs you to forgive her if she isn't able to wish you a safe journey. I'll ask Susan to pack a box of sandwiches for you, and a Thermos of tea, to see you as far as London. I'm to send a telegram to your father to meet you there."

I could hardly tell him that I would rather leave in the morning than arrive in London so late. Instead I thanked him and added, "I'll write Mrs. Graham as soon as I reach Somerset. Please tell her she's been more than kind."

I didn't know what else to add.

He nodded, and was gone.

I packed my belongings for a second time, and looked around for Elayne's letter to me, to read again on the train. I'd forgot the name of the man she was so sure she'd marry. But it wasn't in my case, and it wasn't in the little desk between the windows. I'd last seen it in the sickroom, and I went there to find it. It wasn't on the table by the bed nor on the mantelpiece, and I knew that if Susan had found it, she'd have brought it to me. As a last resort, I got down on my knees and lifted the coverlet to look under the bed. And there it was, the three pages scattered there. I chuckled. Susan hadn't used the carpet sweeper—my fingers came up with dust clinging to them. I looked again for the envelope, but it wasn't with the pages. That she might well have found, without the enclosed letter, and tossed it in the grate. I took the letter back to my room, and after closing my case, I left it outside my door with my valise for Robert to take down.

I was ready when he came for me, and in the dogcart I saw the box with my sandwiches. He handed me warmed rugs as I stepped into the cart, and I settled myself as comfortably as I could. He draped a length of canvas over my baggage and my lap, handed me a large black umbrella, and then mounted the box. No one had come to see me off.

I watched the house disappear and then the church dwindle to a distant smudge as we turned away, and The Bells with it. And then Owlhurst was gone. I felt like crying. Nothing had happened the way I'd hoped or even expected. And somehow I'd lost Arthur as well. I had liked Dr. Philips and the rector and was sorry not to say farewell to them, but surely they would understand.

Soon the asylum loomed ahead, in daylight a grim place with no redeeming softness—*as grim,* I thought, *as a prison.* At least Peregrine was free of it, and his suffering over.

Like Ted Booker, he would be buried in a wintry churchyard and forgotten before the spring.

I was thoroughly miserable when we finally reached the station in Tonbridge, and the train was already there, white plumes of smoke curling about the booking office roof as the engine worked up a head of steam. Robert left me in the cart while he went quickly inside, speaking to the stationmaster. I could see them through the grimy, lamp-lit window. The winter darkness had come down, and it fit my own dark mood.

And then Robert was back again, my tickets in his hand, hurrying me toward the train. I had forgotten my sandwiches, and with a muttered word, he went back for them, then caught me up. All the while, the stationmaster was fingering his watch, impatience in every line as he stood by my compartment.

I expected Robert to leave me then, but he helped me up into the train, settled me by the window, then stowed my case and valise where I could reach them if I needed them. That done, he stood for a moment, looking down at me, as if he didn't know what to say. Finally he took my hand and held it for a moment, like a gentleman telling a lady good-bye. Without a word, he touched the brim of his hat and was gone, and the train started with a lurch almost before his boots had touched the platform again.

I sat back in my seat and prepared myself for the long journey ahead.

We were just coming into Sevenoaks when a thought brought me out of my drowsiness.

I remembered Timothy and Jonathan arguing in their mother's presence about who should inherit when Peregrine was dead.

Well, they would soon know.

I found that I didn't care.

In Sevenoaks, I got off the train to send a telegram to my father, telling him I would like to stay in London a few days with Elayne. He had no way of knowing she was in France, and I needed a respite before I faced his sharp eyes or my mother's intuition. So much for longing for their comfort. That had been a moment of weakness, and I was rather ashamed of it now that I'd put some distance between myself and Owlhurst.

The train was slow, a troop train taking precedence up the line, and I listened to two elderly women comparing notes on the funeral they'd attended in Tunbridge Wells. I knew Tunbridge—it had once been a garrison town, and I'd visited friends of my parents there on one of my father's leaves. But dissecting a funeral was not a comfortable subject for me, and I tried to shut out their voices with a book I borrowed from the gentleman across from me. He had just finished it and was stuffing it back in his case when I asked to see it.

It was a treatise on the history of the Turkish Empire, and I found it quite absorbing. Our P&O boat had stopped in Istanbul on our return from India, and I had spent an afternoon in a carriage, touring the city.

I fell asleep all the same.

And then we were pulling into London, the outskirts a series of back gardens and small industries, depressing in winter garb. But mostly I could see only my own reflection in the glass as I looked out from our brightly lit carriage, and there were circles under my eyes nearly as dark as those I saw in the glass on my way home from Greece in November.

The two ladies were met by a young man with one arm, his sleeve pinned to his coat. Without a word, the man from whom I'd borrowed the book helped bring down our bags, and then a porter was there to pile them on his cart.

"There's no one to meet you?" the book lender asked as I gave in my ticket and stood there, wondering how I was to arrange to have my heavier valise delivered.

"I daresay they're late," I answered, smiling, not wanting a portly knight in shining armor to see me home. The relief at not finding my father on the platform made me feel giddy.

"Then let me summon a cab and see you into it."

I thanked him, and in ten minutes I was in the cab and on my way to the flat. I was tired despite my brief nap, it was late, and I would be glad for a night's sleep.

Mrs. Hennessey wasn't there, and I asked the cabbie to leave my luggage outside her door. She'd see that it was taken upstairs. The dustman always stopped for an early cup of tea, and the promise of a slice of cake or tart would be enough to send him up with it.

I went up the steps, feeling each one, thinking that all I required would be a warming cup of tea, and then my bed. That is, if Elayne had thought to replenish our dwindling supply of tea. After all, it was her turn. I'd learned long since to do without milk, but we kept a tin of sugar.

I took my hat off as I passed the landing and had it in my hand as I reached into my pocket for the key. It slid into the lock, the door opened, and I stepped into the silent flat with a sigh of relief. I was home.

I set my hat on the table near the door, and felt for the light switch.

It didn't turn on, which meant that Elayne hadn't replaced the bulb when it burned out. I fumbled for the candle and matches we kept on a shelf. As it spurted into gold and blue flame, and the candlewick flared and then steadied, I began to remove my coat.

The flat was chilly, as it always was at night, and for an instant I regretted not going home to fires on the hearth. But never mind. I made myself a cup of tea, drank it to warm me, and then went down the passage to the room at the back that was mine.

The quiet was comforting, and the sense of being in familiar surroundings was what I needed.

There was a small package on my pillow—Elayne's gift.

I opened it, feeling a surge of happiness. One never knew what Elayne might consider a gift.

This time it was a pair of black French gloves—heaven only knew where she'd found them—with tiny pearl buttons at the wrist and leather soft as silk. And they actually fit. I smiled. Elayne had borrowed my opera-length gloves often enough to know my size perfectly. I'd have to return the favor next time I saw something that suited her as well as these suited me.

Feeling more cheerful, I bathed my face and hands, undressed, crawled between damp sheets, and huddled under the layers of comforters until I had warmed a space for myself.

My last thought as I drifted into sleep was, *We must find ourselves a cat—my feet are cold.* I didn't have the energy to heat water for the bottle I kept in the little table by my bed.

It was close on to three o'clock when I came awake with a shock, hearing something in the front of the flat.

Elayne. Or one of the others. They'd seen my things downstairs and were trying not to wake me. Which of course is noisier than going about their business quietly.

I threw on my dressing gown and cringed as I put my warm feet into cold slippers. Opening my door, I walked down the passage.

A candle burst into life just as I reached the end of the passage, and I caught my breath in alarm.

There was a man standing in what we euphemistically called the kitchen, his back to me. He was rummaging through the box of sandwiches I'd brought with me. I'd eaten only about half of them on the train. My other luggage was at his feet.

"Anthony?" I asked, thinking this must surely be Elayne's staff officer. How had he slipped past Mrs. Hennessey? He turned sharply. "Thank you for—"

I broke off, knowing in that instant that my heart would surely stop.

The single candle illuminated his face now, and I couldn't believe—I was dreaming, there wasn't—it couldn't be—

Feeling faint for the first time in my life, I put out a hand to touch the passage wall beside me.

"You're dead," I whispered finally.

"I nearly am," he said, holding one of the sandwiches in his hand. "I haven't eaten for three days. Do you mind?" He sat down suddenly in the nearest chair. "I've lived on tea and that small box of biscuits I found in your cupboard."

It was Peregrine, looking as pale as his own ghost, the hand holding the sandwich shaking as if with a palsy.

He was wearing an ill-fitting suit of clothes, his hair tousled from sleep, and his face drained of all feeling as he watched my changing expressions. The heavy shadow of his beard gave him a sinister cast.

As my brain began to work again, I could feel a ripple of fear run up my spine.

"What are you—how did you know—*Mrs. Hennessey!*" She hadn't been there when I came in earlier. And this man was a murderer.

"Is that who she is? I saw her stepping out the door, and waited until she was down the street. I've heard her since, coming and going."

"She owns this house. She's my—" I paused, not wanting to tell him too much.

He was frowning. "Why did you say just now that I was dead?"

"I saw Robert—it was just after the inquest for Ted Booker—Robert came to find Mrs. Graham and Jonathan. I could tell he brought bad news—Mrs. Graham and Jonathan were very upset, as was Timothy. I saw them from the church as they were walking home—"

"Ted Booker is dead?"

"Yes. I thought—they were so upset—"

"I expect they'd learned I'd escaped from the asylum," he told me grimly.

"Did you—you're wearing someone else's clothing—what happened to the man they belong to?"

"I didn't kill him, if that's what you're thinking. I gave him a handful of the powders I took at night. They must have been sedatives—he probably slept the night through in my bed."

"Who was he?"

"One of the doctors—look, do you mind if I eat this? If not, I'll pass out at your feet."

I nodded, and he bit hungrily into the sandwich. I waited, and as he swallowed the first mouthful, he said, "I told them I thought my fever was back. I'd rubbed my face until it felt warm, flushed. The staff doctor was just leaving, and he came to my room to see what the matter was. I'd been given my powders, or so he thought, and I was hardly likely to attack him. He asked me to open my mouth, and as he bent forward to see my throat, I had him in a headlock. No one heard him cry out—there's too much of that at night, anyway. I knocked him down, turned off the light so that my room was dark, and forced him to eat the powders. Then I changed my clothes for his, and left. That's the only time the main doors aren't watched—after everyone has been locked in. The staff can come and go without disturbing the house. I walked through the fields until it was safe enough to return to the road. About three miles on, a farm cart offered me a lift to Cranbrook."

He went on eating, his hands hardly able to bring the sandwich to his mouth. I stood there, not knowing what to do—whether he would kill me or let me live. Whether I should find a weapon and try to overpower him while he was still light-headed from hunger or try to talk him into going back to Owlhurst.

Picking up the Thermos, he could hear tea sloshing about inside, and he drank nearly half a cup in one gulp. It must have been lukewarm, but he didn't seem to care. "God, I don't know what I'd have done if you hadn't brought food with you," he said. "What did my relatives do, send you packing?"

"They told me they'd had distressing news. I thought—from their faces, I thought they'd been informed of your death. And so I left, to be out of the way. Robert Douglas took me to Tonbridge."

"There was money in the doctor's pocket. I used it for the train, and I walked here from the station." He gave me a twisted smile. "I'd tied a bandage around my head, so that people would help me. I didn't remember how to take a train, much less how to reach London. But there wasn't enough money for food."

"They'll trace you to the train. It won't be long before they come looking for you."

"Not in this direction. I bought a ticket to Dover when I reached Rochester. Then I asked a woman if she would purchase my ticket to London for me. I told her I couldn't see well enough to know if I was being charged the correct amount. She took pity on me and told me her brother was in France."

He could pass for a wounded soldier—he hadn't fully recovered from the pneumonia, his eyes sunken, his face pale from long years in the asylum.

"They'll be looking for a man with a head wound."

"Not at first. I expect you're wondering what to do with me."

"You can't stay here—others live here. They'll be back soon."

"Yes. Elayne. It was her bed I slept in. She's still in France, I expect."

The letter.

"Still, Mrs. Hennessey is prying. She's never allowed men up here. She'll hear you, and report to my father that there's a man in my flat. He won't like it."

"I don't intend for Mrs. Hennessey to hear me. And I've no more money, I have nowhere else to go."

"But what brought you here? To London, I mean? You could have disappeared in Canterbury or Dover just as easily."

"I came to London to relive what happened to me." The timbre of his voice had changed. There was a harshness now that worried me.

I couldn't stop an indrawn breath.

He laughed bitterly. "Not in that way. I was fourteen, frightened out of my wits. I saw things that I can't remember except in my dreams."

To distract him, I asked, "How did you unlock the flat door?"

"Your friend Elayne hadn't locked it in her haste to leave. If I'd had to, I'd have found a way to persuade the dragon at the gate to let me in. I could hardly sleep on the landing."

"You must go. I've done you no harm, I did my best to save your life. You have no reason to hurt me."

"I've told you. I'm here for reasons of my own. Look, lying there in a bed I haven't slept in for nearly ten years, my mind was playing tricks on me. I expect it was the fever, but that doesn't matter. I need to know—certain things. I'll spare you the details. They aren't pretty. Help me, and I'll either go back to the asylum or put an end to an already wretched life. Your only fault was in nursing me too well. For that sin, you must put up with me for a day or so longer."

"You can't stay here! My father—"

He had started the second sandwich, and I could see he was stronger—I'd missed my chance.

He said, his gaze holding mine, "I have a pistol with me. Jonathan's war souvenir. It only has four bullets in the clip, but I'll use them if I'm forced to."

My shock must have shown in my face. "You can't have—you were barely able to stand, much less rove through the house looking for a weapon—and Jonathan will know it's missing. You'll be considered armed, mentally unstable, and you'll be shot on sight!"

"That's my worry, not yours. Go back to bed. Lock your door if you wish, but I won't do you any harm." He laughed, a grim laugh that frightened me. "I couldn't lift a finger if I had to. Still, I'm going to bring bedding out here. You can't leave without stepping on me. Remember the pistol, and don't try."

The door of my room didn't lock. I'd never given that a thought until now. Colder than the cold of the flat, I turned and went back to my bed, shoving a chair under the knob of the door. I huddled in the bedclothes, listening for snoring that would tell me he was asleep.

Chapter Eleven

The next thing I knew, a watery sunlight shone through the curtains and splashed across my bed.

I sat up with a start, dressed hastily, and removed the chair from my door.

Peregrine Graham was asleep across the threshold of the outer door, and the instant he heard me, he opened his eyes and stared at me as if he hardly knew me.

"I'm awake."

"I'm cold. I want my tea. Will you let me prepare it?"

"Go ahead."

I busied myself with the tea things, then said, "You've got yourself a small problem. There's no food in the flat. We'll both starve."

"I've considered that. You'll go and buy what we need. If you call the police or in any way betray my whereabouts, I'll kill Mrs. Hennessey. If she's out, I'll shoot the first three people I see on the street, and then myself. I'm a murderer. What can they do to me? A man can only hang once."

I couldn't tell whether he was mocking me or not.

"Your family will be hurt—it will bring up all the old gossip and make their lives a misery."

"Except for Arthur, who is dead and beyond hurting, I don't really care."

"That's a vicious thing to say—"

He rose from his bedding, then faced me, taller, malevolent. "My stepmother treated me worse than an animal. She slept with her cousin before and after my father's death. I don't know if any of my half brothers are related to me. What do I owe any of them?"

"Her cousin—"

"Robert Douglas. He was always decent to me, I give him that— but he did nothing to protect me."

Well, I thought, *that certainly explains a good deal . . . if it's true.*

He saw the surprise in my face, and added, "I should have thought you'd guessed. You must have seen them together. You must have seen the resemblance between Timothy and Robert, if not Jonathan."

But I'd thought they favored their mother . . . I said as much.

"Yes, yes, I know," he responded impatiently. "But you haven't lived with them and watched as I did when we were young. Look at their hands, they're his, and the way their hair grows. The way their upper lips curl when they say words like *church* or *children*."

It sounded more like obsession than observation, and he must have sensed my disbelief, because he went on earnestly, persuasively.

"I had no idea until one day I caught them in bed together. I was a child, I didn't know what that meant. But that evening I was locked in my room and seldom allowed to join the family again until we were taken to London."

I didn't know whether to believe him or not. The only confirmation I had was the ease with which Robert came and went in that house, and his familiar attitude toward Mrs. Graham. But of course they *were* cousins—

"You have a devious mind for someone the world claims is half-witted."

"I was told often enough that I was slow, stupid. I had trouble concentrating, and Jonathan took pleasure in taunting me about it. Mr. Appleby—our tutor—did nothing to stop him. I'd be tongue-tied with anger, and I must have seemed dull and belligerent and unable to learn. But in the asylum, I saw how half-witted children behaved, and I knew I wasn't like them. Still, I'd been told the alternative was hanging, and I stayed in that God-bereft place and held my tongue. Literally. They thought after a time that I was mute, that it was the shock of what I'd done, or where I was. They got used to not hearing my voice from one month to the next."

I hadn't heard him speak when he arrived or as he left my care. Only in the privacy of the sickroom had he talked to me. And then not in the beginning.

The teakettle began singing merrily, jolting both of us. I made the tea, and while it steeped, I said, "Surely you remember what you did that sent you to the asylum."

"My memory isn't clear. Some of it was shock. Some of it was the nightmare of being taken from London directly to the asylum and never going home again. I was kept at the rectory until arrangements were made. I was dazed, confused, frightened out of my wits. I do remember being led away from something too ghastly to look at anymore. I could smell the blood on my hands and feel the stiffness of it on my shirt. And I remember vomiting on the stairs as we started down them. Robert took me away and tried to clean my face and hands, then shut me up somewhere. They were amazed to find me asleep on the floor when they came back for me. I remember they were shocked that I could sleep after what I'd done. I remember all that, but not what happened in that room—only in my dreams does it come back again, and for years I'd wake up screaming. I also remember standing in the drawing room of the London house, and my stepmother was telling someone—a policeman, I think—that she blamed herself for allowing me to accompany the family to London. She said that shutting me away in my room had made me resentful and angry, and twisted something in me, but she had thought London might be good for me. She'd wanted me to see a doctor there. It was the first I'd heard of it. She said—I can hear her voice now—that I'd killed the woman the way I'd have liked to kill her. That she'd found the pocketknife that my father had left me buried deep in her pillow one night, and never spoken of it."

I felt cold, despite the tea. Peregrine *was* mad . . . however lucid he might seem at times.

But what was the difference between this man and Ted Booker? My conscience wanted to know. *You were sympathetic enough to the soldier. . . .*

I tried to think of something else to talk about, something to take his mind off killing.

"Did you know where you were in London? Did you know the house where all this happened?" I was sure he couldn't tell me.

"We were to spend the autumn in London. A month. My stepmother had friends there, relatives. We went up by train, and I was allowed to look out the window as long as I didn't speak to anyone. The house in London seemed small after Owlhurst. But Timothy and Jonathan shared a room, and Arthur and I were put together. Robert took them to the zoo, but I stayed behind because I might make a scene. I was never allowed to see people, and my tutor told me that I was different and mustn't make a fuss when I was told to stay in my room. He said people would stare at me and be unkind. I didn't want to be stared at. And so they went to the Tower, and Arthur told me afterward about the cannon and the ravens. Everything was the same, I'd come to London but I might as well have stayed at home. There was an upstairs maid. She was pert, teasing, when no one else was about. I didn't like her and told her so to her face. My stepmother put me in a room by myself, as punishment. One night there was a dinner party, and my stepmother went, taking Robert with her. I wasn't well, I hadn't been since I was put in the room alone. My head swam, and my stomach was queer. I remember lying on the floor, because it was cold, and it felt good. The rest is hazy, a botched jumble of images."

He rubbed his face with his hands, scrubbing at it. I could hear several days' growth of beard rasping against his palms, and his voice came through his fingers in an odd sort of echo that made it sound like someone else's.

"That's why it haunts me. I can't make sense of things. What happened when, and who was there."

"Are you trying to tell me you didn't kill that young woman?" I thought he was hoping to win me over with a lie.

"I killed her. Of course I did. When the police showed me my knife, I told them the truth. Do you think I'd have lived nearly fourteen years in that godforsaken asylum if I wasn't sure what I'd done?"

The admission was shocking.

"But you just said—you haven't come to London to remember, you already have—" If I hadn't been afraid before, I was now.

"You aren't listening. I want to remember why I wanted to kill her. Why I picked up that knife, and when. And how it felt to do what I did that night. I've shut it out, it's all missing, and when I was so ill, when I thought I was dying, I realized that I had to know. I had to put it all together and look at it in the light."

His eyes were intense, and I wondered if I would live through his nightmare. Or since he knew what murder felt like, whether he would be eager to experience it again. I'd read somewhere that when men kill, as in wars, they lose a little of their humanity each time until it becomes easier, less awful, and they accept killing in a way that civilized people can't tolerate. Whether it was true or not, I didn't know. But in front of me was a man who had killed not in war but on a quiet London street, without provocation or, as far as I could see, a drop of repentance.

Peregrine Graham must be as dangerous as his family claimed— it would behoove me to be very careful, or I could trigger his anger and suffer the consequences.

A part of my mind said, *They should have hanged him when they had the chance. . . .*

I asked, clearing away the tea things in an effort to keep my hands from shaking, "Peregrine. What good will it do to remember? What will you have gained, bringing it all back again?"

"I can heal."

It was such an unexpected answer that I stared at him.

"You don't know what it's like to look in the mirror every time you shave and see a normal face when you know that beneath the flesh and bone there's a monster inside. I told myself there in the bed in Owlhurst that if God forced me to live, I'd find a way to force myself to face myself."

I caught my breath. It was all so logical. And so macabre I didn't know how to respond.

He smiled crookedly. "This is a poor recompense for saving my life. But then I didn't want it to be saved." He reached into his pocket and pulled out the crumpled envelope from Elayne's letter. "You gave me the means. Unwittingly."

I wanted nothing more than to turn back the clock, arrive on my doorstep and find the flat empty—or filled with my friends and their friends, all of them real, all of them normal.

I was allowed to go and do the marketing, a little later in the morning. I was reminded that Mrs. Hennessey would suffer if I talked to anyone, or sent a telegram to Kent. She was there at her door when I came back, smiling at me, asking how my arm was faring, and if I'd come to London to take up my next posting.

I answered her questions, smiling as if nothing had happened to change my world or hers. I told her that I'd been in Kent and had returned to London to spend a little time with friends, that I had missed them, shut away in Somerset.

She nodded and told me that I had only to ask, and she would bring me anything I needed.

I thanked her and went on up the stairs, feeling Peregrine in the darkness at the top, watching and listening. He had the door open for me, and then shut it behind me. "That was well done."

Ten minutes later, he was asking me how to go about finding a particular house in London.

"You don't remember where you were staying?" I asked, surprised.

"You don't understand. I was never told these things. I was taken to the train, I was taken to the house, and I never left it until we returned to Kent. I can only tell you what I saw from my window—a fenced square with trees, a walk, several benches, and a gate on four sides. The house across from ours was a pale cream, with six chimneys, a false balcony on the upper floors—no more than an ornate iron railing in front of the windows—and a black door with a brass knocker and short iron railings up the two steps to the door."

"There are any number of houses in London that match that description."

I debated how far I should go in helping him, whether dragging my heels would wear him down or if helping him would buy some protection in the end.

"Then we'll walk the streets until we find the right one."

"You aren't in any condition to walk the streets. This is winter, and London is damp, cold. You could find yourself ill again. Pneumonia can come back."

"It behooves you to help me. The sooner the better."

I made up my mind. "I'll take you to a place I know that fits your description. It may be the wrong place. But it's somewhere to start."

"Fair enough."

I had bought a razor for him while I was out, and he used it, ridding himself of the dark beard and, with it, some of the sinister expression that I hadn't seen while nursing him. I'd kept him reasonably well shaven then because of the need to wash his face after his fearsome coughing fits.

We left the flat together. I expected—dreaded—Mrs. Hennessey popping out her door and asking who my young man was.

An escaped murderer, Mrs. Hennessey. My father will be horrified.

But she didn't come out her door, and then we were in the street.

London in winter *is* cold. The damp from the Thames pervades the city, and the wind seems to sweep down the long streets without hindrance, as if blowing across Arctic ice floes. A bitter and penetrating cold, the sort that makes life miserable for those who live here.

We found a cab in the next street, and I gave the driver the only address I could think of, the one that Mrs. Clayton had mentioned in her enthusiastic account of nearly visiting London. But would Peregrine know it now? Would he recognize the square or the houses?

We said very little to each other—from the time we left my flat, our conversation had been limited to necessities. I could feel his presence beside me, determined, and surely dangerous if crossed.

We got down by Carroll Square. In the center of it, the garden was winter bleak, trees that blossomed in spring showing bare branches to the steel gray sky, and the earth of flower beds looking like the burrows of fat, invisible animals. I began to walk along the street, looking up at the houses as we passed.

I could see Number 17 now, across from the southern gate into the square. It was a handsome house, white with black shutters, and there were two small evergreens in pots on either side of the black door. I looked across to the other side of the square. Number 17 was almost a mirror image of the house directly opposite, across the garden. In place of the ornamental pots, there were decorative mock wrought-iron balconies at the first-floor windows and railings at the shallow steps to the door.

I didn't draw attention to either house but watched Peregrine as he gazed from one to the next. Let any flicker of memory be his and not a reflection of my knowledge. But I thought perhaps this was where the murder had occurred, and wondered what might be stirring in Peregrine's mind.

Peregrine looked about him with a frown on his face. "The trees in the square are different—"

"It was probably early autumn, when the trees were in leaf."

"Yes. Of course."

There was no one about at the moment, and we had the street to ourselves.

We strolled around the square as he sought to find something familiar.

"I don't think this is the right place," he murmured to himself. And then as we went around for a second time, he said, "I should be in an upstairs bedroom looking out. At this level, nothing is the same. . . ."

"I don't think we would be welcomed—"

"No."

We had come back to Number 17. Peregrine stopped to gaze up at the chimney pots of the house across the square.

A constable strolled into Carroll Square and came toward us. I could feel the tension that gripped Peregrine Graham at the sight of him.

Did he have that pistol with him? My throat was suddenly dry.

Peregrine said under his breath, "If you do anything to attract that policeman's attention, I'll kill him." There was no emotion in his voice. I believed him.

We walked on, two people enjoying a companionable silence. I could feel the smile plastered on my face begin to crack from the strain of keeping it in place. But the constable looked at us anyway. I realized that I was a respectably dressed young woman, while the man at my side was wearing a suit that didn't fit him and his face was still pale, with dark circles under his eyes.

Oh, my God. Does he look like a convict—or someone just escaped from an asylum?

Or will he pass for a wounded soldier in civilian clothes he's outgrown?

The constable walked on, in spite of the second glance he'd given Peregrine. I started to breathe again.

"If we're to promenade around London like this, you must have decent clothes," I said, my voice angrier than I'd intended. But I could see again in my mind's eye how that constable had stared, and if he'd stopped us, it didn't bear thinking of.

Peregrine turned to me, amusement in his eyes. "You don't care for the good doctor's taste in clothes?"

I retorted, "If you attract attention to yourself because you don't appear to belong in a neighborhood like this one, it won't be my fault."

He looked down at his clothing. I don't believe he'd given a single thought to his appearance, except for the beard.

"I have told you. I have no money. There's nothing to be done about it. Can we go into the square? It has benches. I need to sit down."

"Only the residents have a key to the gates."

"Ah." He did look exhausted. "All right, I want—" He stopped. The sun had come out from behind a cloud, and suddenly the windows on the far side of the square were lit as if from within by the golden light. "Look!" His exhaustion vanished in his excitement. "I remember now. That chimney pot, the one on the left side— see, there's a missing tile, and when the sunlight hits it just so, the shadow resembles a small dog."

I couldn't see it. But he crossed to the square, the better to see Number 17 and stare up at its windows, as if expecting to find himself at fourteen gazing down, then he positioned himself on the walk, and turned toward the house opposite.

"They've painted the door a dark green, but it was black once. As were the shutters. But, by God, this is the right street!"

"There must be others just like this one."

"No, I'd stake my life on this."

Across the square, the constable stopped to speak to a housemaid just coming up from the tradesmen's entrance. Then he turned our way and began to stroll back toward us, as if he hadn't a care in the world.

"Come away, Peregrine, please! We've loitered here long enough. Please, before that constable catches us up."

Peregrine seemed not to hear me, his mind on something else. Then he turned, took my arm, and we walked on, toward the corner. I wanted to hurry, to look back over my shoulder, but I dared not draw attention to us again. At the corner we turned away from Carroll Square, and I felt my heart begin to beat normally again.

Peregrine's grip on my arm tightened until his fingers felt like they were bruising the skin. "How did you know?" he asked. "Who told you where to find that house again?"

Surprised by the unexpected attack, I said, "It was Mrs. Clayton—"

"I don't remember anyone of that name. You're lying."

"No, truly, I'm not."

"Did you live here before, is that it? Is that why you came to visit the Grahams? I asked you if you were Arthur's wife. You told me he was dead. Why were you in Owlhurst?"

"Peregrine. Mr. Graham. I was the nursing sister with Arthur when he died onboard *Britannic*. I came to visit Mrs. Graham, to—to talk to her about the day Arthur died. He had asked me to. It was his dying wish."

"He wouldn't have asked you to come to Owlhurst. Unless there was more to your relationship than nurse and patient."

"You aren't required to judge any relationship of mine," I retorted coldly. "I'm helping you because you are here, you are armed, and I have no choice."

"You saved my life," he said sardonically. "And your letter gave me a place to hide in London. And you must have been asking questions about me, or you wouldn't have known about a house my family lived in for only a few weeks nearly fourteen years ago."

I could feel myself turning red, and not from the cold wind.

"I admit to some curiosity. Arthur Graham told me he had three brothers, but he said almost nothing about them. When I arrived in Owlhurst, there were only two, and no one told me anything about you. When you were being carried to Owlhurst, and I'd volunteered to attend you, your mother explained in the briefest terms what I was getting myself into. I should have trusted my instincts and let you die!"

He chuckled. It was the oddest sound, coming from a confessed murderer. I hadn't expected a sense of humor and looked up at him, startled.

"Some curiosity, indeed," he repeated, mimicking me.

We were standing on Radcliffe Street, waiting to hail a cab.

I felt a touch on my shoulder. "Miss?"

I turned, alarmed, and found myself face-to-face with the constable we'd seen in Carroll Square.

"Constable?" It was all I could manage. Peregrine's fingers were still digging into my arm, their iron grip biting through the cloth of my coat and my sweater.

"Is this man annoying you, Miss?"

My eyes moved to Peregrine's face. He had turned toward the constable, and was waiting for me to answer.

"His name is William," I said in a voice I knew wasn't my own but prayed the constable would think I was shrill as a rule. "He worked for my family before the war. He wanted to see where his— his brother had been in service before volunteering for the army."

"He's not in the army himself?" the constable asked.

"I'm home on leave," Peregrine answered. "Pneumonia. Not as glorious as dying, is it?"

The constable nodded. "You oughtn't be out of uniform," he admonished Peregrine.

"It's just for today." He indicated his cuffs and the shortness of his trousers. "I've outgrown them. My mum says I'd added an inch since I've been in the army."

The constable smiled. "Good luck to you, son." He touched his cap to me and walked on.

Before I could fall down in relief, I caught the eye of a cabbie coming toward us and hailed him.

"I see what you mean about the clothing," Peregrine said after I'd given the man the address of Mrs. Hennessey's house. "Will you buy me a new suit of clothes, for your sake and the sake of the police? I have no money. I can't pay you back."

There was the shop where my father bought his clothes and had his uniforms tailored. I leaned forward and told the cabbie that I'd changed my mind and wished to go to Oxford Street. He nodded, and we turned toward Piccadilly.

Peregrine sat back and closed his eyes. His face was gray with fatigue.

I sat there counting the lies I'd told to the police. I'd be an accomplished liar before Peregrine Graham and I were done.

I leaned a little forward. Where was the pistol? In his coat pocket? If he was being measured for a new suit of clothes, he'd have to remove that heavy coat. . . .

When we arrived at Gladwynn and Sons, I was grateful to find that young Mr. Gladwynn, who knew my father very well and who must be nearing eighty years of age, was not in the shop that morning. The clerk who greeted me, a Mr. Stanley, informed me that Mr. Gladwynn would regret not having seen me and would surely wish to know how my father fared.

"Very well," I said. "He's in Somerset at the moment. Meanwhile, I have brought a friend who finds he's outgrown his prewar clothes. This is Mr.—Philips, and he's in need of something to finish out his leave."

"We've a backlog of uniforms on order," Mr. Stanley informed me, and my spirits plummeted. "But," he went on, eyeing Peregrine like an undertaker eyeing his next customer, "I think we just might have something to fit his size. . . ."

I sat down in the chair before the tier of mirrors, and Mr. Stanley went off to find whatever he had in mind. He was a thin man, with thinning hair, and close to sixty. I wondered what tale would get back to my father.

Peregrine stood there, ill at ease. It occurred to me that Peregrine had never come to London to have his clothes fitted. He'd either been shut away at home or shut away in the asylum, everything he needed ordered for him. I felt a wave of pity for the child, if not for the man.

Such shops as this one have an air of their own. The smell of wool blended with the beeswax polish that gave a rich luster to the wood of counters and a wall of drawers containing everything from collars to buttonhooks to handkerchiefs. The bolts of cloth on the other side were mostly khaki now or in the colors of various dress uniforms from scarlet to naval blue. Someone had just been fitted with the dress uniform of a Highland regiment, and there were trays of buttons and braid ready to go back into their respective shelves. The tweeds and woolens from before the war were sadly missing, and there were only a few civilian hats to choose from, the rest being military caps of various ranks and services. They were lined up above the bolts of cloth with the precision of Old Mr. Gladwynn, who was legendary.

Mr. Stanley came back, wringing his hands in apology. "I fear there's nothing in civilian clothes to match the gentleman's height," he said. "But I have uniforms that might fit. Alas, they were ordered by someone who died on the Somme. What regiment is the gentleman?"

The gentleman, I informed Mr. Stanley, was in my father's old regiment and held the rank of lieutenant.

Half an hour later, Peregrine and I walked out into Oxford Street again. Mr. Philips had been transformed into Lieutenant Philips, and I wondered if I would be shot at the Tower for making it possible for him to impersonate an officer.

But the streets were filled with officers and men, and as long as Peregrine remembered when to salute and when not, we had a good chance of getting by with this charade. And a young lady in the company of an officer would attract no attention at all. Such couples were everywhere.

I found us a cab as quickly as possible and wondered how I would smuggle my officer past Mrs. Hennessey.

Chapter Twelve

I NEEDN'T HAVE worried. She was out, and the flat was still, blessedly, empty of my flatmates.

While I removed my hat and coat Peregrine sat down in the nearest chair and leaned his head against the cushion. It had been a long morning for him, and I hoped he would sleep the sleep of the ill. I hadn't had an opportunity to search his coat pockets while he was being measured. He had carefully hung the coat in full view. His stolen clothing had been neatly boxed up by Mr. Stanley. I could tell from the man's expression that he thought it should be put out of sight as quickly as possible. The good doctor had an unknown tailor.

I made tea and sliced bread for sandwiches, but tired as he was, Peregrine Graham slept with one eye open. The box was under his feet, and when I touched it with my foot, he was alert on the instant.

"Sorry," I said, moving a small table closer to his chair. I brought a tray with his food on it and sat across the room from him.

As he ate, I asked, "Did seeing the house again rouse any memories?"

He shook his head.

"It's going to be a hopeless task, Peregrine. What will you do then?"

"I still have the pistol," he said, and I shivered.

"Please, not here—" I said before I could stop myself.

He stared at me, then shrugged. "One place is as good as another."

"Do you remember the name of the dead girl? It might help if we could find her family," I said into the empty silence.

"Lily. She told us she was named for Lillie Langtry. I was laughed at because I didn't know who she was."

Peregrine looked across at me, surprise in his gaze. "I couldn't have told you that yesterday. I couldn't remember her name. I'd blotted it out, somehow."

"And her last name?" How many hundreds of girls had been named after the Jersey Lily, once the mistress of Edward VII when he was Prince of Wales, and so famous for her beauty that even her lackluster acting skills brought her fame and fortune?

But it was no use. Peregrine couldn't bring it back. He'd said something about powders they'd given him when he was first put in the asylum. Surely they hadn't kept him drugged all these years? But then there were the powders he hadn't taken but had used to keep the doctor quiet while he escaped.

We ate our sandwiches in silence. Clearing away afterward, I said, "You've found the house. Or so you believe. What are we to do now?"

"I have no idea." He put his head back against the cushion again. "I've got to get some rest. Remember what I told you. Betray me, and others will pay the price for it." He lifted his shod foot and placed it on the box with the doctor's clothing. "I've got nothing to lose."

If I could find a telephone, and call my father, he could alert the police—but even as the thought formed, I knew I wasn't about to do it. I'd survived so far, and I was beginning to think that if I waited Peregrine Graham out, he might return to the asylum of his own accord. Where else was there for him to go?

He was watching my face as the thoughts passed through my mind.

I found it difficult to judge him. His brain appeared to be clever, able to connect events and reason his way through a problem. I couldn't put my finger yet on what it was that was wrong with him, what his tutor had seen, what Mrs. Graham might have used as an excuse to keep him segregated from his half brothers.

"What was the Christian name of your tutor?" I asked just as Peregrine was drifting into sleep. Appleby was a fairly common name, surely.

Rousing himself, he said, "His name was Nathan Appleby."

How would I go about finding someone who had been a tutor fourteen years ago and might be anywhere now, including in his grave?

I sat there thinking as Peregrine slept. I had no idea where else to turn for information Peregrine Graham needed. For that matter, I had no idea whether he would be satisfied if he learned what he'd claimed he wanted so badly to discover.

And then I remembered the journals that Rector Montgomery's predecessor had kept. But how to get to *them*? And what excuse could I use to go back to Owlhurst?

It would surely arouse suspicion. . . .

Well, then, who could I send? Mrs. Hennessey wasn't up to traveling that far in midwinter. Could I ask Dr. Philips to bring the journals to me in Tonbridge?

I was going around and around in my head, trying to see my way through the problem, when the door opened and Diana James, who was another of my flatmates, came in with a smile and a cry of welcome.

"Bess! How good to see you. And how is the arm?"

Before she could reach me to embrace me, Peregrine was on his feet, his eyes wild and his hands clenched.

I leapt into the breach, taking Peregrine's arm as I said, "He couldn't find a room anywhere. I had to smuggle him past Mrs. Hennessey. You won't give him away, will you?"

Diana looked from Peregrine's face to mine.

"He's wounded, Diana." With my free hand I touched my fore-head, and after a moment she relaxed.

"As long as he isn't sleeping in my bed," she said. "Hallo, Lieuten-ant."

"Philips," Peregrine answered. "Lieutenant Philips. Sorry. I was asleep when you came in." His hands were trembling, but he stepped back and sat down in his chair again, as if his legs were unable to support him.

Diana brought in her valise and said, "I hope there's something to eat. I'm starving. The train was so crowded coming up from Dover I could hardly breathe."

"Yes, there's food. How long are you here, Diana?"

"Four days. Worst luck. Ralph isn't here, he's been sent back. I'd hoped we'd overlap for a day or two."

I made her a sandwich as she sat down across from Peregrine. "Ralph is my brother," she was saying. "Where were you wounded, Lieutenant?"

"The Somme," he said. It was the battle Mr. Stanley had men-tioned. "I don't remember much about it, I'm afraid."

"Not surprised. Head injuries are the very devil." She went on, unwinding as she described working at the dressing station along the Ypres line. "Frostbite, trench foot from all the rains, dysentery, fevers, rat bites, lice, even a case of measles. And that's not counting the wounded."

She rattled on, a pretty girl with tired blue eyes and blond hair that she had refused to cut even when ordered to do so. It was pulled tight into a bun at the back of her neck, but anyone could see how lovely it was. She'd maintained that the men she treated liked look-ing at it. I didn't doubt it.

Peregrine was pale with exhaustion, but he kept up his end of the conversation as best he could, falling back on his head injury when pressed about something he had no way of knowing.

Diana ate her sandwich with zest and asked me about *Britannic*, and I told her briefly what it had been like. Then she handed me her empty plate and her teacup, saying, "Would you mind if I left you to wash up? I'm going to fall flat on my face if I don't get a few hours of sleep."

I sent her off to her bedroom, then said in a low voice to Peregrine, "She won't be difficult, and she won't be here very long. And she might be able to help us."

"Why should she?"

"Because she owes me a favor. Will you be willing to go back to Kent? Will you risk it?"

He watched my face, as if trying to see beneath skin and bone into my brain. "I don't trust you. I can't trust you."

"The sooner you're satisfied, the sooner I'm rid of you," I said. "I protected you when you were ill. But I can't condone your escape from the asylum—you aren't trying to make amends for what you did, you aren't even trying to start life anew. You want to relive it."

"I don't want to relive it," he said, his voice tense. "I want to understand it."

"I'm going back to Kent. There are some things I must do, information I must find. Will you stay here with Diana, and not harm her? She'll do your marketing, and she'll be my hostage, if I betray you."

"I can't sit here waiting. I'll go with you."

"If you do, and you're recognized—"

"I'll chance it," he told me grimly.

And so that evening we set out for Kent again. When we reached Tonbridge, I found a hotel on a side street, bespoke two rooms, and asked if there was anyone who could take me to Owlhurst in the morning. They found a man who was willing, and after breakfast, I left Peregrine cooling his heels in his room while I set out, wondering what I was going to say to anyone.

I watched the villages come and go in silence, for I hadn't slept well, worried about Peregrine taking it in his head to walk away. He was two people, the sick man I had watched over day and night for nearly a week, and a man obsessed with a bloody moment in his childhood.

I tried to shut out Peregrine, but he was there, a dark figure in the back of my mind. I turned to the middle-aged man driving me. His name was Owens.

"Do you know Owlhurst?"

"Oh, yes. My Aunt May lived there for a time," he said. "I visited her often enough, boy and man."

Oh, dear. *Mind your tongue,* I warned myself.

"Did you know an Inspector Gadd?" It was the first name that came to me, other than the Grahams and Dr. Philips. After all, the man had been dead for some time. It should be safe enough to claim acquaintance there.

To my surprise, Mr. Owens replied, "He lived next house but one to my aunt. Taught me how to ride my first bicycle. Shame about his dying so young. A good man."

"Yes. Er, do you know if his widow is still living in Owlhurst?"

"She went to stay with her brother in Rye. She couldn't bear that house afterward."

Rye.

I said hastily, "Will you take me to Rye instead?"

He turned to look at me. "You said Owlhurst."

"Yes, but that was before I knew Mrs. Gadd now lived in Rye. Will you take me there, and bring me back again?"

We settled on a new price for his trouble and were soon on our way south to the small town that had once been a Cinque Port, one of the five major harbors during the great days of the wool trade.

It was a journey of several hours by motorcar, but I soon found myself at the foot of a high bluff on which sat a gray stone church. We looked for the local police station, and I went in to ask the desk sergeant if by chance he knew where I could find a Mrs. Gadd. Oh, yes, he said, he knew her well.

"Go up to the church, Miss, and turn to your right. At the corner of the churchyard, turn left, and at the next corner, turn right again. You'll have a lovely view of the water from there. Her house is on the left, the small one with black trim and an anchor for door knocker."

I thanked him, went back to the patient Mr. Owens, and passed the directions on to him. We climbed the hill, went around the large, gray stone church, and found ourselves on a street that seemed to be eager to run straight down into the sea. From the heights, we had a wonderful view of gray water, rough with the turning of the tide. I located the house easily and told Mr. Owens to find himself tea and something to eat while I went inside.

"Knock at the door before I go," he suggested. "She might not be to home."

Good thinking. If I was as brilliant in questioning Mrs. Gadd, we might actually accomplish something, I told myself ruefully.

Using the anchor, I tapped briskly. After a moment someone came to the door. She was not young, perhaps in her middle fifties, but her hair was still fair, and her face unlined. She'd been a pretty woman in her youth, and that hadn't faded with time.

Before I could speak, she peered over her spectacles at the man in the motorcar. "Is that you, Terrence Owens?" she asked.

"Yes, Mrs. Gadd, it is. How are you faring? I haven't seen you in a good many years."

"Well enough. Harry died, you know."

"Your brother? That's sad news. My aunt is gone as well."

"Oh, my dear. I'm sorry to hear it. Won't you come in?"

"I think this young woman would prefer to speak to you privately. But I'll step in when I come to fetch her."

"Fair enough." She turned to me, frowning. "I don't believe we've met, my dear."

"My name is Elizabeth Crawford. I've come to speak to you about something that happened in the past. While you were living in Owlhurst."

There was the briefest hesitation.

She knows what I'm here to ask her. . . .

"Do come in out of the cold, then. The wind is brisk here on the bluff."

Indeed it was. I followed her inside, and after she had taken my coat and gloves, we sat by the fire. My fingers and toes were instantly grateful for the warmth.

"I was a nurse on *Britannic,*" I began, "and one of the men in my care was Arthur Graham. You probably remember him as a child. I knew him as a man, a very brave one. He died of his wounds, and I was with him until the end. I spent some time in Owlhurst until a week ago. A guest of the Graham family, in fact. What I've learned about Peregrine Graham during my visit has been confusing—contradictory. I didn't like to ask his family more than they were willing to tell me. But it has become rather important to me to understand about the murder of the girl called Lily."

Mrs. Gadd spread her hands to the fire, and at first I was sure she wouldn't answer me. Then she said, "Is it just idle curiosity that brings you here?"

"No. You see, I carried a message from Arthur Graham to his brother. No one told me what the message meant, but I came to believe it might have something to do with Peregrine. And I had the strongest impression that the family chose to ignore what amounted to Arthur's last wish. Were they right to do so? I'll tell you something else in confidence. While I was visiting the Grahams, Peregrine was brought to the house suffering from pneumonia. I nursed him back to health. He was so different from what I'd expected—I couldn't— he seemed normal. As normal as Arthur or Jonathan or Timothy Graham. That troubled me."

"What will you do with this knowledge, once you have it?"

"I've come back to Kent, and now here to Rye, to settle my own conscience. I have no right to pry, and I respect the possibility that you have no reason to confide in me."

I'd tried to be honest—just leaving out the fact that Peregrine had fled from the asylum and only I knew where he was.

"Your concern does you credit, my dear. A duty to the dead is a sacred matter." It was an echo of what my father had said to me. "What is it you want to hear?"

"What do you recall about Peregrine and the decision to send him to the asylum? How much did your husband tell you?"

"Very little at first. He came home that night shocked and grieving, refusing to tell me anything. Several months later, he was reminded of that night. We'd just finished our tea, and it was beginning to rain when Mrs. Graham sent for my husband. He was gone for hours. It seems that young Timothy went missing. We learned afterward that he'd set out on his own to find Peregrine. I have no idea how Mrs. Graham explained the situation to her other children, but it appeared that Timothy really didn't know what had become of his half brother. Come to that, most of us weren't told in the beginning where Peregrine was or why. And to tell you the truth, the boy was so seldom seen by that time that few of us thought twice about his absence. But back to Timothy Graham. My husband learned that Timothy was very upset that day. He'd been sent to his room for disobeying Robert Douglas, and some time in the late afternoon he left the house without being seen and simply vanished. Everyone was frantic; they had no idea where he was or why he'd told no one where he was going."

"There were search parties?"

"Oh, yes, as many men as my husband could muster. Mr. Craig rang the church bell to gather them. And they were out until late into the night. Finally someone came from one of the outlying farms—a man named Hutter—to say that Timothy had been found in his barn, asleep in one of the horse stalls. My husband asked the boy why he'd run away, and he said that he wanted to find Peregrine and stay with him. It was after he was brought in that Mrs. Graham finally admitted to her sons where their brother was and that he would never come home."

"How sad!"

"When Henry finally walked in the door, he couldn't sleep. He paced for two hours, he was that upset. And because he couldn't put it all behind him, he told me about Peregrine."

"Did he tell you about how they'd gathered—your husband, Mr. Craig, Lady Parsons, and Dr. Hadley, together with Mrs. Graham—to decide Peregrine's fate? And then apparently London accepted their decision? Did Inspector Gadd believe it was a just solution?"

"Yes, and I'm sure he felt it was, or he wouldn't have been a party to it. Still, I was horrified. I'd known those boys, you see, most of their lives."

"Can you tell me anything about the tutor? Nathan Appleby?"

"I didn't know him well, but I was of the opinion that he didn't have the character to rule four lively boys. But Mrs. Graham appeared to be satisfied with him."

"What do you mean, the character?"

"He was rather pompous, for one thing, and I—well, to put it bluntly, I overheard the rector question Mr. Appleby's qualifications, when the Grahams could afford the best. Mr. Graham replied that his wife—the present Mrs. Graham—had selected him, and there was no more to be said."

Why would she willingly choose an incompetent tutor? Unless she felt he would do as she asked?

"Did he stay with the Graham family, after Peregrine was taken away?"

"Yes, until the boys went off to school, and then he moved to Chilham, to a family there."

"Did your husband tell you the name of the girl who was— murdered?"

"How could I ever forget it? Lily Mercer."

"Did anyone ask her family how they felt about Peregrine going to the asylum rather than standing trial?"

Mrs. Gadd looked surprised. "I—I don't believe they were consulted—nothing was said—the London police were in agreement about the asylum. Even though there were no witnesses, the evidence spoke for itself. Peregrine's bloody hands and clothes, his mental confusion, told their own story. And of course there was his youth. No one wanted the boy sent to prison, if treatment was available at Barton's."

"Yes, but no one has explained why he should have killed Lily."

"I doubt that anyone knows except perhaps Peregrine himself, if he's able to understand his own actions."

"You said the evidence pointed strongly to Peregrine."

"Mrs. Graham and her cousin had gone out to dine that evening. They came home to find the other boys in bed. Lily wasn't waiting for them, as she was supposed to be. Mrs. Graham went to Lily's room and found Peregrine on the floor by her body. They asked him, of course—the London police, Lady Parsons, the rector, my husband—everyone. He seemed dazed. And all he would say to them was he wanted his knife back again, the one his father had given him. And of course they couldn't give it to him, the police had taken it away because it was a murder weapon."

I swallowed hard. "And his brothers? They hadn't seen or heard anything?"

"Apparently not. But we had the same laundress, Mrs. Graham and I. And I heard her tell my cook that when Susan's mother unpacked the boys' luggage, the night they returned to Owlhurst, she found blood all along the cuff of Arthur's nightshirt. She pointed it out to Mrs. Wallace—the laundress—and asked if such a stain would come out."

"Arthur's? Are you sure of that?" My voice was sharp, I couldn't make it behave.

"Yes, I'm certain. He'd had a nosebleed, he said. It seems he was prone to them as a child."

Mr. Owens chose that moment to knock at the door, and Mrs. Gadd went to let him in.

I sat by the fire, cold to the bone. And all I could think of was the message I had carried home for Arthur.

Tell Jonathan that I lied. I did it for Mother's sake. But it has to be set right.

I was silent on the long drive back to Tonbridge. Mr. Owens tried once or twice to draw me into conversation, but I told him I was tired.

The truth was, I was tormented by what I'd learned.

I should have risked everything and turned Peregrine over to the police the first chance I had. The police could have disarmed him before he'd killed anyone. Surely—

And then I would never have come to Rye to hear Mrs. Gadd's account of what had transpired in London. I would have gone instead to Somerset, my father's daughter, and been told I'd been very brave and very foolish at the same time, and I could have forgot Peregrine Graham in a few months. I'd have gone back to war, and put him out of my mind.

Instead I'd taken up the challenge of finding out more.

Arthur hadn't wanted to put his last wishes into a letter. He'd trusted to his brother to set things right for him. He'd been certain that Jonathan would understand his message and see that justice was done.

But neither Jonathan nor his mother had seemed to understand it—Mrs. Graham had asked me questions about it.

To find out how much Arthur had told you, my mind retorted. *To see if you were aware of what ought to be set right.*

Had she let me nurse Peregrine because she thought I would fail to save him? A young nurse, where a doctor's training was needed? She'd turned away the doctor when he came to the door. And the rector as well. Or had she only been afraid that in his delirium, Peregrine might remember more than he ought?

I was condemning her because of my own hurt, and that was hindsight, and not fair at all.

Arthur couldn't have killed that girl. Not the man I'd known on *Britannic,* not the man everyone remembered as brave and stoic? He was his mother's favorite, she'd said as much.

But then she'd protect her favorite, the dead son's memory, with all her might, wouldn't she? Peregrine had always been blamed, why do anything now?

Surely she couldn't have known from the start—

I huddled in my seat, listening to the cold wind whistling by, my fingers already stiff with cold, my feet barely warmed by the tiny heater. Even the rug Mr. Owens had handed me for my knees wasn't enough.

I was reminded of that dreadful ride in the dogcart from Tonbridge to Owlhurst, when the cold knifed through my coat and the rugs, no motorcar to break the wind or offer a modicum of protection.

The cart had nearly dumped me on the verge of the road, on my broken arm, when Robert fell asleep and the wheels went into a ditch. Had that been deliberate, and then he'd changed his mind at the last possible second and held me on the seat?

My mind was running away with me.

But in a short time I would have to face Peregrine Graham, and I had no idea what I was going to tell him.

There's no proof that Arthur—*You've jumped to conclusions, my girl, and you're paying the price of it,* I lectured myself.

I'd wondered why Peregrine had killed. I could ask the same question about Arthur—or any of the other Graham sons. Why kill Lily?

It was useless, I was going around in circles for nothing.

What was it Arthur felt must be set right? What did he lie to his mother about? Or to put it differently, since he too was only a child at the time, what lie did he let his mother tell to protect the son she loved best?

We were pulling into the outskirts of Tonbridge. I roused myself to thank Mr. Owens for taking me to Rye, and I counted out the money I owed him for the journey. As I gave it to him in front of the hotel, he said, "I have you to thank as well. I'd not have visited Mrs. Gadd, else. It was good to see her again."

And all the while I wished I'd never heard her name spoken this day.

Peregrine was pacing the floor when I tapped at his door and stepped into his room.

When I'd left that morning, I'd feared he might do something foolish, perhaps walk away and never be seen again. Now I wished he'd done just that.

"Where the hell have you been?" he was demanding. "You couldn't have been in Owlhurst all this time!"

"I didn't go to Owlhurst after all. I went to Rye instead."

"Rye? What were you doing in Rye?"

"Do you remember the policeman who talked to you that night?"

"Inspector Gadd? Yes. He was kind. I think he believed I was some sort of monster, but he treated me gently."

"Well, I've just spent half an hour with his widow. She gave me the name of the girl who died. Lily Mercer."

"Yes, that's right. I don't know why I couldn't recall her last name."

"Did she like Arthur more than anyone else? Did she seem to favor him?"

"I have no earthly idea. I was in my own room most of the time. I don't know how they got on."

I took a deep breath. "I was just wondering. Peregrine, I want to go back to London tonight. I want to see if I can find Lily Mercer's family."

"What could they know that would be helpful? They weren't there."

"But they knew their daughter, I expect. They knew what manner of girl she was. A person of your background doesn't just decide from one minute to the next to strike down a servant in his household. I mean to say, there must be more to the murder than we know—than you can remember."

"She teased Timothy about his clubfoot. I heard her, in the passageway. She asked me what was wrong with me, why I was left behind when my brothers had gone to the zoo and to see the Tower."

Timothy was the youngest. Vulnerable. Would Arthur defend him? But you don't go round murdering someone just because she's cruel. Unless this was the first time Timothy had been tormented in such a way and Arthur—

No, he'd have spoken to Robert—to his mother. Wouldn't he have?

"What else do you recollect?"

He frowned. "I was given my meals in my room. As I always was. I saw the staff only in passing."

"Peregrine. Was your tutor attracted to Lily Mercer?"

"Mr. Appleby?" He smiled. "I can't imagine him condescending to a flirtation with a servant girl."

Mrs. Gadd had said that the tutor was pompous. Still, anything was possible. London was a long way from Owlhurst.

"I've changed my mind, Peregrine. I want to go to Chilham tomorrow, instead of London. To see if I can find your former tutor. To see what he could add to the story."

"I thought someone in Owlhurst had the rector's journals?"

"Yes, but think—if there had been anything in those journals that the police ought to know, Mr. Montgomery would have told me. He'd read them over. He said as much to me."

"Who is Montgomery?"

"The present rector. No, I think it might be more helpful to speak to Mr. Appleby. Let me see if I can persuade Mr. Owens to drive me there tomorrow."

"This time I'll go with you."

"You'll be seen—recognized—"

"Hardly. I doubt Appleby will know me. Not in this uniform. It's been fourteen years, after all."

He had a point.

We had a late tea in the hotel dining room, with me on tenterhooks that someone might see in the rather attractive young officer across from me a dangerous escapee from an asylum. But of course no one did. Peregrine complained of being shut up in his room all day and needing exercise, so we went for a short walk down the quiet street. Afterward Peregrine saw me to my door, and said, "Something you learned today disturbed you. Will you tell me what it is? I ought to know, if it has any bearing on my situation."

I tried to smile, but it faltered. "It was just something—odd, that's all."

I opened my door, and he followed me into my room, shutting the door behind him. I tensed.

He said, "Don't look like that. I'm not going to hurt you. Have I? In any way?"

"No."

"Then tell me."

"The housekeeper—Susan's mother—showed the woman who was the family's laundress a stain she'd found on the sleeve of Arthur's nightshirt, and asked if it could be gotten out. She'd found the nightshirt in the valises as she unpacked after everyone returned from London. There must have been no time to do anything about it—or else no one noticed it. It was just—she said he was prone to nosebleeds. Arthur."

"Was he? I don't know. Surely my stepmother was told about

the blood. Or the London police would have seen it and questioned Arthur."

They might have, if he'd been wearing the nightshirt when Mrs. Graham called the police. Had he changed it before his mother got home?

Stop it! I ordered myself.

Answering Peregrine aloud, I agreed. "Yes. Of course. I'm tired. It was a long, cold journey. And stressful."

"I'm sure." He nodded, and was gone. I stood where I was, listening to the sound of his own door opening and then closing.

I wondered if he believed me.

Chapter Thirteen

THE NEXT MORNING, Mr. Owens was there with his motorcar when we came out of the hotel after breakfast. He touched his hat to me, then shook hands with Peregrine—Lieutenant Philips.

Eager to hear about the war firsthand, Mr. Owens was disappointed to find that Peregrine's wound had affected his memory. We were silent, watching the rain clouds build over Dover. In the distance we could see Canterbury Cathedral as we climbed the hill to Chilham and came out into the wonderful square with its Elizabethan buildings. The gates of the Jacobean manor house marked one end of the square and the churchyard of St. Mary's the other. Where to find Mr. Appleby?

I decided to try the flint church first, walking through the gates to the arched west door. It creaked as I opened it, and the interior was icy, as it must have been for centuries. But I had been right to come here. There was a woman on her knees by the altar, arranging green boughs in bronze vases. At this time of year the arrangement was mostly sprays of holly, its red berries bright among the greenery.

She turned at my footsteps, and smiled. "Hello. Are you looking for Rector?"

"Actually, I'm looking for someone who may have lived here some years ago. He was a tutor, his name was Appleby."

"Mr. Appleby? Yes, of course, he tutored the Laurence boys. But he's no longer teaching."

My spirits sank. "Do you know where he might have gone from here?"

"Oh, he liked Chilham so much he stayed on. He married one of the Johnstone girls. Mary, the eldest. Go back to the square and the little lane that runs down to your right, just after you leave the church gates. The third house is his."

My spirits rose again. "Thank you. I'm very happy to hear that."

"Do I know you?" she asked. "Your face is familiar."

"I was here some years ago. My father was returning from India, and we were traveling with him, my mother and I. Colonel Crawford."

She stood, her smile widening. "Colonel Crawford. The handsomest man at the dinner party. Of course, I remember now."

That was the Colonel Sahib. In his dress uniform he was quite remarkably handsome. And had the charm to match.

"Let me finish here, and I'll show you the Appleby house myself," she offered. "I'd like to hear how your parents are faring."

"They are both quite well," I answered. "But I have friends waiting. If you don't mind—"

"Of course. Give my regards to your parents. Tell them Sarah Cunningham was asking for them."

I promised, and made my escape.

Peregrine was pacing beside the motorcar, a frown on his face. Mr. Owens had walked up to The White Horse on the corner, to wait for us. I told Peregrine what I had learned, and together we walked down the curving lane past a lovely stone house where I'd had cookies and milk when we called there, my mother and I. The tutor's house was easily picked out, and I went up the short walk to lift the knocker.

"Peregrine. Whatever he tells us, promise me you won't—"

At that moment the door opened. Peregrine sucked in his breath but said nothing.

Appleby was of medium height and thin build, his long face

marked by a scar on his chin. His hair was graying, but his short mustache was darker, like his eyebrows. A scholarly man, at first glance, but his eyes were weak and his mouth was small. My father had always held a theory about small mouths—that they indicated spitefulness.

"Mr. Appleby?"

"Yes, indeed. How may I help you?" He looked from my face to Peregrine's, without any sign of recognition.

I introduced us and then said, "I was one of Arthur Graham's nurses when he was wounded, and he entrusted me with messages to his family just before he died."

"I read that he'd died of wounds. What a tragedy that was. He was a fine young man."

"May I spend a few minutes talking to you about him?"

He was surprised. "To me? Er—what information can I give you about Arthur?" He seemed confused.

I said quickly, "I spent a few days with the Grahams, as Arthur had asked me to do. But there were questions I felt uncomfortable bringing up—"

"You're here about Peregrine Graham, aren't you?"

"I—yes."

"Why are you prying into the past?"

"I'm not prying, Mr. Appleby. I was very close to Arthur Graham at the time of his death. I can't help but believe he died with something on his conscience—"

"You had better come in." He stepped aside, and we followed him into the parlor of the house. It was prettily decorated, a woman's touch with floral covers on the chairs and small china figurines on tables and the mantelpiece. I could hear someone humming in another part of the house.

A small dog was curled on the hearth rug. She lifted her head, considered us, and went back to sleep.

Appleby offered us chairs and then said, "Look, I've put the past behind me. It was a fearsome situation, and I felt somehow responsible because the boys were in my charge while we were in London."

"Yet you continued to work with them for several years afterward."

"Of course. Continuity is what children need when their world has been turned upside down. Mrs. Graham begged me to remain there until her sons were sent to public school."

"Did you know Lily Mercer well?"

That took him aback. "Well? Of course not. I'd never seen her before we arrived in London," he answered indignantly. "She was a member of the temporary staff."

"I understand that. But you must have spoken to her in the servants' hall—"

"I never took my meals with the servants. I ate in my room or with my charges or in the small room off the study."

I recalled that someone had told me the tutor kept to himself.

"I'm not trying to stir up the past, Mr. Appleby. But if Arthur had doubts about what happened in London, I'm honor bound to put the matter to rest."

"You are honor bound to do no such thing. Peregrine Graham did a wicked thing, and he was put in a place where he couldn't hurt anyone again. We feared for the family, if you must know—there was no other choice but to send him away. No one wanted a trial, it would have been devastating for the other boys. That they had a brother in prison for murder would have damaged their lives beyond measure."

I glanced at Peregrine, whose face remained impassive. It was as if he accepted everything that Mr. Appleby was saying.

"What did Lily Mercer's family want?"

Mr. Appleby opened his mouth to answer me, then shut it smartly. After a moment, he said, "I have no idea."

"Were you satisfied that Peregrine Graham had done what he was accused of?"

"Miss Crawford. I know you mean well. But let me tell you this.

I only saw the body briefly, but the girl was covered in blood. Mrs. Graham told me later that Lily Mercer had been disemboweled. I also saw Peregrine Graham kneeling there beside her, splattered with her blood. What conclusion would you have drawn, in my place?"

Peregrine Graham flinched, shutting his eyes for an instant.

"But I understand that Arthur also had blood on his nightshirt."

I could tell from his reaction that this was something he was unaware of.

But he said, "You can't change history, Miss Crawford, however good your intentions. I think you should go now."

"Mr. Appleby, I'm not trying to change history. I'm trying to get to the truth, and decide in my own mind what the message Arthur charged me with really meant. I have given this message to Jonathan Graham. But I bear some responsibility in seeing that Arthur's wishes are carried out."

"That's your personal choice, my dear. If you cared anything for Arthur Graham, you will put this behind you and move on with your life. Arthur was a fine young man, and it is to his credit that he was concerned for his brother. He went to the asylum one year, learned that Peregrine was not allowed either books or writing implements, and complained to the doctors. They refused to give him either pen or pencil, but they brought Peregrine books to read. I was surprised that he even grasped what was in them—he had shown no aptitude as a child."

"What do you mean, no aptitude? Was he—mentally incapable of reading?"

"No, Miss Crawford. I'm surprised no one has told you that Peregrine Graham was unable to focus his attention on anything for more than a few minutes at a time. His father's death had been a great shock to him, and by the time I arrived when he was seven, he was nearly unmanageable. We felt it best, Mrs. Graham and I, to separate him from his brothers and try to keep him as calm as possible. I made every effort to teach him, but I was never sure how well he had comprehended his studies. He wouldn't answer my questions, he wouldn't write out an examination, and he refused to accept my guidance."

And yet the man that Peregrine had become could read.

"Did you like Peregrine Graham, Mr. Appleby?"

"As to that, there was little likable about the child. Mrs. Graham had warned me that I would find him difficult, a liar, and given to throwing tantrums. I was not surprised to discover that she was correct."

"And for this reason you were able to believe that a boy who had been kept from his family for—what? Seven, eight?—years was capable of murder?"

"Miss Crawford. The boy's father had given him a very nice pocketknife as his last birthday gift. It was a man's knife, Peregrine's grandfather's—and Mr. Graham insisted that he be allowed to keep it. The boy used it incessantly—to carve any wood that came to hand, whether the table at which he sat or a bit of tree branch that he found in the garden. He wished to use it to carve his meat but was forbidden. It was taken away, but he managed to find it again, and hid it. But he took it to London with him, and that knife was in the body when it was found."

"Yes, so I was told—"

"And his only remorse was that the knife was taken from him for good. No feeling for that pitiful young woman."

"I'm a nurse, Mr. Appleby. I can't believe that a pocketknife could do the sort of—butchery—that you described."

Appleby's face was unfriendly. "I'm not a fool, Miss Crawford. There was of course another knife, one from the kitchen, that did the butchery as you called it. But it was Peregrine's knife in Lily Mercer's throat that mattered. She couldn't have screamed if she'd wanted to."

No one had told me such details. I felt a surge of nausea but collected myself and said, "Everyone knew that this knife was a favorite of Peregrine's—"

Appleby was on his feet.

For an instant, I thought Peregrine, also rising, was going to strike him down.

And then Peregrine had taken my arm in a firm grip and said, "Miss Crawford. You're getting nowhere. I suggest we leave now."

I thanked Mr. Appleby, for manners insisted that I should. But I was furious with him.

He didn't say good-bye, nor did he see us to the door. We were outside, shutting the door behind ourselves, and standing in the street before I could say anything.

Peregrine spoke first. "I took that knife to London," he said in a tightly controlled voice. "But I gave it to Arthur when I got there, in exchange for a promise that he would speak to his mother and ask her to allow me to go with my brothers to the Tower."

I stared at him. "Peregrine? Are you certain?"

"I hadn't remembered what happened to it. I saw it in Lily's throat and wanted it back. I told you, I don't remember much about that night. It comes in bits and pieces, like a puzzle. But I gave that knife to Arthur. I'd swear to it. On my life."

I could feel my heart turning over in my chest. It was medically impossible, and yet I felt it.

He was a murderer. He had every reason to lie. Even Mr. Appleby had told me that Peregrine lied.

And yet—and yet. I looked into his eyes and knew he was telling me the truth.

"You've had years to remember this. Why now?"

"I shut it all out of my mind for years. When I refused to talk to the doctors, and they finally decided that I was mute, that shock had robbed me of my voice, they left me alone. If I couldn't answer their questions, how could they judge my progress? They tried for the first two years to bring me to a sense of my own guilt, but I'd had that drummed into me by the London police, everyone in Owlhurst— my own family. I was dazed when they found me. I admitted to everything, to make them leave me alone. You don't seem to understand—I could smell drying blood, it was everywhere, all over my hands, me, and I couldn't escape it. But no one would let me wash my face or my hands. They hired a carriage and drove me back to Owlhurst, still covered in blood. I would have agreed to everything in the hope that they would let me go to my own room and shut the door."

"You're saying you didn't kill her."

"No. I'm saying that there must be more to this than I've remembered so far. Something happened that night. Something appalling. I can't think why I walked into that room and killed Lily Mercer. But there must have been a *reason*."

He turned to look up at the church, his face hidden from me. "I want there to be a reason. I want to believe that I didn't suddenly run amok, striking down the first person who got in my way. What if it had been Arthur? Or Timothy? That's madness of a different order, don't you see?"

"It never happened before that night. Or since that night."

He turned back to me. "Since that night, my dear Miss Crawford, I was locked in a room, put into a straitjacket to be taken to the offices where my doctors examined me, and given nothing sharper than a spoon. I was handed a sedative as soon as I'd had my tea, because my history of violence occurred at night. I couldn't have killed again. They saw to that."

"Did you ever want to—to kill?"

"I spent most of my childhood alone. I saw my brothers sometimes, Mr. Appleby, the housekeeper, my stepmother, Robert. And that was it. It never occurred to me to hurt them."

"Have you felt the urge to do violence since you left the asylum?"

He smiled suddenly. "Just now. Speaking to that fool. I was afraid of him as a child. He could decide whether or not I'd deserved my dinner or was to be denied it. He could allow me to sit in the garden for an hour every afternoon, while my brothers were at their lessons, or leave me locked in my room. It was Appleby who refused to take the responsibility for me to accompany my brothers to the Tower. I heard him tell my stepmother that the night before. He was a bully, but I wasn't to know that, was I?"

He walked on, and I hurried to catch him up. "If it had been my tutor who was found butchered, I could understand it. I would have reveled in it."

Mr. Owens was waiting for us, stamping his feet and clapping his hands together to keep warm.

"This is a pretty town," he said as we came up the lane and into the square. "Look at those houses, now. If old Queen Bess was to walk through here this minute, she'd feel right at home."

Peregrine helped me into the motorcar, and then seated himself beside Mr. Owens.

"I'm sure she would," I answered him, my mind elsewhere. The black and white buildings with their beautiful diamond-shaped windowpanes reminded me of the rectory in Owlhurst.

"It's the oak," he went on. "Good English oak, that's kept them so fine. Nothing like it, I say. Would you care for a cup of tea to warm you, Miss, before we start back?"

I thanked him for his kindness and told him I was warm enough. All I wanted was to be back in London, a place I knew, where the world made sense.

We drove back down the hill, looking across the Juliberrie Downs toward Canterbury, and wove our way through the countryside toward Tonbridge. We made a stop along the way at a tiny village where the pub offered tea for me and ale for Mr. Owens. Peregrine took nothing, his face gray with fatigue. I saw Mr. Owens glance at him once or twice, concern in his eyes.

A rainstorm on the way delayed us, but we reached Tonbridge just before dusk.

After I'd settled my account with Mr. Owens, I went to my room but felt smothered there, as if the walls were closing in. A certain sign of fatigue and worry. Nevertheless I caught up my coat and went out to walk, past the boys' school and up to the handsome gatehouse to what was once Tonbridge Castle. The gatehouse, part of the curtain wall, and a broken tower were all that was left, but I walked through and into the grounds, crossing to the cliff that looked down on the Medway and another part of the town.

I hadn't been there long when someone came up behind me. It was nearly dark now, the dusk fading quickly in an overcast sky. I turned, and found myself face-to-face with Peregrine.

"You should be resting," I said.

"I could say the same for you."

We stood in silence, staring down at the lower part of the town, watching a pair of ducks paddling along the quiet river.

"Are you still afraid of me?" he asked.

"I wasn't in Owlhurst. I was in London. You threatened Mrs. Hennessey, remember, and then any three strangers you met on your way out the door."

"I was more afraid of you. I didn't think you'd help me. And I needed that help. I had to trust you, and I wasn't certain I could."

"Would you have shot Mrs. Hennessey?"

"I'd have shot myself, I think, if the police came to take me away."

"I haven't had many dealings with murderers. Though there was one I knew in Rajasthan. An old man who would sometimes let me ride his camel around the market. He was hanged for killing his young wife's lover. I didn't know that until much later. I just wondered why he never came to market again."

Peregrine was silent for a time. Then he said, "What next? I want to see those journals."

"I've lost my nerve. I don't want to go back to Owlhurst." I straightened and turned back the way I'd come. Peregrine fell into step beside me.

"Why not?"

"I don't want to learn any more. About you. About Arthur. About the Graham family."

"Arthur didn't kill Lily Mercer. If that's what worries you."

But I couldn't be sure. The way he had made me learn his message by heart—the intensity behind demanding my promise, the refusal to write anything down . . . It had seemed unimportant then, I'd been too worried to ask questions, prepared to do anything to bring him peace of mind at the end. The Arthur I *thought* I knew would have confessed, he'd have written it and had his letter witnessed, and sent it to someone—Lady Parsons? He'd have stood up to everyone and cleared Peregrine's name.

Wouldn't he?

Why had he told Jonathan that he'd lied? Surely Jonathan already knew about the pocketknife? And what had to be set right, if it wasn't clearing his brother's name?

Neither Jonathan nor his mother seemed to be disturbed by the message—that made me wonder if Arthur had tried before this to make his feelings known, and found his mother dead set against changing the status quo. That was a rather chilling thought. That they had made up their minds to ignore any protestations on Arthur's part long before I'd appeared on the scene.

And where did Robert stand in all this?

It made sense that Mrs. Graham and Jonathan had agreed to let the matter end with Arthur's death.

But when had she confided the truth to Jonathan? Or had it been Arthur himself?

Look, Jonathan—if anything happens to me . . .

No, it wouldn't have been that way. There was too much passion in Arthur's determination to set matters right. As Death came to collect him, he tried to clear his conscience in the only way left to him.

But when was Jonathan told the truth—and why?

All I could think of was that he'd known from the start, and said nothing.

It was more comfortable not to. Everyone looked up to Arthur, everyone called him a fine young man, even the tutor. After all, Peregrine had been found beside the body. Why look any further? Yet until the moment Peregrine had been taken to the asylum for testing, Mrs. Graham had been distraught with fear. Not for what was to become of him but because somehow the truth might slip out and wreck all her careful plans.

I sighed.

Peregrine, a dark, looming shadow beside me, said, "What is it?"

"I was thinking that truth is a very illusive thing."

He was silent for a moment, and then he answered me, his voice muffled. "I'm not sure truth exists. Perhaps we only think it does. But in reality it's only what you believe and I believe and Mr. Owens believes—the rest is merely compromise."

I couldn't sleep that night. At every sound my eyes flew open and I waited—for what?

My door was locked. Peregrine couldn't get into my room without waking half the guests on this floor. And yet I was on edge, unable to feel safe.

At one point, on the brink of slipping finally into a drowsy peace, I thought I heard Arthur calling me. It was so real my heart leapt, and I was wide awake again. That was the last straw.

It was nearly dawn by then, and I got up, dressed, and for a time walked the dark, silent streets of Tonbridge.

At one point a constable stopped me, asking if anything was the matter, if I needed help. I told him the truth—I was too troubled to sleep.

He said, "Aye, my daughter's husband's at the Front. I find her out and about at all hours. But mind where you go, Miss. There's not much to worry you here, but one never can tell what's lurking in the shadows."

I watched the night turn into a gray dawn, I watched candles flicker into life in attics where servants dressed in the cold. I watched the milk cart making its rounds, watched as sluggard schoolboys made their way to their lessons, and then watched merchants unlock their doors and set out their goods for the day. I saw the gate of the castle rise above the mists of the river, and quiver there, like a disembodied vision.

It was nearly time for breakfast when, cold and courting sleep, I turned back to the hotel at last. I was just walking up the steps of The Checquers, when someone came bounding through the doors, nearly bowling me over.

"I beg your pardon, madam—" he started to say, and then broke off in astonishment.

Beneath the officer's cap, above the scarf, I recognized the bandaged face of Jonathan Graham. Or to be more precise, I recognized the bandaging.

"Miss Crawford—"

"Good morning, Lieutenant Graham," I managed to say. "How is your family?"

"My family? Yes, well enough. What—brings you back to Tonbridge?"

"A personal matter," I replied. I wanted very much to ask him the same. We stood there, confronting each other, neither willing to give the other satisfaction.

Finally Jonathan said, "Will you be returning to Owlhurst?"

"I've considered it," I said slowly. "Perhaps to call on Dr. Philips."

The words lingered in the air like the morning mists, going nowhere.

Jonathan Graham frowned. I realized, too late, that it sounded as if I were pursuing the good doctor, a very bold thing for a single woman to do. My mother would have been appalled. I could feel my face flush as it was.

Trying to recover, I said, "We had a professional connection, in regard to Ted Booker and cases like his."

The frown deepened.

I took the plunge. "You weren't called at the inquest, and I can't help but wonder why. You visited Mr. Booker, didn't you, the night before he was found."

I managed to make it sound like a documented fact.

"All right. Yes, I did. I felt—a fellow invalid's compassion."

He'd hardly shown compassion when he'd called Ted Booker a coward.

"I've wondered why you didn't speak up at the inquest. It could have given all of us a clearer picture of his state of mind later in the evening."

"I spoke to the police. I told them he was asleep when I got there. That I'd turned around and left straightaway."

I couldn't have said why, but I didn't believe him.

And why had Ted Booker killed himself, if he could sleep?

"I'm sorry," I said. "I truly believed he'd turned the corner. It's heart wrenching, to lose a patient."

"As you lost Arthur."

Touché.

"Do you know when you'll return to France?" I asked him.

"They remove the bandages tomorrow," he said. "It should have been sooner, but there was concern about infection. Thank God, their worry was misplaced. Another week, and I'll be declared fit."

"I wish you well. Good-bye, Lieutenant Graham."

I held out my hand and he shook it.

"Good-bye, Miss Crawford."

I went upstairs and knocked on Peregrine's door. He was dressed and shaved, preparing to meet me in the dining room for breakfast.

"Jonathan is here in this same hotel," I told him in a low voice. "It would be best if we left for London as soon as we can find a train."

"Jonathan?"

"Yes, he's here to see his doctors. They expect to remove his bandages tomorrow. That means he'll be in and out, and we're likely to run into him."

"I didn't know he'd been wounded."

"Across the face. It's going to leave a terrible scar."

"I'd have liked to join the army."

"Be glad you were spared," I said shortly. "I'll go and see about tickets. But it might be best if you stayed here, in your room, until we're ready to leave."

"Jonathan won't recognize me. Not after all these years."

"I wouldn't wager your freedom on it."

"No."

He closed his door and I went to the station, found that there were tickets for the morning train, and before Tonbridge was stirring, we were on our way back to London.

Once on the train, I drew a sigh of relief. It wouldn't have done for Jonathan Graham to find me with Peregrine. It was dawning on me that the cost of helping this man could well be my reputation. Was there a law forbidding aiding a desperate fugitive from an asylum? I shuddered to think.

As we were nearing London, Peregrine opened his eyes and turned to me.

"Will your friend be at the flat?"

"Diana?" I felt a chill. "I—don't know. Why?"

"She's very pretty."

Oh, dear.

He was saying, "The only women I've seen for nearly fifteen years are other inmates and matrons. I've noticed too how the world has left me behind. The women are dressed very differently, there are more men in uniform than in civilian clothes—only the very old and the very young aren't, in fact. There are more automobiles, and very different ones at that. And this morning, while I was waiting for you, there was a flight of aeroplanes I could see from my window. I feel like a stranger in my own country. It's daunting, frightening, and fascinating, all in one."

I could imagine. Peregrine had managed remarkably well. I was beginning to realize the tragedy of his childhood. Mrs. Graham had done a cruel thing, whether out of maliciousness or out of an honest belief that he was different, I couldn't tell. Mr. Appleby had aided and abetted her treatment of Peregrine, the fault was surely not entirely hers.

We were arriving in London. Back in the crowded, anonymous world of people who had things on their minds other than spotting my companion and taking him back to his jailers.

How do you make up for a lost life? I couldn't think of a way.

Diana was delighted to see us, demanding to borrow Peregrine for an hour that evening, to escort her to a dinner party. He flatly refused, and she was hurt, saying to me later, "He's the most attractive male I've seen in weeks, and the only whole one as well."

"I've promised to see that he doesn't overdo. Next visit, he'll be well on his way to recovery."

"I think you merely want to keep him for yourself."

I laughed. Little did she know. But I didn't want a blossoming romance on Diana's side or any temptation on Peregrine's. After all, by his own admission he'd killed one young woman. Whether it was true or not.

There was a knock at the door, and I went to open it, thinking that Elayne must be back and had forgot her key again. She'd find a man in her bed. But knowing Elayne, she'd be amused and not angry.

It was my father standing there on the threshold, concern on his face.

"I came to see you yesterday. Your mother was worried. Your friend told me that you'd gone to Kent. Back to Owlhurst?"

My mouth had dropped open at the sight of him. I shut it. Over my shoulder, Diana said, "Ah. I forgot to tell you that your father was in town."

My father smiled. "I can see that you did. Er—am I to wait on the threshold, or am I allowed into your flat?"

"Come in, of course," I said, but one part of my mind was praying that Peregrine, hearing a male voice, would stay where he was, in Elayne's room. All my father had to see was that uniform, and Peregrine would be finished. "Is Mama with you?"

The Colonel Sahib stepped in, his frame filling the room in a way I hadn't remembered before.

Guilty conscience, a voice in my head pointed out.

"She's at home. I needed to be in London for a few hours and wanted to ask if you'd decided to come home again. We could travel together."

I said in a distracted way, "I'm thinking of staying on a few more days."

"Do you feel your social calendar might accommodate an elderly relative desirous of your company at lunch?"

I smiled in relief. "If the elderly relative is my father—of course."

For an instant I thought he was about to ask Diana to join us. But she said, "I've things to do to get myself ready. Go, and leave me to see to them."

And then I was instantly suspicious. Had she and the Colonel planned this between them?

I said, "Let me fetch my coat," and all but ran to my room. I found paper and pen, jotted a brief message for Peregrine, telling him that I'd be back as quickly as I could, and was ushering my father out the door in short order.

Chapter Fourteen

My father had his motorcar waiting, with a familiar driver. I'd grown up knowing Simon Brandon. He'd been in and out of the house so often that my mother said that she felt he must be related. From lowly soldier-servant to my officer father, he had risen to the heights of his profession: regimental sergeant major. There were not many people who argued with him. My father was one, and I was the other.

Simon greeted me warmly, as if he hadn't seen me in many months, though I'd had lunch with him in his cottage a few days before I'd left for Kent.

He helped me into the rear seat, and my father followed me. Simon closed the door, resumed his place behind the wheel, and my father asked, "Where would you like to dine, my dear?"

"Your choice. Most of the restaurants are struggling to survive these days."

He gave Simon instructions, and we drove off. The streets were crowded, and the weather was fair for a change, though cold.

"In your haste," my father was saying, "you forgot your gloves."

I grimaced. So I had. Depend on the Colonel Sahib to notice.

"Tell me about the visit to Kent."

"It went very well. I honed my nursing skills on a man with pneumonia—who lived—and another with shell shock, who didn't."

He raised his eyebrows at that. "And how did you find the Grahams? Did they take your message in the spirit Arthur had intended?"

"I don't think they did," I said honestly. "I was disappointed in that."

"Perhaps they disagreed with young Arthur."

"It appeared they did."

"Bess."

I knew what was coming.

"You don't look well. I think Kent was perhaps too much too soon. How is the arm?"

"Healing. I can do a little more each day."

"Then if it isn't your arm that's worrying you, what is?"

Oh, yes, I could hear myself now telling my father of all people that I was harboring an escaped lunatic in my flat and that we'd had a brief journey back to Kent in each other's company to find out what had possessed him to do bloody murder when he was only fourteen.

Instead I said, "I'm learning that you can't save everyone in this world. I thought that my shell-shocked patient was convinced that he could heal. And I was wrong."

"Yes, well, sometimes there are miracles, and sometimes there are not."

Peregrine surviving had been a miracle. And I was paying for it even now.

I said, "Let's not talk about guessing wrong."

He said nothing more until we'd reached the small restaurant not far from St. Paul's. I'd been to The Regent's Table only once, and the food had been good. That was before the war.

Women had been warned that they must do their part against the Hun. That they must sacrifice their men, their comfort, their necessities, and anything that brought them pleasure. That included most foodstuffs. God knew what even the chef at such a restaurant could do with the only cuts of meat available in wartime.

Simon joined us as soon as he'd seen to the motorcar, and we enjoyed a table set in one of the windows, with a view down to the street below. My father ordered for me, and Simon made his own choices.

I'd been right. The mutton was as old as the Kaiser and nearly as difficult, but the wine sauce was exquisite.

My father waited until we were nearly finished with our meal, and then said to me, "I want to take you back to Somerset with me. Will you come? I find it hard to know what could be keeping you in London. I can understand that after such a difficult time in Owlhurst, you might need a day or two to settle yourself. Your mother wants your opinion on cuffs and collars and God knows what."

"I can't leave just at the moment," I told him. "Please don't ask me why."

"Why not? Bess, you can talk to me. Simon will leave if you wish, and you can tell me what's put those circles under your eyes and the strain in them. I'm not imagining things—and if you're fair, you'll understand my concern."

I went rapidly through all the problems facing me at the moment and chose the one least likely to worry either the Colonel Sahib or Simon Brandon.

"I want to find someone. The family of a girl who died in service nearly fifteen years ago. And I don't know how to begin."

My father's eyes met Simon's across the table. "And if I help you find this family, you'll come home with me?"

"Yes. No. I don't know. It will depend on many things."

"Does this have to do with Arthur and his message?"

"Arthur must have been all of eleven at the time Lily died," I replied, evading his question.

"I see." I don't think he did. But one could never be sure with my father.

Finally he added, "All right. Simon knows people. Give me the name of the family and we'll see what he can discover."

"I think it's hopeless. But I have to try. The girl's name was Lily.

Lily Mercer. And she was murdered in a house on Carroll Square, Number 17. I want to know what became of her family."

Simon had finished his flan. "I'll leave the motor with you, then, shall I?" he said to my father, and then to me, "I'll bring whatever I can learn to the flat. Tomorrow morning. Will that do?"

"How are you going about this?" I asked, more than a little alarmed.

He grinned. "One of the lads in the regiment is now a sergeant in the Metropolitan Police."

Before I could ask him to be circumspect, he was gone—a tall, slender man striding through the restaurant as if he were about to lead the regiment into battle.

"Who is Lily Mercer?"

I turned quickly to face my father. "Let me do what needs to be done. And afterward, I'll tell you what I can."

"I don't care to find you involved in a murder, even an old one."

"I'm not involved. I just want to know what became of this girl's family afterward. Whether they were satisfied that justice had been done."

"Why is it so important to you? Tell me that?"

"You'll learn soon enough, if Simon speaks to the police. It had to do with the Graham family."

"You told me it had nothing to do with the message you carried."

"No, I told you that Arthur was only eleven at the time."

He smiled. "You are no better at lying to me now than you were at seven."

"I don't want you taking charge and doing it all your way. I want to satisfy myself in my own fashion. I can't do anything about the past, I can't bring back the dead, but I think Arthur was—changed by what happened in Carroll Square, and perhaps he'll rest a little easier at the bottom of the sea if I finish what he never could."

"All right. That's fair enough." He signaled to the waiter, and we left the subject of Lily Mercer until we reached the street. As we walked to where Simon had left the motorcar, my father said, "We'll say nothing of this to your mother. Is that agreed?"

"Yes. Oh, yes."

"And if you should find yourself in over your head in this business, you'll remember to call in the cavalry, won't you?"

"I promise." He handed me into the motorcar, and as he walked around to the driver's side, I thought, *This is my chance.* I could tell him about Peregrine, and let him see to finishing what I'd inadvertently begun in Owlhurst.

But I couldn't. It wasn't clever to deal with a murderer, let alone a man who has spent years in an asylum. It wasn't clever to hide an armed man with a history of murder in his background. It wasn't at all clever to think I could do what I'd set out to do, alone and in the dark.

Yet if I sounded the alarm now, Peregrine would be returned to the asylum to live out his life there. And the truth would be locked away with him.

If Arthur had had any part in what had happened to Lily Mercer, I wanted to know.

He was only eleven, the little voice in my head reminded me.

Who was I to say that a child of eleven could or couldn't kill. I didn't even know if a child that age really understood the significance of killing.

I remember one summer morning in India when the box wallah came to tell the cook that his favorite grandson was dead. The boy had been bitten by a cobra that had been called out of its hole in the roots of a tree near the river by the boy's own cousin with a flute he had made for himself from a reed. It was called an accident, a tragic accident, but other children told me later what the adults hadn't known, that the cousin had been eaten up by jealousy and wanted the boy out of the way. They were both nine.

I had told my ayah, my Indian nanny, what I'd learned, but she said to me, "It was the boy's time to die, don't you see? If it hadn't been, the cobra would never have come, no matter how much the cousin had played his flute."

Her fatalism had frightened me far more than the death of the boy. It claimed that the universe I knew wasn't run by a benevolent God, as I'd been taught, but by Chance, a system where one's turn was dictated by forces over which one had no control.

My father was saying, "You must get this altruistic nature from your mother, not me."

I laughed in spite of myself. "That indicates a choice in the matter," I told him. "This wasn't so much choice as it was thrust in my face when I wasn't looking."

The Colonel dropped me at my flat.

As I watched him drive away, I wished I'd had the forethought to ask him to stay in London, within reach, and not return to Somerset just yet.

Then I turned and hurried into the flat, where Peregrine and Diana were comfortably discussing a visit she'd made to Rochester shortly before the war. But his eyes as I came through the door flicked to my face on the instant, searching for any sign of betrayal.

Diana went out that night to dine with friends, and I made dinner for Peregrine and myself.

"What did you tell your father?"

"That I was in London to discover what had become of Lily Mercer's family."

He started up, sensing betrayal.

"Sit down. I can't track them alone. Nor can you. The best chance we have is to use my father's connections. You don't know the Army, Peregrine—the regular Army. It's as tightly knit a group as the Knights Templar—or the Masons or the Catholic Church. If there's a way to find them, my father will." I had left out Simon Brandon. *Don't muddy the waters too far, my girl.*

Besides, no military plan should be without a line of retreat.

But Peregrine was nothing if not astute.

"Who was the man with your father? The one waiting with the car?"

I would have sworn, if I'd been my father's son instead of my father's daughter. As it was, I was sorely tempted.

The windows of Elayne's room looked down on the street. I had forgot.

"His batman. My father retired as a Colonel. Simon had risen to sergeant major. But they served together when my father was a lowly lieutenant, and the bond has lasted all these years. Simon drives my father, he always has."

"But he didn't drive you back here, did he?"

The temptation to swear was overwhelming now.

"He had other business to attend to. He left us while we were still in the restaurant."

Peregrine wasn't convinced, though he said nothing more. But I could feel him watching me for the rest of the evening, speculation in his eyes.

Diana left the next day, and I was grateful not to have to consider her in my dealings with Peregrine. She gave him a good-bye kiss on his cheek, though, a dancing dervish in her eyes, and blew me one, then was gone, back to France, leaving silence behind her. I saw that Peregrine was staring at the door with an unreadable expression on his face.

At teatime, Mrs. Hennessey brought up a folded note. "From your father, dear," she said.

I thanked her and read it quickly.

Lucy Mercer's family had emigrated to New Zealand soon after she was killed. Their passage had been paid for them by the Graham solicitors.

They had traded their daughter's death for a better life for themselves.

I turned to Peregrine as he came up from Elayne's room. "Not the best of news," I said, and gave him the message.

He read it and swore.

"A dead end," he said, finally.

"But it's odd, isn't it? That they should take the money offered them, and leave England on the heels of their daughter's murder."

"Desperate people. She wasn't coming back, and something good—for them, at any rate—had come of it."

"I expect so." But I couldn't rid myself of doubts. Still, I had no children, and I couldn't judge whether a grieving mother might well take the chance to better the lives of her remaining children while she could, even at the hands of the murderer's family, or whether she had been willing to sacrifice one for the good of the others, making the best of what life had brought her.

Had that been the bribe? Had the family accepted a new life in lieu of demanding that Peregrine be sent to prison? The police of course had decided Peregrine's fate, but without the Mercers demanding an eye for an eye, they might have been more easily persuaded to be lenient with a disturbed boy.

"I'm going back to Carroll Square," I said on my way to my room to fetch my coat and hat. "I'll see if anyone there still remembers Lily."

He was at the door before me, his own coat over his arm as I came out of my room.

"No, Peregrine—"

"Yes. They aren't going to know me, for God's sake. Why shouldn't I accompany you?"

Reluctantly I let him come with me. We found a cab and arrived at Number 17 as a few early flakes of snow began to fall.

An elderly maid answered our knock, and I asked her if there was anyone still employed in this house who remembered a maid here some fourteen years ago, by the name of Lily Mercer.

She stared at me for a moment, and said, "You must ask Mrs. Talbot, Miss."

And so it was that we were admitted to the presence of Mrs.

Talbot, a formidably fat woman in her later years, swathed in shawls and seated like a toad in the largest chair in a very fashionable drawing room. Her trim feet rested on a stool.

She had an eye for Peregrine and asked him where he'd been wounded.

"On the Somme," he said, but didn't elaborate.

She nodded. "Indeed. I lost a son at Mons and another at Ypres. I didn't want to live myself, at first, but it's not in my nature to die. Which of my many committees and sponsorships brings you to my door tonight?"

"I'm afraid it's none of them, Mrs. Talbot. We're trying to find anyone who might have known a young woman by the name of Lily Mercer. She worked here in this house as an upstairs maid for a time some fourteen years ago."

"And why do you wish to find this young person?" Mrs. Talbot asked, her eyes narrowing. "Is it in her interest or yours, this search?"

"Mine," I admitted. "I never knew Lily Mercer. But her family moved to New Zealand, and so I'm unable to contact them. I was hoping one of your present staff might remember her. Lieutenant Philips is as interested as I am to learn more about the girl. One of his friends was accused of harming her, you see, and I'd like to know if it is true, or if he was falsely accused."

We had discussed in the cab coming here what to admit to and what not.

Mrs. Talbot considered us a moment, then picked up the silver bell at her elbow. The maid who had admitted us answered the summons. Mrs. Talbot sent the maid belowstairs to question the staff.

Mrs. Talbot, meanwhile, turned her attention to me.

"You are doing nothing to help with the war, Miss Crawford?"

I could see myself leaving here as part of any number of committees, or dispatched to Hampshire to grow vegetables on the lawns of some great estate.

"I was serving on *Britannic*, Mrs. Talbot, when she went down, and my arm was broken when she was struck. I can't return to duty until it's fully healed."

She nodded approvingly. At that moment there was a tap at the door, and the maid was back.

"There's the laundress, Mrs. Talbot. She remembers the young person in question."

"Then bring her here."

"If you'll forgive me, she might be more comfortable speaking to us in the servants' hall," I suggested quickly.

But Mrs. Talbot wouldn't hear of it. "Nonsense. Bring her here, Mattie."

And in due course, Mattie returned with the laundress. She might have been young and pretty fourteen years ago, but hard work had toughened her skin and reddened her hands and taken away her youth.

Her name, Mattie informed us, was Daisy.

"Hallo, Daisy," I said. "It's kind of you to speak to us. We're concerned about Lily Mercer. Did you know her?"

"She's dead," Daisy answered bluntly. She was clearly ill at ease.

"Yes, I know that. But as her family has left England, I'm hoping to find someone who can tell me a little about her."

"We was employed here, when this house was let to visitors to London. That was when Mr. Horner owned it, and didn't want to live here anymore. He said it was haunted by his wife's ghost. Which is absurd, o' course. But he believed it. And so we stayed on as staff, those that chose to stay, and went with the house, so to speak. When Mr. Horner died of his grief, the house was sold to Mrs. Talbot's brother, and then she inherited it from him."

"What happened to the rest of the staff?"

"Some stayed. Others gave in their notice."

"Tell me about Lily?"

"There's nothing to tell. She died here—" Her eyes slid toward Mrs. Talbot's face. "And soon after, her family went away. Like you said."

I tried another approach, but Daisy remained tight-lipped. I was surprised that she'd even admitted she knew Lily. I thought it likely that curiosity had got the better of her, and she was here to satisfy it. Or see if there was anything in it for herself?

"Speak up, Daisy, the lady and the gentleman want to hear what you have to say."

But Daisy stuck to her story, and that was that.

We thanked Mrs. Talbot after she was dismissed, and Mattie came to see us to the door.

"Damn!" Peregrine said as it shut behind us.

The snow was a little thicker, but not intending to last. I thought the temperature had eased up a very little.

We were about to walk toward the corner in search of a cab when the tradesman's door opened and closed quietly, and there was Daisy, a shawl thrown over her head, coming quickly toward us.

"Miss!"

I stopped, my hand on Peregrine's arm. "Daisy?"

"Yes, Miss. I'm sorry, but we were all sworn to secrecy when Lily died. Mr. Horner didn't want the story getting about, scaring off people wanting to let the house for the Season. I couldn't tell Mrs. Talbot, could I?"

"No, of course not." I looked around, searching for somewhere we could stand and talk without freezing to death. But there was no place except the square and we didn't have a key.

"Did you like Lily?" I asked, trying to learn as much as possible while Daisy was in the mood to talk to us. But she hesitated, and I said, "There's five pounds for you, as a reward for helping us."

Her eyes lit with avarice. "Thank you, Miss, I could use the money."

I took a five-pound note from my purse but held on to it.

Daisy said, her words coming quickly, "She didn't just die here, did she? She was murdered. The staff had the evening off, except for Lily, who was set to looking after the little boys. But she was to meet the young man she was walking out with, and she wasn't happy about missing him. Still, she went upstairs to see the lads to bed. It was the last time I saw her. She hadn't come back down again, by the time I was leaving. Later we heard that one of the lads had killed her, that he'd used his pocketknife on her, mutilating her something fierce. But I don't see how that can be, do you? A pocketknife? He must have come down to the kitchen for something larger. At any rate, the family left London sudden-like, and Mr. Horner paid off any of us that wanted to leave, but swore us all to secrecy. Bad for business, he said. That's what murder was." She finished, eyeing the five-pound note.

"What was Lily like?"

"She was always out for herself. Always looking to better herself. She'd study the photographs in the London *Gazette,* and carry herself like them, head up, back straight, and copy their style of clothes for her day off. Silk purse out o' a sow's ear, that's what it was, and her telling me that my hands were too big and my fingers too thick. And how was I to help that, I ask you, when I was the laundress!" Her grievance might have been old but it was fresh. "She had a temper too."

"Was Lily good to the children in her care?"

Daisy shrugged. "I can't say. But I remember one of the lads leaned over the upstairs railing one day and called her a nasty name, and she told him he was a monster and God would see to him one day."

I could feel Peregrine stirring beside me.

"Which one? Do you remember?"

"Lord if I know," she said, "*I* was never abovestairs. We come home at eleven that night, as we was told to do, to be ready for church service the next morning, and there was police everywhere, and Mrs. Graham crying as if she'd never stop, and Mr. Graham was pacing, his face black as Satan, and I don't know where the lads were, but I heard they'd been clapped up in their rooms. I came to the servants' door to bring hot water to the housekeeper, and I could hear Mrs. Graham begging them not to take her son from her."

Mr. Graham—Peregrine's father—was long dead by that time. It must have been Robert who was pacing.

"Do you remember anything else?" I asked.

"They said someone had cleaned away most of the blood before the police got there. That was strange, wasn't it, but Mrs. Graham claimed she couldn't have the poor girl seen like that, it was indecent and horrid. All I know is, there was three sheets missing, the next time I counted the wash, and I got the blame for ruining them and hiding it."

"Did you go to the services for Lily? Did you see her family there? How did they take their daughter's death?"

"There wasn't no one but her mother, her sister, and her brother. There was no church service that I heard of. And I asked." She was stamping her feet against the cold now, and casting anxious glances at the door behind her, as if half afraid someone would see her talking with us. "It was the talk of the servants' hall. Everyone felt she didn't deserve to be abandoned like she was, by her own family. I heard they went out to New Zealand before she was hardly cold. If it had been my daughter, now, I'd have had her ashes and taken her with me."

"Perhaps they did," I said. Part of the agreement with the Graham solicitor, to remove all traces of the girl, even a gravestone?

I couldn't imagine such thoroughness to protect Peregrine, already in the asylum. It would make more sense if the murderer had been Arthur.

I gave the woman the five-pound note, and she bobbed her head, thanking me, and quietly opened the door. With a glance into the passage behind her, she said, "I said I didn't know one boy from the other, and it's true. But the one that killed her, he was the apple of his mother's eye. It like to have killed her too."

✦ ✦ ✦

Waiting for a cab, Daisy's voice echoed in my ears. ". . . He was the apple of his mother's eye . . ."

Even under great stress, I couldn't envision Mrs. Graham referring to her stepson in that fashion. But she had called Arthur her favorite.

Stop now, I told myself. Arthur's dead, and what good will it do to bring down his reputation now? He can't be punished, and if there's judgment beyond the grave, he's long since been judged.

But what about the man beside me? He would never have his freedom or his reputation restored.

Jonathan I could accept as a murderer. Wasn't that odd? His callousness was only too evident, and for all I knew about murderers, that must count as one of the indications that a man could kill. But he was a soldier now, and bitter, and disillusioned. He might have been very different before the war.

Peregrine spoke, startling me.

"I was never the apple of her eye. . . ."

"What was she to tell the police, then? That she welcomed her stepson as a murderer?" My voice was harsher than I had expected.

He looked down at me. "You don't want it to be anyone else."

"You told me you didn't doubt that you'd killed that poor girl."

"So I did. I still don't doubt it. But it would be comforting in the dark of the night to think that someone believed in *me.*"

I felt the blow of that comment almost physically. "I'm sorry—"

"But you aren't, are you? You're afraid that it might have been Arthur, and you were half in love with my brother, weren't you?"

"No. But I was fond enough of him to want to believe he couldn't have killed anyone." Even as I spoke the words, I was ashamed.

He reached into the pocket of his coat and brought out something that caught the light from the nearest streetlamp.

It was the pistol. It had been there all along, and I had almost stopped believing in it.

"It wasn't Jonathan's. I lied to you there. It was in the pocket of the good doctor's coat. I think he was afraid of us, his patients. And so he went armed, in case."

"But that's disgusting! A doctor would never—"

"You haven't spent a great deal of time in a madhouse, have you? Barton's Asylum has a locked ward where the most dangerous patients are kept. I was there, in the beginning. Until Dr. Sinclair ordered me to be moved to another floor where I was kept in a locked room by myself. Do you have any idea what it was like for a fourteen-year-old boy to be at the mercy of what must surely have been the most depraved men? I fought one off one night, screaming for help, and help never came. That's when I gave up all hope."

If that was true, I thought, then Peregrine Graham had been lucky to come out of that place sane.

He was holding out the weapon to me. "Take it. I was going to use it on myself, if they tried to return me to Barton's."

"I don't want it. Put it away, Peregrine, before someone sees it!"

I could tell he was smiling, a flash of white teeth under the shadow of his cap. But not in amusement. The pistol disappeared. "Yes, of course. I might still need to shoot Mrs. Hennessey."

There was such bitterness in his voice that I said, "I'm not about to carry a weapon in my pocket—besides, the pocket isn't big enough. When we are back at the flat—"

"What are we to do now? Will you call your father, or the police?"

"No, this isn't finished. I'm going back to Owlhurst, and I'm going to see the rector's journals."

"Not alone. I'm going with you. What have I to lose?"

CHAPTER FIFTEEN

GETTING THERE WAS easier said than done. Once more we hired Mr. Owens and his motorcar to drive us from Tonbridge to Owlhurst. As we passed Barton's Asylum, I could see Peregrine's shoulders tense. He was in the seat beside Mr. Owens, and it was another five miles before he relaxed again.

I directed Mr. Owens to the hotel in Owlhurst, a part of the little village I hadn't seen before. The Rose and Thorn was a small Georgian hotel with a handsome reception and lounge where two or three other travelers were enjoying their tea.

No one took note of the young soldier with me, and we were given two rooms overlooking the street.

My intention was to visit the rector, and ask him to let me borrow the journals to read in my room, which I could then share with Peregrine. And so I walked down the High Street toward the church, my mind on what to say to him to explain this sudden reappearance.

And the first person I encountered was the doctor.

Dr. Philips stopped in his tracks.

"Am I dreaming?" he asked with a smile. "I never expected to see you again. We used you terribly, didn't we?"

"I was only doing my duty," I said lightly. "How is Sally Booker?"

"Her mother took her to visit a cousin in Oxford. Probably for the best. What brings you back again? The Grahams?"

"I've come on my own account, actually. Did you hear about Peregrine Graham's escape?"

"My God, yes. The village was in turmoil. The general thinking was, he would come here to wreak havoc on his family. Jonathan was as grim as I'd ever seen him, and Owlhurst was combed by the police. It was thought Peregrine might try to live in the wood where the owls are. That proved to be a false lead. A watch was kept on the house. And then word came that he'd gone to Dover. They lost track of him there. One young soldier went missing, and it was thought that he'd been killed for his uniform and that Peregrine had reached France, posing as the missing man. But then that soldier turned up—apparently he'd had second thoughts at the last minute and gone to Canterbury to wed his sweetheart there before embarking. Later a body washed ashore, rather decomposed, but Jonathan went to identify it anyway. He couldn't be sure it was Peregrine, or so I was told. But the hunt was called off. The police had other matters demanding their attention, and the feeling was, the poor man couldn't have survived very long in this weather, out in the open. In his shoes, I wouldn't have gone back to the asylum, once out of it. And the sea is merciful."

"That's a very compassionate opinion."

"Is it? That's the way Ted Booker chose."

"Did they actually declare Peregrine dead?" I asked, thinking what that might mean to the living Peregrine.

"With reservations. Until new information comes along."

"Oh."

"You said Peregrine brought you here?"

For an instant I was so stunned, I couldn't speak. Then I realized that Dr. Philips had drawn conclusions from the direction the conversation had taken.

"Actually I wanted to ask the rector a question. Nothing to do with the Grahams." At least, not directly . . . it wasn't a complete fabrication.

"I promise I won't drag you to my surgery every other day. At least not this visit. We've got a new nurse, an older woman who seems to be steady as a rock. And thank God for that."

He had turned to walk with me toward the rectory, and after a moment he said, "Speaking of reservations. I must admit I've got my own about Ted Booker's death. I've kept that to myself. I'd appreciate it if you did the same."

I stopped in the middle of the street, right in front of a woman pushing twins in a pram. "Reservations. That's a strong word."

"Look, come and have tea with me, will you? There's no one I can speak to here, without stirring up the devil of a fuss, and I can't afford to do that. But you'll leave Owlhurst, and carry my secrets safely away with you." The last he said with a quirk of an eyebrow, and laughed.

"Back to war, you mean."

We went into the little tea shop within sight of the hotel and ordered tea and small sandwiches.

"I've not had my breakfast," Dr. Philips said ruefully. "Another lying-in. I can almost count on a baby arriving nine months after the soldier husband came home on leave. And this one was an eight months' wonder. Still, it had his father's nose, according to the fond grandmother, and who am I to tell the world otherwise?"

When the tea had come and we were alone in the corner of the shop, watching the cold wind bowl down the street in gusts that had men clamping a hand on their hats and women's skirts blowing about their ankles, Dr. Philips began in a low voice, "Do you remember the smudged footprint I saw in the passage the morning I found Ted Booker dead?"

"Yes. I do."

"I've given a great deal of thought to that footprint. And it worries me."

I told him about the conversation I'd had with Jonathan, but he shrugged it off. "All the more reason, if Booker was asleep, to wonder about this print. I have come to the conclusion that Mrs. Denton, Sally's mother, must have come to see him, and she distressed him to the point that he finished the botched job."

"Oh, dear God." I remembered my conversation with Mrs. Denton, and I thought she might well have come and undone all the good I'd felt I'd accomplished. Or had I simply been congratulating myself over my skills, and not seen the fact that Ted Booker was trying to put my mind at ease, not the other way around?

"I can't believe—I mean, that's tantamount to murder!" I whispered.

Dr. Philips looked around, then said softly, "I doubt she knew what the outcome could have been."

"But she'd watched him for weeks—she'd seen how fragile his state of mind was—she *did* know. She told me that both her daughter and her grandson would be better off if Ted had blown his head off with that shotgun."

"Yes, but what am I to do about this?" Dr. Philips asked, leaning back in his chair, lines of worry etching his face in the pale light from the windows. "Do I go to the police? What if I'm wrong? I've caused trouble for her for nothing. And it wouldn't do my own reputation here any good. A good many people sympathized with Sally and her mother. They knew Booker could be violent, and they forgot he was a soldier who had been wounded in spirit rather than flesh."

"Did you speak to the rector?"

"No. He's not—worldly?—and would feel obliged to go to Mrs. Denton and pray over the state of her soul. What good would that do either of them?"

"I take your point," I answered slowly. "And you can't go to the police." I sighed and watched a small boy racing down the street, spirits high as he and his dog chased a goose that had escaped from the farmer's wife lumbering in their wake. "Ted Booker is dead.

Nothing is going to bring him back again. And he'd probably refuse to come, even if by some miracle he could be offered the chance. And Sally is probably better off. She'd never learn to cope with his moodiness, even if he tried to heal."

"Are you saying I should just keep my mouth shut and try to forget this whole business?"

"No, of course you can't do either. But since the only proof is a footprint that was there then and now isn't, there's nothing concrete to support your suspicion. And you did give testimony at the inquest that Ted Booker was not in his right mind. You'd be changing that, in a sense. I don't see that you can accomplish anything by raising the issue. In time, Mrs. Denton's conscience might get the best of her."

"A deathbed confession? I was hoping you might have a brilliant idea I could use," he said. "I've exhausted even my own patience."

"If Mrs. Denton meant no harm," I said, "then while it was foolish to visit Ted so soon after his attempt at suicide, she might have wanted assurances." I added, "However glad she might be now, to have him dead, it will come to haunt her."

But Dr. Philips was more realistic. "I doubt it. Well, I've burdened you, and neither of us has come up with a solution. Still, I'm relieved in a way. It helps to talk through one's troubles."

I wished I could talk through my own. But I dared not tell this man that the missing Peregrine Graham was alive and probably standing at a window not fifty yards from where we sat.

He paid for our tea and he saw me as far as the rectory before returning to his surgery.

The rector was quite surprised to find me at his door. He offered me tea, but I refused as politely as I could.

"What brings you here, my dear? I know a troubled spirit when I see it. If I can help—"

"I've been thinking," I said, careful how I began, "about the journals your predecessor kept. Do you think—would you mind if I read them? I attended Peregrine Graham when he was ill, and now they tell me he's dead. It would do no harm if I learned more about the crime that put him where he was."

"They reported that he'd stolen a pistol from the asylum," the rector said, "and they feel he must have used it on himself. How sad. I asked Mrs. Graham if perhaps she would consider a memorial of some sort—a private service, a marker in the churchyard, whatever might suit the family. But she felt that it would be rather—a reminder of something the family preferred to leave as a closed subject."

"You mean the family didn't wish to inter the—er—remains?"

"Jonathan Graham couldn't be sure, you see. I expect Mrs. Graham felt that a memorial would be rather—premature."

And the family of Lily Mercer had been paid to emigrate to New Zealand. I wondered suddenly if they had prospered there, or if the change had made them wretched.

"I can appreciate the Graham family's feelings, though I don't share in them," I replied. "But for the sake of my own conscience, I'd like to know why I felt that the man I treated had—er—paid for his sins and deserved credit for that."

"I see." He hesitated. "The journals were solely for the purpose of guidance. I'm reluctant to take a broader view of my charge to keep them private."

"And private they should remain. I'll be taking up my new assignment shortly, and there's no harm I could do, surely—even inadvertently."

After a moment he went up the stairs and I sat there, looking across the churchyard to what I could see of the Graham house. Timothy limped through the gate at the far end of the churchyard and paused for a moment at a fresh grave, the earth still raw, waiting for spring to give it new life. And then he went back the way he'd come.

Ted Booker's grave? Or a friend who'd died in the war? At this distance, it was hard to tell.

The rector returned with several bound books in his hands and said, "These cover a longer period before and after the time you're interested in. But short of tearing out the pages, there is little I can do but to trust to your good faith."

"It won't be misplaced, I promise you."

After a few more minutes of conversation, he gave me a small case to carry the books, and I took my leave.

He saw me to the door, and I could feel him gazing after me as I walked back the way I'd come.

Peregrine must have seen me walking in his direction, and as I waited to cross the High Street he must have come to meet me, because I found him waiting at the top of the hotel stairs, his gaze going directly to the box under my arm. I shook my head, and he followed me in silence to my room, where we pulled the tea table to the window and I opened the box.

The bound books were a little musty, as if they'd been stored on a study shelf for years.

I opened the first, after asking Peregrine if he knew the date of the murder. And of course he did, it was seared in his memory forever. But the volume I opened was a later date, and so I tried the second in the stack.

It covered the right period. I skimmed over comments about the births and deaths and marriages of various Owlhurst inhabitants, about the business of the parish, and a brief record of whatever had happened on a particular date that was notable. I saw that the owner of The Rose and Thorn had died and his son had taken over management of the hotel, that the man who cleaned the stained glass in the church had fallen to his death one morning, as his ladder tipped over. Many rectors were amateur historians, more passionate than trained, and their privately published works were often very readable.

Moving on, I came to the comment "Mrs. Graham departed for London this morning, and I shall have my choice of the offertory hymn while she is away. Very kind of her." I thought that last was a dry commentary rather than an expression of real gratitude.

I was already learning that the rector, Mr. Craig, had a tendency toward tongue-in-cheek remarks. And so I was prepared to see an additional remark on the first Sunday of her absence, where he wrote, "The service went smoothly and there were several people who spoke kindly about the anthem. If I were a betting man . . ."

I interpreted that to mean that the people who spoke kindly would also say something to Mrs. Graham on her return.

There were more entries, and then a lapse of a day, and when the writer took up his pen again, it was with shock and disbelief.

The most ghastly thing has happened. Mrs. Graham returned from London, bringing her sons with her, and she asked me if I would keep Peregrine at the Rectory, under lock and key, while she spoke to Inspector Gadd and Lady Parsons. I could see that the entire family was in great distress, and I was grateful when Robert Douglas offered to take the other boys home and see them put to bed. He came back after that was accomplished, expecting to find Mrs. Graham here, but she hadn't returned. I asked him what in the name of God had brought them back to Kent in such a state, for I had also seen the bloody clothing Peregrine wore, and no one had thought to bring the child a change. Douglas told me that he and Mrs. Graham had returned from a dinner party to find no servants in the house. They went in search of the housemaid and finally came upon her in her own quarters. And Peregrine was there as well, striving to remove a knife from the poor girl's throat. It was his pocketknife, a handsome large one that had belonged to his father. The girl was quite dead. The only conclusion, considering his condition, was that he must have killed the girl in some fit or other. He'd never been well, but no one had ever expected such a turn of events, and the police asked Peregrine what he was about. He said he wanted his knife back, and that the girl wouldn't give it to him. After much discussion and consideration, the London police agreed that the boy should be admitted to an asylum as soon as feasible, and that trying him, with his limited range of understanding and emotional response, would be difficult. I have never seen a child so ill and shocked as he was—he hardly knew where he was or why, and though Lady Parsons had questioned him most forcefully, he was in no state to answer her. Inspector Gadd took Peregrine into my study and questioned him privately but had no more success than Lady Parsons. The doctor had come in the meantime, and he was in agreement that this boy was both exhausted and in a state bordering on catatonic. It was nearing morning, and Douglas took Mrs. Graham and the doctor to Barton's, to speak with the staff there. Before noon, Douglas returned with the doctor, who had prescribed a sedative for Mrs. Graham and left her at her house to rest. The two men then took the dazed lad into the carriage, and I never saw him again.

And then in an addendum dated some weeks later:

On several occasions, I went to the asylum to offer pastoral care to Peregrine Graham, and I was told that the doctors had determined that it was best if he continued the regimen of care they had devised, and that the chaplain at the asylum would see to the lad's spiritual needs. I have no such faith in Mr. Newcome, and although I spoke to Mrs. Graham about this, she told me that the London police had told her that Peregrine shouldn't have visitors of any sort. I left it there, though I was very distressed. The other Graham boys have seemed to come through this nightmare with few scars, but Arthur was very subdued when first he came home from London. Some time afterward, he was sent away to school, and I saw him only on holidays.

I thumbed through some twenty ensuing pages, but there was nothing more about Peregrine Graham.

I was disappointed that the rector had only been able to describe events as he was told them by the Grahams, but his remark about Arthur cut me to the quick. Subdued . . .

Peregrine read the sections again. "I don't recall much about any of this, I was half sick and too dazed to take in what was happening to me."

"Had you been sedated—given anything to calm you?"

"I don't know, I hardly remember my conversations with the police. My stepmother brought me a cup of sweet tea that made me drowsy. Still, I can recall that Inspector Gadd was very kind. He asked me why I had done such a thing, and then again, what Lily had done to me that made me want to harm her. I could only stare at him, but he didn't shout as the London police did. He put his hand on my knee, and told me not to worry, that I would be all right. But I wasn't, was I?"

I was nearly sure that Peregrine had been drugged. To keep him quiet on the journey to London, and while he was there, so he wouldn't trouble anyone. But then why take him? There had been the excuse of seeing a doctor, but nothing had come of it. I was left with the only logical answer. If he was left at home alone with only the servants, someone might have discovered that the public view of Peregrine Graham was not the real truth.

Whatever my feelings about Mrs. Graham, this was a horrible supposition, that she would have treated her stepson so cruelly. But then I remembered something else—something Peregrine had told me.

He had found his stepmother in bed with her cousin Robert Douglas.

I sat back in my chair.

"My good God," I whispered.

Peregrine looked at me. "What is it?"

"I—it's nothing. Just—look, I need to be by myself for a while. Do you mind?"

"I'd like to take these to my room and read the passage again. Is that all right?"

"Yes, of course. I'm tired, Peregrine, that's all."

I thought he saw through me, but he turned and went to his room, and I sat there staring out the window, not seeing the traffic in and out of the shops, not seeing the sun fade behind gray clouds, looking inward at something rather terrible.

Peregrine believed that Jonathan or Timothy—or both—were the sons of the liaison between Mrs. Graham and her cousin Robert Douglas.

Was Timothy's clubfoot the mark of that liaison? I had no idea if a clubfoot was a result of inbreeding. But it might be, for all I knew. It might also run in families.

I tried to picture each of the sons in turn. That got me nowhere. I hadn't been looking for indications of their ancestry when I was speaking to them face-to-face. But even if they weren't Robert's off-spring, Mrs. Graham might have been so frightened that Peregrine would tell his father what he'd seen, she'd done her best to destroy his credibility. And what better way to do that than by indicating he wasn't really right in the head? However cruel that was, it would be nothing to what she might have done years later to protect her own child and blame Peregrine for a crime he hadn't committed.

Everyone agreed she had been terribly distressed by the death of Lily Mercer—and she'd paid the girl's family handsomely to leave England. Would she have felt so strongly about protecting Peregrine, or gone to such lengths to hide what had been done? She had kept him out of prison, not from kindness but because his brothers would have suffered the shame of being related to a murderer. And I hardly thought Mrs. Graham was the first person to send an un-wanted family member to an asylum. Little better than a prison in some ways, it could at least provoke a measure of sympathy for the family of the afflicted.

I thought about the young Prince John who had had seizures, and how he'd been removed from the public eye very quietly, until he'd been nearly forgotten. Mrs. Graham had succeeded in doing much the same with Peregrine.

I was still trying to understand the full impact of my thinking when there was a knock at the door. It was Peregrine, and he held one of the rector's journals in his hand.

"I think you ought to read this," he said, and walked into my room.

I took the book and carried it to the window, reluctant to turn up the lamp. Peregrine followed me and pointed to an entry some years after the murder of Lily Mercer.

I read it quickly, and then again.

Inspector Gadd died this morning in spite of everything the doctor could do to save him. He had gone very early to one of the outlying farms to investigate a rash of small fires and other destruction that had been plaguing Herbert Meadowes for several weeks. The inspector had hoped to catch the culprit in the act, and was lying in wait for him. He must have seen the culprit and given chase, but as he tried to climb the stile, a blood vessel in his brain burst from the effort he was making, and he died where he fell. Meadowes found him there some hours later. God be with him, he was a good man.

I turned to Peregrine. "I don't understand. What does this have to do with your situation?"

"None. Except that I know Jonathan boasted that he'd raided Herbert Meadowes's henhouse for eggs, and not been caught. 'He thought it was a fox,' he told me, 'I'm as sly as a fox.' And Arthur had said, 'That's not brave. You must give him a fair chance to catch you. You must do it three times.' This was in London."

"And how did Jonathan answer him?"

"He didn't. I think he was put out. Timothy taunted him too, saying, 'No, it must be six times, to be fair.' And Arthur said, 'Six it is, then.' Timothy asked him, 'When will you try? When we go back to Owlhurst?' But Arthur answered him, 'Not then. When I'm ready.'"

"But that's not proof of anything. Boys boast, striving not to be outdone." Even the young subalterns under my father's command took foolish risks and accepted dares, to prove they were brave. More than one was given a dressing-down for imprudent conduct. Come to that, I'd heard my father and Simon Brandon wager on the outcome of a fight between a mongoose and a cobra.

"But no one came forward to admit to being there. And no one got help for the inspector, when he went down."

For fear of being punished for trespassing.

"You're telling me that Arthur did this?"

"No. Now read this."

He held out another diary, and I saw that it was some six months after Inspector Gadd had died.

> Doctor Hadley coming home from the bedside of Daniel Furston died when a startled horse ran away with his carriage, overturned it, and threw him out on the roadside, where he broke his neck. He was a good man. We shall miss him. God rest his soul.

"I don't know, Peregrine, you're leaping to conclusions. Accidents happen—"

"Read this."

He had marked another passage in that same diary.

Lady Parsons had had a close call. She had been out riding in the woods where the owls lived, when her horse stumbled and rolled on her.

> She broke her collarbone, her right arm, and her right leg in the fall, and the wonder was, she wasn't killed outright.

So ran the rector's account.

"No, Peregrine, you're trying to make connections that aren't there."

"Indeed." He retrieved the book from my hand and left the room with a final comment. "I lost track of events here in Owlhurst. These journals make for interesting reading."

I thought, *He's playing mind games. He offered me that pistol, knowing I wouldn't take it then or later. He's trying to show me other deaths that he couldn't possibly have been responsible for. He knows I suspect Arthur, though. And that will be his salvation.*

I returned the journals to the rector just after dusk had fallen. He thanked me formally, and then asked, "Have these set your mind at rest?"

"They were very informative. While I was a guest in her house, I could hardly ask Mrs. Graham to relive what must have been a very painful past. And Peregrine Graham was too ill to tell me anything, even if I'd asked. I don't much care for mysteries; I just used whatever skill I possessed to see him well again."

"And the same for Ted Booker, I think. Only he was beyond human help."

"Sadly," I agreed.

"I'm glad you came to see me, my dear Miss Crawford. It's why I am here."

"Tell me," I asked, "how did the man who wrote these die?"

His eyebrows went up. "Are you suggesting he wasn't in his right mind when he made his entries here?"

"No, no. I just—I felt I came to know him, a little, through his words. I was told that he had nearly worn himself out, caring for his flock."

"That's true. He was in the church one morning, and went up into the pulpit to find something he'd left there. He tripped over his own feet and went down the stairs headfirst. He lived for several months afterward but hardly knew where he was or what had happened to him. It was a blessing for him when he died. He wouldn't have wanted to linger. He'd put a note with these journals years earlier, that they should go to his successor for guidance. A very thoughtful gesture."

I said, "An unfortunate mishap. Like the burst blood vessel that killed Inspector Gadd, like the carriage overturning and killing the doctor. The fall that injured Lady Parsons so badly. Have there been other incidents of this nature since the war began?"

He pursed his lips, thinking. "In fact, no. Unless you count young Peter Mason. But that's ridiculous—"

"What happened to him?"

"He was swimming in the pond on his father's farm, when he apparently got a cramp. He drowned. Arthur was at home, just before being sent to France, and he and his brothers swam in that murky water looking for the body. Jonathan found it, but it was hours too late. He was a promising lad, Peter was, and my first service for one so young."

I thanked him and said good-bye. But I couldn't go back to the hotel straightaway. There was too much on my mind. Peregrine's doing.

I walked in the wood where the owls nested. The trees were tall and sturdy, the last of the ancient forest that had once covered this part of Kent. The forest that had stood at Harold's back in the Battle of Hastings, on the main track that led from the sea to London.

I counted. Inspector Gadd. Lady Parsons. The doctor. The rector. But surely not the boy Peter. Without him, Lily Mercer made five.

Six, Timothy had suggested, and Arthur agreed. But that was six times taunting the farmer Meadowes, to give him the chance to catch the culprit. Not six murders. Or near murders, if we counted Lady Parsons among them.

But to look at it another way, six opportunities for the police to catch their man. And Peregrine locked away in his room at the asylum could only have been blamed for one of them.

It was dark under the trees, but peaceful. A little wind rustled the dry, bare branches, and once I thought I heard an owl glide past me, after other prey. They are silent, owls are, as they fly, but there's something, a disturbance in the air, a sixth sense, that catches one's attention sometimes.

It was time to turn back. I was nearly out of the wood when someone stepped from the shadow of a tree trunk and confronted me.

I drew in a breath, I was so startled, and he could hear that. He laughed, and then my eyes adjusted to the barest glimmer of ambient light, and I saw that it was Timothy Graham.

"It is you," he said then. "I thought I saw you walking toward the wood, but I told myself it was impossible. What brings you back to Owlhurst?"

"You gave me such a fright!" I declared.

"Guilty conscience, I'll be bound."

That was too close to the mark for comfort. I laughed, more an admission than a denial, I was certain.

"I—a personal matter brought me back. And so I stayed the night. But I'm leaving tomorrow."

He fell in step beside me. "I saw you coming from the rectory. If I were to guess, I'd say it was Ted Booker who has been on your mind."

"I'd rather not discuss Lieutenant Booker."

"You tried to help him. I think it was unfinished business on Ted's account."

I answered. "Sometimes when you try to save a patient, and you fail—even if it isn't your fault, you still take it more personally than you should."

"As you did in Arthur's case."

Surprised, I answered, "In a way, yes. He sent me here with a message, and I felt honor bound to bring it. However it might be received."

"I can understand that." He hesitated, then asked, "What did you make of Arthur? I don't mean what you told my mother, but what you really felt?"

"He was a good patient. We often talked—I'd be coming off my shift, and I'd stop by his cot and he'd tell me what he'd been reading. Or I would tell him about some part of my day. He was restless, his foot hurting him like the very devil, and I knew that any distraction was welcomed."

"Did he talk to you about Owlhurst or his family?"

"Only in the most general terms. You see, the wounded often live in the present, because they've been very badly frightened, even if they refuse to admit it. And so they hold on to the present. The past is still too—I don't know—precious."

"Did he tell you about his brothers?"

"I knew he had three, and no sisters. That was all."

"Not that I was lame, or that Jonathan has a cold streak in him that I've never fathomed, and I doubt if Arthur did either? Or that Peregrine had been clapped up for murder?"

"In a hospital ward, with other ears hearing every word, men seldom bring up such personal things. I knew Jonathan was also in the army—I heard Arthur telling someone that."

"Yet you came all this way . . ."

"I made a promise, Mr. Graham. I have told you."

"And so you'd have traveled to Yorkshire, if a patient asked you to."

"Kent was much easier. But yes. I'd have tried."

He nodded. "Yes, that's honorable. I'm angry that I'm not allowed to join the army. I resent the bonds that soldiers share. Arthur and Jonathan wrote often to each other, but less often to me. Or to my mother. It was as if we didn't exist because we weren't *there*."

I could sympathize with what he was saying. My father, during his years as a commanding officer, cared for his men like a stern but loving father. I doubt they saw it that way, especially those who felt the sharp edge of his tongue, but my mother and I did. We sometimes felt pangs of jealousy, and my mother would say, "I married a regiment, my dear. If you are looking for single-minded love, find yourself someone in civilian life. A nice banker, perhaps."

I said to Timothy Graham, "I think it isn't so much the bond between soldiers as the fear that to tell the truth to those one loves would be too painful, and so letters must be brief, before other things spill over. I've written to wives and sweethearts and mothers, putting down what I'm told to write, and even knowing it for kind lies, I add nothing of what I know."

There was the young Welshman who assured his mother that the trenches were quite comfortable, despite what she read in the newspapers, and that he had clean sheets and a good pillow for his bed.

"Did Jonathan tell you about Peregrine?"

"No. Your mother did, when I was asked to care for him. You were there."

"I'm surprised you could bear to be in the same room with him."

"A nurse is only concerned with the health of a patient. I wasn't there to judge Peregrine Graham, only to heal him."

"What did he tell you?"

"He was so ill. I think once he asked me why I was there—he thought I must be Arthur's wife—and again he asked where he was, and I told him. He had to fight for every breath, even to tell me whether he felt like drinking more broth, or if he needed another pillow to help ease the coughing. And I was far too busy to worry about what he might have done years before." It was such a narrow line between truth and falsehood.

Timothy nodded. "I didn't want to see him. None of us did. He was the painful past, come creeping back. I wouldn't recognize him if he spoke to me on the street. He must have changed beyond recognition. It explains why he killed himself. I wouldn't have wanted to be shut away, as he was."

"No." We had reached the churchyard wall, and he opened the gate for me.

"I'm glad Arthur had someone with him at the end. It must be rather frightening to die alone. I can't imagine it, to tell you the truth."

I went through the gate, and after closing it, he turned toward his home. Then he came back to me. "I won't mention the fact that I saw you. I can do that much for Booker. And his death did me no good. Mrs. Denton took Sally away with her, and it may be months before she's home again."

"Just as well," I said. "She has a great deal of healing to do before she thinks about any future."

"You're a wise woman, Elizabeth Crawford, did anyone ever tell you that?"

I smiled but didn't answer. And he was gone, limping across the uneven, winter-dead grass in the churchyard.

Chapter Sixteen

Peregrine was waiting for me, and I said as I reached the head of the stairs, "I walked in the wood for a time, and Timothy saw me there. I came back as soon as I could."

He was silent. We went down the passage to the door of my room and paused by common consent.

I hadn't told him what I'd learned about his disappearance and possible death. I couldn't have said why, except that it had erased Peregrine's identity, and I wasn't sure it was for the best to tell him that. He could take passage now to half a dozen countries that wouldn't ask too many questions, he could create his own past, and walk away from Peregrine Graham. Would he be as eager to learn about Lily Mercer, if he knew all that I knew?

He waited. I said, "Peregrine. We should go back to London. We've learned all we can learn, here."

"You know how the rector died, don't you?"

"Yes. He tripped and fell down the pulpit stairs. Do you remember? It's very high and the steps turn and narrow as they descend."

Frowning, he looked for the memory, then nodded. "Yes. I do remember."

I had opened my door and was about to cross the threshold, when he said, "You still think Arthur may have killed Lily Mercer, don't you? I've seen your face when you're afraid the evidence points in that direction. Tell me, how would you choose between Arthur and me, if it came to that—if the only way you could protect him would be to sacrifice me?"

I said, "Arthur is dead. Nothing can harm him now. You are alive."

"Fair enough. Then I'll be honest with you as well. If I didn't kill Lily Mercer, why do I dream so vividly about her death?"

He turned and walked away, going into his room without looking back.

I had dinner sent up to both of us, for fear that someone might recognize Peregrine in the dining room or ask questions about the man who accompanied me. And so I ate alone, and Peregrine did the same.

We left Owlhurst behind and went back to Tonbridge, to take the train to London.

We hadn't been in the flat for five minutes before Mrs. Hennessey came puffing up the stairs. I made certain Peregrine was safely out of sight before opening my door.

"There's someone to see you, Miss Crawford. I declare, Mr. Hennessey might have something to worry about, if I were thirty years younger. But after those stairs I daresay I'm thirty years older." She had brought up the post as well and was fanning herself with it as she caught her breath.

"Is it my father?" What if Peregrine and I'd encountered him as we arrived? It was such a close call I felt weak.

"No, my dear, I know your father very well. It's the other one. He's very anxious to speak to you, though he was inordinately polite when he asked if I'd mind going up to fetch you for him."

Simon Brandon. And that would have been just as bad.

"Yes, I'll be there in a moment. Let me collect my coat."

She turned to descend the stairs again, smiling at me over her shoulder. I stepped back into the flat, promised Peregrine that I'd return in a few minutes, and went down to meet the sergeant major.

He greeted me and held the door for me. "Let's sit in the motorcar—it's warmer."

The hall was cold. I went out and got into the motorcar, wondering what was afoot.

As he got behind the wheel, he said, "How are you faring with your search for Lily Mercer?"

"Um—well, I know her parents went to New Zealand shortly after she died."

"Then you may not know that one Peregrine Graham was charged with her murder. He stabbed her in the throat with his father's pocketknife. And it was agreed by all parties that he should be remanded to an asylum for the rest of his natural life."

"Indeed." It was all I could think of to say.

"Indeed. And said Peregrine Graham is now missing from said asylum, and the authorities have every reason to believe he shot himself on the coast of Kent, somewhere south of Dover. Winchelsea? Dymchurch? And his body is still missing, though they did find someone near his size and age."

Something he'd just said struck me.

"She was what? Stabbed in the throat, you say?"

"My friend at Scotland Yard tells me that's what the report says."

"But—I thought—I mean, someone told me she'd been disemboweled—"

"Now that's a nasty thing to be telling a lady," he said, turning to look at me, his dark eyes unreadable in the dimness of the motorcar's interior.

Oh dear. Simon was frighteningly astute. Had I given myself away? Still, I had to ask.

"Are you very certain, Simon? It's important to know this."

"As certain as the report filed at the time of death. I don't know how your Mrs. Graham managed to protect her stepson the way she did, but the police were in agreement that in his present state, taking him into custody would only aggravate his condition. A number of other cases of a similar nature had been sent to Barton's, they knew the doctors there and respected their expertise. The upshot of it was, the boy was given into the care of his stepmother to be transported to the asylum, where doctors evaluated the facts, examined him, and reported to the police. The inquest was held, the documents were placed in evidence, and that was the end of the matter."

"Does the Colonel Sahib know any of this?" I asked after a moment.

"Not yet. That's why I came to see you first. Want to tell me what's going on?"

My heart sank. Simon would never accept my assurance that I was as safe with Peregrine Graham as I was with him.

"I learned something when I was in Owlhurst. I don't know that Peregrine did what he's accused of. If my information is reliable, it's possible that his half brother let Peregrine take the blame for what happened to Lily Mercer. If that's true, Peregrine may have spent nearly fifteen years in an asylum for something he didn't do."

Simon whistled. "My God, Bess, you do manage to get yourself into a tangle. Don't tell me you found a way to spirit Graham out of that asylum yourself. It would be just like you."

I sighed. "He escaped the day I left Owlhurst. I didn't know—I thought the family had been told he was dead of pneumonia. There was the death of Lieutenant Booker, you see, and I was so distressed by that—"

"Who is Booker?" Simon asked suspiciously.

"While I was in Owlhurst, I was asked by the local doctor to help him watch a patient suffering from severe shell shock. He was threatening to kill himself, you see, and in fact he did."

"I thought nursing would keep you safe. How wrong I was. *Britannic* sank under you, and now Owlhurst involved you in murder and suicide. I'm taking you back to Somerset with me."

"No, you can't—" I began to say, then stopped short.

"Pray, why can't I?"

"I—I want to do something first. Are you sure Lily Mercer was stabbed—that there was nothing else?"

"You've already asked me that," he pointed out. "Who are you really trying to protect, Bess? Arthur? Peregrine? This man Booker? Are you in love with any of them?" His voice was exasperated.

"Ted Booker is—was—married, and he has a son. Arthur is dead. And you just told me that Peregrine was dead."

"I told you the authorities believe he could be. For all I know, you have him hidden in your flat, while you sort all of this out. If it weren't for Mrs. Hennessey and her rules, I'd march up there and see for myself."

I was glad I was looking away from him, watching a large man walking a little dog with pretty brown ears. Simon would surely have read the alarm in my eyes as I scrambled to think of a response.

"I'll ask her to do my marketing and then smuggle you into the flat. What a story that would make for the Colonel. Just promise not to tell her what you find, or she'll never allow me to live here again." God knew how much trouble I'd had smuggling Peregrine in and out. It was a miracle we hadn't been caught long before this.

Simon laughed, and I could breathe again.

"All right, Bess. Stay in London if you must. But your father's no fool, and he'll soon be on your doorstep again with no allowance for your wishes. I'll give you twenty-four hours before I tell him what the Yard told me."

"But—that's not enough time!"

"You don't have time, Bess. Your father was notified that your orders will be cut within the week. You'll be sailing for France in a fortnight."

Oh damn.

I thanked Simon and went back to the flat, my mind racing.

Peregrine was behind the door when I walked in, and I could see that he was on edge.

"That wasn't your father," he told me flatly.

"No—that was Simon Brandon. He might as well be my father. Sometimes he's worse!"

"He's not old enough to be your father."

He wasn't. I hadn't given it a thought before.

"Peregrine. That doesn't matter. Listen to me." I was taking off my coat, reaching for the kettle, making tea. The English panacea for stressful moments. "Somehow Simon got a look at the official report on Lily's murder. It says—it says that there was a pocketknife in her throat—but no other wounds are listed. If you'd—well, if you'd butchered her, there would have been *something* in the file."

"My stepmother—"

"I know. Whatever she told you, she didn't have the power to change the official record. Are you sure you remember—that you see in your dreams—something so horrible?"

He stared at me. "I don't know," he said slowly. "No. Yes, I dream I'm touching her entrails."

Dear God. "Peregrine, it could be that you dream about it. But that it didn't happen in life. The police can't be wrong."

He put his hands to his face, covering it. "You can't make up a dream. Not like that. Not unless I'm mad as a hatter. I used to wake up screaming, I tell you. It was that real."

I turned around. "Are you alone? Is someone else in the dream? Who is there in the dream with you?"

"I hear my stepmother's voice, she's speaking to me, telling me I should be ashamed, making me face what I've done. I am nearly sick from the smell, but she won't let me go, she's *there*."

The kettle was beginning to boil, I could hear the soft rumble of bubbles forming in the bottom.

"She found you by the body, trying to retrieve your knife from the wound—is that when you see the entrails?"

"I don't remember." He crossed the room to sit down heavily in the nearest chair. I was pouring the hot water into the teapot now, splashing a little on my hands, unaware of the pain.

Remember Ted Booker—a little voice in my head reminded me.

Shock can do terrible things to the mind. And a fourteen-year-old boy with limited experience of life might easily be made to remember something that wasn't real. But how? With words?

I couldn't quite grasp what had been done. Or how Mrs. Graham could have allowed it to happen. But a mother will do anything to protect her own child, and destroying Peregrine Graham was the surest solution to the thorny problem of presenting Arthur or Jonathan or even Timothy to the police as the murderer.

I cudgeled my wits, but no brilliant solution offered itself.

Handing Peregrine his cup, I sat down across from him with my own. The hot, sweet tea was reviving. "Peregrine? You asked me if I'd sacrifice you to save Arthur's good name. But the facts point to Arthur as the killer—he was Mrs. Graham's favorite, he was next to you in age, you were already damaged, and so it was a short step to substituting you for him. But I need to know why Arthur would kill?"

"To protect one of his brothers?" But he was unconvinced.

I on the other hand leapt for that explanation.

"It could happen. If Lily, in the house alone with you and resenting that she couldn't have the evening off with the other staff, taunted the four of you for being in her way—"

He shook his head. "Don't."

"Peregrine. I'm being ordered back to active duty within the week. Time is slipping through our fingers."

"It doesn't matter. I can go somewhere else and start another life. The Mercers must have done that in New Zealand, and it would have been harder for them than for me. After all these years in Barton's, I don't need much. I could survive."

Peregrine was already thought to be dead. There were ways it could be made to happen, this new life. There were people in India I could send him to—

But it solved nothing. There was Lily, deserted by her family, however desperate they'd been to accept the offer of passage away from England. If I had thought it was my duty to Arthur to bring his message home, what duty was still owed to Lily Mercer?

"Talk to me, Peregrine. Please—if you didn't kill her, someone else did. Do you remember what you told me about that conversation where Arthur and Jonathan discussed doing something six times to give the victim—or perhaps the police—a fair chance to catch you?"

"I've already considered that. Lily. The policeman Gadd. The doctor. The rector. Lady Parsons."

"You can't count her. She survived."

"The boy who drowned, then. That's five. And about as far-fetched as a fairy tale."

"Add Ted Booker. Six."

"Arthur couldn't have killed Booker."

"To my knowledge, Jonathan was the last person to see him alive." Unless I was wrong, and Mrs. Denton went to the surgery.

"Jonathan?"

Unless Jonathan had completed Arthur's six. It would have to be Jonathan. But he was never Mrs. Graham's favorite.

He was her son, all the same. And she would be rabid to protect him.

Could he kill at that age? He must have been what, ten? A little younger, perhaps. If he'd caught Lily off guard, he could have struck her with the knife, just happening to find the right place to kill her. Or lashed out and was unlucky enough to cut an artery.

I hadn't liked Jonathan very much, but that didn't matter. The truth did.

But what if it was not the boys? What if it was Mrs. Graham? Or Robert? If he'd tried to seduce Lily, and she'd told him she'd complain to Mrs. Graham, he might have been in a panic. Or to twist it another way, if Lily had seen Mrs. Graham and Robert together—or perhaps guessed that one of the Graham children was his—she might have been killed if she threatened blackmail. What were the laws on inheritance, if it could be shown that a child might not be the legal father's son?

The trouble was, I hadn't known Lily Mercer, and I hadn't been able to speak to her family. I was blind when it came to her nature, her way of seeing life, and what she wanted from it.

Daisy had claimed she was ambitious, and that fit nicely with the theory of blackmail. But Lily might well have been innocent of any wrongdoing. I mustn't make her the villain without evidence.

"I'm going back to Owlhurst. I'll speak to Lady Parsons, and see if she had any doubts about what happened to you. If Mrs. Graham had already received permission from the London police to take you directly to Barton's, why did she call in so many people after she reached Owlhurst? The doctor—the police—the magistrate—the rector. To erase any doubt in the minds of people whose opinion mattered in Owlhurst? Or to make certain that you, Peregrine Graham, were seen with blood all over your hands and shirt, so that she and not her stepson would be the object of their sympathy?"

"I'd rather go away now, and not look back."

"But you're a witness, Peregrine. You can't disappear, if there's to be any justice at all."

This time I found Simon at his club and asked him to drive me back to Kent. Peregrine was determined to go, but I didn't want him taking the risk. Or to have to explain to Simon.

Curious, Simon agreed, and he took me to the flat long enough to fetch my bag. Peregrine, in Elayne's room, didn't come out, though I was nearly certain he'd call my bluff and find a way to accompany us. I expect if he'd had any uniform but that of my father's old regiment, he might have tried to do just that.

I half expected to find him gone from London by the time I got back. I wasn't sure how I felt about that. What if it was all taken out of my hands, and I didn't have to face what Arthur might have done?

Simon was silent for most of the journey, and I was grateful, lost in thought as I was.

We found Lady Parsons just outside Cranbrook in a very lovely old Jacobean house with a pedimented porch and graceful stonework around the windows. The estate was called Peacocks, and on the gates were two magnificent stone peacocks, the hen demure and the male with raised head, above the spread of that glorious tail.

I remembered Lady Parsons from the inquest. But I had forgotten how formidable she was.

She received me in her drawing room, austere in mourning black, with jet beads and only a touch of white at her collar and at her cuffs. A pince-nez on a silver chain was pinned at her shoulder.

"You're the young woman who worked with Dr. Philips trying to save Lieutenant Booker. What brings you here, second thoughts about your testimony? As I recall, it was an impassioned plea for understanding. Remarkable, I thought. We have no room for compassion in a war such as this one. A shame."

"I'm afraid that it's another matter that I wish to discuss, Lady Parsons. The fate of Peregrine Graham."

The door opened, and a little dog trotted into the room, taking his place at Lady Parsons's feet.

"Peregrine Graham, is it? You do have a taste for lost causes, my girl. The odds are, he's dead."

"So I've been told. But I happened on information that confused me—I'd heard that the body of Lily Mercer had been—er, butchered, for want of a better word."

"We did not ask for such unpleasant details, Miss Crawford. Mrs. Graham was nearly incoherent with shock by the time she reached Owlhurst. I was summoned, along with Inspector Gadd, because she was unable to continue at that hour to the asylum and attend to all the details of admitting her son. Inspector Gadd and I decided the boy was safest at the rectory until he could be moved again, and the doctor determined that he was stable enough to wait a few more hours."

"According to the information that Scotland Yard has in hand, Lily Mercer died of a single stab wound to her throat."

"And how did you come by such information, Miss Crawford?" Her voice had taken on a chilly note, and the dog stirred at her feet.

"My father, Colonel Crawford, was able to discover it for me."

"And is he aware of the use you are now making of this information?"

"He—is aware of my interest in the fate of Lily Mercer."

"I see."

"I believe there might have been a miscarriage of justice, Lady Parsons. And I am seeking advice from you on how to proceed in this matter."

"My advice, if you will take it, is to leave police business to the police. As I did. Inspector Gadd handled a most difficult matter with admirable skill and discretion. That's all there is to say. It does you credit to want to set the world to rights, my dear, but as Peregrine is dead, I see no point in investigating a tragedy that lies in the past where it belongs. Fifteen years is a long time, witnesses die, attitudes change, and it is almost impossible to make a judgment on new facts when the old ones can't be reconstructed."

"I'm not asking you to make a judgment. I'd simply like to know if you were aware of a discrepancy in important details."

"The nightmare here, Miss Crawford, was that of a child committing murder. We were appalled, and we did what we could to make Mrs. Graham's hideous duty as simple as humanly possible. You cannot know her state of mind at the time. I witnessed it. I saw the young man myself, and his own state was pitiable. It was I who suggested that Mrs. Graham's cousin, acting in loco parentis, remove the child the next morning to Barton's while the doctor treated Mrs.

Graham for exhaustion. She had done more than any woman might be expected to do in such circumstances, and I admired her courage in seeing the matter through. But she had three other sons who were in desperate need of her care, and her place was naturally with them. A man's steadying hand was what Peregrine Graham most needed, and that is what we were able to provide for him."

"What did Peregrine have to say for himself?" I asked.

"Very little. He was quite naturally dazed by the turn of events, and on that score, it isn't surprising. I asked him how he had come to kill, and his answer was that he wanted his father's knife returned to him, he was quite upset that it had been taken away. I asked him how he felt about what he'd done, and he said that he didn't care for the smell. I asked him if he'd liked the unfortunate victim, and he replied that she was spiteful when no adult was present, and that he had disliked her for it. All very consistent, according to the doctor, with the boy's inability to tell right from wrong. He couldn't seem to grasp the severity of his actions. There was no malice, no cunning, no viciousness. There was no doubt in my mind, as there was no doubt in the minds of the London authorities, that prison was inappropriate and that Barton's Asylum was the proper choice, where he could be evaluated."

"Why not a London hospital?"

"I believe that the doctor, a man called Hepple, who was a specialist in mental derangement in children, had recently removed to Barton's. Mrs. Graham was very persuasive. She felt that her stepson had no prior history of violence, no indications of a violent nature, and that it had most likely been a disagreement over a pocketknife, about which he was obsessive, that might have triggered this event. In supervised circumstances, it was likely he would never kill again."

I could see that I was speaking to a wall. Lady Parsons had made up her mind that night, and she was not accustomed to changing it. I could also see that Mrs. Graham had been terribly distressed but had somehow kept her wits about her as well. And that would be indicative of a shocked and horrified mother who had to fight for a child she loved with every tool at her disposal. Nothing else mattered, not even her own near collapse.

I thanked Lady Parsons for her time and prepared to take my leave.

She said, "My dear, when one is young, one sees dragons everywhere, and one is prepared to fight them. That's an admirable trait. But as one ages, one often sees that injustice is rare, and that what had appeared to be dragons are merely the shadows the mind creates when it wishes to avoid a bitter truth."

I stood there for a moment, then asked, "Did you feel I was fighting dragons when I made the plea for Lieutenant Booker?"

"In a way, I did. Shell shock is little understood, although I believe that in young Booker's case, it was clear that both Dr. Philips and you had fought hard against *his* dragons. But the dragons won, and that was neither justice nor injustice, but the simple fact that in the end, he didn't have the strength to endure."

She hadn't used the word *courage,* but it hung in the air between us.

The little dog accompanied us to the door of the drawing room, either ready to defend his mistress or hoping for a walk, it was hard to say.

Which brought me to another matter I hadn't intended to broach.

"I understand you had a terrible fall from your horse some years ago, Lady Parsons."

"Oh, my dear, I was frightened to death that I wouldn't walk again! I don't know why the horse fell—my groom found cuts on the mare's knees, and he very rightly called in Constable Abbot, but I could swear that there was nothing on the path that might have tripped up Henny. We had ridden through high grass before we reached the wood, and she might well have encountered something there that I couldn't see. I don't wear my spectacles when I ride."

And that was Lady Parsons's dragon—that no one would dare touch her or her horse. She was sacrosanct.

Simon said as I walked out to the waiting motorcar, "You don't appear to be happy with the outcome of your visit."

"I've been fighting dragons. Or so I'm told."

Simon put the motorcar into gear and drove several miles until he came to a place wide enough for us to pull to the side of the road. The view across the Downs was wonderful in the cold light of a winter's day.

He said, simply, "What can I do?"

"Dear Simon, I thank you, but it isn't a position the army can take with full cavalry charge in support of the infantry."

"Try."

I shook my head.

"Bess—"

"Do you remember some twenty years ago, there was a scandal about a steeplechase where a favorite lost to a horse with no record of winning—and suddenly in this one race, he was a phenomenon, ahead of the field by some ten lengths? And much later, it was discovered that the horse who won had actually taken the place of the one legally entered in that race? My father was angry when the truth came out. He'd had a wager on the favorite."

"As I remember the substitution wasn't discovered for five years."

"Exactly. I think this must have happened when Lily Mercer was found dead. The wrong boy was blamed, because it served everyone's purpose for *him* to be sent to an asylum."

"That's a rather strong accusation. The police don't often get things wrong."

"And they didn't. It was a child in that house. Only, the real killer was protected, and the scapegoat was not missed by anyone."

Simon was silent for some time. And then he asked, "Has this boy—the real murderer—killed again?"

"I don't know," I answered honestly. "Circumstantial evidence says he may have. I'm not a policeman, I can't prove what I believe."

"You're too close to the people involved—too close to be objective."

"And if I'm sent to France in a fortnight, it will all be swept under the carpet again, and an innocent man will continue to be blamed for something he didn't do."

Simon turned to look at me. "Are you in love with this innocent man?"

I laughed. "Hardly." The laugh faded. "But I see the injustice here, and I'm helpless to change it. And what about the dead girl? What does she deserve? Even her family abandoned her, in a way. She wasn't the victim, she was the problem, to be swept under the carpet as quickly as possible."

"You were ever taking pity on the halt and the lame and the lost."

"I know. I've seen so much death, Simon. I'm glad I took up nursing—I've been able to do something about the war by saving the lives of wounded men—but there are things I'll remember until I die, and memories that come in the dark, when I'm trying to sleep."

He got out to crank the motor. "You should have been a son, Bess Crawford. It would have made life much easier for the rest of us."

"No, it wouldn't have done any such thing. You'd have been following me into battle to keep me safe."

CHAPTER SEVENTEEN

I TOLD PEREGRINE that shifting Lady Parsons's belief in her own judgment was going to be an uphill struggle. "And one I don't think we're likely to win."

He got up and began to pace. "I don't even know what I believe. Logic tells me I could have done it. Honesty says I probably killed her. The problem comes back to what I remember. And memories are difficult to refute."

"That's probably because you were drugged to keep you out of the way and manageable while in London. And it turned out to be a godsend, that you were acquiescent to whatever was asked of you."

Stopping at the window, he lifted the edge of the white lace curtains that my flatmates and I had hung there, idly glancing out. And then his interest sharpened, and he stood there, watching something or someone in the street below.

After a moment, he said, "Come here, will you?"

I went to stand beside him, reaching to pull the curtain wider so that I could see the street. But he caught my hand, pulled me in front of him, and said, "No. Through this crack. Don't disturb the curtain!"

I could feel him behind me, tense as a steel rod, and the hand on my shoulder was gripping it hard.

"I don't see anything," I said uneasily. "The street. The houses opposite, the carriages and motorcars and people—"

"There. At the house across the way. There's a man loitering there. See, the one with the cane."

The house he spoke of was closed up. The children had been taken to the country for safety from the zeppelin raids, staying with their grandparents for the duration of the war. Mrs. Venton was nursing burn victims at her sister's country house near Winchester. Her husband was serving in the Navy, the gunnery officer on a cruiser.

I looked again at the man. He was moderately well dressed, but the cane he was carrying caught my eye. "That's not a cane," I said, intrigued. "Well, it is, if you like, but I recognize it. My grandfather had one—it's a sword stick. A twist of the handle, and the blade slides out."

"Your father has set someone to watch over you. What have you told him?"

"Nothing—truly, I haven't betrayed you. I wouldn't. Besides, the general view is that you must be dead."

Just at that moment, Mrs. Hennessey came out of our house and crossed the street, her market basket on her arm. The man stepped out of the shelter of the Venton porch and tipped his hat to her.

I could see then that he was older than he looked, his head bald save for a ring of graying hair like a laurel wreath worn rather long. He looked more like a hopeful poet than he did a menace. And perhaps that was by design.

Mrs. Hennessey listened to him for a moment, then shook her head. He asked other questions, and she again told him no. After that he let her go, walked in the other direction from the one she took—and just as he was about to pass out of sight, he turned and came back again to the porch across from us.

I moved away from Peregrine and the window. "I'll collect my coat and walk out. See what he does. Whether he follows me or stays where he is. We need buns for our tea, and the bakery is just in the next street. You've been there."

"What if he stops you, as he stopped Mrs. Hennessey?"

I smiled as I pulled on my gloves and reached for the market basket we kept in the flat. "I'm forewarned, aren't I?"

Peregrine was uneasy with my going. "I still don't like this idea."

"No, I want you to see that I had no part of this watcher, and that we're both beginning to imagine things."

Before he could argue, I was out the door and down the stairs.

This house had four floors, three of them let to people like my flatmates and me—in need of a base in London but seldom there to enjoy it.

I went down the stairs and out the door without looking in the direction of the watcher—if that is what he was. Instead, I walked briskly to the corner of our street, turning toward the small shops huddled together on the main road.

When I got to the corner, I risked a glance behind me, and to my surprise, no one was following me—and the watcher had vanished.

"Tsk. I've come out into the cold for nothing," I said to myself. But I had come this far, and I went to the bakery to see what was available. We were all doing without the niceties by this time, and it depended entirely on what the baker had been able to find in the way of sugar and flour and eggs as to what was for sale. He put all his resources into bread, which everyone needed, and what was left over went into the tea cakes and buns and an occasional surprise, like the Sally Lunns on sale last week.

We weren't as fortunate today. I bought bread and looked at the pathetically thin arrangement of sweets on trays that now dwarfed the selections and that used to be filled to overflowing with good things. There was a little white gingerbread left, and I bought two cakes of that for our tea.

Mr. Johnson, serving me, said, "You aren't at the Front yet, Miss

Crawford, nursing our lads? They must be heartsick without your sunny presence."

He was a string bean of a man with thick white hair, black brows, and a pleasant disposition. I didn't think I'd ever seen him in a foul mood.

"Alas, they must wait another week, Mr. Johnson. I've no word yet on where I'll be sent."

"If you see my grandson, God forbid he should be hurt, but if you do, tell him I send him my love."

It was his greatest fear, that his grandson would die in the war. A fear that too many people shared.

"I promise," I told him as he handed me my tidy little square of cakes. And then someone else was holding his attention, and I went out the door.

The man, when I approached the flat, was walking back up the street, toward me. But he stopped to watch a small boy trying to make a toy horse set on wheels crest the uneven cobbles of the street. I went on to our flat and opened the door.

Peregrine was standing there, his face a thundercloud.

"He came into the house," Peregrine said before I'd even crossed the threshold. "I watched him cross the street, heard him climb the stairs, and he went to each door, listening and then trying the latch. I'd locked your door. But I could hear him fumbling with it."

"Then he wasn't sent by my father. My father knows which flat I occupy. He must be looking for someone else."

"You saw Jonathan in Tonbridge. You saw Timothy in Owlhurst. You called on Lady Parsons, the rector, and the doctor. Someone set a watch on you."

"No, I was circumspect. Except with the rector and Lady Parsons. I don't see either of them running to Mrs. Graham, telling tales. I gave your brothers—and Dr. Philips—the impression that I was still concerned about Ted Booker's unhappy death."

And then it occurred to me that we had counted Ted Booker among the six dead. Because Lady Parsons had survived.

"Dear God. Peregrine, what if we were right about the killing continuing? And I let it be known I was concerned about the Booker suicide. . . ."

He said nothing, but behind his dark eyes, his mind was racing. I could see it in his face.

"Then I'm still in the clear," he said finally. "That is, if they still consider me dead as you said. But you are most definitely in danger."

He tried to persuade me to go home, where my parents could protect me until I left for France. Here, alone in London, I was vulnerable. If, that is, the man watching the flat was indeed here because of me.

And before long, through me, someone would surely discover that Peregrine wasn't dead in Winchelsea but alive and in London. That would never do.

"Don't you see?" I said to Peregrine. "The first order of business is to get you safely out of London, and I don't know where to put you. Not at home—I won't involve my father or Simon in this business. They'll do something rash."

I wouldn't put it past either of them to kidnap our watcher and make him tell who had hired him, and why. They had served on the Khyber Pass—kidnapping there was something of a local pastime. Not among the British, but the wild tribesmen who lived on either side of the pass had no compunction about treating their foes as they were accustomed to being treated in their turn.

"I can protect myself."

"With the doctor's pistol? And this time you *will* hang. Be sensible."

He rubbed his face. "I wanted nothing so much as to leave that asylum and get at the truth about that night in London. Afterward—well, if I didn't like what I learned, there was a way out. And then when I was free of the gates, trudging through the cold night, I was tempted to turn back. Much as I hated the asylum, I was afraid.

Of the night, of myself, of what lay ahead. I told myself I might never have another chance, and so I kept walking. It took more courage than I ever knew I had. And I don't know much more now than I did when I started this search. You've done all you can—all anyone can do. But there are more questions than answers still."

I asked, "If you could prove you were not the murderer, and you were set free, what would you do?"

He dropped his hands. "I don't think I'd ever considered the future. But then I met Diana. I'm not in love with her. But I saw in her what I'd missed."

"You know that if you were cleared, and you could return to Owlhurst, the army would be on your doorstep tomorrow. And you'd be sent to France or somewhere to fight."

He considered what I was saying. "I'm not afraid of dying."

"War isn't about dying so much as it is about horror."

He shrugged. "Living in an asylum, I knew what horror was."

We came back, then, to the man standing patiently in the cold, waiting.

For what? For me, for Peregrine, for answers?

"I came to believe it was Arthur who had killed Lily. I didn't want to, but the facts pointed almost as strongly to him as to you. Now I have to ask myself if he could also have killed the others—if it's true they were murdered. But if we count Ted Booker among the six, it couldn't have been Arthur, could it? If it wasn't one of your brothers, who, then? Robert Douglas? But he was with your mother the night Lily died. I'm not a policeman, Peregrine, I'm not trained to sort out the sheep from the goats."

"Robert Douglas?" Peregrine's voice was bitter. "He's no murderer. He's just made a habit of looking the other way. That's his failing, if you like. He swallowed his pride and his self-respect when he followed my stepmother to Kent, and he knows the price he's paid to stay near her. He's willing to live with that. He was kind when he knew she wouldn't care. He sat with me at my father's funeral, and held my hand when I cried. He brought me cake on my birthday. When he took me to the asylum in her stead, he told them that if I was mistreated, she would see that they answered for it. He persuaded Inspector Gadd to insist on a warm meal, a bath, and fresh clothes straightaway. Little things. But he wouldn't take my part to her face."

It had been Robert who had insisted that the dying Peregrine be cared for at home.

"Then we can't expect him to be an ally. All right, we'll set any other suspicions aside and concentrate on Lily. Why was her family given money to leave England so quickly? So they wouldn't make a fuss and bring you to trial? And why was Mrs. Graham so persuasive, convincing London that you should be committed to the asylum for observation as soon as possible? Because she feared that once the shock wore off, you'd remember too much? And why bring in Lady Parsons and the others, unless it was for the same reason— to see you in such a state that they were convinced beyond any doubt that you were the killer?

"What's more, I begin to wonder why you were drugged to keep you quiet in London. You could have been shut up in your room there, just as you had been in Owlhurst. The only explanation is that your stepmother really did want you to see a specialist, with an eye to having you committed, even before the murder. And you wouldn't have been in your right mind. Another thing—her own state just after the murder. If you'd really been guilty, she'd have jumped at the chance to be rid of you. She was beside herself because it was one of her sons, and in the midst of her horror and grief, she saw the only way out of her nightmare was to put the blame on you. And if you're right about Robert, he stood there and let her do it."

He had listened carefully. But at the end he said, "She told me that if I caused any trouble, then or in the asylum, that I'd be taken away and hanged. I believed her. I didn't know any better."

"In prison, they wouldn't have kept you drugged. And at the

asylum, if you tried to tell anyone that she'd slept with Robert Douglas or that one of your brothers was not your father's son, they would put it down to your madness. And if you remembered too much about London, they wouldn't listen. After all, the police had what amounted to your own confession, that you wanted your knife back after using it to kill the girl. You said yourself that little effort was made to help you get well. You were in that place for a lifetime, and even if they had restored you to sanity, the only option was a prison cell."

Peregrine shook his head. "You make it sound logical. But how do you explain the dreams?"

"I don't know," I told him truthfully. "But tomorrow we're leaving London. In the dark before dawn, if we have to. There's one person I can think of who would keep you safe. I don't know why it hadn't occurred to me before. And I promise you, as soon as I have leave again in France, I'll find a way to prove what I just told you. And the watcher will have nothing to tell whoever hired him. He'll be called off."

"I dragged you into this at the point of a gun."

"That's water over the dam. Let it go."

"Do you still brace your door with a chair at night?"

I opened my mouth to deny I ever had done, and then said, "No. Not now."

Peregrine smiled, and this time it reached his eyes, but he said nothing.

We ate what I'd brought from the bakery, and I cleared away the dishes. Peregrine watched me, and as I dried the cup that I'd used for my tea, he reached out and took it from my hands.

It was the cup with Brighton Pavilion on it, that exotic palace that the Prince Regent had built for himself not so very far from here, his cottage at the seaside.

"I'd like to see that," he said wistfully. "It's very un-English."

"If we can clear your name," I answered him, "I'll take you there myself."

✦ ✦ ✦

When Mrs. Hennessey returned later in the day, I went down to ask her what the man who had accosted her earlier had wanted with her.

"He was looking for a flat to rent for his daughter. He thought I looked to be the sort of person who would keep her from getting herself in trouble."

"When you were away, he came into the house and went up the stairs to try every door."

"Did he, indeed!" She was quite angry. "Is he looking to murder us in our beds? Or to rob us blind?"

"I thought perhaps you ought to know. Especially since I'll be leaving quite early in the morning—"

She was quite exercised at the thought of someone coming into her castle and threatening it. It made me feel guilty for frightening her. But it was true.

"Is he still out there?" She went to her window and peered through a slit between the curtains. "By Judas, so he is. Just you wait—when Constable Brewster comes by on his rounds I'll have a word with him, see if I don't! And we'll see then who is the clever one." She let the curtains come together again. "Did you say you were leaving? Oh, my dear girl, you will be careful, won't you? Those Huns are cruel, they shot that poor Edith Cavell, just for staying at her post with the wounded. And look how they sank *Britannic*. A hospital ship! You must stay as far away from them as you can."

"I'll keep myself as safe as possible. We're behind the lines, it will be all right." I didn't tell her that sometimes when the shelling began, we were too close.

She embraced me, saying, "Of all my girls, you are the closest to my heart."

I left her with tears in her eyes and went back up the stairs, feeling a certain elation.

The constable would see to our watcher just long enough for Peregrine and me to slip out of London.

There was no one watching when Peregrine and I quietly let ourselves out the door an hour before dawn. I had spent most of the evening removing any trace of Peregrine's presence from the flat. The sheets were set out for the woman who did Mrs. Hennessey's wash and ours, all the cups and dishes we'd used were in their accustomed places, and Elayne's bed had fresh linens from our cupboard.

I'd borrowed a valise from another of my flatmates for Peregrine's belongings, and repacked my own. When we crept down the stairs, I could hear Mrs. Hennessey snoring gently from her rooms, the house was so quiet.

There was a misting rain this morning, cold and wet on the face, as we walked several streets over in search of a cab to take us to the station. I had thought of everything, and I was rather pleased as we stepped into the train at Victoria Station, on our way to Rochester.

I had even fashioned a bandage for Peregrine's head, so that he wouldn't be required to speak, and I'd told him he was my brother, going home from hospital to complete his recovery. He had looked in the mirror and said, "It's more believable than the bandage I contrived."

"Well, of course, what did you expect?" I demanded.

We left the train at Rochester, walking up the hill to the old heart of the city. The squat, powerful Romanesque cathedral and the keep of the castle across from it were floating in disembodied splendor above the fog that had swept up from the Medway's estuary. I needed transportation to my final destination, the home of a woman my parents had known for some years. The best place to find a driver was at an hotel. The long winding High Street was still nearly empty, though it was close on nine o'clock in the morning, but the shops had opened, and a chimney sweep walked by, whistling.

We were just by a butcher's shop when I saw coming toward me an officer I knew, now a captain in my father's old regiment.

I clutched Peregrine's arm and steered him into the shop. "Wait here," I said, in a low voice. "Whatever you do, don't come out."

To the astonished butcher, I said, "We're eloping—can my fiancé wait in a back room? Someone who knows my parents is coming up the street!"

The butcher, a burly man with thick graying hair, nodded, and beckoned to Peregrine as I stepped out of the shop and walked on.

Captain Raynor recognized me, waved, and we met in front of a milliner's, well beyond the butcher's shop.

"Bess? Is that you?"

"Of course. What on earth are you doing in Rochester?" I asked. "I thought you were the terror of the Hun?"

"I could ask you the same. Your father isn't here with you, by any chance. I thought I saw you with an officer."

"Someone who was my patient on *Britannic*. He walked a little way with me, catching up on news. But tell me, how is Margaret?"

He grinned from ear to ear. "We've a son! I was here for the birth—nasty shoulder wound, and they sent me home. I never thought I'd ever be glad of German marksmanship. His name is William, and he's beautiful."

"I'm so happy for you." I embraced him lightly. "That's for Margaret. Tell her she's wonderful."

His eyes were bright with pride. "So she is. She could ask for the moon tomorrow, and I'd do my best to reach it for her."

"How long is your leave?"

The brightness faded. "Ten days, and I'm off again. I don't know how I can bear to go. I never hated the Germans until William came. And now I'm not very happy with the French either. And what about you?" he asked, quickly changing the subject. "I heard what happened. Are you all right? Are you returning to duty? The Colonel must have been beside himself."

"I survived with nothing more than a broken arm," I said. "And I expect my orders will be here next week."

"I'm sure this break from blood and death has been good for you. But I must say you still look a little tired."

If only he knew!

"The arm was slow to heal."

"Don't tell me. They worked on this shoulder of mine until I wished it had been blown off. But see, I can almost reach above my head." And he demonstrated how far he'd come.

I made congratulatory noises, all the while praying that he'd be spared and come home safe to William and Margaret.

He asked after my father and Simon, and sent his dearest love to the Colonel's Lady, and then we parted. He embraced me warmly, saying, "Keep safe, Bess. I'll do the same, trust in that."

And he was gone. I walked on as far as a small bookshop, stopping there to look in the window while surreptitiously watching Captain Raynor turn a corner and disappear.

Weak with relief, I hurried back the way I'd come, and opened the door to the butcher shop, still smiling at our close call.

The butcher was nowhere to be seen, nor was Peregrine.

But at the sound of the bell above the door tinkling its warning, the butcher appeared from the back, his ruddy face nearly as white as his shirt.

"You'd better come," he said, and gestured toward the back.

I had no idea what was wrong, but I almost ran through the shop to follow him.

In the room behind the shop where the butcher worked, out of sight, there was a long wooden table, a block for a top, and beside it an assortment of knives and other tools.

Peregrine was on the far side of the table—rigid with shock, his face a mask of horror.

"I don't know what's wrong—I was cleaning a brace of geese—what happened to him in the war, then?"

I had nearly forgot that Peregrine was in uniform.

"I—a head wound—" I managed to say, and then my training asserted itself, and I put my hand on the butcher's arm. "Could you leave us, please? For a little while? I'm a nurse. . . ."

The butcher all but fled the workroom. I looked at the blood on the worktable, the entrails of the geese lying in an ugly heap. That hint of rusty iron that was the smell of blood caught in my throat.

I went around the table without speaking. I was afraid to touch Peregrine, and the shared knowledge of war that had helped me deal with Ted Booker was no use to me here.

"Peregrine?" I spoke softly. "It's Bess Crawford. What's wrong?"

He started back as I spoke. "No, I won't put my hands there—you can't force—"

I looked from his staring eyes to the bloody entrails, and my heart turned over.

I hadn't been there when Mrs. Graham found Lily Mercer. But I was seeing the scene now as Peregrine must have seen it.

"Peregrine—" I reached out for his arm, to turn him away, but he flung his arm out at me, knocking me halfway across the room, where I ended up next to a large basket of live chickens, their startled cackling adding to the nightmarish scene. This wasn't a slim, dazed, and frightened fourteen-year-old. He was a fully grown man, and I was winded from the blow.

He was screaming, "No, don't touch me! I won't, I tell you, I won't—!"

I had helped Ted Booker by taking part in his nightmare. I tried it now.

"But this is what you did, Peregrine. Do you hear me?" I said in a voice as near to that of Mrs. Graham as I could make it.

"*I didn't touch her.* I only wanted my knife—"

"You can't have it. The police must take it. Look at what you did.

Put your hands in her body, Peregrine, and touch what you have done! Your father would despise you, if he'd lived to see this. Here, hold out your hands, and I'll show you how it feels to be ripped apart—"

He screamed and went on screaming, and then began beating at the front of his uniform, as if frantically trying to rub something off, his eyes wide with horror and revulsion. And he kept on beating at his chest before turning with such loathing in his face that I nearly fell back again into the basket of chickens.

"I hate you," he said, no longer screaming, his voice cold and hard and young. "I have always hated you—"

He broke off, as if he'd been slapped, his head jerking.

And then to my astonishment, he began crying, silent tears of anguish rolling down his cheeks, and with a bravado I hadn't thought possible, he reached out and buried his hands in the bloody mass.

"There," he said. "I'm my father's son, which is more than my brothers can say."

I hurried to him, caught his hands, and with a cloth that hung from a hook by the table, I cleaned them as best I could. Then I made him dip them in a bucket of water standing beside a sheep's carcass. I was crying myself now, tears of pity for a child who hadn't been able to defend himself, tormented beyond bearing.

He seemed to shudder, and after a moment he said, "Bess?" As if he couldn't see me there beside him. It was the first time he'd used my given name.

I dropped the cloth to the floor and took his arm.

"I'm here, Peregrine. It's all right, come with me."

He moved like a sleepwalker, and I led him like a little child back out into the shop. The butcher was standing there, hands to his sides, his expression one of pity mixed with horror.

I think he believed Peregrine was reliving some war experience, for he said to me in a low voice, "I'd not marry him, Miss. Not if I was you. Not in this state. He belongs in hospital, where they can see to him."

I thanked him, telling him I would reconsider, and I led Peregrine out of the shop. The damp air clung to our faces as I guided him to the nearby side street, and we climbed the hill to the cathedral. It was the only quiet, empty place I could think of. We walked to the side door that I could see was open, on the south side, crossing the lawn wet with dew.

Inside it was cold and quite dark, the massive pillars almost ghostly sentinels against the windows. I found a bench in the back, and we sat down.

Peregrine was calmer now. As if the nightmare had receded and left him drained. I think I could have ordered him to jump from the squat tower and he'd have done it, his will destroyed.

We sat there for some time. I didn't touch him, but I was close beside him, where he could sense my presence.

Gradually he seemed to recover. I could almost watch the progression of emotions. In the distance someone came in from another door, a woman, lifting the holly branches and fir boughs out of the vases by the altar and going off with them. I doubted she could see us here beneath the west doors. But I said nothing until she had come back for the vases and carried them away as well.

"Peregrine?"

"Where are we?" he whispered, looking at the cavernous nave and the long row of columns, the only light that small one in the altar and the rain-wet windows reflecting the dark day. "I don't know this church."

"Rochester Cathedral," I replied. "Did you ever come here?"

He frowned. "Once. With my father. We saw Becket's tomb—"

"That's Canterbury."

He didn't answer. I thought perhaps he must have been very young at the time. His father hadn't lived very long after Timothy's birth. I could see them walking along together, man and child.

Arthur would have been too young to accompany them. Peregrine would have still had his father to himself.

"Do you remember what happened in the—er—the shop where you waited for me?"

"There was someone who knew your family. . . ."

"Yes. He'd have been curious about this uniform. He's in my father's regiment. And I couldn't pass you off as a brother or a suitor, or he'd have known it was a lie."

He turned to me, the first spark of the man I'd seen yet. "You don't have suitors?"

I felt like laughing out loud. "Not at the moment, at least."

"I'd forgot. You were in love with Arthur."

"Hardly love." Yet I could hear his laughter, remember the warmth in those blue, blue eyes, and still feel, sometimes, the touch of his hand, how it had seemed to open a world of happiness. No shadows, no secrets, just a good man, what people often called a natural leader, who had put aside his own pain to make the others in the ward believe they would all survive together.

"Well, then. You felt something. There was a softness in your voice when you spoke his name." He paused. "It's not there any longer."

"No." Which was the real Arthur? The dying man who gave others the gift of his spirit, or the devious man who had concealed the ugly crime of murder? Were they one and the same? How could they be? How could I care for one—and not the other?

I shook off that train of thought and went back to my probing. I wasn't sure how far to press.

Then I remembered something that Daisy, the laundress in London, had said. *"Someone had tried to clean away most of the blood—"*

That hadn't been what I needed to learn at the time, and so I had ignored the words. But now I began to see a picture of such hideous behavior that I felt ill.

Mrs. Graham had so terrified Peregrine that he had never really recovered from it—as much a victim of shock as Ted Booker cradling his dying brother in his arms. The dreams—

How could a woman commit such an act of betrayal? But there had been a choice. Peregrine—or her own son. And so she had destroyed her husband's child with a cold and malicious trick.

And then she had displayed him to the London police and after that to everyone who mattered in Owlhurst—Inspector Gadd, the rector, Mr. Craig, Dr. Hadley, and Lady Parsons—to leave them in no doubt that Peregrine was a monstrous boy whom she had saved from prison but lost to the asylum. And all the while, the child who had really killed was safe at home with Robert Douglas.

He must have loved Mrs. Graham very much to allow himself to be used as he was—or perhaps it *was* his own child he was protecting, at any price?

I'd guessed what she must have done that night—but I couldn't have imagined the cruelty of the scheme she had used to make the changeling work.

I said to Peregrine, "What were you served at the noon meal the day of the murder?"

He gazed at me as if I'd lost my mind. Then he said, "I don't remember." He sat there for several minutes, his thoughts elsewhere. And then he said, "Yes. Yes, I do, it must have been a goose, because there was a fricassee of goose for dinner. It made my stomach queasy. I couldn't finish it. And later I lost it, and Lily told me I ought to be made to clear the vomit up myself. Timothy told her to smear it on my face, the way one shows a dog he mustn't soil the carpet. She was angry with all of us because she had so badly wanted the night off. She felt that Mr. Appleby ought to have been forced to give up his evening instead."

His eyebrows rose. "I hadn't thought about that. I heard her call Arthur a spoiled mama's boy, and later she told Timothy that a cripple ought not be so prideful, that he had only to look at his ugly, misshapen foot to know that he had an ugly, misshapen nature. I don't know what she said to Jonathan, but he slammed his door and wouldn't unlock it again, however much Lily wheedled, until she threatened to send for Robert."

A girl disappointed because she couldn't have an anticipated free evening, four boys teased and called names—and then some final exchange that must have triggered fury and finally murder.

But if it wasn't Peregrine, someone had had the forethought to use his pocketknife.

Someone, perhaps, who was jealous that it had been given to the eldest son, and wanted to punish Peregrine for being his father's firstborn.

I said, breaking the stillness, my voice almost overloud in the quiet cathedral, "Peregrine. You were very young at the time. Do you know how your father died?"

"My father? He'd gone to Cranbrook. On the way home his horse bolted and the carriage overturned. He was dead when he was brought to the house and laid on his bed. All I knew at the time was that he lay there with his eyes open, and I couldn't understand why, when someone tried to close them, they wouldn't stay closed."

"Who found him?"

"I don't remember that, if ever I was told. Later I overheard my stepmother talking about Gypsies, but it was a child who ran under his horse's hooves."

Peregrine remembered his father's corpse with sadness but without terrors. He'd have remembered Lily Mercer's in that same way, if he hadn't been made to put his hands in what he'd thought was her bloody body. It had never occurred to him in those few minutes with Mrs. Graham that the offal was not a human being's, and she'd counted on that—counted on his state of mind warping all he saw.

"Let's find the hotel," I said, getting to my feet. It was cold as a tomb in here, with the stone walls and stone flooring locking in the frigid January air. "We could use a cup of tea while the hotel finds someone to drive us."

CHAPTER EIGHTEEN

A MR. FREEMAN agreed to conduct us to the home of Melinda Crawford.

She was a connection on my father's side, her ancestors army officers who'd fought at Yorktown with Cornwallis, followed Old Duro through Spain, and danced with my own great-grandmother—so the story went—on that fateful eve of Waterloo.

As a child in India she had lived through the siege of Lucknow, where the British were nearly wiped out during the Great Indian Mutiny. She had seen death and disease close-up, and survived to marry her own cousin against all advice—and been extraordinarily happy with him. When he died, she returned to England by a roundabout route that would have made the hardiest explorer blanch to contemplate. At least those were the stories I'd been brought up on, and I'd believed them. When one knew Melinda, one did.

With that past, I was hoping she'd accept an escaped lunatic with equanimity if not precisely with enthusiasm.

I'd omitted the polite telegram signaling my imminent arrival. She just might take it into her head to telephone the Colonel Sahib and ask him if he knew what his errant daughter was up to.

She still might.

But it was worth the risk. No one would think to look for Peregrine Graham in Melinda Crawford's lair, and if they tried, she was more than capable of dealing with them.

Her house was closer to Tonbridge than to Rochester, but I was wary now of Tonbridge, after our encounter with Jonathan Graham there. Better a long drive across Kent than the worry of a confrontation at the train station or the hotel.

A cold rain had started again as we set out, and the countryside, winter bleak, was colorless and dreary: muddy roads leading through brown, fallow fields, apple trees raising twisted limbs to the gray sky, sheep huddled wherever they could find shelter. And any people out in the weather were hurrying about their business with heads down.

Not far from Marling, we found the turning that led to the Crawford house, and shortly after that, the stone gates with their elephant lanterns loomed through the mists. As the drive wound up the knoll, the views were shrouded in rain.

I had heard many British exiles in India describe the "cottage" they would have when at last they could go home. Roses and daffodils and wisteria and all the beauty that the brown and tan and cream shades of Indian dust made impossible out there. Melinda's gardens were beautiful in season, and she indulged herself with arrays of color. Not for her single beds of pinks and red, beds of yellow and gold, beds of blues and lavenders. Here flowers mingled in rampant glory, a rainbow of blues nodding to cream and yellow, lavenders touching rose and pink and dark blue, golds indulgently shoulder to shoulder with white and purple and red, all striking to the eye and visible from every window. Now of course the beds were dormant, but a bank of holly trees and a dramatic cedar and the leathery green of rhododendron softened the scene.

To a child, coming home on leave from India, this was heaven.

All the way here I'd debated with myself what I should tell Melinda Crawford, and how to explain Peregrine. Nothing believable came to mind.

We rang the doorbell, huddling close under the small porch. I had paid off the driver but asked him to wait until we were certain someone was at home.

The door opened, and in it stood Shanta, the Indian woman who had served Melinda for so long she could speak her mind without reprimand.

Now she took one look at the orphans of the storm on her doorstep and raised her eyebrows.

"I do hope," I said, mustering a smile that had more of Cheshire cat in it than I'd have liked, "that Melinda is at home. It's been a wretched drive!"

"Miss Elizabeth," she said severely, "if you are eloping, you can go home now and be sensible."

Thank God I'd warned Peregrine that the household was a little eccentric, but still I felt myself flushing.

"I'm not eloping. The lieutenant here is a patient, and he has nowhere to go. Er—the zeppelins destroyed his flat in London—"

He did look every inch the wounded hero—his eyes dark-circled and tired, his shoulders thin from fever, and his skin without much color. I found myself thinking that as my choice for eloping hero, he was off the mark.

"If that is the case, come inside and be warm."

I turned to wave good-bye to Mr. Freeman and followed Shanta inside, taking Peregrine's arm and ushering him ahead of me. I could feel his silent resistance—the muscles in his arm were corded bands.

We were taken to the study, where a fire blazed on the hearth and the room was suffocatingly hot. Melinda Crawford's blood still yearned for the heat of India, and I could remember as a child thinking that all old people must be on the verge of freezing to death. Two other widows my father had visited over the years, wives of officers who had died out there, lived in the same tropical environment. They were the only people I knew who kept roaring fires in high summer. One had suffered from malaria on and off and was always feverish.

Melinda was seated in a chair, draped in lovely silk Paisley shawls, and she registered no surprise at seeing me in her doorway. I wondered why.

"I've had a letter from your mother," she said, rising to kiss me.

"She was worried about you. She said you haven't been the same since you went to visit the Grahams."

I kissed her cheek and smelled the scent of sandalwood and roses in her hair.

She was tall and straight, with the bearing of a soldier.

"And this is . . ." She turned to Peregrine and held out her hand like an empress greeting a new and interesting courtier.

Before I could stop him, Peregrine gave her his real name.

She turned to me again. "I thought the Graham boy you were so fond of died aboard *Britannic*?"

I could feel my heart fluttering into my throat. "This is his eldest brother," I said, trying to appear nonchalant.

Melinda nodded. "Welcome to my house, Lieutenant Graham. Come and sit by me. I see you're in the colonel's old regiment. My husband's as well. Wounded in France, were you?"

We sat down as far from the fire as was polite.

The room hadn't changed much, crowded as it was with Melinda's Indian souvenirs as well as objects she'd discovered on her travels. There was a tall porcelain Russian stove in the left corner of the room, a gigantic ceramic affair in blue and cream that she'd seen in Leningrad and shipped home. A samovar from Moscow—often used to brew her tea—stood on a table between the windows, and above it were two great African elephant tusks that curved around a Garuda mask from Bali.

I couldn't help but wonder what Peregrine made of it all. If he'd thought the Prince Regent's Pavilion intriguing, this must seem exotic in the extreme.

Melinda was asking him how much action he'd seen, and he was answering, "More than I care to recall," and she nodded, satisfied.

"What brings you here, my dear girl?" she asked me next. "Your mother says your orders have been cut and should arrive at any moment. And I've yet to thank you for the letter you sent from Athens. Most reassuring, let me tell you."

I said almost bluntly, "Peregrine needs somewhere to stay. Would you mind? He doesn't wish to go home, and there are no beds to be had in London. He's good company, and as soon as he's well enough to manage on his own, he'll be rejoining his regiment."

"Of course he may stay. We're a quiet house. If he doesn't heal here, he never shall."

I felt distinctly uneasy. Had she heard about Peregrine's escape? Surely not. Truth was, I'd expected more resistance on her part. Damn Peregrine for not remaining Lieutenant Philips.

It was much later, after a light luncheon, that Peregrine was shown to his room by Shanta, leaving Melinda to cross-examine me at her leisure.

"Child, what are you playing at? The truth, if you please!"

"There's nothing—"

"Balderdash. I'm not senile yet, Bess Crawford, and I'll thank you to give me credit for knowing you well enough to see through your happy little charade. I do read the papers, you know. That man's an escaped lunatic, and here you are roaming the countryside in his company."

"He's escaped from the asylum, but he's not mad—you have talked with him for two hours or more, Melinda. Tell me you believe he's crazy, much less a murderer!"

"What I believe is beside the point. There's his family to consider. The world believes he must be dead. You can't leave them to grieve. It's unconscionable."

"No, it isn't. Not when everyone is glad to be rid of him at last. I don't think he killed anyone. Did you know his father? Ambrose Graham? He was twice married, and Peregrine is his son by his first wife. . . ."

I found myself telling her everything, trying my best to make what I'd done seem reasonable and logical under the circumstances. And all the while her dark eyes seemed to bore into my head to look beyond my words and find the truth.

"So you now think it must have been Arthur who did these terrible things? Except for the fact that someone else died after Arthur himself was dead."

"I don't know. It must be one of the sons. Everyone else was away that evening. Robert Douglas had accompanied Mrs. Graham to a dinner party. Lily Mercer was still alive, then. As she was when the tutor left the house. Peregrine feels he was persecuted by his stepmother after he found her in bed with her cousin Robert. I think she took Peregrine to London because she was afraid to leave him at home. Not because he was dangerous, but because someone might discover that he wasn't what everyone thought he was and perhaps believe what he had to say. He was angry and violent sometimes, I'm sure, but not in that way—more frustrated and unhappy than mad or murderous. And I strongly suspect he was drugged part of the time he was in London, to keep him quiet. Especially between the time of Lily's death and his arrival at the asylum."

"So you would like very much to believe."

"What else is there to believe?"

She sat there, thinking it over.

"Did it occur to you, my dear, that Peregrine was taken to London to die?"

I opened my mouth and closed it again.

"Yes, I know. But consider. He was desperately unhappy, his brothers were being treated to the sights, and he was left alone with a staff no one knew well. What was to prevent him from walking out the door and disappearing? But in London, without money or friends, where would he go and what would become of him? His chances of surviving were not good. How long would they have waited before calling in the police? Do you think this Robert Douglas could be counted on to see that Peregrine's disappearance was permanent?"

I shook my head. "No. Robert is easily led, but he isn't cruel. He lets things happen without demur, but he doesn't initiate such things."

"Then he must love Mrs. Graham very much indeed. Or know which of her children he fathered. Another point. Why was the maid Lily left in charge that fatal night? She was young for such responsibility—she couldn't have been much older than Peregrine. Add to that, she was angry, rude to the young gentlemen, and she retired to her room, rather than remain belowstairs on duty, as she should have done. Peregrine could have been gone for hours before anyone noticed. It's the only explanation, you see. But Lily went too far in her rage at being left in charge, and she was murdered. What a shock for Mrs. Graham, to come home and find Peregrine still there. You must ask Peregrine, indirectly, what his thoughts are about this view. It could be enlightening."

I was still trying to digest her comments. I wanted to go straightaway and speak to him. But she put her hand on my arm and said, "No, let him rest. Is there no one else you could ask about events in London?"

"The tutor. Mr. Appleby. He was in London with the family. He *must* know more than he was willing to tell me earlier."

"Well, of course, you must visit him again," Melinda said.

"I let Mr. Freeman go—"

"I have my own motorcar, my dear, and Ram Desikhan to drive it. Leave Mr. Freeman and his like out of this." She looked at the little watch she wore on a diamond brooch pinned to the left shoulder of her gown. "Too late today to make the journey—it will be dark soon. But tomorrow you shall go to Chilham and ask him. But carefully. Remember that."

"But who killed Lily? If it wasn't Peregrine?" I told her about events this morning in the butcher shop, expecting her to be as horrified as I was.

She said, "It's an old trick. Carried to extremes here, of course. I remember once on the Northwest Frontier that a Pathan rebel was led to believe he'd killed one of his own family by mistake. It saved a feud, you see. The eye that offended was his, not ours. My husband was very pleased with the outcome. He was rid of two birds with only one bullet, as it were."

"What became of the Pathan rebel?" I asked, intrigued.

"He went home and kept to his tent, like Achilles at Troy. They said his first child after that incident was born deformed and lived only a few hours, and he believed it was his curse for killing his own blood. He put away his wives, went into the hills, and died many years later as a hermit."

"But surely there was someone to take his place?"

"Sadly there always is. But the point remains, my dear, that the brain can be fooled. I'm not saying it was in Peregrine Graham's case, but if you introduce a horror that the mind can't cope with, it runs away."

"Shell shock," I said, thinking of Ted Booker.

"Precisely. There were women at Lucknow who weren't right in their heads afterward. We all thought we were going to die, but what was far worse, we knew it would be a ghastly death, an insupportable horror."

Like watching the lifeboats being sucked into the screws of *Britannic*, and knowing that it could be one's own fate as well. I shivered.

"I will keep your Peregrine Graham here. But this situation must be resolved. Tomorrow morning, go and see this tutor. If he can't help you, then you must go home and leave your black sheep with me for the duration. You can't take him to Somerset, and you can't avoid your duty when your orders come. You owe your parents a little time with you, with no worries."

It was early when I set out for Chilham. Ram, Melinda Crawford's majordomo and chauffeur, was tall, graying, and very protective of his mistress.

He said over his shoulder as we turned into the main road, "This man you have brought, he is no danger to the Memsahib?"

"I wouldn't have brought him if he was." But Peregrine still possessed his pistol. . . .

"It's as well to ask. There is something in his eyes."

We drove in silence after that, and as I watched the countryside pass by, I thought about the fact that Peregrine Graham was the heir to his father's estate, but he didn't have the wherewithal to buy a loaf of bread or a pair of shoes. I'd leave money with him, if I had to go. Whether he wished it or not.

We drove into Chilham late in the morning. I couldn't send Ram into The White Horse for tea. He wouldn't be welcomed there. But I brought him a cup and asked him to wait while I went to speak to Mr. Appleby.

"I shall be here in the car, if anything untoward happens. You have only to call," Ram reminded me.

I thanked him and went down the lane between the pub and churchyard, trying to decide how best to approach the Grahams' tutor.

And met him coming out his door as I started up the walk.

He wasn't best pleased to see me.

I said, "Mr. Appleby. If you would walk with me for a little? In the churchyard perhaps? We won't distress your wife."

"I have told you, I have nothing more to say to you, Miss Crawford."

"I've learned a great deal more about the events that put Peregrine Graham into Barton's Asylum. I think it might be wise to hear me out."

He had no choice but to fall in step with me as he turned the way I'd just come. At the head of the lane, he saw Melinda's Rolls, and the Indian driver.

"Who is that, and what is he doing here?" He stopped short, staring.

"Waiting for me."

"I see." We continued into the square and paced toward the

Jacobean manor house at the opposite end. "What is it you want to know, Miss Crawford? And why?"

"I'm just trying to understand the sequence of events that led to Lily Mercer's death. Mrs. Graham and her cousin were attending a dinner party. You were given the evening off—"

"I was given no such thing. It was my *usual* day and evening free."

"I see. And the servants were also given the evening off, since there was no one to dine at home except the four boys. Is that true?"

"Yes, yes, what's your point?"

"It seems rather odd, to leave four active boys in the house with only a young housemaid to supervise them."

"She had merely to serve their dinner, which was already prepared, and draw their baths. They weren't small children, Miss Crawford, in need of tucking in and a bedtime story. They could see to their own needs. They were the sons of a gentleman, after all, not barrow boys."

"But one of them, Peregrine, was known to be—difficult. He was fourteen, not ten, and Lily couldn't have been more than eighteen?"

We had reached the gates of the manor house and turned to walk the other way. Even in the dreary light, the lovely Tudor houses gleamed white and black.

"It was Mrs. Graham's decision to make, not mine. It was my *usual* free day."

"Peregrine could have walked out, rather than attacking Lily. He could have gone anywhere. Anything might have happened to him. He wasn't used to being on his own."

Appleby stopped short.

"You are pressing your luck, Miss Crawford. We can't change the past. Why rake through it? I should think that you would find the subject unpleasant enough to leave it."

"You didn't like Peregrine very much. You punished him at every opportunity."

"Who told you that?"

Oh, dear . . . how to answer?

"It was rumored in Owlhurst."

He turned away from me. "Peregrine was the most difficult pupil I've ever encountered. It took all of my skill and most of my patience to teach him. You have no way to measure what I endured."

"You could have quit. You could have walked away."

He turned to face me. "I liked the three younger sons. Why should I refuse to teach them? Why should I punish them for their brother's deficiencies?"

"That's rather arrogant, don't you think?"

"Not at all. I'm a good teacher."

"What if I told you that it's very likely that it wasn't Peregrine who killed Lily Mercer, although he was judged and punished for it. If you were such a good teacher, why didn't you question his guilt? Why didn't you see through the tangle of evidence and realize that it was not Peregrine, that it couldn't have been him. Couldn't you tell that he was drugged while he was in London? Surely there were signs, some indication in the character of one of the other boys that warned you to look in his direction. And what about that visit to a specialist, who could help Peregrine? There had been excursions to the zoo and the Tower, why hadn't there been time to take Peregrine for examination?"

"I was well paid to educate four youths," he retorted angrily. "I wasn't paid to tell my employer that one of her sons was deficient in character—"

"Then you did doubt Peregrine's guilt."

"Not for an instant. I walked in the door, found the police in the house, and Peregrine Graham spattered with the girl's blood. It was the most shocking experience of my life, let me tell you. The atmosphere was highly charged. Mrs. Graham was very emotional, on the verge of breaking down. The police were as shocked as I was. And Peregrine stood there with a dazed expression, not a word of regret, not a word in his own defense. Robert Douglas was a rock, I stood in admiration of his quiet ability to keep the household calm. I wasted no time on doubt, I saw the proof with my own eyes."

"Perhaps not then. But later. Later you wondered. If you were a good judge of young people, as a teacher should be, you began to question what you'd seen and been told. Other things happened, to cast doubt on Peregrine's guilt. Why didn't you do something?"

A flicker of acknowledgment crossed his face. For the first time I saw the truth exposed—he couldn't hide it, however much he tried. It was gone in a flash. And then rage took over. I thought for an instant he would strike me, he was so furious. I wondered how much of that fury was shame, because he hadn't liked Peregrine, and at first had been glad to be rid of him. And later, he still said nothing, because he enjoyed his comfortable position with the Graham family too much to jeopardize it.

I wanted to ask him which of his charges was a murderer, but I didn't dare.

He walked away from me, his shoulders so stiff with his anger that he seemed to strut. But I thought it was more the desire to lash out at me, held in check because I was a woman and this was a very public place.

I waited, in the expectation that he might turn, that he might get himself under control and protest that I'd got it wrong. But Mr. Appleby knew he'd already betrayed too much. He wasn't going to risk betraying more.

I went back to the motorcar, drawing in a deep breath as I took my seat.

Ram said, "That man was very angry indeed." He turned, his eyes anxious. "Is all well?"

"I don't know," I said slowly. "Take me home, if you please."

We drove sedately out of Chilham, down the hill and toward the road west. I had stirred up a hornet's nest. Pray God I wasn't the one who was stung as a result.

✦ ✦ ✦

We stopped on the way back to the Crawford house. I wanted to make sure that Peregrine had all he needed for a visit there.

It took me three quarters of an hour to find everything on my mental list, and I was rather pleased with the result. I'd had no luck in finding evening dress, but then Melinda had never been a stickler for dressing for dinner. She would accept Peregrine's uniform.

Ram was waiting for me near Rochester Castle, and I paid the boy from the haberdashers a shilling for carrying my bundles and packages for me. He had struggled up the hill under his burden and was breathing hard by the time we'd stowed them safely in the motorcar.

He stared at Ram and said, "Who's that, then?"

"My driver. He's from India."

"Does he have an elephant?"

"Once upon a time, he may have."

Satisfied, the boy ran off.

Ram chuckled. But I was struck by something else.

Melinda Crawford's driver must be unique in Kent. . . . I should have insisted on hiring someone else. Someone who attracted no attention.

I settled back for the drive to Melinda's house. It was too late to worry about today, but tomorrow I'd do things differently.

As we turned up the drive, I realized that I'd missed my lunch and was looking forward to tea.

Shanta greeted me and took my coat and gloves.

"Ram has packages that belong in Lieutenant Graham's room," I told her.

"Memsahib is in her sitting room. Will you have your tea now or later?"

"Now," I said, and walked on to the sitting room. I discovered our tea had already been brought in.

"Peregrine will be down shortly. He was asleep when Shanta

went to his room. Are you sure he's well? That he doesn't need to see a doctor?"

"I think he's surviving on his will alone. But he's not coughing as much, and I don't think he's feverish. Sleep is the best medicine, and good food."

"What did you accomplish today?"

"I made Mr. Appleby very angry," I said. "When I suggested that, after Peregrine had been dealt with and the household had returned to nearly normal, he had doubts about what had been done so quickly and without fuss."

"But he gave you no feeling for which boy he suspected?"

"Sadly no. He's an arrogant man, he takes great pride in being a good teacher, but I agree with what someone else said—he's really second-rate. I don't think Mrs. Graham wanted a sharp mind seeing through—"

I could hear the rasp of the door knocker.

"Who can be calling at this hour?" Melinda demanded testily. "No, don't get up, my dear, Shanta will send them away."

"My father—"

"—is in Somerset, I should think."

But the sitting room door burst open, and brushing Shanta aside, there stood Jonathan Graham, backed by two burly police constables.

The raw, puckered scar across his face accentuated his determined expression. He knew what he wanted, and he was set on getting it.

"I've come to fetch my brother," Jonathan said.

Melinda drew herself up to her full height and said, "I beg your pardon. Constable Mason, what is the meaning of this abrupt and very rude intrusion?"

I stood there, astonished, unable to believe my eyes. And then I collected my wits.

He's guessing—he's not sure—

The Colonel Sahib firmly believed in a sharp counterattack when the enemy began a tentative probe.

And so I did just that. "Your brother is dead. So I've been told. If you wish to know why I've been asking questions about what happened in London fourteen years ago, it's because I'm not convinced that the real murderer was ever caught. Then there's Ted Booker's suicide—I have a strong feeling that he was murdered. It's not remotely possible that Peregrine killed *him*, is it? And what about all those other deaths in Owlhurst—Inspector Gadd, Dr. Hadley, the rector? Peregrine was in the asylum during that time, was he not? This begins to shed new light on Lily Mercer's murder, wouldn't you agree, Lieutenant Graham?"

That rocked him back on his heels.

Constable Mason, the older of the two uniformed policemen, ignored me and said to Melinda, "It was reported, ma'am, that there was a dangerous murderer in this house, and we've come to fetch him before any harm comes to you or your staff."

"And why should I entertain a murderer under my roof, pray? I don't know this officer, Constable, and I'll thank you to escort him out of my presence before I make a formal complaint to the Chief Constable. He dined here on Saturday last, and I can assure you he wouldn't have done so if I consorted with murderers, dangerous or otherwise."

I thought we'd carried it off. I thought we had between us put the fear of God into the constables and rattled Jonathan Graham.

Jonathan had looked from Melinda to me as she spoke of the Chief Constable, and there was a flicker of uncertainty in his eyes.

I said, into the silence, "Constable, if you wish to search the house, of course you may. Lieutenant Graham has been misled, maliciously at a guess—"

Just at that moment, Peregrine Graham came unwittingly down the stairs and turned toward the sitting room.

CHAPTER NINETEEN

AT THE SOUND of footsteps, Jonathan Graham whirled, stepped back into the passage, and stared into the face of the half brother he hadn't seen since they were both children.

There was still a chance.

"May I present Lieutenant Philips?" I said quickly. "He's an officer in my father's regiment—he escorted me to Kent—"

But Jonathan saw something in his brother's face that triggered a memory. A profound recognition on both sides that was our undoing.

"That's him!" Jonathan exclaimed, "I told you he was here—"

Peregrine spun on his heel and ran for the stairs. The two constables lumbered after him, shouting for him to stop.

I caught Jonathan Graham's sleeve and prevented him from following.

"Which of you killed Lily Mercer? Do you know? *Tell me.*"

He stared at me as if I'd struck him across the face.

"If it wasn't Arthur—and Arthur couldn't have killed Ted Booker—then it must be you. Or Timothy. *You* were the last person to see Ted Booker alive—"

"You are as mad as Peregrine is."

"*'Tell Jonathan that I lied. I did it for Mother's sake. But it has to be set right,'*" I quoted. "What had to be set right? What had Arthur lied about, for his mother's sake? Had he lied about who had possession of Ambrose Graham's pocketknife at the time Lily Mercer was killed? Did Arthur *know* and cover it up for your sake or for Timothy's? And what about those other deaths—Inspector Gadd, the rector, the doctor. All the people who had acquiesced to sending Peregrine to the asylum. Which one of you decided to right *that* balance, rather than confess to the truth? Or was it done just to see that no one ever changed his mind about Peregrine's guilt?"

He shook me off so forcibly that I fell back against the doorjamb. And then he was gone, up the stairs in the wake of the constables.

"Peregrine!" he shouted, his voice reverberating through the house.

Where was the pistol? What had Peregrine done with it? Was that what he was after? I couldn't stand there, listening for the shots. I was at Jonathan's heels, trying to stop a tragedy that was about to happen.

But Peregrine never used his pistol. He simply ran out of breath, and they caught him as he leaned, coughing harshly, in the doorway of his room.

It was too late to persuade the constables that they had got the wrong man. They would believe Jonathan, not me. There was nothing I could do.

I watched them bring Peregrine down the stairs, without a coat, without a hat, and I could see that someone—Jonathan?—had struck him across the face.

How did they know? How could they have possibly known he was here—unless Mr. Appleby had recognized Melinda Crawford's chauffeur and maliciously set Jonathan Graham on my heels?

He stood there in the hall, triumphant, cold. "I was on my way out the door. My orders have arrived. I would have been gone in another hour, and then the message came."

"Where are you taking him?"

Jonathan didn't answer, but one of the constables said, "He's to be returned to the asylum, Miss."

"He won't remain there for very long," I warned the constable. "There's some doubt now that he killed anyone."

"He's lied to you, Miss," the other constable said. "The police don't make such mistakes." He looked at Peregrine, standing there helpless between them, no color in his face, and something in his eyes that I didn't want to see. "Handsome fellow. Easy to get around a young lady. And here we'd all thought he was dead."

"How dare you—" I began, but Melinda stopped me.

"You aren't taking him from here without his hat and coat," she said, her voice stern. "If he's to be taken back to that place, it's a long drive. Will you fetch Mr. Graham's things, Shanta?"

And Shanta moved out of the shadows and went quietly up the stairs. Peregrine's gaze followed her, and I knew what he was thinking, that the pistol was in his greatcoat pocket.

I held my breath when Shanta returned with the coat. And then I realized what was in Peregrine Graham's mind. He had no intention of using the weapon on his captors, but somewhere between here and his destination, he would find a way to use it on himself.

I said urgently, "Peregrine. This isn't the end of the matter. Do you understand me? I have connections, I'll see to it that this business is settled."

He gave me an odd smile. "Tell Diana I'm sorry I won't be there to see her on her next leave."

And then they were dragging him out of the house and into the motorcar that had brought them here.

Jonathan was the last to go.

I turned on him as he stood on the top step, watching Peregrine being shoved into the backseat, jammed between the two constables.

"Mr. Appleby knows the truth," I said. "He didn't want to admit to it, but he knows. And I know the truth, and my father, and Melinda Crawford, and too many people to be dealt with. It's only a matter of time, Jonathan Graham, before your brother's last wishes are finally carried out."

"Knowing and proving," he said, "are two entirely different matters. Who is Diana?"

I didn't answer him.

"Not that it signifies," he said into my silence.

And with that, he cranked the motorcar, got behind the wheel, and drove off down the drive.

I was so helplessly angry that I burst into tears.

Melinda, behind me, said, "I think we should call Simon. Not your father. Not in this case. Simon will know what to do."

I shut the door on the cold evening air, and turned to her.

"It will be too late," I said. "By the time Simon can get here, Peregrine Graham will be dead by his own hand."

I put in the call to Simon Brandon anyway.

But there was no answer at the other end. He'd gone to dine with my parents, I thought. He did at least once a fortnight.

That was that. The cavalry wouldn't come in time.

I went back into the sitting room. Shanta was taking away the now cold pot of tea, and I stood before the fire on the hearth, trying to warm myself.

"It was Appleby," I said again. "It couldn't have been anyone else. He saw your motorcar and Ram. I was careful, so very *careful* to keep Peregrine out of sight, except on our first visit to the tutor. And he told Jonathan how to find me, out of spite. The penny must finally have dropped."

"It wasn't very clever of me to offer you my car." Melinda sat down, one arm on the table in front of her, a frown between her eyes. "I don't think it was Jonathan who killed that girl. Your tutor, this Mr. Appleby, wouldn't have called him, if he was. Don't you see? He would have been afraid to let anyone know he had guessed the truth. That is, if you are right and the tutor had seen more than he was willing to tell."

"And Arthur sent *his* message to Jonathan. That completes the circle, doesn't it? As for the other killings—they didn't include Appleby, because he was out of reach in Chilham."

"That leaves Timothy, I should think. The only other choice is Mrs. Graham herself. And I find that hard to believe," she answered, musing. "She was devastated, you said, when the murder was discovered."

I hadn't really wanted it to be Timothy. I had disliked Jonathan from the start and could have comfortably concluded that he was the killer.

I said suddenly, realizing the full impact of what we were saying. "It wasn't Arthur. *It wasn't Arthur.*"

"Yes, I should think that would be quite a relief. But how to prove any of this? It won't be easy. The police had convinced themselves that their case was strong enough to send Peregrine Graham to Barton's. They won't wish to reopen the case."

"But it was Jonathan the rector saw leaving the doctor's surgery the night that—"

I stopped. I'd believed all along that it was unlikely that Jonathan had visited Ted Booker. And of course he hadn't. That was why he hadn't spoken up at the inquest.

It must have been Timothy in Jonathan's borrowed greatcoat—and Jonathan had lied for his brother. *Again.*

Shanta came in with a fresh pot of tea and a fresh pitcher of milk.

She poured two cups, passed them to us, and then said, "You are looking very glum. Drink your tea and have something to eat. It will do you both a great deal of good."

I said, "Shanta. What did you think of Peregrine Graham?"

She considered the question and then answered me. "There is a darkness that follows him like a shadow. I'm very glad that you weren't eloping."

I couldn't touch my tea. The feeling that Peregrine would die before he could be taken back to the asylum grew stronger with every passing minute.

Every wasted minute . . .

"Melinda." I was on my feet and heading for the door. "I must borrow your motorcar. I'm sorry, I can't wait for Ram. I must go." Ram drove sedately, not the way I intended to drive. Before she could say anything, I went up the stairs nearly as fast as Peregrine had done, caught up my hat and coat and gloves, and was on my way down the back steps to the barn where the motorcar was kept. I heard Melinda calling to me from a doorway, but I didn't stop to hear what she had to say.

The motor was still warm and turned over with only one revolution of the crank. I drove out of the barn, leaving the doors wide behind me, and went down the drive at a clip that was reckless in this light. I kept my attention on the headlamps as they swept the road while I went through the map of Kent in my head.

There were two ways to reach Owlhurst, or the road leading to it, where Barton's stood. Jonathan would have taken the more direct. And so would I.

I cleared my head of every thought, concentrating on the road. If I could catch them up before they reached Barton's—surely Peregrine would wait until they were almost there. He'd be searched at the door, and then it would be too late. Somewhere before the asylum. I could picture that lonely stretch of road just before one saw the walls around the property. There? Sooner?

The roads were winter poor, and in daylight it would have been mad enough to drive at this speed, but I kept it up. They had a head start of what? Twenty minutes? Thirty? Thirty was too long. I'd never make that up.

I narrowly missed a ewe wandering across the road, and again someone on a bicycle, who yelled imprecations in my wake. I prayed I wouldn't meet anything larger. At this speed, I couldn't stop in time.

Is it worth taking your life in your hands?

I had no answer to that. Would I have agreed to carry a message to Arthur's brother, if I'd been able to look ahead into the future?

I had no answer to that either.

I was within five miles of Barton's, cursing under my breath, knowing I was too late, far too late. And then, over the soft murmur of the Rolls motor, I heard shots echoing across the fields. I'd been close to the fighting. I'd fired side arms myself. I could recognize their sharp reports.

Gripping the wheel hard to hold back my fears, I tried to determine where the sounds had come from. To my right—and surely just ahead.

But to my right was only a tangle of briars and dead stalks of last summer's wildflowers, and on the far side of that, out of range of my headlamps, the flat blackness of what appeared to be a fallow hop field.

I lifted my foot from the accelerator, prepared to find the Graham motorcar stopped in the middle of the road, and I put out my hand for the brake, to keep myself from plowing into it.

But the road ahead was empty. . . .

I was about to pick up speed again when, peering through the windscreen, I noticed that beside me, the tall winter-dry brush along the verge had been flatted by something heavy passing over them and crushing them.

I hadn't even had time to react to that when from the same direction I caught the sound of raised voices, angry and rough.

Barely a minute had passed since I'd heard those first shots, and now there were two more in rapid succession, hardly distinguishable, and someone cried out in anguish.

CHAPTER TWENTY

I WAS ALREADY braking hard, with all my strength, weaving across the road and slewing sideways as the motorcar came to a halt that felt as if it had jarred my very teeth.

Peregrine had walked away from the asylum—he could have remembered this stretch—

Pausing only to pick up the torch that had been sliding wildly about beneath my feet, I was out of the motorcar and running toward the hop field. But the torch's beam was weak, and I had to concentrate on the broken stalks, which caught at my ankles and threatened to pitch me headlong. Then I reached the plowed ground, stiff with frost, and at last could cast my light toward the dark, quiet shape that was a motorcar, barely silhouetted against the sky.

In the silence I could hear my own labored breathing and the muffled sound of my boots as I ran and from somewhere what I thought was someone weeping.

At last my torch illuminated the shining metalwork of the Graham Rolls, the motor still ticking over. But there was no sign of Jonathan or Peregrine or the policemen. Something was glittering in the rear seat, and I lifted the light for a better look.

It caught the buttons of a constable's uniform. The man didn't stir, and I could see as I came closer that he was slumped to one side, as if he were badly hurt.

Oh, Peregrine . . . why didn't you trust me?

But he had never been taught trust.

I shone my light full in the constable's face and realized that he was unconscious, his jaw slack. I could hardly see his features for the spreading mask of blood, almost black in this light, that ran down from a long furrow at his temple and dripped onto his tunic. His helmet was askew, knocked to one side, strap dangling. It was Constable Mason. I pulled off my driving gloves and probed the wound, touching bone. I could even see it briefly, white—and not splintered.

Four bullets. . . . That's what Peregrine had said: he had four shots, and he could kill three other people before he turned the pistol on himself.

The poor, unsuspecting Constable Mason must have been the first victim. But Peregrine had missed his shot, thank God, and the man would live.

Where were the others?

I reached into the motorcar for the headlamp switch, and suddenly there was a brightness that opened up the night.

The other constable was just ahead of the motorcar, perhaps ten feet from the bonnet, as if he'd been trying to follow his attacker. He lay on his face, not moving. I bent over him. He was dead, there was nothing more to be done for him. I moved on.

That made two. . . .

Where was Jonathan? Where was Peregrine?

I turned to scan the fan of light, my own shadow cast like a black monster far ahead of me.

Something moved, then rose from the ground, hunched over as if in pain, and then the figure dashed out of the glow of the motorcar's headlamps, into darkness.

"*Peregrine—!*" I cried. "No, please wait—"

But he was gone, vanished into the night.

I ran forward to where I'd first seen him, and there was Jonathan, lying on his side on the ground, his military greatcoat almost blending into the trampled earth around him. One arm was flung across

A Duty *to the* Dead

his face, concealing it. Falling to my knees beside him, I gently lifted it, and he rolled over onto his back with a grunt that told me he was still alive.

More than anything at that moment, I wished I could bring Mr. Appleby here and make him look at the consequences of his spiteful telephone call. I wanted him to see what men do to each other when goaded beyond what they could bear.

I ran my hands over Jonathan's chest, looking for a wound, and I found it, bleeding freely but not heavily. Pulling off my scarf, I wadded it in a ball, unbuttoned his coat and then his tunic. I shoved the scarf against his shirt, jamming it as best I could against the place where the bleeding was heaviest, then buttoned the tunic over it to hold it in place.

As I worked, I realized that something was hurting my knee, and looked down. There was Jonathan's service revolver—it had been drawn and was lying under him. He must have tried to defend himself and the two unarmed constables.

I had to get these men to a doctor as quickly as possible. And there was no one to help me.

I sprang to my feet, trying to judge whether I could bring the motorcar this far without bogging down, and how best to loop back to the road. And only then did I notice that someone else was lying in the field, outside the perimeter of the headlamp's reach. I could only make out the shape of a man's boot and a lump beyond it that was his body.

I blinked.

Peregrine hadn't made it to safety after all. As I hurried toward where he lay in a crumpled heap, wounded or dead, I knew that Jonathan wouldn't have missed his own shot. He was too good a soldier for that.

Then I was beside him, kneeling in the hard earth again, calling his name. His face was in deep shadow, but as I shone my torch into it, his eyelids fluttered, and he said, quite clearly, "Diana?"

"It's Bess Crawford, Peregrine."

"So it is." He winced and lay still.

I could smell burnt wool, sharp and strong. Setting down the torch to search for a wound, I felt blood warm on my hands on both sides of his shoulder, high up. The bullet must have gone through. To get to his coat buttons, I had to turn him over. He cried out, and said something I couldn't catch. His breathing was fast but steady, and there was no froth of blood on his lips that I could see. I didn't know whether to be relieved or dismayed that he would live.

I rocked back on my heels, thinking. I could do nothing more here, in the dark, without bandages or good light.

But where to find help?

Peregrine had told me once that there was only a skeleton medical staff at the asylum in the evening. Would anyone come back with me? It would take too long to drive to Owlhurst and bring Dr. Philips here.

The best I could do was try to ease the motorcar forward and somehow manage to get everyone in it.

Beside me, Peregrine stirred. "Watch—"

I took his hand. "It's Bess Crawford, Peregrine. Can you stand? If I help you, can you get to your feet?"

"Where's my brother?" His voice was terse, angry.

"Just there. He's badly hurt. Please, Peregrine, you must help me."

He frowned, dark lines across his forehead, giving him a sinister look in the torch's light. I'd seen the same shadows once in his sickroom. "No—"

I turned and hurried back to the motorcar. It was my only hope now. When I got there, I looked at Constable Mason. He was awake, his eyes wide and frightened in the light of my torch. I didn't think he knew where he was, and proof of that came quickly as he lost consciousness again.

No help there. I got behind the wheel, and just barely touching the accelerator, I felt the tires bite and the motorcar move forward. Thank God. A month or so earlier, and the earth would have been soft enough that I wouldn't have made it.

I'd have to leave the other constable. It would be nearly impossible to get the two living men into the motorcar, much less a dead man. But I guided the car toward him and examined him again to be certain.

As I knelt there beside him, the torch in my hand died. I thought, *Oh, God, what next?*

A man's voice broke the silence, from some distance away, and I nearly leapt out of my skin.

"What's happened? I heard shots."

It sounded a little like Robert's voice. The baritone of a big man.

I couldn't see him, but he could see me, quite clearly.

I crouched by the constable, a frisson of uncertainty running through me. *What was he doing here?* "Robert? Is that you?"

To my left, Peregrine tried to shout something, and I was momentarily distracted.

"I say—you there—what's going on?" the man called again, closer this time.

And then something was hurtling toward me from outside the rim of light. I could hear it coming, breathing hard, and as I got to my feet, braced to meet it, a large dog rushed up, tongue lolling, barking as if to say, *Look what I've discovered.*

Its owner stepped into the edge of the motorcar's headlamps and stopped, staring. He carried a shotgun, broken, over his arm.

"What's going on here? Is that a policeman?"

I'd never seen the man before. Relief washed over me and I could almost feel my heart slowing to its normal rhythm.

"I was driving by when I heard the shots," I said. "My own motorcar is on the road. I'm a nurse—these men are badly hurt. Can you help me get them to a doctor?"

"A nurse? From Barton's?" He sounded skeptical. Of course—I wasn't in uniform.

"No, Owlhurst. Please, we mustn't waste time."

He walked nearer, and I could see he was a farmer, broad shouldered and strong enough to help me lift a wounded man.

"Is that one dead?" he asked.

"Sadly. Yes. We must leave him for now. But there are two others." I gestured in the direction of Jonathan and Peregrine.

The dog, disturbed by the scent of so much blood, was frisking around, whining now.

The farmer called him off and waited while I got back behind the wheel. As he glimpsed Constable Mason in the rear, he said in a shocked voice, "There's another policeman!"

I didn't answer him. Driving the vehicle gingerly forward again, I came to where Jonathan was lying, Peregrine just beyond him. The farmer followed on foot.

Peregrine was conscious, though in great pain, trying to raise himself and look the stranger over.

"It's all right," I said, getting out once more. "Can you stand? Between us we ought to be able to help you."

He managed it after a fashion, with support. I thought the shot had struck his collarbone or his shoulder, for there was no touching him on that side. He wasn't coughing, which was a good sign. Still, his face was a ghostly white in the light of the headlamps as we got him to his feet and he walked the short distance to the motorcar, clinging to my good arm. The pain must have been excruciating, each step jarring the wound. Putting him into the rear seat beside Constable Mason was difficult, but Peregrine accepted the situation in grim silence, his jaw set. For the first time I could see a resemblance to Arthur in his last hours, that same will reflected in his brother's taut face, paring all emotion down to one intense resolve.

Mason was awake again, trying to make sense of what was

happening and who we were. I told him I would explain when there was time.

Jonathan was another matter. There would be no help from him. I quickly shoved his revolver into his greatcoat pocket, out of sight, and explained to the farmer what he must do. I heard something behind me and whirled in time to see Constable Mason nearly tumble out of the motorcar, catch himself, and while he was still doubled over, vomit violently before shambling unsteadily toward us, his sense of duty stronger than his dizziness. With his help we settled Jonathan's limp body into the front seat and shut the door. Constable Mason leaned heavily against the wing, breathing hard from the exertion. I felt like joining him there, every muscle in my body complaining from the effort I'd made. Thank God, my arm had healed sufficiently.

As I got in beside Jonathan, I studied his face. I didn't like the look of him, but all I could do was to make certain the scarf was still pressed in place. I thought the bleeding had stabilized, but that could be bad news, not good.

Constable Mason roused himself and joined Peregrine in the rear seat, inadvertently jarring him as he tried clumsily to climb inside.

I heard Peregrine swear fiercely under his breath. He'd said very little since I'd found him. I think he knew there would be no escape now and was resigning himself to his fate.

Turning to the farmer, I said, "Please. You must follow me in my motorcar—out there on the road. We must go to Owlhurst."

For an instant I thought he was about to refuse me. Then he said, "Who shot these men?"

I told him truthfully, "I don't know."

He nodded, whistling up the dog, and went striding across the trampled field toward the road.

It was a bumpy ride, making a looping circle across the field and back to the verge where this motorcar had run off into the underbrush. I could hear Constable Mason breathing hard, and Peregrine grunting through clenched teeth.

On the road the farmer was straightening up Melinda's vehicle and making room for me to pass. The dog's head was turned toward us, ears pricked, as if making certain we were coming.

"Sorry," I said, "I'm so sorry," as we bounced hard back onto the road. And then I was gunning the motor, overtaking Melinda Crawford's motorcar, heading to Owlhurst. In a matter of minutes we were flying past the brightly lit asylum, almost blindingly bright in the moonless night, and then it was gone, and I was gritting my teeth as I tried to avoid the worst of the dips and ridges of the unmade surface. I couldn't help remembering how close I'd come to tumbling out of the dogcart when the wheels went off the road, wondering if any of my passengers would make it back alive if I overturned us. But time was critical, and casting a glance whenever I dared at Jonathan's gray face, I made the best time I could.

Twice behind me, I heard Constable Mason retching as he leaned out his window.

Peregrine asked at one point about Jonathan. "Is he still alive?"

And all I could do was nod my head.

Behind us, the Crawford motorcar kept pace with the farmer at the wheel, its headlamps lighting up our interior, sending shadows dancing around us. Jonathan's breathing was suspiciously quieter. I sent up a silent prayer that we wouldn't encounter anything out here—a wandering dog, a man walking home from a pub, someone on a horse, a lorry. It was a narrow road, with little space to overtake.

Constable Mason said, "I've the devil of a headache." And then to me, "I don't remember you driving us."

I said nothing, concentrating as we came flying into Owlhurst. It was a quiet time of night, the road blessedly empty, and I kept up my speed as we reached the cricket pitch. And then we were coming up on The Bells. By the garden gate was the Graham dogcart, and two men were just coming out of the pub door, staring at us as we passed. I almost didn't make the turning at the church, slowing in the nick of time, and then there was the doctor's surgery just ahead, and I felt like crying with relief.

I came to as gentle a stop as possible, and was out my door, running toward the house, calling for Dr. Philips.

He must have been just finishing his dinner, a serviette still in his hand, surprise on his face as he recognized me and then he saw the Crawford motorcar pulling in just behind the Grahams'.

"What in the name of God—has there been an accident?"

"I have three badly wounded people with me—gunshots." I listed their symptoms quickly, striving to leave nothing out. "The worst case is Jonathan Graham. I'm so afraid he's bleeding internally."

Even as I was describing the situation, we were walking quickly toward the vehicle. The farmer seemed to know Dr. Philips, for I saw him nod as he and his dog approached.

We took Jonathan in first, and Dr. Philips was already at work on him as the farmer—I'd finally asked him his name, and he'd told me it was Bateman—helped first Constable Mason and then Peregrine into the surgery.

Mr. Bateman said, as we settled Mason with a pillow and a basin for the nausea, "Will someone please tell me what's happening? Two army officers, two policemen—"

"Let's make certain they survive," I said, cutting him off. "Then we'll worry about what happened."

We dealt with Peregrine next, and as I closed his room door, I could see that Mr. Bateman was going to cling to me like a leech until he got his answers. Something had to be done about that.

I looked at him, really saw him for the first time. A worried man, blood on his hands and the sleeves of his coat and in a smear across his face. I was suddenly reminded of Peregrine's hands in the offal at the butcher's shop in Rochester.

We wouldn't have made it to Owlhurst without Mr. Bateman. But I didn't want to begin explanations until I was certain myself what had happened on the road. Still, there was one more service he could provide, if he was willing. By that time I hoped I'd be able to question Peregrine or Jonathan.

"Would you mind terribly going to fetch Lieutenant Graham's

mother? Don't frighten her, but his condition is—rather critical. And it might be as well to summon the rector. In the event . . ." I let my voice trail off.

From his expression, I got the feeling that Mr. Bateman knew the rector, and he most certainly recognized the Graham name. But I gave him the necessary directions anyway, and for a mercy, he took himself off, the dog dancing around his legs, as if eager to be out of the surgery and into the night air again.

When I looked in on him next, Constable Mason was beginning to feel a little better, and he insisted that he should be given a chair so that he could sit in Peregrine's room, on duty. But then he retched again, rather spoiling the effect of his claim to be quite recovered, and he lay back, shutting his eyes against the light-headedness sweeping him.

"Mr. Graham isn't going anywhere," I assured him as I closed his door. "We'll be giving him a sedative shortly. It will be more effective than a dozen constables."

Dr. Philips and I worked feverishly for a quarter of an hour. I was right about Constable Mason's concussion. He could remember his name, but he was clearly seeing double when I held up two fingers, and he had no idea what had happened on the road. He asked to speak to Constable Whiting, but before I could answer that, he had drowsed off, and I had trouble waking him again.

Peregrine had a fractured clavicle close to where it met the shoulder, and he lay there against his pillows, his eyes closed to avoid being questioned as Dr. Philips gave him something for pain and strapped the shoulder and the left arm to Peregrine's chest. It was a clean wound, and barring infection, he would be all right.

Jonathan was far more seriously injured, with the likelihood that the bullet had nicked a vein, causing internal bleeding. It was still lodged somewhere in his chest, and the broken ribs made breathing difficult. He was awake, stoically following our movements but saying nothing until Dr. Philips left the room.

"Are Mason and Whiting dead?" He didn't wait for me to answer him. "I shot them all," he managed to add. "I've been recalled to join my regiment. I won't survive France this time. It was best to rid us of Peregrine once and for all. For—for Mother's sake."

His voice faltered at the end, realizing that he had used Arthur's own words.

I'd seen the revolver where he must have dropped it as he fell. I'd shoved it in his greatcoat pocket before we attempted to lift him. But Peregrine too had been armed.

"Peregrine is alive. He'll live," I responded. "Dr. Philips is with him now."

Jonathan swore with feeling. "I want to confess. I want you to write my confession down, word for word. Let the doctor witness it."

"You're in no condition—"

"*I want to confess.*"

To keep him quiet, I said, "Yes, all right, I'll fetch pen and paper for you—"

I left the room, and ran into Dr. Philips in the passage outside.

"I wish you would tell me what this is about. And did I hear you call that other officer Peregrine? Peregrine *Graham*? What's he doing in uniform? I thought—"

I took a deep breath. "The two constables were taking him back to the asylum. Something happened only a few miles from there— that field at the bend. Do you know it? I'm not sure if Peregrine—or Jonathan— Suffice it to say, before they reached Barton's, they went off the road, and somehow, someone began shooting. It was all over when I got there."

"And what in hell's name were you doing—"

"I followed the Graham motorcar from a friend's house, where Peregrine was taken into custody. But he'd been falsely accused, they had no business taking him back there."

"He's a dangerous man, Bess, everyone said so when he escaped.

That he shouldn't be approached. I must send for Inspector Howard—"

"Dr. Philips—he's been sedated. He's not likely to harm anyone."

"There was a pistol in his greatcoat pocket, and a hole there where it had been fired, right through the cloth. I've taken the pistol and locked it in my desk."

Oh, dear God.

"Let me see it. I want to see how many shots are left."

"Three. I've already looked."

"But—" I broke off, frowning. "Did you—did you think to look at Jonathan's revolver?"

"He handed it to me. He said four shots had been fired. He was right."

But that made five, and I'd only heard four.

Dr. Philips was saying, "We should bring Mrs. Graham here as soon as possible. And find the rector. I'm transferring Jonathan Graham to hospital in Cranbrook. She'll want to go with him. I can't probe for that bullet here. If he can survive the journey, they just might save him. It will be touch and go."

"I've sent for them."

"Well done."

I went on to Dr. Philips's office, where I quickly found pen and paper. And then I looked in on Peregrine. The sedative was already working. His eyes were closed, his mouth a tight line of pain and despair.

Touching his hand, I said urgently, "Peregrine? What happened out there on the road tonight? You must tell me—who did you shoot? Was it Jonathan?"

He opened his eyes as I spoke. Then he turned his face to the wall and wouldn't meet my gaze.

"Listen to me! Jonathan has confessed to trying to kill the two constables and you. Is it true? He may be dying, I need to *know*."

There was no answer.

"You fired your pistol. While it was still in your pocket." I reached for his greatcoat, lying across a chair's back, and showed the blackened hole to him. "Look, here's proof."

"I won't go back to the asylum," he said finally. "I can't face it. I'd rather be hanged."

"Constable Mason will be all right in a day—two. He'll be able to speak to Inspector Howard. You might as well tell me the truth. It's the only way I can help you."

"Mason was the first to go down. He won't know what happened after that. I shot Jonathan," he said, and something in the timbre of his voice rang true.

"But that doesn't make sense. He wasn't shot in the back while he was driving—and he couldn't have walked that far from the motorcar, hurt as he was."

He wouldn't answer.

"Peregrine. I promise you, you won't go back there—"

I could read the bleakness in his eyes as he replied, "Bess, you nearly worked a miracle. I'm grateful, truly. But I can't walk out of here. I stood up just now and tried, and it was hopeless. Someone has taken my pistol, and so I can't use it on myself. I'll have to stay and face them. There's nothing more we can do."

I didn't try to argue, but I was far from giving up. My father had always said I was as stubborn as a camel.

"I've sent for Mrs. Graham. She'll be here shortly. I thought you'd prefer to know that."

And then I went back to Jonathan, hoping for a little time before his mother arrived.

Jonathan was waiting for me as I opened the door to his room. When he saw the paper and pen in my hands, he said, "Hurry."

And so I sat there, beside another Graham son, this time instead of writing a letter home, I was taking down a confession of murder.

It was brief, no details, just the stark facts. When I'd finished, he held out his hand for the pen, to sign.

I said, "Did you kill Lily Mercer, Jonathan? I know it wasn't

Peregrine. Arthur knew that too. It's what he meant by his message to you. Surely—surely, if you're confessing to *these* deaths, you will want to tell me the truth of that one as well. Peregrine doesn't deserve to return to Barton's. He's suffered enough. Set him free, while you can."

But he lay there in stony silence, his hand shaking a little as he reached a second time for the pen.

What was it about these Graham men? Stubbornly silent when they might set the record straight. First Arthur and now Jonathan and even Peregrine.

I watched him sign the confession. His signature was a scrawl, but legible enough to suffice.

"Take it to Inspector Howard. Don't let my mother see it. It would be a cruelty."

I agreed and was about to leave when he said, "Let it be finished."

"It can't be finished, if Peregrine Graham is sent back to that place. You never went there, did you? But Arthur did. And still he said nothing. Did nothing. What did he mean when he said he'd lied, for his mother's sake? Did you lie as well? Was *she* the one who killed Lily Mercer, and blamed Peregrine?"

Goaded, he said, "God, no! Damn you, don't even suggest such a thing!"

"Then why did you have to lie, for her sake?"

"I lied because the police were there and they frightened her. She'd been crying. When they asked me about the pocketknife, I told them that it was Peregrine's, that none of us ever touched it because it was left to him by his father. I didn't know—I was *ten*, I didn't understand what it was I was doing."

But that must have meant he knew who had had possession of that knife.

"Take the paper—go." He was insistent, the urgency reflected in his eyes.

I looked at the man lying on the cot.

He hadn't confessed until he'd realized Peregrine was still alive. . . .

With Peregrine dead, the police would easily have come to the conclusion that the dangerous lunatic had run amok. They might still feel that way.

And Peregrine was claiming he'd shot Jonathan—but not the policemen. If he wanted to hang, why not admit to three people? Then where was the need for Jonathan to take the blame?

It was dark out there in the field. When he'd run off the road, why hadn't Jonathan left the motorcar's headlamps burning?

So that the other occupants of the motorcar couldn't see what he'd seen—that someone else had been there?

And the Graham dogcart was standing in the yard of The Bells. It had been used tonight.

I said, "This confession is a lie. Who did you meet on the road tonight?"

He shut his eyes, not answering me.

"I saw him running away—I thought at first it was Peregrine. But Peregrine was already down, wasn't he? He fired at someone, and missed. While you were struggling for control of your own revolver. That's why I thought I'd only heard four shots. It wasn't Peregrine who wounded you, it was Timothy, wasn't it? *And you're still protecting him! How many people must he kill before he's stopped?*"

"My brother—he's my brother."

"So is Peregrine, and you left him to the horrors of an asylum."

I took a deep breath, feeling a wave of exhaustion sweep over me. There was only one other thing I wanted to know. But Jonathan was having difficulty breathing and I moved his pillows to make him more comfortable.

Dr. Philips was at the door, saying, "The ambulance is on its way."

I turned to Jonathan. "Will you at least tell me what Arthur had done that distressed him so? I brought his message—"

Someone spoke from just behind Dr. Philips. It was Mrs. Graham, her face starkly pale, her gaze on Jonathan. "He didn't confide in you after all. I was so sure he had. The police asked him if Peregrine had ever been violent before. And Arthur answered that we were all afraid of him. Arthur had been standing outside the parlor where the police were questioning me, he knew what had been said. He knew I'd claimed that I'd found that same knife deep in my pillow one night. It was a large pocketknife, a man's. The police were appalled. I knew they would be. Arthur saw that I was close to breaking down, and he lied to make them leave me alone."

Two boys, barely understanding what was happening around them, telling lies because they were afraid, confused, and trying to please the adults who were interrogating them. And with their words, damning their half brother to a lifetime in a madhouse. But they'd never been taught to think of him as their brother, had they? Mrs. Graham had purposely kept them apart.

"What did Timothy tell the police?"

She took a deep breath. "He told the police that Peregrine had once threatened to carve him like a Christmas goose with that same knife."

I wanted to bury my face in my hands and cry. On the lies of these three children, their mother had been able to protect her own son and keep him safe all these years, even knowing him for what he was. And no one had given a thought to Peregrine. He was the outcast, he was the eldest, and this woman had convinced herself that in the end his life would not have amounted to much anyway.

She couldn't have loved Robert that much. But she had loved Timothy. And Timothy was only nine at the time.

"Why would Timothy wish to kill Lily?"

"Apparently that night she saw his foot after his bath. Jonathan was there later when she told Timothy—a child, mind you!—that it was ugly and hairy and useless. He never showed that foot to anyone. She told him it was the devil's club and he was the devil's spawn. When I heard that, I felt nothing for her, I owed her nothing." Her voice was harsh, cold.

"Did he understand—did he realize he was killing her?"

"I've never asked him."

She came into the room and took her son's hand. She simply held it and told him she loved him, that nothing else mattered to her but that.

I slipped away, and in the passage came face-to-face with Robert Douglas. He stood there, stark anguish in his eyes.

"You can go in," I said gently.

He shook his head. "No. I loved him as my own. Arthur too. But they were Ambrose's sons."

It was an admission, in his own fashion, that he'd protected Timothy because the last Graham son was his.

And that explained so much. The love child, the deformed child, the child of guilt. No wonder Mrs. Graham had guarded him so fiercely.

I turned away, to allow him the privacy to grieve, and went to stand beside Peregrine's bed. I could hear them working with Jonathan, preparing him for the journey to Cranbrook. My training told me he wouldn't make it.

Mr. Bateman, the man from the hop fields, came to the doorway. "I wish someone would explain what's happened," he said, beginning to show signs of angry frustration.

I turned to ask him to be patient a little longer, just as a voice beyond him said, "Let me try."

It was Simon Brandon. "You're the devil to keep up with," he went on plaintively to me. "I've searched half of Kent for you. Why did you have my poor watcher arrested? He was there to keep an eye on you and make certain you were safe. You're covered in blood. And there's a dead policeman in a field not far from Owlhurst, and three men here in the surgery who've been shot." And then he asked in a lighter tone, "Did you do it, Bess? No, don't answer that, I don't want to know." He gave me a weary smile.

Rattled, I said, focusing on one word, "*Your* watcher? But—I thought someone else had hired him. Why don't you ever *tell* me these things?"

CHARLES TODD

He swore under his breath and took away the man and his patient dog. As I was shutting the door again, I saw Mr. Montgomery hurrying by, on his way to Jonathan's room. Robert, realizing what that must mean, followed him.

But so far no one had fetched Inspector Howard.

I said fiercely to Peregrine, "You must listen to me. If you go on saying you shot Jonathan, they'll believe you. They'll want to. Wait until they've retrieved that bullet and know if it was from your weapon or Jonathan's revolver."

He gave me a twisted smile. "Why should I lie?"

"Because you don't want to go back to Barton's. But I think—I'm nearly sure—you were aiming at someone else. We must clear that up, don't you see? You've trusted me this far." But it was a measure of what he'd suffered there that Peregrine would rather hang than go back to Barton's. I could feel his resistance like a stone wall. I still had Jonathan's confession in my hands. I couldn't rip it up until I was sure. It couldn't have been an hour since I'd found the Graham car in that field, but once Jonathan was in an ambulance on his way to Cranbrook, Dr. Philips would have time to remember Inspector Howard. And then it would be too late. Clutching at straws, I said, "Peregrine. What am I to tell Diana?"

He lay there, drowsy from the sedative, thinking it over. I wanted to hurry him, but all I could do was wait.

And then he said in a dead voice that concealed whatever it was he was feeling—love, hate, disillusion, grief, I couldn't tell—"Timothy. Timothy came out of nowhere. He was suddenly there—in the middle of the road—and when Jonathan stopped, he walked up to the window. He said something to his brother—I think it was, 'You can't do this, Jonathan'—and Jonathan got out to talk to him. All at once there was a scuffle, and Timothy had Jonathan's revolver. Without a word, he just turned and shot Mason. After that, it was chaos. Jonathan threw himself back behind the wheel and rammed the motorcar into the field when he should have run his brother down. Timothy followed us, and the other policeman got out, trying to reason with him, and Timothy shot him as well. Jonathan said to me, 'Run!' and I ran for the shadows just as Jonathan switched off the headlamps. Timothy came after me, and Jonathan after him. They fought, and I fired at Timothy as soon as I had a clear shot. Jonathan's revolver went off at the same time. I thought I'd hit Timothy, but it was Jonathan who went down. Timothy cried out, dropped to his knees beside his brother. Before I could move, he stood up again and deliberately shot me. I struck my shoulder as I fell, and that's the last thing I remember until I saw you there. I couldn't understand why you'd come. I was afraid Timothy might shoot you as well."

I shivered, remembering how he'd tried to shout a warning. And I'd misunderstood it. I'd believed he was running away. But it was Timothy I'd seen. The brothers were nearly the same height, the same build. . . .

Carefully folding Jonathan's confession, I thrust it into my pocket.

Dr. Philips came in. He said to me quietly, "I don't suppose Peregrine Graham can understand what's happening. But he ought to go with Jonathan to hospital in Cranbrook. Do I need a police escort? They'll want to know."

"An escort?" I went on briskly before Peregrine could speak. "Mr. Graham will be represented by his solicitors in London, and they'll be assuming all responsibility for his welfare." And if *his* solicitors refused, I knew a firm that would take him on. "As for comprehending his circumstances, you can tell him yourself what's expected of him."

Dr. Philips stared at me, and then said slowly to Peregrine, "Are you aware of what I'm saying, Mr. Graham?"

Peregrine responded, his voice thick with sleep, his eyes closed, "I wouldn't argue with her if I were you. It does no good."

Dr. Philips gestured for me to follow him into his office, where we couldn't be heard.

"Madmen can sound perfectly sane some of the time," he warned.

"He isn't mad. Any more than Ted Booker was mad."

"I just looked in on Constable Mason. He told me that some-one by the name of Timothy shot him. Does he think Peregrine is Timothy?"

"Of course not. Timothy Graham stopped the motorcar tonight before it could reach Barton's. He didn't mean to shoot Jonathan, but he did intend to kill the others."

Before he could say anything more, down the passage we heard the door to Jonathan's room open, and Mrs. Graham came out, leaning heavily on the rector's arm. She was in tears, such grief in her face that I pitied her. And I knew that Jonathan wouldn't travel to Cranbrook after all. Robert followed her, and I thought about what was to come, the next blow to fall, when Inspector Howard had been summoned.

As soon as they'd passed the office, on their way out the far door into the cold night, Dr. Philips went quickly to Jonathan to do what needed to be done. I leaned against a chair, too tired to think. I had a decision to make, and I wasn't sure I was clearheaded enough to do it.

Jonathan's confession would only muddy the waters. It wasn't true, for one thing, and for another it was imperative now to speak to Inspector Howard before Mrs. Graham could find another way to subvert justice. But I would keep it. I owed Jonathan that.

Simon came looking for me just then, saying, "Mr. Bateman has gone home. I took him in Mrs. Crawford's motorcar. What do we do about that poor constable lying in a field?"

"I was just coming to that. I'll have to speak to Inspector How-ard, he should have been here before Jonathan died, but—but. . . ." I took a deep breath. "But it was just as well. Constable Mason and Peregrine Graham will live, they can tell him what happened."

"Do you want a cup of tea first? You look out on your feet."

I shook my head. "I'll just find my coat. I can't remember now where I left it." But it was on the rack in the passage where I must have flung it as we arrived in such a rush. There was blood on it as well, crusted over now.

Simon helped me into it, then said, "It was never Peregrine, was it?"

"Why are you so sure?" I asked as we walked out of the surgery and I looked up at the stars, wishing that I were back on *Britannic* and none of this had ever happened. But no, I couldn't wish that, for Peregrine would still be shut up in a madhouse.

"You're a damned good judge of human nature," he said.

We had started toward the police station just as the ambulance arrived to carry the wounded and the dead to Cranbrook.

I helped to settle Peregrine on the stretcher, although he regarded the attendants with suspicion, and small wonder.

At the last, he put out a hand, and I took it, knowing it was a promise between us that all would be well. He didn't say anything, he didn't need to.

We were watching the ambulance make the turning at the church, in the direction of Cranbrook, when we heard someone calling for Dr. Philips. It was the rector, running toward us with coattails flapping and his hat gone. He was ashen in the ambulance headlamps as they swept over him, and we hurried to meet him, Dr. Philips, Simon, and I.

"It's Mrs. Graham—" I began. She'd been on the verge of collapse. And I was fairly certain the rector would be hopeless in the face of that.

But I'd misjudged him.

"I was on my way back to the rectory," he said disjointedly. "Susan had taken Mrs. Graham to her room—Mr. Douglas is with her. Timothy—I went to comfort him and couldn't find him—and just now—he's—*Timothy is hanging from a tree in the churchyard*!"

One of those ancient trees that stood by the wall. Where I'd seen Robert Douglas bring Mrs. Graham the news that Peregrine had escaped from the asylum.

We rushed to follow the rector, and then Simon was there with his knife, and we could cut Timothy down. It was too late. He must have gone out as soon as he saw his mother return home with the news about Jonathan.

My first thought was for Mrs. Graham and Robert. And then for Peregrine.

Dr. Philips said, "My God—" as if echoing my thought.

We took Timothy to the doctor's surgery, and then the rector and the doctor went together to hand a grieving mother the final blow.

And Robert Douglas? How would he face the death of his own child? As he had always done in a crisis—with silence.

I couldn't go with them. I didn't think Mrs. Graham would want to see me now any more than I wished to see her. Instead I stood there in the room where Jonathan had died, looking down into the face of his brother. A murderer. Yet it was unmarked by anything he'd done. As if his conscience had always been clear.

He'd worn a coat—rather like an officer's greatcoat—to the tree, to throw the rope over a heavy bough and tie the end to the bole of the tree. He'd even brought a stool with him to stand on. And then he'd folded his coat and set it aside before putting the noose around his neck. I'd brought the coat back to the surgery with us, and reached for it now to cover his face.

It was then that I saw the tear in the sleeve near the shoulder. I touched it gently. A bullet had passed through the thick fabric just there. I opened Timothy's shirt and looked at his arm. Here was a bloody crease where the shot had grazed the skin as well. It had hurt, but it would have healed on its own without anyone else the wiser. Now it was proof that he'd been on the road near Barton's tonight.

Simon had come in and was saying, "There's something in his hand."

I looked down, praying it was a note, a message, something—but it was too small, only a square clenched in his palm, hardly noticeable.

When I took it out to unfold it I saw with shock that it was nothing more than a list of names, and at the top was *Lily Mercer.*

At the bottom, just below *Ted Booker,* was scrawled in anguish *My brother.*

I refolded the note and put it back where I'd found it.

Simon nodded. "Best that way," he said. "The police . . ."

"There's something I must do first," I said. "It's important. Will you wait?"

"Yes."

I walked alone toward the church. As I came to the west door, in the distance, carrying on the quiet night air, I heard one of the owls call from the wood that had given this place its name.

It was cold as the grave inside, and dark as death. I could just see my way. I remembered Mr. Montgomery, in the organ loft, repairing his precious church. He would be on a ladder tomorrow, looking for new tasks to keep his mind off the suffering he'd witnessed.

I came to a halt in front of the memorial to Arthur. This time I put my fingers out to touch the brass plaque, running them along the words engraved there, feeling the sharp edges of letters that spelled out the dates of a man's life and death, but not the sum of the man himself.

He had tried once to visit Peregrine in the asylum and been turned away. It was more than anyone else had done. He'd told the staff to allow Peregrine to have books, because as the oldest of his three brothers he remembered a time when Peregrine was normal and bright. He had lied for his mother's sake, but at the end of his life, he couldn't go on lying. And yet he'd trusted to Jonathan to see matters right. He hadn't put his plea on paper to be shown to Lady Parsons or the police. He hadn't had the courage to stand up for Peregrine in the face of family loyalty. But he'd hoped that Jonathan might—Jonathan, the unfeeling brother, who might find it easier to step forward on his behalf.

It could be argued that small boys couldn't have changed what was happening to Peregrine that night in London or here in Owlhurst. Even with the best will in the world. And none of them had witnessed what their mother had done to sear Peregrine's guilt into his mind. They had lied for her sake. That was all they knew. And yet when they were older, when they could understand what their mother had done to Peregrine, they had never questioned her actions or their role in what had happened. They'd simply turned their backs on the truth. They had been well taught to shield Timothy.

What if Arthur had survived the war, and asked me again to marry him, even with one leg? If I'd said yes, I'd have believed, like everyone else, that Peregrine was a murderer. And Arthur would have let me believe that.

That was what hurt the most. That I would have been drawn into the conspiracy of silence, unwittingly and therefore willingly.

He'd had feet of clay after all.

I had been fond of the man I thought Arthur Graham was. I had mourned him with my whole heart. Visiting Kent had brought him closer for a short time, and I'd been grateful for that. Now, being here made saying farewell easier.

I dropped my hand from the memorial brass, standing there for a moment longer.

"Good-bye, Arthur," I said softly, and turned away.

Simon Brandon was waiting for me at the church door. He didn't say anything until we had reached the police station, tucked away on a side street.

"He must have had some good in him, Bess, or you couldn't have cared for him the way you did," he said, offering what comfort he could.

"For a time I wanted to believe that," I answered. "You couldn't help but like him. But Matron was right. We know them for such a brief space. And so they are ours to heal, but not ours to love."

Chapter Twenty-one

Somewhere in France, March 1917

I HAD COME to the conclusion that French rain was worse than any other—barring of course the monsoons of India—and I was feeling a little down at the end of another long day at a forward dressing station. We had had rather severe cases, three possible amputations and one of pneumonia, sandwiched between more trench foot than I ever hope to see again in my lifetime.

I had been sent back to France, and in some ways I was very glad. I'd been a little uneasy on the crossing, remembering too much. And when my feet touched the solid stone of the quay, I drew a long breath of relief. *Too soon to find the sea friendly again,* I told myself. The memories of *Britannic* were still too fresh.

Slipping and sliding through the mud as I made my way to my quarters, I waved to stretcher bearers huddling under a tent flap trying to smoke. *They must be,* I thought, *as tired as I am.*

During the day, someone had brought up the mail—letters were lying on my cot blanket, still damp from the weather, and I pounced on them like a hungry cat on a handy mouse.

Letters from home, letters from the Front, letters from Egypt and India. I hadn't had anything for so long that I'd been wondering if anyone knew where I was—we'd been moved four times in the six weeks I'd been here, and the post was never dependable as it was. Excited, I completely forgot how I'd been longing for a cup of tea to warm me, and I sat there devouring each letter in its turn.

Between a letter from the Colonel Sahib and one from Dr. Philips in Owlhurst, I discovered a small postcard. On the front was a pen-and-ink sketch of the Pavilion at Brighton. I turned it over quickly and saw Diana's bold penmanship racing across the card, just as she raced through life. I hugged it for a moment, glad to know she was well, then read the message.

Dear Heart,

This is Brighton, as if you didn't know. I am seeing it through new eyes. The young man with me sends his very best love, and I am green with jealousy. The doctors weren't certain he was ready for France, and so he is being sent to Dover Castle after his training. How clever of them! How convenient for me! He's taking over the Dower House in Owlhurst, and you can write him there.

With much love,
Diana

The Dower House, where the eldest son lived when he married. It was his way of telling me just how much he'd healed already. A nursing sister had written to me for him as soon as Peregrine's name was cleared, adding that he wasn't sure where he would go on leaving hospital—he couldn't bear to set foot in the Graham house, even though his stepmother had been sent back to her family in disgrace.

I picked up the card again. Beneath Diana's signature was a handwriting I didn't know, but a name I did.

God keep you safe out there, dear girl.

Ever,
Peregrine

I looked out at the cold, dismal rain. My heart sang for both of them, and suddenly I wasn't tired any longer, I was crying with joy.